NEVER MIND MURDER

Frances Wosmek

The Westminster Press
Philadelphia

Wo

COPYRIGHT © 1977 FRANCES WOSMEK

First edition

Published by The Westminster Press ®

Philadelphia, Pennsylvania

PRINTED IN THE UNITED STATES OF AMERICA

9 8 7 6 5 4 3 2 1

10-78
Josten's
6.36

Library of Congress Cataloging in Publication Data

Wosmek, Frances.
Never mind murder.

SUMMARY: A young girl and her mother rent an old Victorian house in a small Massachusetts town and are haunted by the ghost of a young artist who was murdered there.
[1. Mystery and detective stories] I. Title.
PZ7.W8884Ne   [Fic]   77–7950
ISBN 0–664–32620–X

NEVER MIND
MURDER

Chapter 1

When we left Boston there had been only a little fog. We had no idea it would turn out to be a stormy night. Mom had been driving all day. She wasn't exactly in the mood to cope with bad weather on top of strange roads and night driving, which she hated anyway. Mom's sense of direction, even in the broad daylight, wasn't the greatest, so heading out into the boondocks on a stormy night with Mrs. Douglas as the captain seemed a clear invitation to disaster.

We should have stayed in Boston for a good night's sleep, then gone on to the Cape in the morning. But, of course, Mom had to call her old college roommate the minute we hit town. Nancy whatever-her-name-was had begged Mom to come on out and spend a couple of days, as we might have expected after all those years.

There seemed to be no good reason why we shouldn't.

"After all, Sandy, we do have the whole summer," Mom said, "and Nancy has always bragged that the North Shore is very special."

"It's O.K. by me." I shrugged. "We might as well take in all the sights going."

So here we were on our way out to who-knew-where with the little bit of fog having switched to a steady downpour.

Mom reached into the glove compartment and pulled out a road map.

"You're the navigator, Sandy," she said, dropping it into my lap. "It's up to you to see that we take the right turns."

"Thanks a bunch," I replied. "The blind leading the blind, if ever I saw it."

"Just let me know when we get close," Mom said. "I don't

want to overshoot the mark. I'm not too good at finding my way on a night like this."

I unfolded the road map and smoothed it out across my knees, smiling to myself. That had to be the understatement of the century. Mom could get hopelessly confused going to the supermarket a new way.

I peered at the map in the dim light of the dashboard, trying to pinpoint Hope's Crossing.

"Are you sure it's big enough to make the map?" I asked. "Hope's Crossing doesn't exactly sound like one of the top ten."

Mom frowned and turned up the radio. She already had doubts enough of her own. She wasn't prepared to listen to mine.

After the divorce, Mom and I had been more like sisters than mother and daughter. When she was down I cheered her up. When I was down she did the cheering. There was a lot of cheering going on from both sides for the first couple of years until Mom got her feet planted firmly on the ground.

Dad was Meredith Douglas, an actor—a pretty good one too. At least the reviews for the most part, said so. It was just that he had never included a home and family in his list of things he most needed.

Mom was an artist. From the beginning, I guess, I felt she was pushing for me to study art someday too. I really wasn't all that good. I wasn't sure I wanted to spend the rest of my life bent over a drawing board or slopping paint in an attic.

The trouble was, I couldn't think of anything else I wanted to spend the rest of my life doing either. Unless I came up with something pretty fast, I would probably just drift into art.

On the other hand, from the time I was old enough to listen, I had heard all Mom's views on the subject, and all her artist friends' as well. I'd have a real head start if I went into art.

Mom had promised me a whole summer on the Cape for ages. Mom had gone to art school in Boston and was always raving about the seashore. Now, with college coming closer and closer, it seemed like a better idea than ever.

So we had rented a summer cottage in Hyannis, sight unseen, and sublet our apartment in Cleveland. We had started off feeling free as a breeze—like kids skipping school.

Now, here we were, feeling not that breezy, heading out into the unknown on a dark and stormy night.

I watched the long line of headlights blinking into the black like Christmas lights in a wet watercolor. Forty minutes, Mom had said. Well, at the snail's pace we were traveling, it would probably take twice that long.

So I settled back, with my finger on Hope's Crossing, reading off all the signs I saw, just to prove to Mom that I was on the job.

I tried to remember what I knew about Mom's old roommate. A name on a Christmas card, the kind with photos of the kids pretending to make a snowman or sitting under last year's tree. I seemed to remember two or three from the last card. Little kids. Oh, well, I thought, better than no kids at all. At least there'll be some action.

The rain, by this time, was coming down in sheets. The highway, beaded with strings of oncoming lights, looked unreal and endless.

"Why didn't we have the brains to check the weather report?" Mom was groaning. "We're out of our minds to be out on a night like this!"

We were getting close. I peered into the inky night, reciting the signs as they loomed up suddenly into the light.

It was easy enough finding the right exit. Once off the

main highway, however, it was a different story. Lights were few and far between. Nothing was marked. There was no way of knowing if we were heading in the right direction or not. With Mom's homing instinct there was a pretty good chance we were not, I thought.

Then a low, hollow moan sounded from the thick of the night.

"Listen!" Mom cried in the kind of voice one might use to welcome a long-lost lover. "It's a foghorn! That means the ocean must be nearby!"

"An amazing deduction!" I congratulated her. Then I shuddered. "Sounds like a late, late movie—sound effects for a murder!"

Just the same, I couldn't help thinking how beautiful it all must be by daylight. I caught glimpses here and there of high fences, great iron gates, and long tree-lined drives that melted mysteriously into the black night.

"Nancy said this was once a sort of playground for the very wealthy," Mom explained, "but of late years, with high taxes and the shortage of help, it has changed into a pot-pourri of people with just one thing in common—a leaning toward the unusual. Why, even Nancy lives in an old con-verted carriage house."

An old converted carriage house! I liked that. It had a quaint, romantic ring to it. For the Douglases, living, as we did, in a high-rise apartment with swimming pool and sauna, it was bound to be a change, if nothing else.

"We might as well find a house and ask," Mom said. "There's no point in just wandering around."

She turned suddenly into the next driveway. We wound in and out, following the curves, snaking through the dark, aiming our headlights between the trees marking either side of the road.

The road came to an abrupt end. Mom stopped the car, rolled down the window, and peered nervously out into the soupy night.

Now, as well as the pelting rain, we could hear waves hammering the rocks and spray hissing up onto the shore.

Spooky, I thought. I couldn't blame Mom for being nervous. I would have been too if it hadn't been for a kind of corny, melodramatic thing that kept getting to me, like something so overdone that it loses its seriousness. If I hadn't been quite so exhausted, I might have laughed.

"Just our luck!" Mom groaned. "It's probably a dead end. It's awful. I'm turning around."

She started the engine and backed cautiously against an overgrown hedge. Suddenly, in the thin beam of our headlights, a monstrous house loomed into view. In spite of its dilapidated condition, it was still a pretty impressive sight. It was plainly unkept and uncared for. Everything was overgrown—weeds, vines, uncut grass, and shaggy hedges.

We stared.

"Nobody has lived here for a long time," Mom said.

Then, to our complete amazement, a light went on. There was no mistaking it. One of the windows cast a steady, unflickering beam.

I caught my breath. I could feel my heart thumping like a bongo. "There's a light!" I cried. "Somebody must be there!"

Mom nodded. There was no denying the evidence.

"I'll go," I said quickly, not giving myself time to reconsider. I had opened the door and had slid out into the wet night before Mom could voice an objection. My curiosity was just too much. I had to know who would be living in a house like that, and why.

I paused to look back at Mom's anxious face. "Keep the

motor running!" I called as lightly as I could manage, partly to bolster my own courage. "We may need to make a quick getaway!"

I turned, shielding my face against the driving rain, dashed up the broad steps, and ducked under the porch roof.

The foghorn sounded loud and clear. I could hear the waves. The ocean must be very close, I thought.

There was no bell. I lifted the heavy knocker and let it fall. I waited for what seemed like hours. Not a sound came from within. I turned to go. We must have been mistaken about the light, I thought. Nobody in his right mind would live in a ramshackle place like this.

Then suddenly the heavy old door creaked open.

My first impression was of light and warmth in contrast to the dark, wet night. Then I noticed a girl standing quietly before me, holding the heavy door ajar.

It seemed right to follow her gesture inside toward the friendly fire crackling in the big stone fireplace.

The door closed. The girl walked over and stood by my side in front of the fire.

I had thought, at first, that she was about my age, no older. But, although we were about the same height and build, I could see that her face was not quite that young.

"It's a perfectly dreadful night," she said. "Let me dry your coat."

It seemed, at the time, perfectly natural for me to slip off my wet coat into her waiting hands. I watched her spread it across the back of a chair facing the fire. I untied my scarf and handed it to her. She smoothed and folded it carefully, and then laid it on the chair beside the coat.

I sat down. She sat opposite. It never occurred to me then to wonder why I felt so completely relaxed and at home under such unusual circumstances.

"Mom and I lost our way," I told her. "We saw your light

one of the chairs. It was the biggest cat that I had ever seen. He stared at me with eyes that looked just like cold, blue ice.

I shivered with a feeling that I could not have explained. "He's the most fantastic cat I've ever seen," I breathed. "I have always wanted a Siamese cat. I don't know why, but I just have always wanted one."

"That's Rama," the girl said. "He is very nervous tonight. He doesn't like stormy nights like this one." She looked at him anxiously, and, I thought, a little sadly.

She gave me directions for the Masons'. It was not far off. We had only taken the wrong turn at the main road.

I stopped with my hand on the door. The fire was dying. The girl looked, somehow, terribly alone and lonely. The cat had leaped from his chair and was pacing back and forth, making the low throaty yowls that only a Siamese cat can. His eyes seemed to have changed from ice to blazing blue fire.

"I hope that I see you again," I said. "For some odd reason, I feel that I have known you for a long time."

The girl touched my sleeve with her hand. "To know is to become another," she said. "What is the instant of beginning—or end? Does anything ever truly begin or end?"

Only the thought of Mom having a stroke outside forced me out into the stormy night. The heavy door closed softly behind me. I stood for a moment feeling that I had stepped from one world into another. Then, wrapping my coat close, the wind whipping my hair, I made a dash for the car.

The car door was open. The engine was running. I slid onto the seat and braced myself, armed for the onslaught.

Mom was slumped over the steering wheel. I couldn't be sure, but she was probably asleep. I smiled to myself. Poor old Mom! I had felt the same way before my visit with the girl. Now, strangely enough, I was bristling with energy. In fact, I had never felt less tired in my whole life.

Mom jerked to an upright position. She seemed to be

having trouble figuring out who I was and where I had come from.

Then she smiled. "Well, Sandy," she said, taking a noble shot at cheerfulness. "Thank heavens you wasted no time! I knew nobody could possibly live in that run-down old house. We were mistaken about the light too. It was only the headlights reflecting on a window."

I stole a glance at Mom's relaxed face. She was being absolutely serious. I looked back at the house. Every inch of it was wrapped in total darkness. Not a single window sent forth a single gleam of light. I began to get a squirmy feeling in my insides.

"But, Mom." I shivered. "There *was* someone there, a girl, an artist. We sat by the fire while my coat dried. We talked about painting for a long time."

Mom fastened her eyes on me with a steady look. "If this is your idea of a joke, Sandra," she said in her most no-nonsense voice, "then it isn't funny. I am much too tired to play games."

"But it's not a game, Mom," I continued to protest. "She *was* there. We talked while my coat dried."

"You were gone only a couple of minutes," Mom stated flatly. "You did all that in a couple of minutes?"

"But, Mom—" I replied weakly, "you were sleeping."

"Nonsense!" Mom snorted. "I know perfectly well how long you were gone, and it wasn't more than a couple of minutes!"

One of us had definitely flipped. That much was clear. But which one of us?

I looked back once more at the old house, silent and dark. Evidence was plainly pointing the finger at me.

Mom leaned over to pat my hand. "We're both overtired, dear," she said. "Neither of us is thinking straight. Everything will clear up after a good night's sleep."

I said nothing. Suddenly I was feeling just as tired as she seemed to think I was.

I sensed that Mom still felt as uneasy as I did about the whole thing. After all, to see your own daughter cracking up must be almost as bad as cracking up yourself. Neither of us said another word about it. When I directed her at the cross-road, she made no comment. I suppose we were both trying to sweep our disturbing thoughts under the rug and pretend they weren't there . . . at least until morning. But it didn't work for me. My head was like a hive of bees.

The Masons lived only around the bend. Mom's joy at the meeting seemed to me to be a little strained. I could see that she was confused and worried about me. I kept catching her glance. Of course, neither of us said anything to Mrs. Mason. There was no point in starting right off as a couple of ding-dongs.

Mrs. Mason was a nice enough, pleasant, housewifely type. Her dark hair was carved and sprayed into the latest style, and her eyes were a scrutinizing brown. She fussed over us more than either of us would have preferred. She was hardly the kind you might expect would understand a kooky story like ours. At least Mom liked to fool around with things like yoga and astrology. She was probably more prepared to accept a far-out idea than her friend might.

We got only a glimpse of the kids, who had been allowed up until we came.

Eric was a friendly little blond boy of about seven. He was curious, like most kids, and bursting with questions which he had obviously been instructed not to ask. So he compromised by taking in everything with his eyes.

Margie was quite different. I supposed that she was about twelve, although she could have passed for much younger. She was too skinny, and, poor kid, I thought, she really didn't have too much in the way of beauty. Until she looked at me. I was really startled. I thought her eyes were the most unusual I had ever seen. It wasn't just the color—a funny mixture of brown and yellow that turned out almost amber —but the expression. Scared, I thought right away. They were not just shy, but scared to death. It gave me a jolt to look into them.

Her straight brown hair was slippery finĕ, and when she hung her head, which she did most of the time, the hair slid down the sides of her face like a curtain, hiding her scared expression. Creepy, I thought. She made me feel positively creepy. When she left the room, nobody noticed. She moved like a mouse. She disappeared more than went out.

Getting Eric off to bed took a little more doing on Mrs. Mason's part. It was pretty clear which one was her favorite. Eric seemed to have all the confidence that Margie lacked. He was noisy and laughed easily. He literally bounced out of the room with everyone's attention on him.

Mrs. Mason watched him go, glowing with motherly pride. "He is a character!" She laughed.

After a lot of reliving the old days, Mom finally got around to explaining why we had arrived so late. "We took the wrong turn," she said, "and came out by that big old house at the end of the drive."

It was more of a question than a statement. Mom's face was a picture. I could see that she was hoping for a nice, sensible answer from nice, sensible Mrs. Mason that would explain everything. Poor Mom! It was right out of the frying pan into the fire!

"Oh." Mrs. Mason shuddered. "You mean the old Saunders place. It's been empty for more than two years."

I caught Mom's quick I-told-you-so glance.

"You wouldn't catch me anywhere near that spooky old place," Mrs. Mason went on. "There was a young artist strangled over there a couple of years ago—dreadful thing—

terrible!" She laughed a short laugh, glancing out of the window. "There was a storm a lot like this one the night before they found the body," she added.

"Artist?" I managed to squeak out in a tight voice.

Mrs. Mason nodded. "Her name was Valerie Cameron. Can you imagine, she lived over there all by herself? She was an odd girl. I never met her even though we were neighbors. She never wanted to mix. Never really seemed to belong to the neighborhood. She had a cat though, a great big thing. Siamese, I believe it was."

Mrs. Mason, turning from the window, looked thoughtful. "Nobody ever found a clue," she said. "Peculiar, after more than two years, never a single clue. But it's better to let the matter rest. This is a peaceful neighborhood. It would rather forget."

You had better believe I was feeling pretty queer by this time. If I was all mixed up before, well, this was more than I needed! I had to have time to think.

I was glad that I hadn't mentioned the cat to Mom. It might have been just one thing more than she was prepared to handle. I could see that the bit about the artist had shaken her up pretty much as it was.

Mrs. Mason reached down and picked up one of our bags. "Well, come on," she said. "It's a gloomy enough night without dwelling on gloomy things."

She led the way up the stairs.

I was glad that she gave us separate rooms. I felt I needed time to go over the whole thing piece by piece. Could someone dream with his eyes wide open? Maybe so, I thought, but more than likely, those were the ones who were locked up in padded rooms.

Chapter 2

Ask Mom. Sleeping is one of the arts I have mastered, or, at least, so I always thought. But who, in a sane moment, could picture a night like that first one at Hope's Crossing?

Whether I closed an eye or not I really can't say. My experience at the old house raced round and round my exhausted brain like a caged squirrel. I was never quite sure if I was this side or that side of dreaming.

The darkness seemed like thick, black syrup that oozed through the windows and trickled into every corner, swallowing shapes as it went. Thunder rumbled and grumbled constantly in the background, and the Masons' nice, practical spare room kept coming and going between quick flashes of lightning.

I wondered, now and then, about Mom, and if she were doing any better. Somehow, I just couldn't see her drifting off to a peaceful slumber with such choice bits of a mystery as she had to chew on. For some weird reason the thought soothed me.

With the first ray of sun I was up. I unlatched and opened my window to a new day that I would never have believed. I should have remembered that daylight, like the good fairy, can change a toad into a prince without even half trying.

The sky was cloudless and blue. For as far as I could see there were green lawns, hedges, and flower gardens—all carefully arranged, clipped, and cared for. Everything looked freshly washed. I could hear gulls screeching in the distance, and birds singing their hearts out in every tree and every bush.

Jeepers! I thought, it even makes it all worthwhile.

I found my way downstairs and followed the sound of voices out through the wide-open French doors to the garden in back.

What a super place to have breakfast! was my first thought. It looked like something out of the movies. There was a brick patio with a wrought-iron table and chairs. I thought I had never seen so many pots of red geraniums in my life. The glass-topped table was laid with thick, red woven mats. The whole impression was one of geraniums swimming in sunlight.

Mom was already there. It took only one glance to tell how she had spent her night. Even with her cheery chatter, that droopy, never-slept-a-wink-all-night look was there, stamped on her face for all to see.

I saw Mr. Mason for the first time. He stood up and shook my hand. He looked friendly, but a little stepped on, I thought. He looked a lot like Margie. Maybe not quite so scared-looking, though you couldn't tell, really, because he was wearing glasses. But his slippery-fine brown hair was the same. It kept sliding off the bald spot on the top of his head, and he kept carefully stroking it back.

Mrs. Mason bustled around in a blue-flowered robe. She seemed to get very excited about things nobody else cared about—like how brown your toast was.

Eric was dropping spoonfuls of cereal into his orange juice, watching me out of the side of his eye, and making hissing sounds as loud as he dared with each drop.

Margie was the last to appear. She slipped into the chair beside me in her mouselike way. If you hadn't been watching, you would never have noticed. It was pretty clear that she intended to ignore me and would probably be happy if I would do the same for her. But I get nervous with even a mouse slipping around not talking to me, so I decided to make the move.

"Good morning, Margie," I said.

She might have been deaf for all the response I got. She just paid a little more attention to smearing jam on her toast.

"Margie!" Mrs. Mason was right on.

The curtains of her hair slipped aside as Margie raised her head. "Good morning," she said, looking back down.

If a mouse could talk, I thought, it would have said it exactly like that.

Mrs. Mason perched her coffeepot—red like the geraniums—on the table and sat down beside Eric. She gathered his game into one sweeping motherly glance. She slapped his hand, but it was really more of a pat than a slap. "Stop making a mess," she said, "and eat!"

Mr. Mason was fumbling with his glasses. He cleared his throat. I could see that he was getting himself ready to enter the conversation. I soon found out that Mr. Mason never just tossed off words. He gave birth to them.

"I understand," he said, turning to Mom with a manufactured smile, "that you had a little trouble finding your way out last night."

"They got lost," Eric offered, "in the storm."

"That will do," warned his mother. "Wait until you are spoken to."

Before Mom had a chance to reply, Eric quickly threw in one more bit of juicy information. "They stopped at the spooky old Saunders house to ask the way."

Mr. Mason raised his eyebrows. He concentrated for a while on the inside of his coffee cup, then he looked up over the tops of his glasses, which had slipped down over his nose.

"The old Saunders place?" he asked. "Nobody lives up there."

I glanced quickly at Mom. I could see by her expression which one of us she had concluded needed straightening out. See? she was saying to me as plain as words, you didn't really see anyone or talk to anyone in that old house. There was no one there. You imagined the whole thing.

I was determined to find out all I could in a roundabout way without admitting to the whole crowd that I was subject to hallucinations.

"I thought it was beautiful," I said, "or, I'm sure that it used to be."

"Used to be." Mr. Mason nodded after a pause. "It was empty for years even before the girl moved in. It wasn't in the best of condition then, but it's gone to complete rack and ruin in the last couple of years."

"There must be someone who looks after it," I kept going, "a caretaker, maybe?"

Mr. Mason shook his head. "No, I don't believe anyone has even been inside since the funeral. They gave the key to George Gilligan, a local policeman who lives in the area— due to be retired soon, I understand. I guess that is where the matter rests, until they figure out what to do with the old place."

I heard a rustling from the mouse by my side. She arranged her knife and fork flawlessly in position across her plate and folded her hands in her lap. She waited for her mother's attention, then asked to be excused in a flat, expressionless voice.

If there had been anything out of place, Mrs. Mason would have found it, as evidently Margie well knew. I could see Mrs. Mason's frown, and her eyes taking in Margie from head to toe—every hair. There was nothing to find fault with, so she nodded. Margie scurried soundlessly out of sight.

I was beginning to feel awfully sorry for the kid. With Mrs. Mason fussing and buzzing around every day, it was probably a wise thing to become as unseen and unheard as possible. In fact, I was beginning to think that Margie might really be the smarter of the two kids.

"Strange thing to have happened in a nice, quiet place like this," Mr. Mason still rambled on. "Terrible—dreadful shock to the neighborhood."

There was a silence. I watched Eric feeding crumbs to the sparrows, daring them to come one hop closer with each crumb.

"I do want to see the house by daylight," Mom said carefully. "There was just something about it—"

Good old Mom! I hadn't expected she would let the matter drop. She was all ready to go back for another look. Well, so was I. Daylight had smoothed off some of the dangerous edges. Here in the bright morning sunlight who could resist an adventure like that?

"Go on over any time you like," Mrs. Mason said. "There's nobody there."

"Is there any chance at all," Mom bulldozed ahead, "that I might be able to get the key and show Sandra the inside? She is thinking of taking up interior design, and I would just love to have her see one of these charming old Victorian houses."

I almost chuckled out loud. Foxy old Mom! I wondered what she would say if I announced that the thought of interior design had never crossed my mind. I couldn't help admiring her maneuvers. So I just sat back waiting, with every confidence that she would see it through and us inside the house.

"I don't see any reason why not," said Mr. Mason. "I'll just give George a ring and ask him to let you have the key. Margie can take you over."

He picked up the newspaper scattered on the bricks around his chair. He folded it neatly and laid it beside his plate.

"The best thing to do," he said, checking his watch, "is

to go right on over first thing. George goes on duty at nine o'clock."

That sounded to me as though we might be able to go by ourselves. I was sure that Mom was not prepared any more than I to share our investigation with Mrs. Mason. If she flipped over toast a shade too brown, what would she do in an uninhabited house with inhabitants?

On the way out I caught Mom's eye. She winked. Sometimes I'm almost afraid to think. Mom knows everything that's going on inside my head.

I found Margie curled up in a chair in the living room with her nose in a book—and I mean it really was!

On top of everything else, I thought, the poor kid is nearsighted! I could just picture her in a few years' time with glasses slipping down over her nose like Mr. Mason's. I was surprised Mrs. Mason hadn't noticed. Maybe, I thought, she is so taken up with little things that she doesn't have time for the big ones.

Margie glanced up from her book as I came in. It was almost a friendly glance. I wasn't prepared for that. I was sure that she would have to be won over inch by inch. I was almost looking forward to the challenge. I had done a lot of baby-sitting, and I knew how to get along with most kids younger than myself.

"It's a great day!" I began. A statement like that can cover a broad range of interests. You can narrow it down later, when they open up.

Margie closed her book. She sat up very straight and smoothed the skirt across her lap with one hand.

Actually, in the daylight she was kind of pretty. Her eyes were absolutely sensational. A lot of the best models have that kind of scared, doe-eyed look. She was too thin, and straight up and down, but it was mostly her clothes that were wrong. They were too plain and colorless. She could have done with a lot more color.

"I don't like storms," she told me, "but then, it's always so nice after."

I nodded. "I wish I could have seen the ocean last night," I said. "I have never seen the ocean in a storm. In fact," I added, "I have never seen the ocean at all."

Those way-out eyes opened wide with surprise. "Never?" she asked.

"Never!" I replied.

Suddenly she smiled a real, genuine smile. It was almost as if a light went on inside. Right then and there I decided to be her friend. Maybe she needed one. Maybe that was the whole trouble.

Mrs. Mason worried into the room. Mr. Mason was late. The butter had melted in the sun, and for heaven's sake, what was Margie doing with a book this time of the morning?

I watched Margie curl back into her shell like a little brown snail. There is nothing left, I thought. The shining person I had seen inside had disappeared and left only the creepy little mouse in its place.

Mom was wasting no time. She charged in, all dressed and ready to go. Mrs. Mason was still in her blue-flowered robe. I suspect Mom felt safer having it that way. Mrs. Mason was perfectly fine in her place, but her place definitely wasn't on the kind of expedition we were about to undertake.

"Margie," Mom addressed the ball in the chair, "do you think you could show us where George lives? You know, we need to get the key to the old house from him."

Margie uncurled enough to look Mom squarely in the eye. "I don't know where he lives," she said.

Mom looked a little blank. "But you must," she said. "If he lives just down the street, then you must know where he lives."

"No," repeated Margie, cool as a cucumber. "He must be somebody new. I don't know anybody by the name of George."

I must say my respect for her was growing. Anyone who can lie through her teeth in as cold-blooded a fashion as that can't be all mouse, I thought.

"Never mind," Mom said. "We can find it. We don't mind at all going alone."

I guess we were both sort of relieved that it would be just the two of us.

We asked directions from Mrs. Mason, getting Margie off the hook by saying we had decided to leave her behind in case she was needed.

Mrs. Mason pointed the way. It was only a short walk down a pleasant little road, she told us.

She was wrong. It wasn't just pleasant. It was superpleasant.

"They should bottle this air!" I said, actually daring to draw a deep breath. "It would be a sellout in Cleveland."

Living in the city, one grew up believing that air came in shades from middle to deep gray. Here it was as clear as crystal. You could see for miles. The water sparkled in the sun like billions of diamonds, and the sky was blue . . . blue . . . blue.

It was the first chance Mom and I had had to talk alone since we had arrived at the Masons'. It was reasonable to suppose that, by this time, each of us would have come to some kind of terms with the scrambled events of the night before.

"Well, what do you think?" Mom started me off.

I had my answer ready.

"I think exactly the same as I did last night," I declared positively. "Whatever anyone says makes no difference. I saw what I saw. I heard what I heard. The girl was as real as you and I. I sat by her fire, and we talked for a long time, maybe half an hour."

"That's impossible!" Mom exploded. "You were gone from the car for only a couple of minutes. If you say you were there for half an hour, then you are absolutely mistaken!"

The confusion was back. We started helplessly at each other. Then, by mutual agreement, neither of us said another word about it for the rest of the way. The best thing seemed to both of us to wait and see what the old house would reveal in the bright light of day.

Hope's Crossing was a mixture of ornate and stately old mansions facing the shore, and a sprinkling of smaller places scattered here and there, mostly hidden from view behind rhododendron bushes, flowering hedges, tall rustic fences, or closely planted trees.

These smaller places had once been part of estate grounds and had been converted, like the Masons', from carriage houses and servants' quarters to homes. It was picturesque and elegant in a nice dignified sort of way.

George's house had been an old brick gardening shed. He lived on the loft level.

Charming, I thought, following Mom up the steep staircase that led to George's door, but definitely on the minus side to anyone loaded down with a bag of groceries. Oh, well, I thought, maybe George is not that big an eater!

We didn't have time to knock. George must have heard us coming. The door opened when we were halfway up.

Maybe the perspective of seeing him from the feet up distorted the image. Or maybe he really was ten feet tall. Anyway, I felt he had some kind of an advantage over us, looking down, as he did, in a curious, suspicious kind of way.

When Mom asked for the key, I caught a fleeting glimpse of how we must be appearing to George—two females in city clothes, with cameras dangling, looking for a good snoop in their quiet little neighborhood. It wasn't any wonder he wasn't welcoming us with open arms.

George, as I said, looked ten feet tall, but of course, he couldn't have been. He was thin and gangly. Maybe that was why he looked like the green giant—only not very jolly—or green. Red, mostly. His hair, or what he had left of it, was a sandy red, and his face was freckled and splotched red from the sun. His eyes were pale blue. Creepy eyes, I thought, that bored right through to your unspoken thoughts, like a ray gun.

"Knew the girl, did you?" he asked, handing the key a bit reluctantly to Mom.

"Oh, no!" Mom said. I could tell by her nervous laugh that she wasn't feeling any too comfortable either. "We are only interested in old houses."

We turned to go back down the steep flight of steps to the ground.

"Looking for anything special?" George's voice was crisp and not any too friendly.

While Mom was fumbling for a reply, I decided to help her out.

"We just like old houses," I said, trying to sound light and breezy, "that house or any other. It really wouldn't make any difference."

It was obvious that my reply did not completely satisfy George.

"I am an officer of the law," he said. "I went over that place with a fine-tooth comb. I couldn't find a single clue."

"I am sure you did." Mom smiled sweetly. "I'm sure everyone did. But we aren't the slightest bit interested in the murder. It's the old house that we want to see."

Just as we reached the ground, George, from his great height, tossed down one final remark.

"This is a quiet, respectable neighborhood," he said. "We

don't like trouble. We mind our own business. We like other people to mind theirs."

We both felt relieved when George went back inside and closed the door behind him.

The winding road leading up to the old house looked quite different by daylight. We could see the ocean shining like tinsel in the sun between the sedate rows of trees lining the drive.

We hardly spoke. I guess we were awestricken as much as anything. We weren't used to such magnificence. Even in its run-down and uncared-for condition, the place still looked pretty grand to us.

When the house itself came into view, I had a very sad feeling. I'm sure Mom felt it too. We just stood and stared. It was like seeing someone old and sick who used to be young and very beautiful.

The shutters sagged on rusty hinges. Everything needed paint. Gutters, clogged with leaves, had spilled water through the seasons, leaving ugly stains on the once beautiful bricks. The hedges were shaggy and overgrown. But what struck me most of all was the incredible silence. It seemed to me that you could almost reach out and touch it.

There is nobody here. This was the thought that came to me first of all. Nobody lives here, and nobody has for a long time.

I must hand it to Mom. She didn't start up with a lot of I-told-you-so's. I guess she felt she didn't have to. The evidence was there to speak for itself.

I must have had some kind of a weird dream, I thought. Maybe I had hit my head and freaked out into some kind of a fantasy world. But then, the thought kept nagging me, How come the girl in my fantasy world was an artist and had a Siamese cat exactly like the girl that had been murdered there? I had no answer for that. All I knew was that my insides felt like warm jelly, and I wasn't sure I'd ever believe anything I ever saw or heard again for the rest of my life.

The door was locked, tight as a drum. In fact, Mom had a very hard time getting the key to work. The lock inside must have been rusty. But we weren't about to give up at that point, so we kept at it until it finally gave way.

It took a few seconds for our eyes to get used to the dim light inside, coming in from the bright sunlight. What I saw gave me no reason for surprise. It was exactly as I knew it had to be. The walls were dark paneled, with shelves of books on two sides. There were chairs in front of the big stone fireplace. There were even canvases stacked and leaning against the wall.

The sunlight, filtering through the unwashed windows, winked on hammocks of cobwebs swinging in the corners.

I avoided looking at Mom. I could imagine what she was thinking. My daughter is some kind of a nut who dreams when she is wide-awake. I was glad that we had had the sense to keep still about it at the Masons'. I wasn't quite ready to have Mrs. Mason try to figure me out.

Then I saw Mom, white as a sheet, looking for all the world as though she had spotted a ghost. She walked across the room toward the fireplace. She reached down, taking something from the seat of one of the chairs. Without a word, she held it up for me to see.

I said nothing. What could I say? It was a blue scarf with yellow chrysanthemums. It was my scarf. It was still damp.

Chapter 3

I needed something. Maybe it was air. Anyway, I staggered outside into the sunshine after Mom. At the time it didn't occur to me to notice her face. Too bad. It must have been something for the books. There we both were—speechless. And I had always thought that, in either of us, speech would be the last of our faculties to go.

The sun felt warm and real. I drew a deep breath, filling my lungs to the brim with a new supply of fresh ocean air. In spite of everything, I remember noticing how fresh it smelled. Probably because it had been so damp and musty inside.

We followed a path that led around the house to the back. A few vicious stabs from the needle-pointed thorns of overgrown rosebushes helped to convince me that I wasn't dreaming. Our footsteps made no sound. The path was a cushion of spongy, damp leaves several seasons deep.

We brushed past overgrown and untrimmed vines that had lost their footing and flopped over in tangled masses. To top it all, birds of every description kept shooting out from unexpected places, fluttering and whirring past with shrill cries that would have jangled anybody's nerves, even if they weren't in the fragile and frayed condition of ours.

We collapsed on a bench in what must have been a superelegant garden at one time. I could see the remains of a network of brick walks, now almost completely hidden by ragged weeds and grass.

There was a water-stained marble cherub holding an empty pitcher that must have stopped pouring a long time ago. What was supposed to have been a pool at his feet was filled with tattered leaves and broken twigs. The old fairy tale of Sleeping Beauty flashed through my mind. Everything that plainly had once been loved and cared for had not only been deserted but, it seemed, suspended in time as well. The whole thing gave me the feeling of a held breath.

An ornamental black iron fence separated the garden from a rocky clifflike bank that dropped sharply to a narrow margin of beach below. I could see the wide, seemingly endless ocean sparkling sunshine and lapping its gentle waves on the white sand. I had never seen the ocean before, but something about it seemed strangely and positively reassuring.

I glanced at Mom. She looked as though she had something to say, but was definitely having trouble finding a place to begin. She was making a lot of motions, but no sound.

"There has to be an explanation," she finally blurted out. "Everything always has to have a perfectly logical explanation."

I nodded numbly. My perfectly logical brain was refusing to function at all, faced with such a muddle of impossible facts.

It was quite a while before either of us spoke again. But something about hearing Mom's voice seemed to help connect me back to the real world. The pleasant sounds of the lapping waves and the sea gulls began to register.

"Things like that happen," Mom finally continued, "but they always happen to someone else. You read about them, but you really never more than half believe them."

I was beginning to relax a little. It was comfortable and companionable having her in this with me. It restored some of my faith in myself. Being all alone in a situation as far-out as that one could give rise to a lot of self-doubts.

"Can't you just imagine," I pondered, "what it is going to be like trying to put this story across to the Masons?"

Mom laughed. Somehow that old familiar everyday laugh

was exactly what each of us needed to reestablish ourselves, once and for all, in the normal world. I could almost feel the real blood rushing back into my veins.

"Tell you what," Mom said, giving my arm a squeeze. "Let's not tell anyone at all until we have done a little detective work on our own. You know as well as I do that not only the Masons but nobody else would believe such a wild story."

"I'm with you all the way," I agreed positively. "If you are plotting any Sherlock Holmes, count me in."

I could almost see Mom's mind ticking away. I might have guessed that she would come up with some far-out, one-of-a-kind, never-to-be-repeated plot before too long.

On the way out of the big old tree-lined driveway, we couldn't resist one good, long, last look at the mysterious old house.

Maybe it was just my imagination working overtime, but, for a minute, the feeling was almost overpowering that the old house was not quite ready to let us go. That we shared something special, and this was only the beginning of more to come.

I was sure that Mom felt it too, even before we noticed the sign. The sign was just an old weather-beaten piece of board nailed to a short stick. The words had been almost completely rained away. But when we had brushed aside the debris, we could still read FOR RENT and a number scrawled across the bottom.

I glanced at Mom. She was looking suspiciously like the cat that swallowed the hamster. I didn't need to ask. She answered anyway.

"You can trust the details to me." She smiled slyly. "Just memorize that number!"

For the rest of the day I did my best to go through the mechanical motions of being a polite houseguest, but all the time my mind was working on the double with other things.

I did not see much of Mom. Mrs. Mason was determined to tour-guide her over every inch of Hope's Crossing, and all its surrounding territory. I suspected Mom's enthusiasm might be a little forced under the circumstances. I wondered what she was planning to do. I felt sure that we had not seen the last of the old house. But the idea of renting it left just too many unanswered questions in my mind. What about the Cape? What about all our carefully laid plans? I knew Mom had sent part payment down on a summer cottage in Hyannis. But all the time she kept stressing the point that the summer was open and free for adventure. The way I looked at it, the adventures we had had so far would be pretty hard to beat.

Mom cornered me later in the day. Things were going her way. I could read the smug expression a mile away.

"Nancy has asked us to stay on here for a couple more days," she announced, with all the glee of having stolen a base.

I nodded, waiting for her to fill me in.

"It won't take more than a day or two to work things out our way," she went on. "I plan to call the number first thing in the morning."

So far, so good. As an operator Mom was proving to be first-rate. But what I could hardly wait to see was the effect her news would have on the Masons. Adventure didn't seem quite their bag.

I have to hand it to fate. When it is on your side, it can deal you a pretty good hand.

Mom's golden opportunity began to unfold that very same evening.

After dinner we all gathered in the living room for a nice, relaxed family evening. When I say relaxed, I mean on the outside only. It seemed to me that Eric was the only completely relaxed one among us. So far as I could see, Mrs.

Mason was always about as relaxed as a cat on a red-hot griddle. Mr. Mason would probably never dare to relax with Mrs. Mason around, and that went for Margie too. Mom and I had been on pins and needles all day and were not about to relax now, with Mom's public announcement in the offing.

It was an impressive room. Everything was waxed and polished to a high gleam. Mrs. Mason definitely had it altogether with her housekeeping. Just as it was, the room would have done justice to a full-page spread in *House & Garden.*

The gold draperies looked crisp and new, and hung just so. The natural wood of the old carriage house had all been carefully preserved, even to the roughhewn beams across the ceiling. There was a big stone fireplace at one end that fit in just right. I did wonder, however, if it had ever been used. Even that was swept bare as a bone, without even an ash showing. Everything else in the room was blue and shades of a kind of lilac.

The more I thought about it, the more uncomfortable I felt. Maybe it was just too perfect. It was quite possible that Mom and I overdid the homey feeling, but there was definitely something about a few unfinished projects, or even an article of clothing that had been dropped in a hurry, that gave a room that inviting, lived-in feeling.

Mrs. Mason had brewed a pot of fresh coffee, and there were scads of dessert snacks—enough to feed a hungry army. All in all, to someone who hitherto had been content with a hamburger or pizza, it looked like a pretty sumptuous spread.

Eric, using his charm as a cover-up, was navigating between the plates of goodies, sampling one and all, and being careful to avoid the eagle eye of his mother.

Margie was doing a surprisingly good job of showing off her skills as the well-trained daughter. The minute someone emptied a cup—zap! She was right there with the coffeepot to refill it. She even looked a lot better. The dress she was wearing was a big improvement. It was a bright turquoise blue. The color helped. She didn't look half so mousy, and it did a lot to bring out the unusual color of her eyes.

I noticed that Mom had maneuvered a seat on the davenport, close to Mr. Mason. She must have felt that he would be her best bet in the way of support, or, at least, offer the least resistance.

The conversation was not exactly taking off. Mom was a little absentminded. I could see that she was waiting for an appropriate break for an opportunity to drop her bomb. The minute it occurred, she hopped right in.

"We saw the old house this morning," she said, straining to make it sound casual.

Mrs. Mason, for the moment, was frowning, concentrating on the stitches of a half-knitted sock.

I could tell that Mom was pretty itchy, waiting for Mr. Mason to respond. He fluffed out the pillow at his back, took off his glasses, breathed on them, pulled a handkerchief from his pocket, and began to polish.

I watched Mom's face turn a pale shade of purple. It was more than she could possibly wait out.

"We fell completely in love with that old house!" She literally exploded. "And what's more, we conjured up a perfectly *wild* idea!"

I held my breath. I could see that she had decided on the sock-it-to-'em approach. But I trusted Mom enough to realize that it was undoubtedly all part of a well thought out plan with perfectly good reasoning—of her variety—behind it.

Mrs. Mason laid down the sock and raised her eyebrows. If there was a wild plan afoot, well, she wanted to be right there to stamp it out.

Mr. Mason just smiled. Maybe he hadn't heard a wild idea in such a long time that he had forgotten what one was.

Mom drew a deep breath. "The house is for rent," she announced. "Well, we want to rent it!"

Mrs. Mason's face was something else. I wouldn't have thought she would ever be at a loss for words. I guess she just hadn't expected an idea that wild.

"Just for the summer, of course," Mom hurried on. "We have sublet our Cleveland apartment and freed the summer for adventure. And what could be more adventuresome than living in that delightful old house with a view beyond all description? I can't explain it," she added breathlessly, "but I'm just hopelessly attracted to the idea!"

She looked pretty much out of wind. I decided it might help if I backed her up before the objections began to descend.

"Isn't it a great idea?" I gurgled with all the enthusiasm I could muster. "It will be just like living in another world!"

Eric had come over from the opposite end of the room. He leaned companionably across the arm of my chair and examined me as though I were some rare, freaky specimen.

"You'd *really* live over there?" he asked with obvious admiration, "in that *spooky* old house?"

Mrs. Mason laid down the sock and stroked it lovingly. Then she turned to Mom, devoting her entire attention to the matter at hand.

"It's a perfectly marvelous idea to stay on in Hope's Crossing," she said. "But, why that old shambles? It's a monstrous old house and would take endless cleaning."

I smiled to myself. If she only knew. Mom's cleaning instinct was not so well developed that it would ever be likely to stand in the way of a good, juicy adventure.

"We wouldn't need to use the entire house." Mom was right on with objection number one. "The smaller wing that we saw would be plenty big enough. Anyway, I doubt whether the rest of it has been used for years."

Eric's interest was bristling. By now he had positioned himself in front of Mom, with his round blue eyes glued to her face.

"I've never seen a ghost," he confessed, his voice soft with awe.

I had noticed a moment before that Margie, on her way out, had paused briefly, then turned quickly back into the room. I could see that she was pretending to be busy, piling and unpiling cups on the serving wagon.

Mrs. Mason reached for her knitting. She tossed a quick glance at her husband.

"I suppose it's rentable," she said briskly. "At least the sign says so. But who in the world would have the authority to say?"

"I have the number to call," Mom put in quickly. "I plan to give it a try in the morning."

Mr. Mason smiled a slow smile her way. "Don't be too disappointed if things don't work out," he said. "Lawyers are notably heartless fellows. The romance of your idea may not be entirely clear to them."

Margie was making the rounds once more with the coffee-pot.

Mom, looking vastly relieved that her ordeal was over, held out her cup and smiled.

Margie, true to form, carefully averted her eyes to avoid Mom's glance.

Eric, on the other hand, was not about to let a good conversation die. He revolved his fists in the pockets of his jeans and rocked on his bare heels.

"Maybe we can find a *clue!*" he chortled. "Maybe we can even find the *murderer!*"

Everyone laughed a bit nervously. In the confusion, Margie tilted the pot a little too far, flooding Mom's saucer and spilling the overflow into her lap.

Mom dabbed and mopped with her napkin in a hurry. "It's nothing," she assured the circle of anxious eyes. "It's hardly more than a drop."

I could see that Margie was standing rigid as a ramrod. That dreadful scared look was back. She was white as a ghost.

"It's all right, Margie," Mom said softly, touching her hand. "It slipped, but it didn't hurt a thing. Really it didn't."

Margie moved across the room like a sleepwalker. She covered her face with her hands and burst into tears. Then, quick as a flash, she darted out of the room like a scared bird.

Mom and I exchanged glances, sympathetic and surprised.

"Well!" Mrs. Mason laughed shortly and apologetically. "You wouldn't think a little thing like that would bring on such a storm!"

No, you wouldn't, I silently agreed. But, obviously, something had scared the poor kid half to death, and I was feeling mighty curious.

Not long afterward I excused myself. I felt that I could use a little time to think. It was still light enough for a short walk. Maybe that would help to clear my head.

I started back to my room for a sweater. June evenings in Cleveland were one thing. But it looked as though June evenings in Hope's Crossing were going to be quite another.

I stopped at the window by the stair landing. Oh, wow! was all I could think. It looked unreal. The greens were all too green and where, outside of a corny calendar picture, had the flowers ever been colors like that? I was used to the murky gray of the city, or scroungy-looking parks at best. I felt as though I had been fitted with a brand-new pair of eyes. I wondered what luck Mom would have with the real-estate man in the morning. Strangely enough, I wasn't at all worried. I had perfect confidence that things would work themselves out.

Margie's door was partly open. I glanced in. I could see a turquoise heap on the white bedspread. No face, just a heap and a maze of thin arms and elbows.

I hesitated for just a second, then I went inside. If I expected an open-arms welcome, I was bound for disappointment. She never moved a hair, although I was quite sure that she had heard me come in. Maybe she buried her face into her arms just a little deeper.

The room lived up to Mrs. Mason's standards in every respect. The windows were wide and sparkling and hung with crisp white ruffled curtains. The wallpaper was a neat blue-and-white stripe—not very exciting, but nice. Everything was superneat and in perfect order.

I felt a slight twinge, remembering my own room at home. Collecting junk was my specialty. Most of it was not the right size or shape to be piled, filed, or stored in drawers. The general effect, more often than not, was the wake of a disaster.

The only thing I could see in this room that gave any indication at all that anyone lived here was a desk in the corner. That, at least, looked used.

I moved soundlessly across the room, ankle-deep in the thick blue carpet. Above the desk was a neatly framed square of corkboard. Pinned and thumbtacked to every square inch were literally dozens of drawings that she must have made herself.

It took only a glance to tell me that they were all pretty good. In fact, pretty darned good. Another glance was enough to show that she was sort of single-minded as to subject.

Cats and kittens were obviously her specialty. Every kind,

every color, every position—she had tried them all.

I could understand that. I had always wanted a Siamese kitten myself. Her interest was not that narrow, it seemed. But a lot of girls her age have a thing about horses, I thought. With Margie, it was cats.

Anyway, I had the clue I needed. I went over and stood by the bed. "I'm an old cat lover from way back," I said as cheerfully as I could. "I am glad to see that you are too."

I waited. No sign.

"Would you believe," I rambled on, "that I have wanted a Siamese kitten for as long as I can remember? The trouble was, we always lived in apartments where animals were not allowed. Maybe, if we move into the old house, I could have one over there."

I didn't know about her, but the idea struck me as first-rate. I definitely planned to return to it later.

I thought I noticed a slight relaxing of the heap, but she was plainly not in the mood for any heart-to-heart, so I went out.

I unpacked a few things and hung them in the closet. We were staying another couple of days, at least. Suddenly I found myself a lot more concerned about things like wrinkles than I had ever been at home. I shook out a sweater and hurried out the door.

I couldn't resist another peek into Margie's room as I went by. The room was empty. That's strange, I thought. She hadn't impressed me as being about to go anyplace for some time. She must be feeling better. Maybe my little monologue about the cats had helped. I thought of all her cat drawings. The poor kid must have had to work out her love for cats in the neatest possible way under Mrs. Mason's iron rule. Nothing real enough to shed hair and make tracks would have had a show.

Almost without realizing, I directed my steps down the

winding road that led past the Masons', on up to the seashore and the mysterious old house. Maybe the whole idea of the walk was just a subconscious cover-up for one more look. Or maybe I just felt drawn toward the ocean. Though we had a pretty good-sized lake in Cleveland, it had never interested me too much. But I was finding the whole idea of the ocean exciting and romantic. The sailboats, the screeching gulls, and the ever-changing tides were all part of a delightful world that I had hardly known existed.

I guess I was more aware of the silence than anything else that evening. I suppose I had taken it for granted that the sounds of traffic, and sirens, and subways were the normal background sounds everywhere. It seemed pretty strange and wonderful to me to actually hear the leaves stirring, birds twittering, and the high-pitched chirp of millions of crickets hiding somewhere in the grass.

I walked slowly, not wanting to miss a thing. One would need a lot more even than a whole summer to explore all the possibilities of this place, I thought.

I went back to the idea of getting a Siamese kitten. That fantastic cat belonging to the girl must have reactivated my old childhood dream. I could hardly believe that it had all happened only the night before. It seemed years ago.

I wondered about time. Why should the same number of hours seem so long sometimes, and so short at others?

I rounded the curve, recognizing George's house a short distance ahead. I thought about George. I hadn't particularly liked him. I was sure that Mom had not felt too comfortable with him either. Maybe, if things turned out, he would be our neighbor. In that case, I had better forget my feelings and give him a chance, at least.

Then I stopped short. As clear as a bell, in the still evening calm, I heard the distinct sound of a hastily closed door.

I watched, startled, while a small figure shot down the

steps and out the driveway leading from George's house.

There was no mistaking the bright turquoise blue that flashed in and out between the openings in the bushes.

Instinctively, I stepped quickly off the road and ducked from sight behind a convenient bush. I watched while Margie darted past like a frightened fawn.

I stood bewildered for a long time, trying to make some sense out of what I had seen. That very morning Margie had insisted that she did not even know who George was, or where he lived. Of course, I hadn't believed a single word of that. But, even so, Margie was definitely shy. It wasn't likely she made friends all that easily. Why, then, of all people, would she choose George to call on by herself, especially when she was feeling unhappy and upset?

I could do without the rest of the walk. I turned back down the road that was already beginning to melt into darkness. I hurried back toward the Masons', by now looking friendly and safe with lights shining through the windows.

Chapter 4

Mom woke me at the crack of dawn. At least, that was the way it seemed to me. A breakfast where everyone sat down and ate the same thing was another whole trip in itself. Mom and I never had leisurely breakfasts. At least one of us was usually late for something or other. My morning nourishment was ordinarily limited to whatever seemed portable enough to hold together between the apartment and the school bus.

"It's the middle of the night!" I groaned, turning over to shield my sensitive morning eyes from the sun that was beaming through the window like a searchlight.

"When you're in Rome—" Mom said. "Besides, we have a lot of things to attend to today."

The whole thing came flooding back into my soggy mind. So it really wasn't a dream after all! With reality that far-out, who needed dreams? I hopped out of bed in a hurry.

The whole clan had already gathered when we straggled out to the patio. That is, everyone but Margie. I noticed at once that her chair was conspicuously empty, in spite of the fact that her place was all carefully laid out as usual. Halfway through breakfast, when she still hadn't shown up, I really began to wonder. One wouldn't ignore Mrs. Mason's neat routine just like that. There would have to be a darned good reason.

Eric was up to his usual games. Obviously, scrambled eggs were something he could have lived without. I watched, intrigued, while he slyly flipped them off the end of his butter knife into the shrubbery.

Mrs. Mason seemed in no mood for games, not even

Eric's. She pounced on him immediately.

"Young man," she snapped, "one more time and it's back up to bed for you!"

It didn't seem like very good timing, but Mr. Mason waded right in anyway.

"Where is Margie?" he asked innocently enough.

Mrs. Mason glared. "She simply refused to come down. She insisted she wasn't hungry."

Then she shrugged in Mom's direction. "I simply don't understand what gets into that child. The last couple of years it has just been one thing after another."

After breakfast Mom called the number. She made an appointment with the real-estate man in the next town for, like, right away, and was positively straining at the leash to get started.

I couldn't see just waiting around, wondering how she was making out, so I decided to go along. After all, if things shaped up, we would be around all summer. So I felt that I might as well fill myself in on a little of the local color.

By daylight the road was really something else. It was narrow and winding, dipping in and out to reveal absolutely breathtaking views of that fantastic, shining ocean. We drove past intriguing driveways, ornamental fences, and fancy iron gateways one after another. We caught glimpses of houses you wouldn't believe.

In town things leveled down to the ordinary. It was almost a relief to discover that not everyone lived like royalty, but that some people actually worked and looked as shabby and down-at-the-heel as they did anyplace else.

The real-estate office did not appear all that inviting. As soon as we drove up, a wizened little man peered out of his unwashed window to look us over.

There was a delicatessen across the street. At least things looked alive over there. So I decided on that.

"Concentrate your charms," I told Mom. "I'll be waiting across the street. When you're through with your wheeling and dealing, we can celebrate over a banana split."

The delicatessen was nothing special. It could have been downtown Cleveland for all the individuality it showed—the same old blurbs on the same old signs propped and leaning against the half-empty sugar bowls. Even the few kids with nothing to do, draped over the stools, looked the same.

When I came in, all eyes turned my way. I felt a little self-conscious. I wasn't exactly used to being a novelty. Though I suppose I would have stared the same way if some new kid had breezed into one of my hangouts where everyone knew everyone else.

I felt that I was making a pretty good impression, so I decided to ham it up a little bit.

I slid onto a stool with a big-city flourish, and ordered an orange-apricot parfait. The boy looked put out, as I had secretly thought he might. Obviously he had never heard of such a thing. As soon as I saw his color rise, I felt a little sorry and hurriedly changed it to a Coke. He was sort of neat-looking—longish, blond hair, and a real cute dimple in his chin. After all, I thought, I'm beginning a vacation, not joining a convent.

I gave him a nice smile in return for the Coke. I think he wanted to say something friendly, but wasn't quite up to it. So he made a big thing of mopping and remopping the counter nearby with an outsize rag.

I felt a lot more comfortable when the conversation started up around me in a normal way. I settled down to sip my Coke and kill time until Mom was ready. I didn't mind. I like watching people and wondering about them. The world is full of characters.

I couldn't help being especially fascinated by one man who came in and ordered a quart of ice cream. I could see right away that he was blind. He wore dark glasses and carried a white cane. Otherwise, he seemed to move quickly and easily. He obviously had no trouble finding his way around.

Apart from his being blind, though, I thought he looked a little familiar. That struck me as odd. I knew that I couldn't possibly have seen him before. He was tall and gangly. He stooped over, which gave him the appearance of an old man, though I didn't think he was all that old. His face literally sagged. In fact, even though a lot of his expression was hidden by the dark glasses, I felt actually depressed just looking at him. I watched while he carefully sorted out his money and reached for the change.

"Thank you, Mr. Gilligan," the boy said as the man turned to leave.

Gilligan? Where had I heard that name before? Of course, I thought, wasn't that what Mr. Mason had called George? I had to find out.

"Is he any relative of George Gilligan's?" I casually asked the boy who had gone back to his mopping.

"Yup," he replied. "They're brothers. Owen is the blind one."

I thought that over, sipping slowly, watching the Coke rise up the straw.

"What happened?" I asked. "I mean for him to lose his sight?"

"That's a pretty long story," the boy said. He came over to stand in front of me. Now that he was more relaxed, he actually looked great. I wondered if he played football. He had the build.

"Shoot," I said.

"He had a son, Charlie," the boy began.

I could see that our conversation was creating quite a bit of interest among the kids nearby. A few of them moved to stools within range of the conversation.

"Charlie was kind of a mixed-up guy," one of them said.

"But he was the best athlete that Edgewater High ever had," another added.

"Was?" I asked. "What happened to him?"

There was a minute's silence.

"He was drowned," the boy said, going back to his mopping.

A creepy-looking boy, who looked superanxious to be included, carried on.

"Charlie and his father always did a lot of fishing," he explained. "This time their boat smashed up on the rocks when the fog came in suddenly. George and Owen made it to shore, but Charlie was drowned."

I stopped sipping abruptly.

"George was there too?"

The boy nodded. "Yeah, and it was pretty rough on him too. Like George never had any kids of his own, so he kind of thought of Charlie as his own son."

So there! I scolded myself silently. Let that be a lesson to you not to judge people before you know all the facts of what they have been through!

"But what does that have to do with Owen's being blind?" I probed on.

"Owen really freaked out," the creepy boy replied. "Like everyone thought he was losing his mind for a long time. Then his sight started to go. Like I guess the shock was just more than he could take. They say he still gets pretty upset at the sound of the foghorn. I suppose that's natural enough —considering."

I could see Mom coming out of the real-estate office across the street. I counted out my money.

"My name's Sandra Douglas," I told the boy behind the counter, along with my best smile. "Maybe I'll see you again. I hope to be around all summer."

I watched the bright-pink color rise over his collar, spread over his face, and settle in his ears.

"Luke Evans," he said, holding out his hand. "Glad to have you aboard."

He was cool. I didn't mind his being a little shy. In fact, I preferred it to the pushy type. Right then and there I decided to include Cokes as a regular thing, once we settled down.

Halfway across the street I knew Mom's news. I could see her face, even at a distance, glowing with a smug, self-satisfied beam.

"I got it!" she squealed breathlessly. "But, believe me, I heard all the objections."

We fell into step with the stream of early-morning shoppers.

Mom giggled. "That poor old New England Yankee will never be the same!" She laughed. "Such a lot of good, sound advice, none of which I took!"

"But it was for rent," I said. "Somebody must have put out the sign."

"In spite of women's new rights," said Mom, "it made no sense to him at all that two females should want to settle down in a big house alone where there had been a murder."

"Come to think of it," I replied, "when you put it that way, it doesn't sound all that bright to me either. Aren't you even a little bit scared?"

"Maybe," Mom admitted, sobering fast. "Maybe just a little. But my curiosity is overpowering, and, never mind the murder, I couldn't rest without having, at least, made an attempt to straighten out that first-night thing in my mind."

"And I've been boning up on the local gossip," I confided. "Just wait till you hear."

On the way home some of the sound advice began to seep through to Mom.

"It's such a *big* house!" she moaned. "I have never lived in a *whole* house. I haven't the foggiest idea how to look after even a *little* one. And just the two of us rattling around out there all by ourselves!"

Though I was having second thoughts myself, I felt that Mom needed a little spurring on. I knew that neither of us was ready to back out at that point, so we might as well start thinking positively.

"O.K." I challenged her. "If that's the way you feel, maybe we had just better forget the whole thing."

Mom shot me a quick, startled glance. Then she laughed.

"You know perfectly well that wild horses couldn't drag me away," she said. "How about you?"

"No way," I replied.

I suppose the Masons, by that time, had concluded that we were some strange new breed who couldn't be expected to think like normal human beings. Anyway, they hardly seemed surprised. In fact, they seemed genuinely anxious to help out in any way they could. Maybe they secretly liked the thought of our settling down close enough for them to watch —a whole summer's free entertainment!

"Who would have thought it would be so easy?" Mr. Mason marveled. "Anyone would think that the whole thing had been planned."

For some weird reason, I guess I had felt that way all along. Things seemed to fall into place just too easily. We hardly even had to try.

"I am coming to see you every single day," Eric promised, "but only in the daytime. Won't you be *scared* when it gets dark? Won't it be *spooky* at night?"

"I hate to disappoint you," I said, "but with us in it, it will have lights just like anybody else's house."

"I'm afraid you'll have a steady visitor." Mrs. Mason laughed. "He's positively eaten alive with curiosity."

Margie said nothing at all. There was no way of telling whether she was pleased or not. She was a genius at blank expressions. She must have had a lot of practice. Just the same, she was fascinating me more and more. I was glad I would be around for a while. Maybe I could figure out what made her tick.

There seemed to us no good reason why we should not move right in. The way was paved, our enthusiasm was at high peak, and maybe each of us secretly wanted to avoid thinking about it too much.

Mrs. Mason's mind worked in more practical ways. "At least give it a day to air!" she exclaimed. "A house closed that long will have a dreadfully stale and musty odor."

She had a point. It definitely had smelled musty. So we decided that one more day wouldn't make that much difference. In the meantime, we could hardly wait to charge over, open it up, and get things in order.

Chapter 5

Early the next morning Mr. and Mrs. Mason, Mom and I, with Eric sprinting on ahead, trooped over to the old house, hammer and hedge clippers in tow.

We watched while Mr. Mason ripped the boards from the windows and cut back some of the thick vines that had run wild, gobbling whole doors and windows and whatever else lay in their path.

Mom unlocked the door with the big rusty old key. The ancient hinges creaked and groaned as we pushed open the door.

I still felt a little weak-kneed and shaky when I stepped inside. It looked a lot more cheery with bright sunlight streaming in through the windows. But, at the same time, it made the thick dust everywhere and the cobwebs swinging from everything more obvious. It underlined the fact that no one had done any housekeeping for a very long time.

Just the same, maybe even more than ever, I had the peculiar feeling that I was a welcomed guest, as though someone was glad I had come. It was a feeling I couldn't quite put my finger on, like trying to hold on to a dream that seemed to be slipping away.

Mom and I had already decided to limit ourselves to the smaller wing. After all, for two cramped apartment dwellers, even that would seem like the Taj Mahal.

"If we used all those other rooms," Mom laughed, "I might not see you for weeks on end!"

"You could write," I replied, leaning out of one of the windows to gloat over the view, "or send smoke signals."

Even though the garden was overgrown and full of weeds,

it was still making out O.K. by itself. I had never seen so many roses of every size and description and color in my life. It was almost too much for my smog-city nose. I positively reeled back into the room.

The furniture was heavy and dark, with a lot of carved legs and fancy doo dads. It wasn't exactly what either of us would have chosen. Tasseled and beaded lampshades seemed a bit much. But altogether it was sort of comfortably quaint. Anyway, who wanted to look at furniture when you could look at the kind of view most people only dream about?

The room I chose for mine was something else. It had a brass bed that would have accommodated everyone in Hope's Crossing—all at the same time. The bed was covered with a green spread patterned with Chinese pagodas and palm trees. For knickknacks there were things like marble busts and vases that would have positively swallowed eight dozen roses. But, oh, wow! You should have seen the view —right over the water, with a couple of little green islands thrown in for good measure.

There was a nice fireplace too. I tried to imagine Sandra Douglas reclining in that bed, looking out of that window, with a fire blazing away in the fireplace! It was more than I could handle. I just had to be dreaming.

Mrs. Mason was sniffing around, flicking dust, thumping pillows, and shaking her head.

"It will take the whole summer to get it back in livable condition," she groaned.

"A little musty smell won't matter," Mom said cheerily. "It will help to remind us that we are in New England, where old things are always more respectable than new."

As a staunch New Englander, Mrs. Mason probably wasn't quite sure whether Mom's remark was complimentary or not, so she chose to ignore it.

"You can never manage all this by yourselves," she concluded. "Maybe you can get Nora to help. If anyone could straighten this place out, it would be Nora."

"Who is Nora?" asked Mom, scooping cobwebs from the corners with a broom handle.

"Just the neighborhood treasure," replied Mrs. Mason. "You will be lucky if she has the time to spare, but," she added, "with your kind of luck, I wouldn't be surprised if you would have no trouble at all."

Mom leaned on the broom handle and nodded thoughtfully. "It would be nice to have someone to steer us off in the right direction," she agreed. "I definitely want to do some painting, and we want plenty of free time to enjoy just being here."

Things were shaping up. Already we practically had a maid. How domestic could anyone get, and all in less than a week, I thought.

Nora lived in a small, barn-red house hidden away in a corner of one of the big estates. Once, in grander times, Mrs. Mason explained, it had been an estate toolshed. More recently it had been converted to living quarters and presented to Nora in return for her cleaning in the big house.

Nora's house was almost smothered out of sight in among the thick branches of some big old elm trees. Even though the sun was shining brightly, the house was in deep shade. Bare patches of ground showed that even the grass didn't consider it worth the effort.

The minute Nora opened the door, I could see that the inside was even gloomier than I had expected. The small windows were hung with limp lace curtains. Any light that might have seeped through was shut out by a collection of huge, potted, green plants.

Nora blinked her pale-green eyes as though she hadn't seen daylight for a long time. She stood in the doorway, pinning some loose strands of her thin, copper-colored hair into a sagging bun behind. When she recognized Mrs. Mason, she smiled broadly with a couple of enormous amber hairpins jutting out from her mouth. She looked slightly flustered to see two strangers. She sounded a little out of breath when she invited us inside. She kept apologizing for her appearance.

While she chattered on endlessly in her thick, Irish brogue, we almost sank out of sight in some deep, dark chairs in the living room.

I looked around, trying to figure out some of the dark shapes lurking everywhere. As soon as my eyes got used to the dim light, I could see that, though the room was tiny, everything in it was outsize. It looked a lot like a church basement the day before a white elephant sale. I wondered how Nora moved around in the maze, considering the fact that she was definitely on the broad side.

I guess she caught me looking. Anyway, she was on her feet in a minute, offering us a tour of the house.

It seemed that everything she had was a hand-me-down from someone or other whom she had worked for. That accounted for the size of everything. In a huge mansion, the pieces would have looked right.

Nora, showing us all her treasures, was as carried away as a kid on Christmas.

"Did you, in all of your born days, ever see the likes of this one?" She fairly chuckled with glee. She pointed to a big old-fashioned drop-leaf table. "If I had bought it meself, 'twould have cost me a fortune! See, 'tis solid as a rock!" She beamed, thumping it proudly.

We all nodded.

"It's lovely," Mom agreed weakly.

"An' nearly as good as brand-new!" Nora puffed. With one mighty shove she heaved the table away from the wall.

"Don't let Nora fool you," she said. "She wouldn't miss being part of this whole thing for anything in the world. Tragedy seems to have some awful fascination for her. Funerals or accidents—you can count on Nora to be first on the scene."

"If that man was her husband," I said, "then she's had some of her own tragedy firsthand."

"You heard?" Mrs. Mason looked surprised. Then she sighed. "Yes, it was perfectly dreadful about poor Charlie— such a nice-looking boy. But I sometimes think that the very quirk in Nora's nature, that fascination for the morbid, helped to protect her from the effects of her own tragedy. She certainly came through with a lot less scars than Owen, poor man."

Wheels within wheels, I thought. I wonder how many more Gilligans there are in this town.

Chapter 6

The next day we moved in bag and baggage. It really wasn't that much of a chore. We had already condensed our necessities to a bare minimum before we left Cleveland.

"We are not going to load ourselves down with a lot of luggage," Mom had warned at the very beginning of our summer plan-making. "Take only the things you can't possibly exist without."

That was easy for me. Stripped to the bare necessities, I could be perfectly happy with a jersey and one pair of jeans, which I was most of the time anyway.

Mom backtracked a little when she saw that I was about to take her at her word.

"Don't forget, it will be for all summer," she had cautioned. "We will need enough summer things."

So we had conjured up a shopping spree to buy a few things like shorts and bikinis.

Anyone in search of a cure for inflated ego should try modeling a bikini in a department store on a cold May day in Cleveland.

While Mom was busy bewailing the new lumps in her figure, I padded back and forth from the fitting room to the mirror feeling absolutely naked. My reflection seemed to have more limbs than a centipede—all long, lanky, and white as dough.

"Jeepers!" I groaned, "I look gross, like I spent the winter under a board."

"You look lovely, dear," Mom lied, shading her eyes from the glare. "Nothing that a good coat of tan won't cure!"

Once in a while even Mom gets caught up in the corny

mother routine, sidestepping the truth to protect her off-spring.

Now, here we were with more closet space than I ever dreamed existed, with practically nothing to hang in it. But it wasn't quite the same as moving into an empty house. Almost everything we would ever need was already there. In fact, in spite of the dust that coated everything, things seemed to have been left pretty much as they were. Little things, like a seashell arranged just so, or a book with the marker still inside, kept reminding us of the girl whose house it had been.

"It could be positively spooky," I told Mom, "but for some strange reason, it isn't. Never mind the murder, I just can't get away from the feeling that we were actually expected."

Mom nodded. "I feel it too," she agreed. "I guess this is just one of the times we have to trust our intuition. Both of us have definite positive feelings about the whole thing. I am satisfied to leave it at that—at least for the present."

We explored the cupboards, finding mountains of clean, folded linens, but all with that same old musty smell. Mom, positively dripping with nostalgia, unfolded them one by one.

"Just look at them," she crooned, "all crocheted edges, hemstitching, and embroidery! Just like my grandmother's! I thought the last of these had vanished a generation ago!"

"You're in New England now," I reminded her. "We left those things behind when we wagon trained out to the new frontier, remember?"

We strung a line between two big old trees in the garden and hung the sheets out to air. There was something awfully satisfying about watching them flap wild wind dances in the sun. Maybe it symbolized a coming back to life of the old house and the deserted old garden. Or maybe it was just the gay touch we both needed after experiencing so much that was old, and sad, and forgotten.

We swept the leaves from some of the main walks, and unclogged the fountain. We shook rugs and washed windows.

Mom spread her meager painting equipment out in a room that was all view.

"I've never had this much room!" she wailed. "How can I ever think with room enough to breathe and a place for everything?"

Everyone had warned us, "If you don't like the New England weather, then just wait a minute."

It was wasting no time in living up to its reputation. By noon the bright morning sunshine had vanished, and a skyful of heavy, low-hanging clouds moved in to take its place. We could see a thin mist rising to a fuzz on the horizon.

We were not quite ready to cope with the gloom of a cloudy day. Things that had seemed quaint and charming in the bright sunlight threatened to look positively sinister on a dark afternoon. However, to feel a little bit chicken was one thing. To admit it was something else. We each made a good try, but our strained lightheartedness wasn't all that successful.

I am sure we both breathed a secret sigh of relief at the sight of Eric skipping up the driveway, positively bursting with friendly curiosity.

"Mom thought you might like these." He beamed, presenting us with a basket brimming with superfresh rolls still warm from the oven.

We literally pounced on him. Food! We had been too involved to even think about it all morning.

"Did you find any treasure?" Eric aimed straight for the heart of his real interest.

"It depends on what you consider treasure," I said. "We

found sheets, and pillowcases, and towels, and dishes, and pots and pans."

Eric looked disgusted. "Not that old stuff!" he scoffed, wrinkling his freckled blob of a nose. "I mean *real* treasure, like the pirates buried."

"We haven't found any gold doubloons, if that's what you mean," I said.

After having demolished most of the rolls, we plunged with new energy back into the chore of putting the house into livable condition. For a couple suffering from droopy spirits, Eric was made to order. The sound of his endless, good-natured chatter echoing through the musty old rooms made everything seem normal and O.K. again.

By the time he was ready to leave, our panic had given way to a nice comfortable sense of knowing that civilization was really only a telephone call away. The thought of the good old down-to-earth Masons just around the corner was a real courage booster.

Later in the afternoon Nora stopped by to check us out. Her expression, as she peered past Mom into the gloomy insides of the house, was something to see. No self-respecting ghost, had one been lurking in the invisible, could have resisted just one little banshee wail.

"I thought I'd drop by," she explained, "to see if ye might be needin' something."

Mom and I exchanged sly glances. What she really wanted to find out, it was pretty clear to both of us, was whether or not we had stumbled across any more bodies.

It took a little, but not too much coaxing to get Nora to come inside.

"No." She backed off when Mom offered to hang her shabby navy-blue coat in the closet. "I can't be stayin' more than a minute."

As she edged cautiously into the library behind Mom, I suddenly caught her quick, startled glance. Her pale-green eyes were round as an owl's. Her hand flew to her mouth.

"Merciful heavens!" she cried. "Standin' right there, sure as y'r born, you were lookin' the spittin' image of the poor murdered girl herself! God rest her poor, unfortunate soul!"

Mom whirled around with the dazed look of someone in a mild state of shock.

"The saints preserve us!" Nora muttered, backing away and eyeing me suspiciously. "For a minute I thought 'twas she—if I hadn't seen with me own two eyes the poor unfortunate girl laid to rest in her own grave two whole years ago!" She ended with a series of clucking noises, and a sigh that shook her soft, sagging body like a small earthquake.

I was feeling a little wobbly, but the more I thought about it, the more I could see that there was something in what she said. Though the girl had been older, I remembered her as about my height and build. Her hair had been blond like mine, and about the same length. In a dim light, at first glance, we probably would resemble each other.

We all sat down a little uneasily. Nora perched on the very edge of the chair nearest the door.

Mom didn't look all that relaxed herself. She kept casting queer glances my way as though she were considering the possibility of my being a changeling.

By this time, I wasn't too sure myself. I felt I was in a new world with new rules. Nothing much could have surprised me anymore.

"Then you knew Miss Cameron?" Mom plunged in, trying to sound normal.

"Ach! That I did!" Nora replied, dropping her voice to an appropriately gloomy key. "Tuesdays and Fridays—those were her days. I can only give me ladies two days apiece each week," she explained grandly. "With so many wantin' me, I try to divide meself equal."

"Then you worked for her?" Mom exclaimed, surprised. "Here? In this very house? No one told us that!"

Nora nodded. She took in our eager faces with her shrewd, pale eyes. It must have been crystal-clear that we were literally dying for her next word. So she took her time. With the choice morsels of information she was dangling just out of reach, she could afford to make us wait—give suspense a chance to build.

"'Twas actually meself who found the body the mornin' after the murder," she announced at last, with a noticeable ring of pride in her voice.

Mom and I exchanged startled glances. I thought of what Mrs. Mason had said. It seemed that Nora had been Johnny-on-the-spot with this tragedy too!

I was beginning to understand why she might be a little more nervous than usual. The house must have positively reeked with unpleasant memories for her.

I guess Mom and I both figured we might as well hear her out. If we were to live in the house, we could hardly avoid hearing the story from someone. Nora probably knew as much as anyone.

Then, too, I reasoned, things are not usually quite so scary, once you know all the facts.

"The murderer was never found?" I started her off again with just the nudge she was waiting for.

She heaved another couple of supersighs and wagged her head mournfully.

"'Twas a terrible stormy night, that one," she recalled. "Windows bangin', lightnin' flashin'! 'Twas not a fit night out for man nor beast, that it wasn't!"

There could be no stopping her now. She settled back in

68

her chair with a far-out gleam in her eye. She had a good
story to tell and some very curious ears to pour it into. To
her way of thinking, the combination was irresistible and
worthy of being enjoyed to the fullest.

"The day followin' was a Tuesday," she related. "With
such a wind as had been ablowin' and moanin', and scatterin'
things about the whole night, the garden was flattened. Little
I could do about that! Then the fog settled in sudden. Ach!
I had the divil's own time in findin' me way to work!"

Even though it had all happened more than two years
before, Nora seemed as carried away as though it had been
yesterday.

"The front door was standin' wide open," she continued.
"I did think that a bit queer right away, with the fog thick-
er'n pea soup, so to speak."

"Did you call the police?" Mom cut in, hoping, I figured,
to bypass the grisly details that Nora had probably reserved
for her climax.

"That I did." Nora nodded vigorously. "I called George.
He came right on out."

"Of course you left everything just as it was until he got
here?" Mom quizzed thoughtfully.

"Glory be!" exclaimed Nora. "I hardly moved from the
spot, I was that petrified!"

Nora's parting words were about as cheerful as her visit
had been.

"The curse of this place is the fog," she complained bitterly. "'Twould like to smother the very breath out o'ye,
closin' in, as it does, night after night!"

Considering the fact that Charlie had been lost in one, it
wasn't too surprising that his mother would have a thing
against fogs, I thought.

Mom offered to drive Nora home and pick up some groceries on the way back.

"See if you can figure out that antique stove," she told me, "or we will find ourselves having the longest picnic on record."

I watched them drive off, my head still reeling from Nora's colorful story. So I had reminded her of Valerie Cameron! I wondered if anyone else would think so. Maybe that had something to do with the fact that I had felt so much at home and welcome in the old house right away.

The fog was really closing in. I could hardly see to the end of the driveway. I looked back over my shoulder, shuddered, and went inside.

From a dinky apartment kitchenette to the kitchen in the old house was a bigger leap than I was prepared to take.

The seemingly endless rows of cupboards and miles of counters must have been designed for an enormous family with even more enormous appetites.

There was a horrendous old metal sink that, it seemed to me, would do just fine as a bathtub, in a pinch. There were also two stoves.

One was an ominous-looking gas stove, which I rejected on sight. It seemed to me that a match within yards of it would create an explosion that could set all the hot lines in the world buzzing. So I turned my attention to the other one.

Basic survival lesson number one coming up, I thought. Would you believe a wood range?

I took a quick mental survey to figure out the principle of the antique. There was some wood stacked nearby, and even some matches. I decided to brave it out.

I put together a neat pile of rolled paper and sticks. I used most of the matches before I finally managed to transport a live one to the rolls of paper.

For a while it looked as though we might have to settle for a barbecue, or maybe just give up and smoke-cure everything.

I tried every possible combination of all the gadgets that apparently made up the draft system. I must have done something right. The air cleared, and the stove began to feel warm.

There is a friendly feeling about a real fire, I decided at once. The kitchen itself was about as homey as a Waldorf Cafeteria. The fog coming in and the dusk falling didn't help. Creepy shadows, like ghosts, had begun to materialize in all the corners.

I hoped that Mom wouldn't be too long. Even two people in a house that size seemed a lot more than one.

Stranded in the unnatural quiet, my brain got busy with the details of our first day. To me it seemed years since morning. I thought about Nora and the fact that I had reminded her of the murdered girl. . . . I thought about the murder. . . . Funny, until then, I really had not given it much thought. . . . That struck me as strange, since it was the one thing that everyone seemed to agree about. Now, suddenly, it was giving me an awfully creepy feeling.

Hey! Wait a minute! I caught myself up short. It was stupid to let Nora's story get to me. Why, even her version of "The Three Bears" would probably be hair-raising enough to give nightmares.

I scooped up another bundle of sticks and crammed it into the stove. I stepped back to watch the little orange flames leap and lick, pretending that my heart wasn't thumping a mile a minute.

It was more than I needed that the next sound was the thud of the heavy front door knocker.

I felt my scalp prickle and crawl. Who in the world would choose that unlikely hour of early evening to call? I thought.

Of course! I felt a great wave of relief wash over me. It would have to be one of the Masons. Who else would even know we had moved in?

None of the doors opened easily. Every movable part of the house had a permanent warp from the years of damp sea air. I clamped both hands on the big old brass doorknob, and pulled. Inch by creaking inch the heavy old door swung in.

I looked out, ready with a cheery greeting. The words stopped halfway. I saw George waiting patiently, his hands behind his back.

I suppose I would have done something brave and noble —like bolt, if he hadn't looked quite so friendly. He looked a lot different from the time Mom and I had first seen him. The suspicious look was gone. He just looked . . . friendly.

He smiled. "I'm sorry if I startled you. I saw that you had moved in. I just wanted to welcome you to the neighborhood."

I was beginning to feel a lot better, though my throat still felt dry as a bone.

"Thank you," I stammered. "That is very nice of you."

"If you need anything," he went on, "don't be afraid to ask."

"You are very kind," I replied. "This is all very new to us. I wouldn't be surprised if something would turn up."

He was being very friendly, I thought. We certainly had not been fair in judging him. It only goes to show how wrong first impressions can be.

Then, all at once, there he was, his hands outstretched, offering me a . . . . tiny, squirming, mewing Siamese kitten!

"It's for you," he said a little self-consciously, "to liven up the old place."

I was flabbergasted! After all those years of wishing, there it was, nestling into my trembling hands as though we belonged together! Its fur was like pale-cream silk. Its tiny smudged nose was cool. It had two of the roundest and bluest eyes imaginable.

I tried to stammer a thank-you. George waved it aside.

Still smiling, he turned and began his way down the steps.

I stood speechless, holding the soft little ball of warm fur against my cheek. I stared after George's tall, bent figure. His arms hung out of the sleeves of his jacket, a couple of inches too short. The top of his head was bald, just as red as his face, and even, I couldn't help noticing, almost as freckled.

He paused at the last step, turning back to add, "Two women alone sometimes need a man for the heavy things. Don't hesitate to call on me."

I nodded stupidly, still speechless.

George disappeared into the fog. Then the thought struck.

Was it all just a coincidence—or had George known that I wanted a Siamese kitten more than almost anything? I was positive I had not told anyone . . . not anyone at all, except . . . Margie!

With a sinking feeling, I remembered the small, frightened figure dashing out of George's place on the night of my walk. It was just possible that, for some odd reason, they had been discussing me and my half-made plans. That was something to think about. They could have fooled me. I would never have figured I was all that important to either of them.

I could see the faint glow of Mom's headlights turning into the driveway. I hugged the kitten close, and tore down the steps to meet her.

Chapter 7

At first Mom was just as stunned as I was with George's gift, but, I must say, a whole lot less enthusiastic.

"You should probably give it back," she told me, being careful not to press the issue, knowing only too well that I would rather die first.

"It's not just *any* cat," she fussed on. "It is a beautiful animal. It must be worth a good deal. I only wish I knew *why* he did it."

"Maybe he was just being neighborly," I said. "Is that so hard to believe?"

Mom frowned, watching the kitten frisk up and down the chair legs batting at shadows.

"People like George just don't *do* things like that," she replied. "I hate to think that we might be under some kind of obligation to him."

Let Mom do the worrying, I thought. There was no way that I would give up the kitten before the end of the summer. And, after that, well, that was a long way off.

"I'm going to call her Cleopatra," I hurried on. "Cleo for short."

I suppose I wanted to clinch my ownership with a name, any name. And Cleopatra was the first exotic name that came to mind. A Siamese cat, if nothing else, is exotic.

Mom scowled and did not reply. She probably wasn't about to involve herself by arguing that it wasn't a Siamese name, which she probably would have done otherwise.

That first night, without actually admitting it, neither of us could quite face turning out the lights and going off by ourselves into separate beds in separate rooms.

"I never knew a night could be that dark." Mom shuddered, peering out into the pea-soup fog and pitch-blackness. "I don't believe there is even a moon or stars out there anywhere."

"When you can't see two feet ahead," I replied, "it isn't likely that anything a few billion light-years away will show."

"I think we'd definitely feel better," Mom ventured, in one of her more rational attempts at bravery, "if we took a good look through the rest of the house. Just seeing for ourselves that all those empty rooms are really empty is going to make both of us sleep a whole lot better."

I had to agree, although I would have been quite happy to postpone the grand tour until broad daylight with a lot of open windows and sunshine. But half of being afraid is not knowing, I thought, and with a whole long, dark night ahead of us, it seemed sensible to prepare ourselves by finding out everything we could.

I followed Mom down the hall, switching on lights as we passed. After the first couple of rooms, our courage began to seep back. There was something nice and comforting about watching all those shadowy corners disappear, and the old house beginning to glow like a Christmas tree.

It was obvious that most of the rooms had not been used for a long, long time. They smelled old, and everything we touched was coated with a thick layer of fine dust. We lifted the corners of sheets that had been draped over some of the things. The furniture was expensive, ornate, and old-fashioned. At one time it all must have been very grand and elegant. There must be a lot of forgotten stories wrapped up in these rooms, I thought, stories that most likely could never be told. Maybe because it was so quiet, or because we weren't used to rooms that big, the echoes sounded almost alive. There was something strange and unreal about human sounds in a place that had been without them for so long.

"We could take a room a day for the rest of the summer," I began to say in what I thought was a normal voice, but the shout that seemed to be coming from me startled us both, so I whispered the rest, "and never see them all!"

When Mom laughed in reply, I had the distinct feeling that everything in the room shrank back. From then on, for the most part, we just kept our remarks to a minimum, and resorted to gestures, frowns, and raised eyebrows to get our messages across.

It was like a breath of unexpected fresh air suddenly to come upon a room that actually showed some signs of being used. It wasn't too surprising, because it must have been something else on a sunny day. It was a corner room, all windows on two sides. To top it off, we could hear the ocean just outside.

Mom had relaxed and was plainly in her element. It was obvious that Valerie had used this room as a studio. There were tubes of paint laid out, looking as though they had just been squeezed. There was even a palette with little mounds of dried-up paint next to a painting propped on an easel. It almost seemed as though someone was intending to come back to them any minute.

We could see, from across the room, that the painting was a portrait. We hurried over to have a closer look.

I was surprised. All the other paintings in the house were abstracts. There was not much question, however, that this one belonged with them. The colors were the same, and handled with a touch that was almost as clear as a signature. The portrait was of a little girl—probably nine or ten years old. She looked happy, with a wonderful smile that made you feel like smiling back.

When my attention shifted to the eyes, I did an unexpected double take. I knew those eyes! There could be no mistaking eyes as unusual as those. They were a peculiar mixture of brown and yellow that turned out almost amber.

I shot a glance at Mom to see if she had noticed. It was obvious by her dropped jaw and bulging eyeballs that she had.

"It's Margie!" she cried. "It has to be Margie! Just look at those eyes!"

"I'm looking," I said, "but I thought Mrs. Mason told you that none of them had even known Valerie Cameron."

Mom nodded. "She definitely did," she replied. "She said that the girl never mixed with the neighbors at all."

"Well, she mixed with one," I said. "Portraits aren't usually painted long-distance."

"I can't understand it," Mom went on. "If Margie knew her, then why didn't Nancy mention it?"

"It could be," I replied, "that she didn't know. It didn't impress me that the two of them shared many confidences."

We looked back at the portrait—a couple of years younger, but there could be no mistaking the likeness, and once you got used to the unlikely smile, a very good one.

"She looks superhappy," I said. "You wouldn't expect a smile like that from the Margie we know."

We stood for a minute staring at the portrait, trying to find a place for it in the confused story that was building in our minds.

Then Mom laid her hand on my arm. "Not a word, now, to any of them," she said. "Let's gather all the facts we can before we begin stirring everyone up."

"Wow!" I laughed. "We're off and running! I have a feeling that however we describe this summer back home, dull won't be one of the words!"

Mom's eyes sparkled their reply. The old sleuthing light was back.

"I'm staking my claim on this room," she announced.

"Could anyone paint less than a masterpiece in a place like this?"

We stared out into the pitch-black night. The branches of a tree outside brushed the windowpane. We could hear the waves crashing on the rocks and the foghorn moaning out from nowhere.

"Come on." Mom shuddered. "The sooner we get to sleep, the sooner it will be morning. And, as for me, that can't be soon enough."

We walked back to the small wing of the big house, too occupied with our own thoughts to talk. We turned out the lights as we went. At least we had forgotten to be afraid. With things shaping up the way they were, curiosity was fast beginning to crowd out fear.

All night I drifted back and forth, in and out of sleep. Images of the girl floated constantly across my mind. They seemed very real. I thought I saw her smiling, pleased that I was there.

The morning's bright sunshine did a lot toward making fear, doubt, and any other dark emotion seem practically an impossibility. The clear light of day seemed to be the perfect time to resolve that, whatever happened, I would keep a tight leash on my imagination. It would be all too easy, in a situation like that, to lose hold of reality altogether, and drift off on a cloud of fantasy. Anyway, with facts that topped my wildest dreams, who needed anything more?

So, I spent the first part of the morning relaxing in the garden and trying to be logical. It wasn't easy. Hope's Crossing isn't a logical kind of place. Thoughts tend to drift with the sound of waves washing up on the sand, and the clear, bubbling whistles of cardinals coming from the trees. But I did the best I could.

As far as I could figure, Margie had to be some part of the action. In that case, I reasoned, my first objective should be to gain her confidence in some way. That was going to take some fancy doing. She wasn't exactly yearning for my friendship. But I decided to try.

It was odd how things seemed to be shaping up with almost no effort on my part—like Cleo choosing that exact minute to come prancing into view, making every kittenish effort to attract my attention.

Well, if that wasn't a ready-made solution to my problem, nothing was! And with a charmer like Cleo, how could I possibly fail?

Gleefully I scooped Cleo into my arms and made off.

I found Mrs. Mason starched and ironed to the ear tips, pacing the patio, raving to Mr. Mason, who had ducked behind his newspaper and probably wasn't hearing a word. Some of her favorite red geranium plants seemed to have come up missing. Evidently it was a big deal, even if she did have a few dozen more. I was surprised that she noticed.

"I don't know what has happened to this neighborhood," she wailed, turning to me, the only one within earshot who might listen. "It used to be such a nice, quiet place. Now, it seems that anything might happen, from murders to someone coming right up on your patio and carrying off your best plants!"

Mr. Mason folded his newspaper and looked up. He couldn't keep the annoyance from seeping through his careful words.

"For heaven's sake, Nancy! Why should anyone want your geraniums? There are more flowers in Hope's Crossing now than anyone knows what to do with."

I found Margie in the backyard, up to her elbows in red paint. She was bent over a small, overturned sailboat, painting up a storm.

"Hi!" I began. "What are you doing?"

Such a stupid question didn't deserve an answer. And it didn't get one.

I stroked Cleo, hoping that Margie might make the next move. I might as well have been the paint bucket for all the recognition I got.

Well, forget your pride, I thought. You have a purpose, so you might as well see it through.

"Is that your sailboat?" was my next highly original question.

I got a nod. I suppose I should have been thankful for that. Then, "Do you sail?" I lumbered on.

This time I was rewarded by a quick, exasperated glance. "Of course," she said.

There was no "of course" about it, I thought grimly. Here I was actually in high school, and I had never even once set foot on a sailboat.

I was hoping that she might notice Cleo by herself. The kitten was clawing her way up and down my front, mewing conversationally. Nobody could have missed knowing she was there.

"I brought Cleo over to show you," I tried.

She stopped slapping the paintbrush long enough to give Cleo the once-over.

"Nice." She nodded, with her usual blank look. Then she went back to her painting.

I was not about to give up, even if the whole thing did have all the signs of a mission impossible.

"When will your boat be ready?" I asked.

"Tomorrow."

"Will you take me for a sail? I have never been."

There was a long pause while she considered this pathetic confession.

"Sometime," she replied.

There was a finality about her voice that told me our visit was ended, not that it had ever begun.

Well, I had not done too badly for a starter, I thought. I could always have another go at it tomorrow. So I walked off.

In Hope's Crossing, nothing was ever done halfway. In spite of an occasional fog, the sun, when it did shine, seemed warmer, more golden, and more plentiful than anyplace else. Add to that a few million rosebushes, rhododendrons, azaleas, and lilacs, all blooming at the same time, the nightly sunsets, and a couple of daily tides thrown in. It was changing two perfectly ordinary individuals into gluttons of the good life. Mom and I were being spoiled forever.

Mom's interest in a meditative existence, alone with her easel, was the first of our practical habits to go. In search of more intellectual company than her daughter was able to provide, she joined forces with the local art school and settled in to teach some summer classes.

"We can't spend our entire time ghost-hunting," she explained. "There's a real world out there, and we need to keep one foot in it."

She was right. We needed a little perspective. So I was really excited when I was lucky enough to find a part-time job as usher in the theater-in-the-round nearby. It was not the kind of a job that was likely to turn you into a millionaire overnight, but you did get to see all the Broadway musicals that spread out from New York in the summer. If you were on the ball, some of those in the know informed me, you might even be offered the chance to play a bit part when extras were needed. That sounded pretty cool to me.

Things shaped up even better than I had dared hope. First of all, I was one of the few lucky ones plucked from the work crew to play a part in some crowd scenes in the very first production—not exactly a starring role, but I did get to share in the excitement of rehearsals, first night, and all that kind of thing. Besides, I wore a fantastic turn-of-the-century costume—buttons and bows, the whole works.

For someone who has lived most of her life in dungarees, learning to walk in a hobble skirt without tripping was really something else. Women's lib took on a whole new meaning.

I guess I always feel best with lots of excitement around. Settling down to a lonely day of painting might be just fine for Mom, but I definitely was a lot happier where things were happening.

There turned out to be other benefits too. Like the afternoon just before a matinee when I wandered outside for a breath of cool air. I will never know how our female ancestors survived the summers, buttoned up in all those belts and bustles, tight as a mummy.

I ducked over to stand in line at the lunch counter for a quick Coke before curtain time.

I was born lucky. Who would have thought that of all the people in Hope's Crossing Luke Evans would be the one with a summer job at the theater's lunch counter?

When he recognized me, which he could hardly have done without a little help, considering my gay nineties gown and my false eyelashes a yard long, his face took on a bright neon glow.

"You're an actress?" he asked, sounding terribly impressed.

I really hated to disappoint him.

"No way," I replied. "Just a jack-of-all-trades most of the time, and a face in the crowd sometimes."

I had to grab my Coke and move out of line. The people behind me were beginning the restless stir of a herd of cattle about to stampede.

That Luke was a superbrain was the first thing I noticed about him. Whatever the subject, he would more than likely turn out to be an expert on it. So it wasn't too surprising that we should find out we had at least one interest in common.

History had always been the world's worst drag to me in school. Here, I was actually beginning to enjoy some of it. It was thrilling to see the old places where history had actually been made.

So when Luke offered to guide a tour of two through the local cemetery, I jumped at the chance.

We had talked about gravestone rubbings in one of my art classes. I was anxious to try some and maybe make a collection to take back home.

A date at the cemetery with anyone else would sound pretty freaky anytime outside Halloween. But with Luke it seemed the most normal thing in the world. There were some great old stones, he told me. A lot of them dated back to the 1700's.

I had a roll of paper and some crayons stashed away in my locker. As soon as I had unbuttoned and unwound my borrowed glamour and become plain old dungareed Sandra Douglas again, I grabbed the roll of paper and bolted off to find Luke.

The cemetery was a couple of miles away, just past the edge of the other end of town. So we drove over in Luke's old beat-up car that would have been a prized exhibit in any American auto museum.

"Don't expect a Forest Lawn," Luke warned me. "This old graveyard isn't used much anymore."

"Gone out of style," I asked, "or out of room?"

"A little of each," Luke replied. "Because it's small and not much of a showplace, the people in town with money enough to do something about it just aren't interested."

It was perfectly obvious at first glance that no one was interested, or had been for a long, long time. It was a dilapidated and depressing sight.

The old gray slate stones lopped and leaned in every direction. Even the newer ones seemed to do not much better. There were a few tattered little flags and some faded artificial flowers in green plastic vases.

"You wouldn't think," I said, thoroughly disgusted, "that a glamour spot like Hope's Crossing would let a disaster like this exist practically in its backyard."

Luke shrugged. "I suppose no one even bothers to look."

"That's just the trouble!" I stormed. "If it doesn't show, forget it! It just illustrates how much they *really* care, apart from building up an image."

It was beginning to touch my favorite cause of all causes, ecology.

We pulled away old weeds and scraped off layers of moss, revealing old stones with blurred and timeworn inscriptions that hadn't seen the light of day for years.

My collection was definitely taking a big step forward. I stacked my masterpieces, each one better than the last.

As time went by, we became totally absorbed in the decaying atmosphere and the faded old memories of a long-dead past. So we couldn't have been more astonished when we happened to notice one blazing spot of bright color in the middle of all that gloom.

We raced over to investigate.

There, in sharp contrast to the neglect all around, was one cleared green plot absolutely vibrating with vigorous red, red geraniums, recently watered, and not a weed anywhere. The effect was positively dazzling.

Odd, I thought right away, that it should be geraniums—and red ones at that. But then, I supposed the world was full of red geraniums.

"Well, what do you know about that?" Luke was saying. "Who says nobody cares? At least one does!"

I leaned over to read the inscription on the plain gray

stone: VALERIE CAMERON.

A chill rippled up my spine. I felt suddenly weak-kneed and shaky.

"Oh, wow! Oh, wow!" was all that came through.

"Hey! Isn't that . . . ?" Luke cried. "Isn't that the girl who was murdered a couple of years ago over at your place?"

I nodded, leaning against a convenient tree to keep from falling over.

I was remembering my visit with the very much alive and real girl on my first night in Hope's Crossing. Now, suddenly, I was faced with the stark, undeniable fact that she had died two years before. I wasn't prepared for that. Being told and seeing for yourself were definitely two different kettles of fish.

"I wonder who keeps it up," said Luke. "It's very odd. I don't think she had any family at all, at least, everyone seemed to think she hadn't. And if you want to believe the stories that went around, she didn't have all that many friends either. She was a kind of recluse, I guess."

"Well, in spite of what anybody says," I pointed out, "at least she had one friend, and a pretty darned good one it seems, from all the signs."

Suddenly I felt Luke's hand grip my arm. I turned quickly in time to glimpse a stirring in the bushes on the other side of the fence.

Just in time I ducked. A rock, hurled from somewhere, grazed by inches away and settled with a dull thud in the unmown grass.

Stunned, I watched Luke bend down and pick up the rock. He untied a small, folded piece of paper tied to it with a piece of string. I read over his shoulder the shaky pencil scrawl:

"Snoopy Sandra Douglas. Curiosity killed the cat. Don't be a cat."

The fence around the graveyard was high and topped with two rows of barbed wire. We rushed around to the gate, and back to where we had seen the movement in the bushes. But, by that time, whoever had been there had disappeared. We could see the flattened grass where someone had crouched, watching us.

It was pretty clear to me that I was being warned by someone that putting the pieces of the puzzle together might be a lot more risky than I had bargained for.

"Don't say a word about this to anyone," I warned Luke. "I know Mom. If she thought for a minute that there was any real danger, she would call off the whole summer. There is no way that I will let anyone scare me away. Running back to Cleveland is exactly what someone hopes I'll do. Well, I won't. At least, not until I find out a few answers."

Chapter 8

To my surprise Margie, true to her promise, did actually come across with an invitation to go sailing.

I hoped I looked the part. I had been very careful to see that my shorts and jersey were the acceptable Hope's Crossing kind and looking definitely on the used side.

It paid off. Margie's first quick glance covered the works. I had the distinct feeling that if my outfit had looked too new, she would have called the whole thing off with a stomachache.

She had brought Eric along for support. That was just fine with me. In fact, it was a great relief. Eric would be perfect to fill in the big holes in the conversation.

The two of them made a good combination. Margie seemed perfectly happy to do all the work if Eric would do all the talking. That arrangement seemed made to order for Eric too.

Margie was obviously an old hand. I watched enviously as she expertly hoisted sail, slipped in the centerboard, and pushed the boat into the shallow water offshore.

I followed behind, wading through the cold water, gradually numbing to the knees. With the grace of a water buffalo, I made an untidy attempt to hop into the boat. By some rare stroke of luck, it did not quite capsize.

"Step in the middle!" Eric shrieked. "If you don't," he chuckled gleefully, "we'll tip over before we even start!"

I saw the two of them exchange amused and knowing glances. Oh, well, I thought, it had almost been worthwhile. Margie had come as close to a giggle as I supposed she ever would.

From the first, I could see that she was aware that she had the upper hand and was enjoying it. In fact, she seemed to be quite interested in making sure that I learned the fundamentals and took great pains to answer all my questions.

That I managed to come through without a fractured skull was nothing short of pure luck.

"Ready about! Hard alee!" Margie would suddenly shout. Then, *zoom!* over would swing the boom, mowing down whatever did not have the sense to move out of its way. But it seemed to me that a few knobs on the head was a small price to pay for the kind of adventure I was having.

We zigzagged a course, tacking back and forth between the islands. At last I knew what it would feel like to fly, I thought. And I didn't mean sealed inside some big old super-jet. I was feeling just as the sea gulls must have, feeling the wind slip past.

In a setting like that, it would have been next to impossible not to feel free and friendly. A nice normal conversation had even developed among the three of us. True, it was limited to just one subject—sailing—but, at least, I was seeing a new side of Margie, actually relaxed and really a very pleasant person to be with.

I must have passed the test. Anyway, she invited me again, and even often. Though it was a little slower than I would have liked, I was definitely making progress with her. Eventually, with the help of her boat and my irresistible Cleo, I wedged even closer. It was a real triumph when she gave me an armload of her cat sketches to take home. They were good enough to impress anyone.

Even Mom.

Every artist needs a protégé. Although Mom was always very tactful, for a long time I had had the uncomfortable feeling that I was not quite living up to her expectations as an artist. Now, here at last was someone she could honestly rave about. Our talents, by comparison, couldn't help but convince even a fond mother's hopes that I was far from being a budding Wyeth.

"She has genuine talent!" Mom crowed with delight. "Why, with just a little training, that child could be a winner!"

I felt positively relieved to see Mom able to unleash all that enthusiasm. It must have been bottled up for a long time, waiting for some spectacular talent to burst forth from me. And I felt just as relieved that Margie the Mouse might be a winner in something besides sailing.

I must say, when Mom has an idea, you can count on action to follow.

It seemed to me that Mrs. Mason looked genuinely surprised to discover that Margie had any positive qualities at all.

"Oh, I don't know," she hesitated after Mom's glowing report. "She does scribble a lot, but then, don't most children?"

"This is different!" Mom declared. "Margie definitely has a special talent that it would be a crime not to encourage."

So it was decided that Mom was to take Margie along to a couple of her classes at the art school.

Margie, apart from appearing slightly stunned, seemed surprisingly willing, and maybe even eager, to go along.

After a busy afternoon of peak tension at the theater, I was always more than ready for the leisurely stroll home through Hope's Crossing. To have Luke walk with me was especially super. I felt I was getting to know him better than I ever could have where everything was a race with time.

To begin, I told him the whole fantastic story of my visit with the strange girl that first night. I guess I hoped that, with all his brains, he might be able to help me work something out.

I could tell by his expression that he was actually believing every word. You can only expect trust like that from a real friend. Probably having seen Valerie's grave and the rock hurled at me from the bushes helped.

When I had finished, I could see that Luke was wearing his Einstein expression. Sure enough, Einstein himself couldn't have come up with a better reply.

"I guess you just stumbled into another dimension," he said. "There must be a lot of other dimensions that we don't know anything about."

I braced myself. If I had wanted a simple answer, I should never have asked Luke.

"With all those dimensions lying around, waiting to be stumbled into," I said, "why doesn't it happen more often? And why me, of all people, to be the one to stumble?"

I could see that I had come up with a real puzzler, even for Luke. But anyway, it made him look at me with a lot more interest than he ever had before, a special kind of interest, as though even I might have a hidden dimension that couldn't be seen with the naked eye.

"The range of our senses is small," Luke brainstormed on. "One of the main functions of them is to prevent confusion by screening out anything not absolutely essential for our earthly survival. So we are 'tuned in,' you might say, to frequencies similar to our own. If we could switch stations or frequencies, we would probably tune in on other worlds or dimensions. Maybe that was what you did—just switched stations."

I thought that over carefully, activating brain cells that had never been used. I liked what he was saying. It made a kind of kooky sense to me, though it probably wouldn't have to a lot of other people.

"If I could just pin down one single person with firsthand information," I sighed. "I have a feeling that there are a lot more legends than facts floating around."

Luke was making a big thing of kicking stones in the dust with the toe of his worn-out sneaker. We had already passed the Masons'. I could see the postman leaving George's place, completely absorbed in thumbing through a handful of letters.

Luke saw him too. "Why don't you ask him?" He grinned. "He must have seen the girl as often as anyone."

"A brilliant idea!" I exclaimed. "Providing it is the same man. Don't forget, it was more than two years ago."

Luke laughed. "By the look of that old scout, he came into the game shortly after the pony express."

He could have been right. It took just a quick glance to see that the postman was well past his prime. In fact, at the rate he was moving, I thought, things were going to be awfully out of date and out of style before he got around to delivering them.

He was probably the cagey New England type, careful about giving out information to outsiders. But then, I reasoned, almost everyone, even an old postman, usually has a pretty active curiosity.

I began by asking for our mail.

"Y're new 'round these parts, ain'tcha?" he asked, peering over a bundle of letters.

I nodded. "I live over at the old Saunders place," I told him. "You know, where the girl was murdered a couple of years ago."

I had been right about the curiosity. There was not very much of anything shining in his eyes, but what there was, was all curiosity.

"Don't say!" he exclaimed. "Pretty spunky, seems t' me, fer a couple of women t' move right in on top of a murder!"

I didn't think that two years later was moving right in on top of one, but I decided not to argue.

"I suppose you knew Valerie Cameron?" I asked casually.

The old man shifted from one creaky leg to the other. He wound his rubbery face into some amazing contortions, and spit into the breeze before he replied.

"Odd sort, that one," he remarked. "Never cared to pass the time of day like most folks. Fact is, hardly ever saw her, but then, guess nobody else did neither."

"That was a pretty big house to live in all alone, completely by herself." I helped him along.

"Yep," he agreed. "Don't know what she ever did with him, but she must've had a husband one time or t'other. A lot of the letters were addressed 'Mrs'. Never did see hide nor hair o' him though."

He took one letter from his bundle. He held it at arm's length, squinting as he turned it from side to side.

"See George's got another of them Mexican letters," he said. "Know anybody collects stamps? George Gilligan must have a lot of 'em."

We watched the old postman totter off on his spindly legs, while we mulled over these new bits of information.

He turned once more, regarded us curiously, then, as an afterthought added, "The girl did have one real good friend, though, Crazy Nate. Saw him over there a few times. Seemed real friendly."

"Who in the world is Crazy Nate?" I turned to ask Luke.

His expression surprised me. For once, supercool Luke looked almost excited.

"He's just the town's favorite character," he replied. "He lived on a boat. He has been spending the summers here for a long time, right up until last year. Nobody saw him at all last year."

"What do you mean he lived on a boat?" I wanted to know. "What kind of a boat?"

Luke laughed. "It was one of a kind," he said, "all patched

together and weather-beaten. He always took the same spot every summer—up the beach about a mile. Rumors of all kinds were always floating around, like his being a professor at one of the big colleges in the winter, or someone famous in disguise. None of them was ever pinned down and proved true. He always made it very clear that where he spent the rest of his time was his own business."

"Why was he called Crazy Nate?" I asked. "It doesn't sound to me as though he was all that crazy."

"You know how kids are," Luke said. "They tagged him because he was different, and the name stuck."

We walked up the long drive to the old house in silence. However you looked at it, the place was definitely an impressive sight. Maybe it had been there for so long that it had just naturally become part of the landscape. Anyway, one couldn't help feeling it had been there forever.

"Who do you suppose George knows in Mexico?" I asked.

Luke shrugged. "Beats me. He doesn't exactly give the impression of a jet-setter with cosmopolitan friends."

I laughed. "It's probably just a pen pal he found in the classified ads of the *Policeman's Gazette.*"

For the next few days I found myself thinking and wondering a lot about Crazy Nate, the one person I had ever heard was friendly with Valerie Cameron. Just my luck that he had vanished!

But little did I realize that the old postman's words had set the stage for a new and surprising development that wasn't too long in coming.

Unless you were a dyed-in-the-wool native of Hope's Crossing, you were bound to feel pretty awkward in a lot of situations that everyone else took for granted. I watched little kids, barely able to toddle, take to the water and swim like little ducks. And mere infants, it seemed to me, were operating every kind of boat in a way that you wouldn't believe.

My own swimming added up to a few turns around the apartment pool, so I hadn't been too eager to display my Cleveland dog paddle to Margie and Eric, who were already a serious challenge to the seals. But they turned out to be surprisingly kind and coached me to the point of a respectable showing, at least.

After a few unbelievably chilly laps one morning, I sprawled on the sand, soaking up the sun and trying to store it up to be doled out over the next Cleveland winter.

Eric, building a sand megalopolis nearby, kept up a running chatter of all the neighborhood goings-on. Apart from having sand kicked in my face from time to time, it was a lot easier than reading the newspaper.

I must have levitated several feet off the ground when his shrill voice suddenly ripped the morning's peace to shreds a few inches from my exposed ear.

"Crazy Nate is coming back!"

In a second, he was on his feet and dashing off like a wild antelope to the water's edge.

His excitement shot through me like an electric charge. Almost before I knew what was happening, I found myself taking off after him, as though I had waited all my life for this moment.

But it turned out to be more than worthwhile.

Talk about staging! How dramatic can real life be?

I could see the boat—if one had the imagination to call it a boat—floating by. I could hear the regular throb of an engine, while small waves slapped the shoreline in a quickening rhythm.

It was pure magic! There, materialized before my eyes, was a fantastic old weather-beaten boat right out of never-never land, complete with captain to match.

It looked to me exactly like the illustration from a kid's picture book. A thin, black stovepipe poked up through the cabin roof, and a wisp of smoke ribboned out behind. Bobbing along at the end of a long rope was a battered old dinghy, straining to keep up.

The old captain, looking proud as any admiral, smiled and waved in reply to Eric's enthusiastic waves from shore. Though he looked just as patched together as Luke had said, the only word I could have used to describe him was—noble.

We watched while the boat moved slowly past and chugged off with impressive dignity.

"He's going to tie up where he always does," Eric squealed. "He's come back! I gotta tell everybody. Crazy Nate's come back!"

He raced off, his excitement still at high peak.

Wow! I was thinking, One thing for sure, the summer was turning out to be a terrific bargain at any price.

Chapter 9

One thing for sure that I have inherited from Mom is an overdeveloped curiosity. So you can imagine the glee of us both when we discovered that, from one of our windows, with the help of a pair of binoculars, we could occasionally zero in on our new neighbor. It was going to help a lot in trying to figure him out.

"I wonder if he ever gets lonely," Mom said with a calculating, faraway gleam in her eye.

"Why don't you bake a pie and find out?" I suggested.

Mom shook her head with a laugh. "The old welcome-wagon approach would never work with him. I'm afraid we will have to be a lot more original than that."

He made things a lot easier for us by paddling off regularly in his old dinghy on frequent fishing excursions. His favorite spot was practically our backyard.

It was nice having a neighbor to watch. The big house with all its grounds was more exclusiveness than we were used to. Having lived all our lives in apartments, we just naturally took watching and being watched by neighbors for granted. I wondered how neighborly the old man was willing to be, because I, for one, was intending to waste no time in finding out.

He was still on my mind when I climbed into my own big old brass bed later that night, feeling, as I did each time, like Marie Antoinette, at least. I arranged Cleo in her usual spot at the foot, and tucked the green pagodas under my chin.

The rising breeze rattled the shutters softly. Moonlight, filtering through the leaves outside, sent a troop of shadowy acrobats tumbling across my wall. The beam of light from the lighthouse on the island swept the room like a giant windshield wiper.

I hoped the old captain didn't mind nosy neighbors too much. I could hardly wait to worm my way far enough into his life to find out what made him different.

I slushed out into sleep with my last thoughts trailing after me and plunged into my most fantastic dream ever. I was chugging through Cleveland's main street on a houseboat with Luke at the helm, while the old captain kept pulling lobster traps over the side, unloading fresh, cooked red lobsters dripping with butter.

I woke suddenly sometime in the pitch black of the night. For a minute I hung somewhere between sleeping and waking. Then my dulled brain snapped to attention at the unmistakable sound of the metal latch being jiggled on the outside of my window.

I bolted upright and aimed my attention toward the sound. Nora's story of the murder flashed across my mind in wide-screen technicolor, sending icy chills charging through my veins.

If I have any natural hero instincts, they must have been still asleep. I slid out of bed and raced to the door. I paused with my hand on the knob. Something about my real feet, on the cold, real floor, let a little reason trickle back into my numb brain.

The only sounds I could hear were the usual beat of the waves and the leaves brushing the outside of my windowpane.

Just a case of jumpy nerves, I thought, plain and simple. If I wanted to last out the summer in a house where there had been a murder, then I had better learn to keep my cool. Mom wouldn't appreciate waking up in the middle of the night with no excuse better than a branch brushing the window.

I tiptoed closer. The pale-blue moonlight slipped over the windowsill and gathered in a pool on the floor.

Then, wow! If I could have found any voice at all, I would have had everyone in Hope's Crossing rushing to my aid!

I saw two luminous eyes, like yellow neon lights, gleaming in from the dark outside my window.

Surviving the first shock, I suddenly relaxed. I chuckled out loud from pure relief. I knew that only an animal has eyes that shine like that in the dark. And to have climbed the tree outside my window, it would have to be a pretty small one at that.

I advanced a few more steps, straining my eyes to see past the moving shadows of the leaves outside.

I breathed easier. Just as I had thought, it was only a cat. Maybe he was cold, or lost.

I unlatched the window, letting it swing out gently.

As light as a feather, the cat stepped over the windowsill and dropped to the floor into the pool of moonlight.

I positively gasped with astonishment. It was an enormous Siamese cat. He stroked his warm, velvety fur back and forth across my legs, purring deep in his throat in the nice chatty way that Siamese cats do. He looked at me with eyes that shone exactly like blazing blue fire.

My heart began thumping like crazy. I had never seen any cat as large and beautiful as that one before—except *one!*

Noiseless as a shadow, the cat slipped through the partly opened door. I could hear the pad of his soft feet dropping from one step to another on the stairs.

Turning on the lights as I went, I followed him. I wasn't too sure that I wasn't dreaming. It wouldn't have surprised me at all to have suddenly found myself waking up right there beneath the green pagodas.

I found the cat in the kitchen chirp-purring a cheery welcome as soon as he spotted me.

I figured that he was asking for food, so I put together a few scraps in a bowl and set it down in front of him.

He couldn't have been very hungry. He barely nibbled the food. I could see that he was sleek and fat, obviously well fed and cared for.

I wondered if he could possibly be the same cat. Rama, I remembered the girl had called him. If he were the same one, where could he have been until now? Two years is a very long time for a cat. No one, that I could think of, had ever mentioned what had happened to him. But, then, more than likely it was just some cat that happened to look a lot like him.

But I couldn't quite convince myself. I knew that of all the Siamese I had ever seen before, none of them came even close to being as spectacular as this one. It wasn't likely there were two like that.

The cat, without even bothering to finish the scraps, sailed out of the door and down the hall, his long tail waving like a proud banner. He seemed to know exactly where he was going. So I followed.

Without a pause, he turned into the study at the end of the hall. I stood in the doorway and watched. He made straight for one of the chairs beside the fireplace, leaped up and curled himself into a ball on one of the soft cushions.

I was quivering from head to toe, and not altogether from the cold. It had to be the same one, I told myself. He had known exactly where to go for food. He was sleeping now in the very same chair where the girl's cat had been sleeping on that first night.

Since he obviously had no intention of going anywhere else for a while, I turned out the lights and went back upstairs.

In the morning I woke to the clatter of Nora's pots and pans. Nora, with some great acting on Mom's part, had finally been persuaded to honor us with a full day's cleaning every week. Her day was unmistakably marked by her own special brand of bugle call. To her way of thinking, once the sun had cleared the horizon, the day had officially begun, and it was time for us all to be up and running, keeping pace with the sun. She announced this with an ear-piercing scraping of pans and a rattling of pots, to rout out the stragglers.

My shadowy room looked gloomy as a morgue. I peered out the window. Everything was wrapped in cotton-batting fog, as it was most mornings. But, at this early hour, who could blame the sun for goofing off behind some nice warm cloud or other?

I wriggled into my old robe and slipped my feet into a pair of slippers. I took off out the door and down the stairs toward the sound of Nora's kettle concert.

I was greeted by an early-hour grunt from Mom, and a sour look tossed over Nora's shoulder.

"Ach! I was about to be lookin' in to see that nothing had happened to ye," she muttered with obvious disapproval. " 'Tis a fair bit after seven."

Mom's early-morning basset eyes met mine over her fourth cup of morning coffee. She grinned. I could see that she was thinking that "a fair bit after seven" on a Saturday morning was nothing short of the middle of the night to either of us.

I had completely forgotten about my little adventure of the night before. After a halfhearted search through the cupboards, I settled for a bowl of uninspiring cereal and slumped into the chair opposite Mom.

I experienced a kickback of my first shock, when I happened to glance up and see the cat standing in the doorway viewing the situation with his icy-blue eyes. He floated into the kitchen, his dark-brown tail rippling clear to the tip.

"Merciful heaven!" Nora shrieked. Then came the deafening crash of a stack of plates smashed to smithereens at her feet.

Quick as lightning, the cat, like a pale ghostly shadow, streaked out the door, down the hall, and out of sight.

Nora's eyes, dazed and bright, stared after him. Her face was white as chalk.

"I forgot to tell you," I began to explain, "the cat—"

"Did you see that?" Nora interrupted in a hoarse whisper, motioning toward the door with her plump, trembling hand.

"It was only a cat," Mom said, looking quite bewildered. "Someone probably left the door open, and he just wandered in."

"I let him in," I hurried to explain, "last night. He wanted to come in . . . through my window."

" 'Twas the same one!" Nora droned on, her eyes fixed in space, totally ignoring my attempts to explain. "Sure as I'm born, 'twas Miz Cameron's cat, and no other!"

Just hearing her so sure gave me an extra jolt. I could see that her remarks had hit Mom with a wallop too, but she made a noble attempt to brush it off lightly.

"Suppose it was," she said. "It was only two years ago. The cat must have been someplace. It's perfectly possible that he just decided to come back."

Nora, a wary gleam in her eyes, glanced over her shoulder to check for listening ears.

"A cat that has been missin' for two whole years doesn't just come back . . . without a reason. Cats are evil," she rasped. "Bearers of bad tidings, they are."

"Nonsense!" Mom exclaimed.

I could see that Mom was getting pretty annoyed with the whole thing. "A cat's a cat. It's no more evil than anything else."

Nora was untying her apron. "I'm leavin'," she announced flatly. "An' I won't be back. Maybe 'tis too late. I should never have come a-tall. Ach! I should have known there'd be a dreadful curse on this place!"

"You can't be serious!" Mom cried. "You're not leaving just because of the cat!"

Nora paused. The muscles in her pale, sagging cheeks twitched.

"Take me advice," she warned, "and do the same. Ye're temptin' fate, that ye are. This place is the devil's own. The cat was a warnin', plain as the nose on yer face. There's another death in the air. Ach! I can feel it too. The cat knows it. . . . There's a death. . . ."

With a sudden muffled sob, she turned and took off through the door.

Mom and I, half stunned and half amused, moved over to the window to watch her zoom down the driveway and disappear around the bend.

"Well," said Mom, laughing nervously. "She was right about one thing. That cat was certainly bad news for us, appearing when he did. Here we are with the whole week's mess to clean up by ourselves!"

Chapter 10

I searched high and low for the cat. I couldn't find him anywhere, which was a disappointment, since I was formulating a sly scheme of dropping him on Margie's lap, then standing back to watch the effect.

It seemed only logical to believe that Margie was no stranger to the house or to Valerie Cameron. She must have, at least, been around long enough to have her portrait painted. It followed that she couldn't have helped seeing the cat. Nobody, least of all a confirmed cat lover like Margie, could ever forget such a spectacular cat as that one. I was tired of tiptoeing around, wasting the whole summer softening up my suspects. It was about time I closed in on some of the principals and probed for some real answers.

But the cat, whoever he was, had vanished without a trace. I couldn't blame him too much. Even an evil cat could hardly be up to Nora's clatter and carrying-on that early in the morning. Oh, well, I thought, maybe he will come back when he is sure that things have quieted down.

I went back into the house to see if I could persuade Mom to join me for an early-morning bike ride. That was another of the long list of things I was going to miss when I got back to Cleveland. In Hope's Crossing, everyone rode bikes. It did a lot more for setting up your nerves for the day than the screeching racket of subway cars.

Just as I had suspected, Mom was only too eager to jump at any excuse to leave the mess behind. The idea didn't appeal to her, any more than it did to me, that we plunge headlong into Nora's grubby kitchen chores. There was no

point in wasting a perfectly glorious morning by straining to
be unnaturally tidy.

We wheeled our bikes out and paused long enough to
watch Owen, as we did most mornings, stride past on his
regular morning beach walk.

"Eight thirty on the dot," Mom noted, checking her
watch. "The sun itself is no more prompt than he."

Owen walked fast and confidently. His white cane shot out
ahead, touching the sand lightly, marking a path for his steps
to follow. It was easy to see that he had long ago memorized
every inch of the way.

"Life demands so much from some." Mom dramatized, as
we watched him disappear from sight. "But what a rare kind
of dignity and courage misfortune often leaves behind."

We took another minute to gloat over the kind of morning
that we could never just take for granted as, it seemed, some
of the old-timers could.

The sun was out in all its glory by now, busy gobbling up
the last few shreds of fog that floated over the islands. We
could hear the lazy squawk of sea gulls as they glided on the
breeze overhead, against a blue backdrop of sky you
wouldn't believe.

The old captain was already out. He had loaded his fishing
gear into the dinghy and was taking off to round up his day's
menu. Some contrast to seafood shopping in the city, I
couldn't help thinking. No supermarket crunch, or worrying
about whether your fish was fresh or not.

We mapped out our route, including a check-in at the
Masons' on the way back. There was no danger that any of
the Masons had late sleeping habits. Mrs. Mason would have
seen to that. More than likely, each one of them was already
routed, fed, and properly dressed, ready to be packed off
right on schedule.

If I live to be a hundred, I could never forget the smell of that fresh, early-morning Hope's Crossing air. It had never occurred to me before that just plain, ordinary air could have such a distinct character of its own. It made rides like this one, breezing past those stately old mansions surrounded by all those grand old New England trees and flowers, pure heaven.

All the locals, going to work, offered us nice relaxed smiles and friendly waves as they passed. It was quite a change from the harried faces we were used to seeing, peering out from the traffic jams.

I rode up beside Mom, and we pulled together to a stop at one of the few traffic lights in town. A car with several people inside eased to a stop beside us. I glanced up, full of the spirit of the morning, ready to smile at whomever.

My nerves, already having been shaken up once that day, weren't ready for what I saw.

I found myself staring into the very same face that had already burned itself indelibly into my memory forever. It was the girl that I had seen at the old house on the first night. There could be no mistaking it.

Realization of what I was seeing, and the implications that went with it, was spreading a cold chill slowly through my rigid body.

The girl smiled with what might have been recognition and lifted her hand. I am not sure whether I responded or not. Probably not. Anyway, the car moved on when the light changed. I just stayed, too frozen to move.

Mom glanced back over her shoulder. "Come on!" she called.

When I still did not move, she pulled over to the side of the road.

"Sandra," she said anxiously. "Is anything the matter?"

I managed to transfer myself and the bike awkwardly out of the way of the traffic.

"You're white as a sheet!" Mom exclaimed. "Whatever happened? You look as though you had just seen a ghost!"

"I think I just did," I replied in a voice that was little better than a squeak. I pointed stupidly in the direction of the disappearing car. "That was the same girl that I saw in the house that first night. I am sure of it."

I could see that Mom was more concerned about me than my news.

"But I thought . . ." she began hesitatingly.

"Don't think," I warbled in a trembling voice. "Just take my word for it. It was."

With Mom watching me out of the corner of her eye, we rode on to the Masons'. Of course, we said nothing at all about what I had seen. But, now that my senses had returned and were functioning reasonably normally, I was determined to try for some real answers.

So I herded Margie off for a private interview at the very first good opportunity. I pinned her down and made a feeble attempt at tactfulness as I pumped.

First I described the cat and dramatized his visit in color-ful detail to capture her interest. I watched her face carefully. Apart from maybe a slight rise in color, she dealt me the same blank look as usual.

This was definitely not the morning that I was about to be put off by a poker face. So I dove in headlong, risking every-thing.

"Look," I said, with as much of Mrs. Mason in my tone as I could muster, "I know for a fact that you knew Valerie Cameron. I am positive you must have seen her cat dozens of times. Now, all I am trying to find out is if this cat is the same one. Can you help me?"

If I accomplished nothing else, at least I got a reaction. Her amber eyes nearly popped out of her head. I was not sure whether it was surprise or fear, probably a mixture of both.

"How do you know?" she hedged.

"I just know," I replied. "So you might as well tell me the whole story."

Maybe I had come on a little too strong. So I decided to ease it a little. "If it's a secret," I added more kindly, "then I promise I won't tell anyone."

Her expression, looking a lot older than it should have, was cagey. She had to be sure.

"Scout's honor," I said, raising my right hand.

She almost smiled.

"Yes, I knew her," she admitted. "So what of it?"

I eased in carefully.

"Did your mother know?"

She winced ever so slightly. "No, nobody knew, except—" She stopped, then hurried on. "She was my very best friend."

"Why didn't you tell?" was my next question.

There was a pause. I was afraid I was losing her. I held my breath.

"People thought Miss Cameron was odd. My mother would not have let me go to see her if she knew."

Right on, I thought. Anything or anybody odd would not have much of a show in Mrs. Mason's neat world.

"She wasn't odd. She was beautiful," Margie offered almost fiercely.

I took it as an invitation to go on and grabbed my opportunity.

"What happened to Valerie Cameron?" I asked abruptly.

The color drained from Margie's face.

"You know," she replied bitterly. "Everyone knows."

I had to take one more shot.

However we chose to look at it, we still were left with an awfully squirmy feeling. It was an enormous house, and while we were at one end of it, there was no way we could keep a watchful eye out on the other.

My next remark did nothing to promote our peace of mind.

"Probably two females in all this space look like an awfully easy mark for anyone," I observed unnecessarily.

"The police!" Mom pounced on the idea. "Maybe they could keep an eye on the house for us."

"O.K.," I said, smiling in spite of myself, "if you would feel better with George out there watching the house, then go right ahead. Don't let me influence you, just because he doesn't happen to be my idea of the Great Protector."

We both felt better after a good laugh. Things couldn't be all that bad if we were still able to laugh about them.

"Just the same," Mom said, suddenly serious once more. "I do think we should report the burglary. Because that is just what it is, a burglary. The police should know if things like that are going on in the neighborhood."

I shrugged.

So after a lot of silent arguments with herself, Mom called George over.

He looked slightly uncomfortable, I thought, confronting the two of us standing there with our forced smiles a mile wide.

But, by the time he had checked out the room and inspected the outside of the house, keeping a one-sided chat with Mom going all the time, I could see that he was looking quite a lot more confident.

When he was ready to leave, he offered Mom his hand. I noticed that he held hers quite a bit longer than he needed to.

"I'll keep a sharp eye out," he promised in a syrupy voice. "Maybe I can drop by now and then. I'm alone. You're alone. Why be lonely?"

I could see Mom's color rising to the danger point.

"That won't be necessary," she said. "We will call you if we need you." Her voice was so cool that I shivered several feet away.

"Anyway," was her hasty postscript, "we are not a bit lonely. We have a great deal to do. It takes our whole time."

George laughed. "Don't you worry about a thing, Joan. You can count on me."

He turned and walked down the steps without looking back.

Mom stood glued to the spot, her smoldering eyes fixed on the closed door. I could see the spark creeping up her fuse.

"Did you hear what he called me?" she sputtered. "Did you hear him call me Joan?"

"That happens to be your name," I replied.

That was all she needed to trigger an attack. Since no one else was available, she turned on me.

"I knew you should have given that cat back!" she snarled. "I warned you! I knew there had to be some motive behind it."

"Don't blame me," I said, ducking out of arm's reach to hide a smile. "Can I help it if my gorgeous mother has attracted another admirer?"

Mom glared. She was speechless. But I knew that speech, and a lot of it, would be arriving later.

The more we thought about it, the more we began to wonder if the portrait was the only thing taken. We hadn't exactly taken an inventory of everything in the old house, which would have taken at least a year or two, but if anything had been disturbed, maybe we could tell.

So we carefully checked all the rooms, looking for signs

that anything had been moved around.

"Does it strike you"—Mom came up with a bright idea —"that it is a little strange we have found no really personal things? The girl was evidently murdered suddenly. It stands to reason that things should be just as she left them, that is, unless someone has gone through and taken some things away."

I wasn't quite ready to believe that Valerie really had been murdered. You don't get yourself murdered and then go riding around in cars two years later. Someplace there must be some big ugly joke ready to laugh in our faces. Anyway, what Mom said did make sense, so it was worth looking into.

We combed through all the desk drawers, and wherever else it seemed likely we would come across something more personal than bills or recipes. And unless the girl had operated without any personal life whatever, which seemed unlikely, Mom's theory appeared to be holding up.

Then, quite accidentally, I happened to scoop out an old envelope that had been squeezed behind one of the drawers. I smoothed it out. It didn't look like much. It was just the unromantic kind of windowed envelope that usually doesn't have very exciting insides.

But there was something scrawled across the front.

It took us a while to figure it out: "V. CAMERON" seemed close enough.

There was definitely a note inside.

"It doesn't seem right . . . reading it," Mom protested weakly, but I could see that her eyes were gleaming with anticipation.

We both leaned over and eagerly read:

"Dear Val,
"Maybe Hope's Crossing is not the place for you. I was only trying to be your friend. If you don't want friends, then you may be sorry.
"George G."

"Jeepers!" I exclaimed. "It seems as though your old friend George Gilligan was out recruiting lady friends long before he ever met you!"

It was a poor choice of remarks. Mom looked positively fierce. She glared at me.

"The whole thing may not be as funny as you think!" she sputtered. " 'If you don't want friends, then you may be sorry' sounds a lot like a threat to me. And don't forget what happened to Valerie Cameron."

That is, I had to add silently, if anything did! But a small shiver slithered up my spine just the same.

"I never did trust that George Gilligan right from the start," I declared.

"Well," retorted Mom, "I suggest you trust him even less from now on!"

She jammed the letter into her pocket. "I, for one, am going to keep an awfully sharp eye on him from here on in! I can just picture him taking advantage of that poor girl over here all by herself!"

I couldn't help smiling. If clumsy old George only knew what a rotten hand he had played! In whatever encounter he might have with Mom in the future, I was wagering on him to come out a mighty poor second.

There was one other thing that I hadn't mentioned to Mom—and wasn't about to. I had recognized that scrawly handwriting from somewhere, and that somewhere, I remembered, was the note that had been tied to a rock and hurled at me over the fence in the graveyard.

Chapter 11

My job at the theater was opening my eyes to a lot of things. More and more I was getting caught up in the excitement of acting. Even when I was going through the motions of ushering, I still felt some part of me was up there on stage experiencing that electric thing which connects an actor with his audience. Applause, even when it was for someone else, charged me with a strange, wild kind of delight that I had never known before.

I couldn't really blame Mom for not being too enthusiastic about the way I felt.

"What we don't need," she often said, smothering out my sparks with her wet blanket, "is another actor in the family!"

I tried to tell her that it wasn't fair to blame the theater for the way Dad was. But she never would listen. To her way of thinking, if he had been a nice, dull accountant, he would automatically have been a quiet, home-loving husband too, who grew tomatoes in his backyard and fixed the leaky faucets on his day off.

Maybe, at Hope's Crossing, I was feeling more security in the make-believe world than I was in the real. At least, on stage, you could depend on all the ends being tied together in time for the grand finale, which was more than seemed to be happening in Mom's so-called real world.

The face I had seen in the car was positively haunting me. Valerie Cameron had been murdered. Nora had seen the body. Margie had watched them burying her, and I had seen the grave with my own eyes. No sane person could argue in the face of all that firsthand evidence.

Yet, on the other hand, who was the artist with the Siamese cat who had chatted with me by the fireside that first night? And who was it that had reappeared to smile at me from a passing car window? No wonder the imaginary world at the theater was beginning to look more and more stable and dependable by comparison.

I was determined to find out more about the old captain, or Crazy Nate, as everyone called him. Though, it did seem to me that he might be a whole lot less crazy than the rest of us. From what I could see through the small circle of the binoculars, he had eliminated a lot of the hassles of supposedly normal life.

So, the first chance I got with a few clear hours ahead, I took off down the beach in his direction. I wasn't quite sure what I intended to do. I don't go around storming moated castles every day. So I was leaving it up to chance to find an opening.

It was a cooler morning than I would have expected. A sweater felt just fine. I couldn't believe that the Hope's Crossing summer was beginning to wear thin in the middle of August. But maybe it was. This was a whole new world to me, and nothing about it could surprise me much anymore. Or so I thought.

Luck was with me. I could see that the old captain was on shore, putting pieces of driftwood into a neat pile by the water's edge.

I breathed a sigh of relief. That took care of one of my problems right away. You can't pretend you are selling magazines to a boat on an offshore mooring. There are usually no doorbells and, unless you plan to swim over, you need to get a little cooperation from the other side.

My first surprise was that he was not so old as I had thought he would be. Close up, his face was weather-beaten and rugged, but not all that old. I liked his face. It was like a doorway you wanted to go through because you knew you would find someone nice living very deep inside.

He was barefooted. He wore only a pair of old gray trousers that had seen better days, but he was so dignified and polite that you almost got the impression he was wearing royal robes.

He was not at all shy and unfriendly as I had imagined someone who was practically a hermit would be. In fact, he was very friendly and even spoke first, saving me the problem of thinking up something appropriate to say.

"So you are the girl who is staying up at the old Saunders place," he said, as though he already knew.

If he knew who I was, then that must mean he had been doing some watching himself. I felt a lot more comfortable right away.

"This is another Hope's Crossing brand of day," he said. "You cannot find such days anywhere else."

I had no argument there, but I had more important things on my mind than the weather, so I swung the conversation around right away to a more important subject.

"What a great way this must be to live!" I exclaimed, sizing up his old boat tied to its mooring a short distance from shore. It was low tide. The boat rocked gently, rising and falling with the regular rhythm of the small waves.

He followed my glance and smiled. "In stripping life down to the bare living," he said, "one eliminates the confusion of dealing with shadows. One must free his mind and his life enough to recognize the true essences. That alone is the real —the eternal."

I was liking him more and more. I wished that Mom could have been there with me, or Luke. If that last remark had been typical of his everyday conversation, then I was going to have a tough time telling them what he said.

"Come aboard," he invited me, motioning toward his dinghy pulled up on the sand, "and see for yourself."

I climbed in without a moment's hesitation, congratulating myself all the time. Things were shaping up beyond my wildest dreams. There I was, almost without trying, folded up in one end of the battered old dinghy, with the captain folded in the other, and a pile of driftwood between.

With the skill of someone who had spent a lifetime doing it, he rowed us quickly and expertly in the direction of the quaint old cabin boat.

The boat was very old, but I could see that it had been carefully worked over and was in immaculate repair. It had been built in the seaworthy tradition of all oceangoing lobster boats. The hull was scooped wide and low. The afterdeck was neatly piled with several much-mended lobster traps. Ropes, which had been coiled with the greatest of care, lined the deck. The boat had been painted white, but it was well on its way to becoming as gray and weather-beaten as everything else. Across the stern I could barely read the faded letters spelling out the boat's name: The Gull.

I was not very expert in clearing the chasm between two boats. But, with an encouraging shove from behind by the captain, I found myself safe on deck without disaster.

I was wobbly-kneed enough. I hardly needed the jolt that was waiting for me, eyeing me with a cold, ice-blue stare.

I nearly pitched right back into the briny deep. There was that very same cat again! There could be no mistaking him. It was the same smooth satin coat, the same incredible size.

"The cat . . . ," I sputtered to the captain, who had effortlessly vaulted over the side of the boat and was now standing beside me. "He belongs to you?"

"No," Captain Nate replied, stooping to stroke the cat's silky fur with his rough brown hand. "I would not say that. No creature should ever think that he can own another. We are friends. We share our lives. That is a much better way."

"I'm sure it is," I floundered. "I just think that I have seen him before."

"When we tied up after our long journey," Captain Nate said, "I am afraid that he took the opportunity to exercise his sea legs."

He motioned me toward the cabin. The door was open, so I ducked to enter. I immediately got the impression of a scrubbed and polished interior, neat as a pin.

Then, with a start, I noticed that there was another person in the cabin. A small, dungareed figure was bent over the old black, potbellied stove, fitting a clawed piece of driftwood inside.

The figure straightened, and turned.

I gasped, feeling my insides turn to water.

It was the girl! The same small figure, the same face, the same gentle smile!

I collapsed onto the canvas folding chair that the captain was offering me. Through the ringing in my ears I heard him say, "I want you to meet my wife. Allison, this is the girl who is staying at the old Saunders place."

"I know," the girl replied, smiling. She held out her hand. "We are already old friends. We met one dark and stormy night when I was feeling very blue. I invited her in because she reminded me so very much of my sister."

I laid my cold, limp paw in her warm hand, and returned her hospitality with a rude, glazed stare. The captain had called her Allison. . . . She had said "my sister."

"Then you aren't . . . ?" I stuttered, clutching for words. "Then . . . you aren't Valerie Cameron?"

The girl looked startled and surprised.

"Oh, no," she said quickly. "Valerie was . . . was involved in a dreadful accident. I thought you would have heard. I am Allison, Valerie's sister. When you stopped at the house, I had only just come to Hope's Crossing that day. Valerie had very few friends here so I did not tell anyone that I was coming, or that I was there. I had my own key, so I let myself in. I wanted to sort out Valerie's personal things and take what she would want me to have. I left early the next morning after the storm cleared."

I needed time to absorb that. So I glanced quickly around the cabin. Captain Nate was pouring steaming black coffee into three thick mugs from a chipped blue enamel coffeepot. He handed one to each of us and then sat opposite.

I needed that scalding black coffee. I sipped it eagerly. I didn't question the fact that I had never even tasted coffee before. It just seemed exactly the right thing at exactly the right time.

I made one more effort to sort things out.

"I thought you . . . Valerie . . . No one believed me. . . . We went back the next day . . ."

Obviously, I needed more time.

Captain Nate and his wife were regarding me strangely, which wasn't too surprising.

Then Allison laughed. "Oh, you poor dear!" she exclaimed. "You must have thought . . . Oh, I am so sorry! You must have been utterly confused. All those legends floating around about my sister, and then me appearing and disappearing . . . and then reappearing again!"

With her laugh, I could feel the whole nutty summer shifting and settling back into place. I laughed too. I had survived one shock, and I was ready for almost anything from there on in.

"Valerie and Allison were very dear friends of mine," Captain Nate said. "Allison had been abroad for years. When she returned, we were married—just a year ago. We both love Hope's Crossing more than any place, but the memories are too painful, so we will be leaving in a few days.

We probably won't be back."

"I have taken all of Valerie's things that had special meaning for me," Allison explained. "The rest will be sold later. And the house is due to be torn down this fall. That makes you a very special kind of tenant. You are the very last occupants of that grand old house."

The sinking feeling that I was experiencing was not all due to the black coffee and the rocking boat. I was thinking of anyone daring to tear down that lovely old house that seemed to have been there forever.

"But, why?" I asked with a trembling voice. "Why does that beautiful house have to be torn down?"

The captain stroked his windswept beard and looked almost as unhappy as I felt.

"A house like that is no longer practical," he said. "Impossible taxes and the shortage of help make it a burden for anyone. At least, all of us who have loved it will always cherish its memory."

I nodded, hoping that I could keep my cool and not disgrace myself further by doing another dumb thing like bursting into tears.

"Valerie was a sad and lonely girl," Allison told me. "Almost no one here knew her at all, so they imagined all sorts of inaccurate and romantic things about her. You see, she came here to lose herself in her work. She had lost everything else. Her husband was killed in a plane crash. Then, a few days later, she had a child and it died too. That was the final blow. She couldn't bear to live among all those memories, so she came out here to that old house that our grandfather had left us. Her painting became her life."

I nodded. What could I say? So I just waited, until she was ready to continue.

"Probably she didn't give them a chance," Allison went on, "but most of the contacts she had with her neighbors here seemed to be disturbing ones. Even the maid who came in once or twice a week, Valerie told me, was overbearing and superstitious. I don't know if she ever got around to letting her go or not. I know that she intended to."

That would have to be Nora, I thought. So it hadn't been all sweetness and light between the two of them. With all Nora's eagerness to explain the situation, it seemed she had forgotten to include that one little piece of information.

"There was just one person," Allison went on, "who meant all the world to Valerie in those last years, a lonely little girl who belonged to one of the neighbors."

"Margie?" I breathed. "Margie Mason?"

"Yes," Allison replied, "that's the one. You see, Valerie's child had been a little girl. I suppose, at first, this one was a kind of substitute for the one she had lost. She needed someone desperately, and the little girl seemed to need someone too. But I believe, as time went by, Little Margie and her own child became confused in her mind in an odd sort of way. She came to mean everything to Valerie."

"She painted a portrait . . . ," I began.

"Oh, yes," Allison said. "I meant to explain about that. I hope you don't mind that I took it. You see, among some of the things that I took back with me the first time, I found a letter addressed to me that had never been sent. Perhaps she had some kind of a premonition at the time. Anyway, she told me about the portrait, and said that of everything she owned, that painting meant the most to her. She asked, in the event she was not here to see to it, that I take the portrait and, when the time seemed right, give it to Margie. Evidently she did not trust the mother to understand. Since you were not home, I used my key again to get inside. You see, it is terribly important to me that I do exactly as she asked."

She had answered most of my questions. There were only

a few more. It seemed that this might be my last chance to ask them, so I forged ahead.

"Do you know who murdered your sister?" I asked abruptly. Then I felt, right away, that I had been too bold in asking.

Her face stiffened with a strange masklike expression. She lowered her eyes and seemed to withdraw inside herself.

"I don't know," she replied at last. "Does it matter? Everyone loved Valerie who knew her. People have said ugly things about her, but they were all untrue. I suspect robbery was the motive. Valerie had a very valuable pendant that had been a gift from her husband. She always wore it. It was missing when they found her. It has never been found."

"It is too late now to help Valerie," Captain Nate added. "We can only pray for the poor, sick mind that was capable of such a crime. It would be of no benefit to anyone to stir things up again. Allison and I feel no revenge, only sorrow, and sympathy for whoever must bear the burden of his terrible deed."

I hated to leave, knowing that I probably would not be seeing them again. They were two such super people, and they had given me back a lot of what I had thought was gone forever—confidence in my eyes and ears.

My head was reeling with a million new angles to think about on the way home.

I replayed the part about Nora. So Valerie had found her overbearing and superstitious! Well, that wasn't too hard to believe. She had done her best to bully Mom and me into her way of thinking too. In a way, I had to admit, she had succeeded. She had the two of us hopping out of bed long before we were ready on the days that she had come. . . . And Valerie was planning to let her go. I wondered if Nora knew that.

Then there was the missing pendant. No one had mentioned that. I wondered how many people knew.

Disturbing thought followed disturbing thought. The "poor, sick mind" that the captain and his wife were leaving behind forever might still be in Hope's Crossing. Mom and I were still encamped in the big old house, and everyone, including her own sister, had insisted that I looked a lot like Valerie Cameron. As I could see it, I had only one positive thing going for me—my lack of valuable jewels. People hardly ever murdered for the kind of jewelry that comes as a prize with bubble gum.

Margie there was no pushing. If she didn't choose to confide in me of her own accord, then I could forget it.

As with every turn of the season, one of the first sure signs was the bargain hunter's gleam in Mom's eye, accompanied by an obsession to scoop up everything in sight with a mark-down tag. Even Hope's Crossing had not been able to cure her of that.

"Count me out," I warned as soon as her plans began to take shape. "Shopping in Boston is no different from shopping in Cleveland—a drag from whatever point of view."

Besides, I thought, with time so short, who would want to waste a single, precious, sun-filled Hope's Crossing moment?

So, without too much argument, she invited Mrs. Mason instead. She had learned, through bitter experience, that I wasn't exactly a bushel of laughs when it came to one of her bargain scavenger hunts.

The day they chose for their big blast didn't turn out to be the best weatherwise.

To top everything, all their careful plans to charge off early and avoid the rush collapsed.

Mom's old wheels, true to form, sensing her impatience, refused to budge. The next hour or so was a scene of frustration that I would rather not describe. Enough to say, she was glad to see even George come by and offer her a push. When he finally, beaming, waved her off, she did come across with the reasonable facsimile of a smile. It couldn't have been easy.

I had planned on spending the day enjoying the sun, maybe rounding up a few of the kids for a cookout, and just, in general, relaxing, now that things at the theater had slowed to a crawl.

In the best Hope's Crossing tradition, the day started off with all the signs of a winner—clear blue sky, warm breeze, and the kind of late-summer sun that could convert anyone to sun worship.

But, before anyone had a chance to enjoy it, zap! the wind picked up, sweeping a whole skyful of clouds right out of nowhere, blotting out everything, including my hopes for a super day.

I was feeling a little gloomy and sorry for myself, standing at the edge of the garden and weighing the prospects of the weather, when Margie appeared.

She was carrying a rolled-up sail under her arm.

"You're not going out?" I asked. "It's going to rain."

Margie scanned the sky with the eye of an expert.

"There's a good breeze," she said. "It won't rain yet awhile. Do you want to come? We won't go far."

I shrugged. Why not? It was better than standing around waiting for the weather to make up its mind.

I helped carry *Whisper,* the boat, down to the edge of the water. Between us, we managed to straighten out the flapping sail and secure it to the mast. We shoved the boat past the uneasy waves breaking offshore and swishing up onto the sand.

The light boat rocked and bobbed. The sail was flapping for all it was worth. We waded out, pushing the boat in front of us. By the time we reached water up to our knees, we were able to climb aboard without too much trouble. I must say I had improved a lot at that sort of thing.

The sail billowed out, tight as a drum. In no time at all, we were skimming over the water as easily as a leaf in the wind.

With a breeze like that, it took a lot of concentrating to keep the boat pointed just right. Fumbling could mean capsizing into Hope's Crossing's notoriously cold water. Neither of us was too anxious for that, especially without the sun to warm us up afterward.

By the time we got around to noticing the sky, half of it was churning with clouds black as ink.

"I think it's going to storm!" I shouted to Margie, above the slap of the waves and the sail, rippling with each sudden gust of wind.

Margie nodded, and shouted, "Ready about! Hard alee!"

We had barely turned the boat around, when we heard the ominous rumble of thunder in the distance.

I measured the space between ourselves and the shore with anxious eyes. By this time, I knew enough about the ocean and its moods to know that I wasn't gung ho for battling a storm at sea in a miniature boat like *Whisper* . . . or any other boat, for that matter.

We were lucky. The wind happened to be blowing in our favor. It blew us obligingly toward shore in a straight and steady line. I breathed a sigh of relief. We made it by a hair.

We hauled the boat quickly up onto the sand. We kept a wary eye on the sky that was obviously churning up to something else. We unfastened the sail, overturned the boat, and got ready to take off.

"Come on back to the house with me," Margie shouted above the shriek of the fast rising wind and the sound of the waves battering the shore.

"Right on!" I shouted back. To be alone in the old house in a storm wasn't all that inviting. Anyway, Mrs. Mason, and probably Eric, had gone off with Mom. That left Margie on her own too.

It was already beginning to sprinkle. The black sky blinked with faraway bursts of lightning, and we could hear the steady grumble of thunder. It wasn't more than a quarter of a mile to the Masons'. We made a mad dash, aimed between the rhododendron hedges, and tore off like a couple of fugitives.

Leaves and twigs lifted from the roadway and spun in

restless little whirlwinds, almost as though they were alive. An ominous, unnatural twilight had begun to nudge out the daylight. Every living being had scampered to shelter.

Then, unexpectedly, from out of nowhere, a man's figure materialized in the gloom and stepped directly into our path.

He seemed in no hurry at all. In fact, I got the distinct impression that he wasn't even noticing the storm. It was us he was interested in. To be precise, it wasn't exactly us. It was Margie. It was pretty obvious from the way he was staring at her.

There was something awfully queer about the way he was looking at her. All my natural instincts bristled to attention and signaled *split!*

I glanced at Margie. She was staring at him with her round owl eyes. She looked positively hypnotized. She radiated terror.

I grabbed her arm. "Come on!" I cried. I felt frightened out of all reasonable proportion.

The rain began to fall sometime during our record-breaking sprint to the house. Shivering and drenched, we watched it beat against the windows in heavy silver sheets. The world outside dissolved to a soggy blob. Lightning crackled and ripped the sky into ribbons. Then came the thunder, slamming it all back together.

I was shivering uncontrollably. It was the most beautiful and terrible storm I had ever seen. Cleveland had its storms, but I had never seen one as awe-inspiring as this.

I was glad of Margie. Another human being in a rampage of the elements like this was a comfort. For the first time, I turned my attention away from the storm and back to her.

I felt a wave of shock sweep through me. This was not the expressionless, frozen-faced Margie I was used to seeing. Her round eyes were glazed and golden. Every inch of her body quivered in a spasm of dry sobs.

"Margie!" I said. "What's the matter? Are you O.K.?"
She said nothing. I wasn't sure she had heard.

"Who was the man?" I demanded. "Was it someone you knew?"

She whirled suddenly to look me squarely in the eye.

Her denial was suspiciously positive. "No!" she declared. "I never saw him before. It's the storm. It's just the storm I'm afraid of."

Somehow that didn't set with me. Margie was used to the weather if anyone was. I had seen her handle her boat, cool as a cucumber, in weather that would have had me praying for deliverance. She had lived with the sea and its weather and moods all her life. I wasn't going to be fooled into believing that a storm could upset her so.

Just the same, I went along with her when she insisted on pulling the curtains across the picture windows. I shrugged and turned on the lights . . . if it would make her feel any better. I prepared for a lengthy and dreary day ahead.

Before long, things were a lot calmer. The wind had died, and the rain reduced to a drizzle. The foghorn had begun its mournful measured moan.

"I suppose that means another miserable fog," I groaned. Of all kinds of weather that Hope's Crossing had to offer, I liked fog the least. It gave me the same smothered feeling I sometimes got in a crowded elevator—closed in and stifling.

Margie wasn't being much in the way of company. She slipped in and out of the corner shadows like the mouse she had first reminded me of. Conversation was out. She still seemed scared to death.

I wasn't feeling too comfortable either, remembering how she had reacted to the strange young man—who must still be out there somewhere. Obviously, she knew something. And, obviously, she wasn't about to confide in me. But that was no surprise.

On a day like this, darkness arrives long before its time. By the middle of the afternoon the white fog had already turned to a dull, murky gray.

I began to wonder if Mom might have trouble finding her way home. Oh, well, I thought, it would be stupid to worry. She ought to be able to cope with something as ordinary as a little fog by this time. Anyway, I already had enough on my mind if I really wanted to worry.

I hadn't realized how isolated we had been in our own little world until the telephone rang. The harsh sound ripped through the silence. My muscles convulsed. I could literally feel each hair rising.

"Don't answer it!" were practically the first words I had heard from Margie for hours.

"What do you mean, don't answer it?" I retorted. "It's probably your mother . . . or Mom. Suppose Mom called home and got no answer. Wouldn't she wonder where I was, especially after a storm like that?" I grabbed the phone.

There wasn't much of even false courage in the queer, cracked voice that trembled into the mouthpiece.

Almost at once, a click on the other end told me that we were cut off. I hung the receiver back on its hook.

"We were cut off," I explained to Owl Eyes.

"I told you," she said. "I told you not to answer."

I muttered something about a branch on the line. I had the feeling I was fooling no one, least of all myself.

The telephone started up again. What could I do? I tried once more. This time I heard the distinct, careful click of someone hanging up on the other end.

This time I avoided Margie's glance. I hiked across the room and turned on the radio—loud. Maybe I was trying to drown out the thunderous thumping inside my rib cage.

If I have any acting ability at all, it was put to the prime, crucial test in the centuries—it couldn't have been less—that followed. It might have been better to admit that I was just as terrified as Margie. It might have been companionable to be scared to death together. But I just secretly prayed that Mom and Mrs. Mason would suddenly be endowed with supernatural speed.

When the doorbell rang, my first reaction was relief. Mom and Mrs. Mason, of course! But, instantly, my better sense leaped in. Mrs. Mason was not likely to be ringing her own doorbell.

I glanced at my cowering companion. If there was to be any action at all, it was going to have to be initiated by me. Somehow, I propelled my frozen limbs across the room. My clammy hand clawed the curtain open a slit. I peered out cautiously.

"It's George!" I squeaked my report. "It's George, and he's in uniform."

I don't know what I expected, but I hardly expected Margie to be right there, Johnny-on-the-spot, flinging the door open, as though he were some old, long-expected guest.

George's tall figure filled the doorway. He swept the room with one quick glance. Then he turned to me.

"You are coming to my place," he snapped. "Both of you . . . now."

I gasped. He had to be kidding. He surely didn't expect to just say the word and have us prance off into the fog and dark with him, just like that!

George was sinister-looking enough in the broad daylight. With the fog wreathing in little swirls over his stooped shoulders, he looked like a villain straight from the pages of a cheap paperback.

"I'm sorry, Mr. Gilligan," I said, backing away. "But we aren't going anywhere with anyone."

I saw George's hand slip to the holster at his side. My jaw dropped in utter disbelief as I leveled my eyes with his across the sleek, steel barrel of a gun—a real gun. And it was aimed squarely at me.

I managed a quick glance at Margie.

There she stood, looking more relaxed than I had seen her for hours, casually slipping into her rain gear. I tried another quick look at George's pale, watery eyes. He wasn't kidding. I reached for my jacket.

Chapter 13

The whole thing had to be some weird kind of a joke. But no one seemed to be laughing.

There I was, feeling cramped and miserable, crouched in one of George's prison-comfy chairs that could only have been a reject from somebody's rubbish sale.

The whole apartment gave the impression of a creepy, gray underground tomb, complete with a sinkful of unwashed dishes. It wouldn't have been the nicest spot on the best of days, but this was ridiculous.

Obviously, the lack of daylight wasn't bothering George too much. He lurked across the room, keeping between me and the door. Not that I would have tried anything. He was making me good and nervous. It was bad enough, the absentminded way he fiddled with his gun. Apart from that, he paced. And I mean, really *paced!* Like a caged lion. He kept looking out the windows—which could have used a little washing. He kept glancing at the telephone as though he were expecting it to ring.

Just to keep me in line, I suppose, every now and then he would bore me with his ray-gun eyes. I got the message. I just sat there like the world's most docile hostage, or whatever I was supposed to be.

By that time, I was convinced he didn't really intend to do us any harm, at least, not intentionally. It could have been just wishful thinking. But once he had us there, he almost seemed to forget us altogether. Obviously, his mind was concentrating on something else. Whatever was bothering him, I figured, had to be a matter of life and death. He looked that grim.

Margie had definitely regained her cool. Watching her, I would have thought that being taken at gunpoint to some weirdo's apartment was a ho-hum, everyday affair, at least, in her book. She wandered around the apartment looking perfectly at home. George didn't seem to worry at all about her moving around. I was the one he was determined to keep nailed to one spot.

Just the same, seeing Margie so relaxed made me feel a little easier. I was pretty certain that Margie knew more about what was going on than I did. If she wasn't worried, then it was a good sign.

I don't know how long I sat there. It must have been hours. It seemed like weeks. I had plenty of time to memorize all the advertising on the calendar hanging across the room from me. There was a supernaturally built female wearing fur. Well, not actually wearing it. There was hardly enough of it to cover a small-sized mouse. I had plenty of time to wonder why she had chosen fur. The weather must have been awfully warm. She would have frozen to death if it hadn't been. What a picture to advertise beer! From what I had observed, beer drinkers hardly ever have hourglass figures.

I wondered if Mom and Mrs. Mason were back. If they were, I could just picture their imaginations working on the double, with both of us missing. The weird thing was, with their combined imaginations, they could never come up with a story as kooky as the real thing.

I could almost see the headlines in the Cleveland newspapers: Sandra Douglas Held at Gunpoint by Crazed Maniac. That startled me a little. I kept trying to watch George, without actually seeming to, trying to figure out if he really was a crazed maniac.

I came to the conclusion that he looked more scared than crazed. In fact, I had the distinct feeling that if I had shouted, "Boo!" he would have gone right through the roof.

He almost did. Not because I shouted "Boo!" but because the telephone rang.

I must say, it jarred all of us. Any sound from the outside world would have seemed bizarre.

George's back was turned toward me. I couldn't see his face. His comments were short and muffled.

He hung the receiver back on the hook slowly. Then he slumped into a chair with his head in his hands. He stayed that way for a long time.

The funny thing was, I never even thought to escape. George just looked so completely sad and harmless. I couldn't help feeling awfully sorry for him. He had forgotten all about his gun. It was lying across the room by the telephone.

Finally, he looked up. He really seemed almost surprised to see us there. He got up. His hands were oversize and freckled. Besides that, they were covered with long red hair, and they hung too far out of his sleeves. He gestured with them awkwardly.

"You can go," he said.

I just sat there, stunned. After all that, without any explanation at all, here he was just telling us to run along home.

"But . . . but," I stammered. "Why?"

George actually looked shy and embarrassed. "I'm sorry about that." He motioned toward the gun. "I had to do it. I had to get you over here fast. I didn't have time for explanations."

I waited. There had to be more to it than that.

He went on. "Margie. . . . He was looking for Margie. He . . . he didn't know what he was doing."

"Who was looking for Margie?" If it took all night, I was determined to get to the bottom of this.

George swallowed. His prominent Adam's apple bobbed over his collar. "Charlie," he said. "But it's all right now.

Margie is safe. Charlie has been found. He had an accident. He was killed."

I was aware of a gasp from Margie, who, until that minute, had made no sound whatsoever.

"Charlie was killed?" she asked, her eyes as round as saucers.

George nodded. He laid his hand on her shoulder, even a little gently, I thought.

"He fell over the seawall onto the rocks. The rocks were slippery from all that rain. He didn't know what he was doing. It's all right now. He won't ever bother you again."

The name Charlie had rung a bell, but it made no sense. The only Charlie I ever heard of in Hope's Crossing had been drowned a long time ago.

By now I was bristling with curiosity. "Charlie who?" I persisted.

George looked at me absentmindedly. He looked as though he might burst into tears any minute.

"Charlie Gilligan," he replied, "my nephew. Owen and Nora's boy."

"But . . . but," I stammered. "I thought . . ."

George nodded. "You might as well know. Everyone will know soon. Charlie wasn't drowned. Oh, we went up on the rocks in a storm all right. We all very nearly drowned, but none of us did."

"Then, why?" I babbled. "Where . . . ?"

"Charlie was a good boy. He was a great athlete over at the high school. He got in with the wrong crowd. He got mixed up with drugs . . . a bad lot."

His voice faltered. I controlled my curiosity, and kept quiet until he was ready to go on.

"Charlie was young, a small-town boy," he explained. "Some of the big boys from the outside figured he was an easy mark. They used him. He got all mixed up in drug peddling.

if I ever told anyone I had seen him, he would kill me." Her voice trailed away, trembling. Then she added softly, "No one knew I saw him but George. Charlie told him. I never told anyone."

"I thought she would be all right," George said. "Charlie was in Mexico for a long time. He came back last week. He wasn't the same Charlie. Something dreadful had happened to him. He said that Margie was the only one who could be a witness against him. So he told me he planned to do something about it. I knew, when he went out today, that she was in danger. I remembered the two of you were alone. I had to bring you here where you would be safe."

I had a lot to consider on the way home. Poor old George. He had gotten the short end of the stick whichever way you looked at it. Even Mom and I hadn't been all that charitable. His worst fault, as I saw it, was that he had involved himself in trying to help everyone. His reasoning hadn't been all that smart, but he had meant to help. Now, maybe even Margie and I had him to thank that we were still alive and breathing . . . or, at least, Margie.

Just as I figured, Mom and Mrs. Mason had accumulated enough shock to keep them in nightmares for the rest of their lives.

"Why didn't you tell me?" Mrs. Mason put it to Margie.

Mom and I exchanged knowing glances. It must have been the trick of the century for Margie to keep the secret, and keep Mrs. Mason reasonably happy at the same time.

The only thing wrong with a vacation that rolls along in high gear is that sooner or later it has to end.

Not that I minded the thought of going back to Cleveland. What I seemed to need more than anything else just then was a good long time to digest the whole adventure. And, it seemed to me, that might be done better from a distance.

He didn't know what he was into until it was too late. [ ]
he couldn't get out. They were putting the pressure on[ ]
threatening his life. Charlie was desperate. We thoug[h]
were helping. It was a bad decision on all our parts[ ]
thought it might be a way—if he could get out of the [coun]
try."

"Did he?" I ventured to ask. "Did he get out o[f the]
country?"

"One thing led to another," George said. "He n[eeded]
money—a lot of money. He wanted to go to Mexico. [He]
did a terrible thing. His mother worked for Valerie Cam[eron.]
Nora is a great one to talk . . . tell things. Well, Charlie [knew]
that Miss Cameron had what he needed."

I felt a wave of nausea when he paused. So he . . .
George read my expression and nodded.

"We should never have covered for him. He needed [help.]
We only wanted what was best for him. It was a mi[stake]
. . . our mistake . . . Owen's and mine. Even Nora th[ought]
he had drowned."

I took the time to consider that. Poor Nora. I got a [sad]
sense of the shock she had in store. On top of thinking h[e had]
drowned, finding out that he was a murderer, and no[w]
this. I only hoped her creepy fascination with the ma[cabre]
would be enough to carry her through.

By this time I almost felt like patting George's hea[d or]
holding his hand. He looked so utterly miserable. But [I had]
to know one more thing.

"Why was Charlie looking for Margie?"

This time Margie spoke up. I noticed a new note of c[onfi]
dence in her voice.

"I thought he had drowned," she said. "Then I saw [him]
coming out of Miss Cameron's. I was waiting for the s[chool]
bus. It was real foggy. I could see that Charlie was aw[fully]
upset about something. He told me to get lost. He said [

Wrapping things up at the theater was especially sad. We kids had been through a lot together—good times and bad. And we knew that, once we had scattered off in our various directions, we might never see each other again.

I had never kidded myself that Luke was destined to be the biggest thing in my life. But, just the same, our friendship had meant something special.

He kissed me good-by. (Wow!) He promised to write, but I wasn't going to count too much on it. Once the routine started up again, we would probably both be swamped. Especially if I expected to keep my marks up as well as my art. And, on top of that, I had almost convinced Mom to let me take a couple of theater classes.

But the hardest thing of all was saying good-by forever to the old house. I tried not to think too much about its being torn down.

When Mom turned the big old key in the lock for the last time, words from either of us were out of the question.

Though the silence was pretty awesome and final, I still had a comfortable feeling that Valerie Cameron would have been pleased with the way things had turned out. Whatever had drawn me into the whole thing in the first place seemed to have been satisfied. And I couldn't have wished for anything more.

Right in the middle of that sentimental moment, a horn's blast from the driveway hurtled us both back into the real world. Obviously, Eric had reached the limit of his patience and was itching for action.

It was like the final curtain zipping across the stage. I should have known the humdrum of everyday living could not lie dormant forever.

We both sneaked one more long, last look back over our

shoulders. For the rest of our lives, I guess, both of us will remember that great old house blending just right into the sounds of the little waves slipping up onto the sand, and the lazy squawks of the sea gulls gliding overhead.

PLACE IN RETURN BOX to remove this checkout from your record.
TO AVOID FINES return on or before date due.
MAY BE RECALLED with earlier due date if requested.

DATE DUE	DATE DUE	DATE DUE
SEP 2 0 2016		
1 2 1 5 1 6		

6/07 p:/CIRC/DateDue.indd-p.1

The Boundaries of
American Political Culture
in the Civil War Era

The Boundaries of America:

The STEVEN AND JANICE BROSE LECTURES

in the Civil War Era   William A. Blair, editor

MARK E. NEELY JR.

olitical Culture in the Civil War Era

THE UNIVERSITY OF NORTH CAROLINA PRESS   *Chapel Hill*

Library of Congress Cataloging-in-Publication Data
Neely, Mark E.
The boundaries of American political culture in the
Civil War era / by Mark E. Neely, Jr.
    p. cm. — (The Steven and Janice Brose lectures in
the Civil War era)
Includes bibliographical references and index.
ISBN 0-8078-2986-2 (alk. paper)
1. United States—Politics and government—1841–
1845. 2. United States—Politics and government—
1845–1861. 3. United States—Politics and
government—1861–1865. 4. Political culture—United
States—History—19th century. 5. Political
participation—United States—History—19th century.
6. United States—Social conditions—To 1865. 7. Social
classes—United States—History—19th century.
8. Material culture—United States—History—19th
century. 9. Political clubs—United States—History—
19th century. 10. Minstrel shows—United States—
History—19th century. I. Title. II. Series.
E415.7.N44 2005
306.2′0973′09034—dc22   2005007817

09 08 07 06 05 5 4 3 2 1

CONTENTS

FIGURES

PREFACE

In March 2002 I gave the Steven and Janice Brose Lectures for the Richards Civil War Era Center at Penn State. The three lectures made a case for the importance of politics in understanding the lives of ordinary Americans in the North during the Civil War era.

It may seem odd that I should have to make a case for the importance of political life in the middle of the nineteenth century, now famous as the period when Americans devised the mass political party and enthusiastic campaigning techniques. Many of the people who heard the lectures, however, knew their modern context well: the currently confused and beleaguered status of political history.

The introduction to a recent book of essays on American political history, for example, recalled the complaints of political historians expressed at a professional meeting in 1995: "Their field was becoming marginalized in the profession, even excluded from it. Back in the 1970s, social history had passed political history as the subfield producing the most doctoral dissertations, so that political historians were now outnumbered in their own departments. More seriously, senior chairs were no longer being replaced, and graduate students could not get jobs."[1] Nine years later, at the annual meeting of the same association, a panel was convened to discuss why political history was dead and whether there were any signs it might recover. Apparently, many at the meeting thought recovery unlikely.[2]

A landmark of the demise of political history is Glenn C. Altschuler and Stuart M. Blumin's *Rude Republic: Americans and Their Politics in the Nineteenth Century*, published in 2000. That book launched the most sweeping attack ever made on the importance of politics to the daily lives of nineteenth-century Americans. My Brose Lectures were originally conceived as an answer to it.

But in the course of revising the lectures for publication I came to see that circling the wagons was an inadequate response. I could not merely reassert the centrality of political life in nineteenth-century America, reminding readers that the national attic remains full of political ribbons, badges, cartoons, and posters from that era. In the first place, the authors of *Rude Republic* made generous exception for the Civil War era itself, saying that politics, though insignificant in the lives of most Americans throughout the century, did reach the apogee of their ability to engage people's attention over the issues that led to civil war, especially slavery and related constitutional issues.[3] And what I was most familiar with was the politics of the Civil War era.

Second, political historians who had never doubted the importance of politics in the nineteenth century had themselves done much to downgrade the political history of the Civil War itself. Surely no survey of the American political system in the nineteenth century had less to say about the Civil War than Joel H. Silbey's *American Political Nation, 1838–1893* (1991).[4] Silbey's interpretation of the important developments in the political parties of the century made a case for the insignificance of the Civil War. Third, it was true also that political historians, whatever their degree of emphasis on the importance of the four-year period of war at midcentury, had exaggerated the centrality of political concerns in the overall period: America was more than a "*political* nation." Its citizens were concerned, as Altschuler and Blumin were justifiably at pains to point out, about family and workplace and schools and religion and other private matters into the consideration of which partisan politics did not always intrude.

So the book resulting from those lectures is more concerned with locating the boundaries between the spheres of political and private life than with making imperialist assertions for one sphere or the other.

❦ The evidence that first seemed to me to call *Rude Republic*'s conclusions into question came from material culture. In the first lecture, "Household Gods," popular prints provided a link between home and public political concerns that *Rude Republic* had overlooked. But material culture soon caused me to reexamine other important arguments about political experience in the period. The second lecture, "A New Branch of Trade," recovered innovations in political technique and in the production of campaign souvenirs based on photography, which in turn suggested an image of political life so vibrant and dynamic as to call seriously into question the dismissive attitude toward Civil War politics taken in *The American Political Nation*. In the third lecture, "A Secret Fund," the production and distribution of forward-looking campaign posters and persuasive political pamphlets by the Union League Clubs during the Civil War provoked a reexamination of the class-bound and hidebound image of these clubs given influential expression in Iver Bernstein's *The New York City Draft Riots: Their Significance for American Society and Politics in the Age of the Civil War* (1990).[5] Finally, the chapter on "Manhood and Minstrelsy," which is entirely new and was not a part of the original lectures, developed from encounters in rare book rooms with tiny and ephemeral presidential campaign songsters. These necessitated a reassessment of the relationship between political parties and popular race prejudice described in Jean H. Baker's *Affairs of Party: The Political Culture of Northern Democrats in the Mid-Nineteenth Century* (1983).[6]

Finally, I am continually surprised by the insight on American society that can be derived by diligent reading of nineteenth-century newspapers. They were so different from the modern press as almost to constitute a class of artifact alongside popular prints, songsters, and old campaign buttons. They were so eagerly and one-sidedly partisan and so completely absorbed in political life that over the years they had fallen out of favor as historical sources. My time in graduate school thirty-five years ago coincided with a low point in the reputation of newspapers as sources. They were regarded as hopelessly partisan and elitist, and I was left for years thereafter with little inclination to pore over the numerous dailies and weeklies of the century. *Rude Republic* helped point the way to rediscovering nineteenth-century newspapers as essential sources, though its authors derived very different lessons from reading them. I have relied heavily on old newspapers for the evidence in this book.

In the end, material culture and the return to reading the popular press of the nineteenth century had caused me to reexamine critically the arguments in four key works of great influence on the writing of political history.

Rude Republic attacked the whole idea of the importance of politics in the daily lives of nineteenth-century Americans. That idea will be closely examined in the first chapter. *The American Political Nation*, in many ways the polar opposite of *Rude Republic*, nevertheless argued for the insignificance of the Civil War to American political development in the nineteenth century—while *Rude Republic* made allowance for intensified interest in politics in that era alone. The dismissive view of American Civil War politics will be put under the microscope in the second chapter.

The New York City Draft Riots may seem a work of such tight geographical and chronological focus as to be in strange company with the other two books, which have great chronological sweep. But Bernstein's arguments transcended the five days of violence in New York City in the summer of 1863 so that his book has been taken as a model of integrating political and social history—in a way, offering a method for bringing together the two different views of American politics we read about in *Rude Republic* and *The American Political Nation*.[7]

In truth, *The New York City Draft Riots* stands as much more a work of social than political history. The index to the book has but one entry for elections, and that an incidental one to the New York City election riot of 1834, an event that occurred a generation before the draft riots. The book offers more class analysis than focus on elections and electioneering, an approach that needs to be examined in detail and will be in the third chapter of this book.

Finally, Baker's *Affairs of Party* stood as an eye-opening attempt to use the idea of "political culture" to bring new life to the political history of the nineteenth century. Like Bernstein's influential work, it sought common ground for political and social history. It similarly diverted the gaze from election results and voting returns. The results of this anthropologically sweeping approach to American politics are examined in the fourth chapter.

It is crucial to remember that all four of these books are excellent and thought-provoking. Only very good books stimulate debate and send us back to the sources to look further into historical questions. Even as I argue with their conclusions, I mean to show respect for their importance and achievement. But ultimately history written in the academy is more an argument than a story. This book began life in the academy, and animated dialogue with other historians is a sure way to advance historical understanding.

❦ The first chapter will focus on the surprising range of political material that might be found in the nineteenth-century home: popular lithographs on the walls, newspapers on the parlor table, statuary in nooks, and collectible photographs of celebrities in albums. The second chapter examines materials found in more public areas: political cartoons in poster format, most notably. It also calls attention to underappreciated developments in political campaign ephemera in the Civil War era, capitalizing on photography in a period that exploded with advertising novelty in politics. All of these materials required talent and money to produce, and the third chapter deals with the rise of a Civil War institution, the Union League Clubs, that adroitly brought money and talent to the spread of mass political culture. In some areas they virtually covered the walls of public buildings with posters, and hardly any part of the Union escaped the reach of their cheap pamphlets. The materials mass-produced for electioneering seasons naturally relied on familiar stereotypes and "melodies"—embodied literally in the smallest and perhaps the most neglected of printed campaign ephemera, songbooks. The fourth chapter explores the indebtedness of these musical materials to the popular entertainment genre of the nineteenth century, the minstrel show. Throughout, the real focus of this book is not on the materials themselves—this is not a book for collectors—but on their meaning for the era and their utility in giving historians a better description of American political culture.

Whatever means historians use to describe American political culture in the period, the effort seems worthwhile, for the real theme of such work is American people, great masses of them who did not leave historians systematic written records in letters, diaries, or memoirs, as the political elites often did. The study of political culture, like voting analysis, is a way to reach those people indirectly through the symbols, devices, literature, and institutions that engaged their attention.

✦ Many of my views on material culture had their origins in interpretations of prints and photographs used in nineteenth-century politics that Harold Holzer, Gabor Boritt, and I formulated in several works published between 1984 and 2000.[8] Association with Professors Edmund Sullivan and Roger Fischer, true pioneers in the study of material political culture, in their efforts years ago to bring life to the Museum of American Political Life at the University of Hartford also gave me some acquaintance with other kinds of political ephemera and their vital meanings.

My familiarity with prints and material culture, generally unfamiliar materials for most academic historians, stemmed from my career before university teaching, when I labored in a museum and rare book library devoted to materials on Abraham Lincoln. Then I could handle such items daily and not merely on brief research trips to reading rooms where these materials can be called up and studied only by painstakingly slow and difficult process. Also because of the two decades I spent at the Lincoln Museum, this book has a special reliance on Lincoln-related sources.

Steven and Janice Brose made these lectures possible by generous funding and made them better by patient personal support, attending the lectures themselves, asking probing questions from the audience, and keeping in touch in the time that has passed since the public presentation, while I have been rewriting and reconsidering my arguments. Harold Holzer, the senior vice president for external affairs at the Metropolitan Museum of Art in New York and my coauthor in previous books, read the manuscript at a crucial stage and provided the sort of advice and criticism that wrought important changes in the book. My other coauthor, Gabor S. Boritt, director of the Civil War Institute at Gettysburg College, likewise read the manuscript at that stage and offered extremely valuable criticism. My colleague Professor William Blair, who directs the George and Ann Richards Civil War Era Center at Penn State and manages the Brose

Lectures, trustingly allowed me to be the first speaker in a three-lecture format. He also provided searching criticism of Chapter 4, which no other historian had read. Anonymous readers at the University of Virginia Press and the University of North Carolina Press commented on the manuscript as well.

Professor Amy Greenberg, another of my colleagues in the History Department, has all along asked prodding questions while offering genuine encouragement. Important advice and criticism on Chapter 4 came from Professors W. Fitzhugh Brundage and John Kasson of the University of North Carolina. Since coming to Penn State, I have been aided in searching for relevant materials in the Rare Book Room of the Paterno Library by Sandy Steltz, James Quigle, and Jane Charles. Thomas F. Schwartz, the Illinois state historian, opened the doors of the Abraham Lincoln Presidential Library and Museum while it was under construction and officially closed. He then took off his hard hat and himself fetched campaign songsters crucial to Chapter 4; Tom provided generous help with illustrations, too. I am indebted to the staff of the Division of Rare and Manuscript Collections, Carl A. Kroch Library, Cornell University, Ithaca, New York, as well. Eric Novotny, humanities librarian at the Penn State University Library, helped me gain access to noncirculating materials for illustrations. Alan Jutzi, curator, Rare Books, Huntington Library, San Marino, California, provided information on Union League broadsides. Karen Ebeling of the Richards Civil War Era Center at Penn State helped me make the proper payments for rights to the photographs which make an important contribution to the book. The research funds so generously attached to the McCabe-Greer Professorship paid for the photographs and reproduction rights necessary for the illustrations—themselves critical, I believe, to a book based substantially on evidence from material culture. As always, Sylvia Neely read the manuscript, listened to the lectures, offered the proper balance of criticism and encouragement, and put the final manuscript into a format that the University of North Carolina Press could turn into this book.

Ultimately, the analytical approach I take to American political history I learned thirty-five years ago as a graduate student from Michael F. Holt, now the Langbourne M. Williams Professor of American History at the University of Virginia. He gave this manuscript a virtually transformative reading, for which I am grateful but to which I cannot do justice.

◆ To dismiss the engagement of Americans in political life in the nineteenth century would, of course, pose the greatest threat to our understanding of the Civil War era. It is, therefore, crucial now to make certain that historians do not somehow demote politics to the margins of the daily lives of Americans who lived in those times. So we must begin by meeting the arguments in Glenn C. Altschuler and Stuart M. Blumin's book *Rude Republic: Americans and Their Politics in the Nineteenth Century*, published in the year 2000.

Mark E. Neely Jr.
Pennsylvania State University

The Boundaries of
American Political Culture
in the Civil War Era

Chapter 1 **Household Gods** Material Culture, the Home, and the Boundaries of Engagement with Politics

⟐ Before the Civil War, the poet Walt Whitman was a beer-swigging Bohemian, but when the war came he finagled himself an easy patronage job in Washington, D.C., and in the abundant spare time provided by that sinecure, he transformed himself into a saint. Instead of patronizing saloons at night as he had done customarily in Brooklyn, he left work early each day in Washington to visit the wounded in Union hospitals. He watched pus run out of wounds and wretched men vomit and waste away with dysentery. After a while, he took a leave to go back to Brooklyn, to visit his old pals from his Bohemian days, and to vote. It was the election summer of 1864.

When he got to Brooklyn, Whitman discovered that he had changed. He did paint the town once again, but he now felt different about nightlife:

> Last night I was with some of my friends . . . till late wandering the east side of the City—first in the lager bier saloons & then elsewhere—one crowded, low, most degraded place we went, a poor blear-eyed girl [was] bringing beer. I saw her with a McClellan medal on her breast—I called her & asked her if the other girls there were for McClellan too—she said yes every one of them, & that they wouldn't tolerate a girl in the place who was not, & *the fellows* were too—(there must have been twenty girls, sad ruins)—it was one of those places where the air is full of the scent of low thievery, foul play, & prostitution gangrened—[1]

Whitman had undergone a profound change in point of view. His old Bohemian life now seemed diseased and immoral, whereas his new life, spent in Washington with real disease and gangrene, seemed elevated by national self-sacrifice.

A political historian cannot help noticing the importance of voting to the Whitman anecdote. The pains the poet took to get home to vote made the scene possible. Whitman was a peculiarly lucky beneficiary of the political system as a patronage officeholder, but casting a ballot was a persistent habit for many others who qualified to vote in the middle of the nineteenth century.

Whitman's letter also offers readers a rare glimpse of lower-class political culture—with a surprising gender twist in the bargain. The path to arriving at this image of political engagement in 1864 turns out to be the low and neglected one of material culture: had the barmaid not been wearing a McClellan political button, this rich election summer vignette would never have been recorded.

Walt Whitman voted regularly and the barmaids in Brooklyn wore Democratic campaign medals because politics engaged the attention and enlisted the emotions of vast numbers of Americans in the mid-nineteenth century. Political history in universities has fallen on hard times in recent years, but it has clung tightly to its claim that politics mattered immensely to Americans then—in fact, that the percentage of voter participation from the 1840s to the 1890s has not been equalled or surpassed before or since. Glenn C. Altschuler and Stuart M. Blumin's *Rude Republic: Americans and Their Politics in the Nineteenth Century* thus took aim at the principal claim made for the importance of American political history in the nineteenth century, namely, people's unparalleled level of involvement in political activities.

The solid foundation of that old claim, not denied by Altschuler and Blumin, was behavioral. It rested firmly on deeds and not mere words: in the period 1840–96 national voter turnout averaged 78 percent in presidential elections, according to historian Joel H. Silbey. The 78 percent represents an average for all the states lumped together. Statistics from individual states could be even more impressive. Between 1840 and 1892 voter turnout in presidential elections in New York state, Silbey points out, was 88.6 percent.[2]

The statistics on nineteenth-century voter turnout remain to this day the bedrock of the modern analysis of American politics in that period. But that remarkable level of engagement can be irrefragably documented on election day only, and what happened in people's lives in the long stretches between elections is difficult to get at—hence the modern debate over the level of nineteenth-century Americans' engagement in politics.

For some historians, those voting statistics have provided the foundation of a view of the wider American culture in Abraham Lincoln's era. In a famous article, historian William E. Gienapp invoked a quotation from a journalist covering the 1860 presidential campaign as the title of the piece and the epitome of the times: "Politics Seem to Enter into Everything." "More than in any subsequent era," Gienapp contended, "political life formed the very essence of the pre–Civil War generation's experience."[3] In a later book on the origins of the Republican Party in the 1850s, Gienapp described the political culture of the era in these words: "Individuals viewed events, facts, and observations through the prism of party identity."[4] That idea has been echoed by political historian Michael E. McGerr, who describes the political party of the nineteenth century as "a natural lens through which to view the world."[5]

Eager to make the best case for our subject, political historians such as McGerr, Silbey, Gienapp, and me have embroidered the hard voting statistics with anecdotal descriptions of the great torchlit parades, barbecues, fireworks displays, and mass political rallies that offered nineteenth-century Americans the time-filling amusement later provided by sport, the ritual provided by state religions in Europe, and the spectacle (minus a great ceremonial military presence) offered by the powerful central governments of monarchical and aristocratic countries.[6]

The authors of *Rude Republic* are justifiably suspicious of claims that the nineteenth century constituted a golden age of "vibrant" and "young" democracy in which there was an unequalled level of political engagement on the part of individual Americans. On the contrary, Altschuler and Blumin argue essentially that the activities of election day constituted an anomaly, an interruption in family and workaday lives. To these social historians, the salient characteristic of the seasons of party activity was their brevity. The periods of election enthusiasm, they say, were the products of feverish attempts by a dedicated but small core of political activists to use every available technique to cajole and nudge and persuade and stampede and hornswoggle an American populace that was generally indifferent to politics and suspicious of political parties—to drive them to the polls for a brief moment of political engagement. The high level of party organizational activity, in this new point of view, proves only how difficult it was to make Americans care about politics and to overcome their natural distaste for politicians. Americans retained suspicions that such ambitious men were not to be trusted with the welfare of the republic. Electioneering and its apparatus were, for the authors of *Rude Republic*, "the efforts of those who were deeply involved in political affairs to reach and influence those who were not. The very intensity of this 'partisan imperative' suggests the magnitude of the task party activists perceived and set out to perform."[7]

Altschuler and Blumin assert "the primacy of the community" as against "the proper limits of partisan conflict." They discern in nineteenth-century American society a "carefully constructed boundary between politics and other communal institutions—the church, the school, the lyceum, the nonpartisan citizens' meeting." At bottom they posit a well-defined and hierarchical separation between home and the public realm. They believe that the worldview of the mass of middle-class Americans can be described as "vernacular liberalism," defined this way:

> It is no more than unreflective absorption in the daily routines of work, family, and social life, those private and communal domains that the small governments of the era hardly touched. . . . We suspect that the radical disconnectedness and "privatism" observed in America by Tocqueville and other European visitors in this period translated in many instances into a primacy of self and family that confined politics to a lower order of personal commitment than is generally recognized. Tocqueville himself argued that Americans were passionately interested in politics, but he would not have seen much or many of those people to whom we

refer. Neither have many historians ferreted them out from their chimney corners and workbenches. Most Americans did vote, and for many historians that has been enough. We would look more closely at "liberalism," not merely as a political theory, but also, for some, as an apolitical way of life.[8]

Such "apolitical" people would stand as the polar opposites of those, described by Gienapp and other political historians, who saw the nineteenth-century world through the lens of party political affiliations. The argument reaches to the most profound assumptions not only about political history but about the very nature of the "people."

⬅ And yet, there is abundant evidence that there was more to nineteenth-century political commitment in America than a quadrennial trip to the polls. The evidence is under our very noses and constitutes one of the principal sources of information relied upon by the authors of *Rude Republic* for reaching contrary conclusions: the daily and weekly press. The American absorption in newspapers caught the attention of nearly everyone at the time—from genre painters (see Fig. 1.1) to census takers. Joseph C. G. Kennedy, the head of the census bureau, pointed out that the 1860 census "strikingly illustrates the fact that the people of the United States are peculiarly 'a newspaper-reading nation,' and serves to show how large a portion of their reading is political. Of 4,051 papers and periodicals published in the United States . . . three thousand two hundred and forty-two, or 80.02 per cent., were political in their character."[9]

Newspapers had doubled in number since 1850, far exceeding the increase in population in the decade. The papers were functions of politicization rather than urbanization. Only 126 communities in the United States in 1860 had a population exceeding 3,200 people. The 3,242 political newspapers, then, must have blanketed the myriad small towns and villages across the land. Illinois provides a good example. The census of 1860 found 259 political newspapers in the state, which contained only 133 towns with populations exceeding 1,500. It follows that nearly every town of 1,500 enjoyed the circulation of two political newspapers, one for each major party, the typical

FIGURE 1.1. Mexican News. *Engraving by Alfred Jones, after painting by Richard Caton Woodville (1853). Reproduced from the Collections of the Library of Congress. The centrality of the newspaper to this genre scene suggests the importance of that essentially political medium to men, women, and children of different ages, social classes, and races.*

pattern.[10] These papers owed their existence, in small communities and large, to the sustained nature of the American involvement in politics.

The editors almost literally redoubled their efforts in election season, producing special campaign editions of the regular newspaper. The periods of intensive electioneering to which *Rude Republic* refers were thus marked by the appearance of still more newspapers specially got up for the presidential election seasons. These campaign papers came atop the weekly and daily drumbeat of political agitation that appeared steadily, year in and year out.

The Whig Party of Illinois provided examples. In its earliest organization, the founding of daily and weekly newspapers was essential. A press was what a party organization needed most. The proliferation of party newspapers in Illinois was remarkable. Before the end of the decade of the 1840s, even Little Fort, Illinois (later renamed Waukegan), sported the Whig *Lake County Visitor* to oppose the *Porcupine and Democratic Banner*. The ambitious Whig campaign for the presidency in 1840—the fabled "log cabin and hard cider" campaign —saw the Whigs of Springfield, the state capital, bring forth the *Old Soldier* (the "old soldier" was the Whig candidate for president, General William Henry Harrison). Eighteen issues of the campaign newspaper appeared between February and November 1840. The *Old Soldier* had its Democratic counterpart, the *Old Hickory*.[11]

The Whig Party of Illinois was relatively feeble. It never managed to elect a governor or senator. But Illinois Whigs were capable of strenuous electioneering. In addition to the *Old Soldier* in 1840, the Whig State Central Committee published seven issues of the *Extra Journal* for the important 1843 elections in the state, contests for the U.S. House of Representatives in seven congressional districts (for which the Illinois Whigs put forward candidates in only six).[12] The existence of the *Extra Journal* reminds us of the important point made by the historian Roy F. Nichols years ago that the election calendar of the nineteenth century did not really allow fallow "off years." The states established the election calendar, and important elections occurred over a broad range of times stretching from March to November and in odd and even years alike.[13]

The newspapers that provided the authors of *Rude Republic* with the names of the small core of activists who regularly attended party organizational meetings and caucuses were steady presences both in election season and out. The steady readership could not have been small. These newspapers bore witness daily or weekly, year in and year out, to the perennial interest of many Americans in political life. How else but through the amazing existence of these party newspapers could Altschuler and Blumin base their study in substantial part on detailed analysis of four small American communities, Greenfield, Massachusetts; Marietta, Ohio; Kingston, New York; and Augusta, Georgia?[14] To use the newspapers in such a way presents a classic case of failing to see the forest on account of the trees.[15]

◄◄ The apolitical vernacular liberalism that *Rude Republic* identifies as the ruling aura in the American home of the mid-nineteenth century was a latecomer to America. Its real heyday commenced at the end of the nineteenth century. Before that, things were different.

The idea of "vernacular liberalism" is related to the notion of separate gender spheres. Historians depicted the home as a "haven" of culture and morality away from the values of business and public life, leaving little room for the idea that partisan subjects were ever considered around the hearth.[16] Patriotism was a central political value in the home, obviously, but partisan politics often stood in popular estimation in antithesis to the values associated with patriotism.

The public and private spheres, thus defined, produced expectations of permissible behavior that differed considerably for each realm. In the public sphere of partisan politics, as historian Robert E. Wiebe has suggested, "lodge politics" created an atmosphere resembling what we might associate today with a fraternity on the eve of the homecoming game — pageantry, noise, fireworks, high jinks, pranks, drinking, swearing, and, at times, fisticuffs.[17] Adversarial confrontation and arguing, dignified as debate in formal public meetings but pitched at the level of the common man, constituted mainstream modes of political discourse. In the private sphere, manners were better, culture was no liability, temperance might keep tempers under control, and piety loomed more important.[18]

The Victorian sense of privacy will forever keep us from knowing for certain what went on within the home in the middle of the nineteenth century. The surviving correspondence of political elites from the period supports the idea that men and women alike had a notion of the limited "proper sphere" for women. No one who has done much reading in such manuscript collections can have failed to notice the great differences in contents of letters written by men and women. The former contain more talk of political matters, and the latter often speak only of domestic and family news.

But the material culture of politics found in the nineteenth-century American home offers proof that the spheres were more like circles that overlapped somewhere near the edges. A good example is political prints, such as those lithographed by the famous print-makers Currier & Ives, which are discussed by Altschuler and Blumin themselves. Could respectability have afforded barriers to such materials, excluding them because of their rudeness? What precisely were the uses of these curious icons? And what are we to make of political photographs and political sheet music?

Did the political parties literally hit a wall when they approached the home?

The very walls of the home, in fact, afford a new picture of the influence that came from the public into the private sphere, rather than the other way around. For the whole span of the era of American history dominated by the conflict of political parties, from 1840 to 1896, there was evidence in the domestic sphere of their influence. Material culture in general will reveal to a degree what went on in the home, a space otherwise largely concealed from historians' view.

For their part, after examining Currier & Ives's image of America, Altschuler and Blumin concluded that Americans lived in "A world beyond politics."[19] In some 7,500 different popular print subjects, *Rude Republic* tells us, the famous lithographers never published a picture of an election day polling place, of a politician giving a stump speech, of a nighttime torchlit parade, or of a political barbecue. No such images qualified, apparently, as American genre scenes among all the "farms and city streets, racing steamboats and heroic firemen, pioneers and sportsmen, beaus and dandies, horse races and boxing matches—seemingly all the things that Americans did." [20]

One body of work published by Currier & Ives, however, is troublesome to such an interpretation: the 259 political prints published by the firm (see Fig. 1.2). These works, according to Altschuler and Blumin, amounted to about 8 to 10 percent of their titles before the Civil War, but, the authors hasten to point out, some of these political portraits doubled as icons of military heroes rather than presidential candidates. Zachary Taylor, for example, was represented primarily as a Mexican War hero and only incidentally as a presidential candidate in 1848. The rest of Currier & Ives's political print production the authors dismiss as products of brief and temporary fits of political engagement, the quadrennial national presidential contest. The firm published few political images in other years to suggest sustained engagement with politics. [21]

But Currier & Ives did not really ignore the American political scene: they were themselves eager participants in it. Far from being apolitical observers of the American panorama, the printmakers realized the commercial potential of capitalizing on the broad American engagement with politics. The firm bet 10 percent of its portfolio on the American appetite for political heroes. Today, those images stand as a distinguishing characteristic of the work of nineteenth-century popular printmakers. Modern publishers still produce cheap printed landscapes and genre scenes to frame for the home, and such images are plentifully available in the frame shops of suburban shopping malls and in art museum shops. But framable images of political heroes nowadays are nowhere to be found.

It is true that the quadrennial presidential contest set the tone for and dominated American politics as well as the political portraits lithographed by Currier & Ives. The U.S. Constitution was ultimately responsible for this dominance by creating the powerful presidential office. Lesser offices representing smaller geographical areas generally created too small a market for campaign ephemera. The distinc-

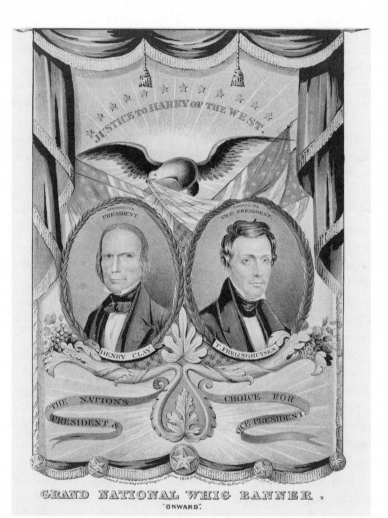

FIGURE 1.2. Grand National Whig Banner. *Lithograph by N. Currier (New York, 1844). Reproduced from the Collections of the Library of Congress. Lithographs promoting the presidential and vice presidential candidates of the major political parties formed a part of the list of images made by the firm that would soon become Currier & Ives.*

tion of market size for the national presidential contest helps explain the relative scarcity of election ephemera from other countries with wide franchise but no presidential contest—such as Great Britain. The orientation of political ephemera in the nineteenth century to the presidential contest constitutes further proof that printmakers and other purveyors of goods for the political market were in fact market- and not politician-driven. If the politicians had generated such materials they would have made them for state and local contests as well.

⤝ Using popular lithography for political evidence requires an interdisciplinary approach, and there is more to do than gather material evidence from another discipline. A true interdisciplinary approach should employ the *methods* as well as the materials of another discipline.

Visual images, properly understood, must be evaluated by somewhat different methods from typographical and written materials. It is crucial to examine their *uses* along with their subject matter—a consideration necessary to understand any printed political matter. It is important as well to examine their *medium*. Medium is as much a part of the analysis of popular prints as the subject matter of the images. We need to know not only who is depicted but whether the image in question is a woodcut, with its telltale rough and broad outlines; a steel engraving, composed of fine lines, crosshatchlike; or a lithograph, with the tonal qualities of a child's crayon.

Enumerating titles is only one part of the method for studying popular prints. It is used in the absence of sales and business records. Currier & Ives and the rest of America's busy printmakers did not bother to leave statistical business records of numbers of each title printed or sold.

Currier & Ives lithographs were conceived as commercial products to sell, not as devices for political persuasion. Though intended *for* voters and other politically engaged Americans, they were created not *by* politicians but by entrepreneurs hoping to exploit a market.[22]

The moment of purchase was the extent of the print's meaningful life for Currier & Ives, who lithographed portraits of Whig candidates for Whigs to buy and Democratic candidates for Democrats to buy. But what happened to the print after that moment of purchase is what really interests the student of politics — and is extremely difficult to determine. The life of the print for the purchaser could be brief or long. The new owner might frame the image, hanging it on the parlor wall at home to "testify" to personal "convictions" about politics, as the student of political graphics Robert Philippe expressed it.[23] Such material testimony might remain well past its corresponding presidential election, perhaps for years. Thus the purchaser would turn the commercial product into something else, an icon. That conversion was an act of individual will and political engagement.[24]

More important than duration of ownership of the lithograph was the place where the owner chose to display it. Currier & Ives usually printed political images in the smallest of the three standard sizes in which their lithographs were formatted. These "small folio" prints were meant for hanging on parlor walls and for intimate, domestic viewing. Most, such as the double-portrait prints of presidential and vice presidential running mates, measured roughly 12 inches by 8 inches. A few were 14 by 18 inches; none were printed in Currier & Ives's "large folio" size, measuring up to 28 by 40 inches.[25]

The public political sphere would surely have demanded large folio images — for placing behind the speaker's podium on the platform at a political rally or for use outdoors as posters on fences or building walls. Currier & Ives produced landscapes and sentimental images in the largest size, but the portraits of political heroes came only in intimate sizes, small or medium folio. The political images were more surely destined for the home than were the larger landscapes and historical images, which might have been suitable also for schoolrooms, libraries, restaurants, or hotel lobbies.[26]

Had political prints been intended for use primarily in public spaces, outside the home, they might well have been executed in a different medium, too. Poster-sized public images from the middle of the nineteenth century were generally woodcuts, rougher and cruder and lacking detail, and not lithographs. To heft a heavy lithographic stone explains much of the reason. In fact, the larger stones were subject to breakage as it was. Very large dimensions necessitated the use of wood as the engraved surface. Besides, the level of illustrative detail permitted by the subtleties of lithographic tones or by the close and careful work of steel engraving was unnecessary for a poster: the fairly crude lines of a woodcut would suffice from a distance.

Currier & Ives's political images printed in domestic format stand as palpable proof that political life penetrated to the very "chimney corners" of the family and that interior wall space was not reserved for domestic scenes only. No antebellum political institution broke down the barriers between home and public life more certainly than these visual devices did. The contents of the prints were political but their format and medium entailed domestic *use*.

From the many political portraits available from the mid-nineteenth century, let us select just one for analysis that properly takes into account subject matter, medium, and use: a print portrait of Zachary Taylor's rival for the Whig presidential nomination, Henry Clay. The print is *Henry Clay*, a steel engraving published in New York in 1843, based on a portrait by John W. Dodge, measuring 191½ by 15 inches (Fig. 1.3).[27]

Although this print was not issued in a presidential election year, there is little ambiguity of intent about it. It is in no way a patriotic icon. It does not depict a victorious general on the battlefield. It does not depict a successful politician transformed into a head of state by election to the presidency and thus moving beyond partisanship and the merely political to reach a status of patriotism and national identity. *Henry Clay* is simply the portrait of a presidential hopeful sitting down. There was not a reason in the world for anyone who was not blood kin to want a portrait of Henry Clay published in 1843 except political fascination.

For all its pastoral trappings, the portrait was conspicuously political. The artist made no effort to dress Clay down to fit into the bucolic landscape that formed the mood-setting background of the image. Clay appeared with his dog and cows in the countryside, wearing a top hat, silk tie, and swallowtail suit with vest and carrying a walking stick. It must have seemed as incongruous to the eyes of Americans of the 1840s, most of whom lived in an agricultural setting, as the modern-day photograph of Richard Nixon strolling the beach in

FIGURE 1.3. Henry Clay. *Engraving by Henry Sadd, after painting by John W. Dodge (New York, 1843). Kentucky Historical Society. The success of the Whig campaign of 1840, with its references to the rustic virtues nurtured by the log cabin, must have influenced this portrait of Henry Clay. Clay's "American system" was a political program meant to bring to rural America the hum of commerce and industry rather than the products of the simple plow (visible in the background). The printmaker, however, was willing to depict a home (Ashland, pictured in the margin) and attire appropriate to a society well past the log cabin stage of development.*

a suit and shiny black lace-up shoes. Like Nixon, Henry Clay was the sort of man who was a politician whatever his surroundings.[28]

Medium matters in this print portrait of Henry Clay also. The fine quality of the steel engraving by H. S. Sadd would have been wasted at long range, high up on a speaker's platform. Engravings were meant for the home, to be appreciated up close.[29]

Reinforcing the notion that *Henry Clay* belonged in a home context was an image appearing in the margin of the print. That "remarque" — a small detail image — offered a representation of Henry Clay's house, called "Ashland." This portrait of the potential presidential candidate for 1844 at his home in Kentucky was obviously intended for the purchaser's home.[30]

Ashland was a grand place, of the sort to which Americans of Clay's era, most of them long since departed from a subsistence economy and desiring "respectability," likely aspired. The role of such aspirations, symbolized in ownership of a political print portrait such as *Henry Clay*, is a crucial one when considering the image of politics presented in *Rude Republic*. The essential theme of Altschuler and Blumin's book, epitomized in its very title, was that politics were "rude" and lacked respectability. "Blatant office-seeking and behind-the-scenes maneuvering, the cultivation of political loyalty among newly enfranchised workers and recently arrived immigrants, the inclusion in political organizations of saloonkeepers, street toughs, and other unsavory characters, the employment of manipulative techniques of mass appeal, and the equation of these techniques with other forms of crude humbuggery, imparted an unseemliness to politics that considerably complicated the simultaneous pursuit of respectability and active political life."[31] Yet the existence of such a steel engraving as *Henry Clay*, which conspicuously banished rude qualities and embodied very considerable artistic craftsmanship, greatly complicates any notion that respectability and active political partisanship were incompatible.

The analysis applied to the Clay print could be turned toward any number of other such images, but surely it need not be to make the point. It is more important to illustrate the range of respectable popular arts that often embodied political themes and entered the home from the brassy public realm of partisan advocacy.

Respectability and political partisanship were by no means necessarily opposed. The idea is obviously false in the case of elected officeholders, who constituted an elite. But the real question is whether the mass of American voters and their families felt they lost respectability by identification with and engagement in the activities of political parties run by eager partisans. In other words, then, did the level of engagement signified by purchase and display of a Currier & Ives political print somehow preclude social respectability?

It is extremely perilous to pinpoint the class appeal of objects. Only the roughest parameters can be drawn. Currier & Ives prints themselves ranged in price from fifteen cents to three dollars. Even the most expensive print was a far cry in value from oil paintings, miniatures, or sculptures that might be purchased or commissioned by the upper classes. Any calculation is also complicated by the advent of photography in the era.[32]

Whatever the reputation of the political methods of the nineteenth-century parties, the prints and other objects that sometimes touched on or embraced political personalities or events were themselves the essence of respectability and more refined taste.

For validating testimony on this point we need only turn to the earlier work of Stuart M. Blumin, *The Emergence of the Middle Class: Social Experience in the American City, 1760–1900*.[33] Through an ingenious and painstaking use of probates of wills, Blumin attempted to reveal the sharp line in consumer goods drawn between the aspiring middle classes of midcentury America and the working classes. Looking at the detailed inventories available from Philadelphia in 1861, he noted not only furniture and carpets but also prints and pianos as possessions that helped to distinguish the emerging middle classes from the manual workers and artisans in the city. In the case of pictures apparently the subject matter of the images was not always listed, and Blumin himself mentions only one "moderately prosperous manufacturer . . . a partner in a lumberyard" who owned a print portrait of Benjamin Franklin and one of Garibaldi. Blumin identified Franklin as the "patron saint of the Philadelphia bourgeois." Garibaldi went unidentified but not without the comment that the meaning of Garibaldi's image somehow "qualified" the icon of Franklin.[34]

The image of Garibaldi, though not partisan in the specific scheme of American politics, nevertheless came from the realm of the political rather than the patriotic and must have indicated a liberalism that was anything but apolitical and private. The liberalism of this Philadelphia lumberyard man transcended the shores of the United States.

Political prints and respectability were not necessarily in antagonism, but the range of images Currier & Ives produced over the years greatly complicates assessment, for some of Currier & Ives's work smacked of rude surroundings. Surely the liberal icon Garibaldi stood higher in the scale of respectability than did the five hundred race horses Currier & Ives depicted over the sixty-three-year history of the firm.[35]

Some prints constituted a badge of respectability and some did not, and we must take our clues on the meaning of such objects from other parts of the culture. An interest in horse racing, as we know from the marginal respectability of New York's sporting newspaper, *Wilkes' Spirit of the Times*, edited by the former pornographer George Wilkes, was not likely to raise one's social status in the Northern states. Scatological references and double entendres about sex—which often appeared in political cartoons, also a niche market for Currier & Ives—were not either. Obviously Currier & Ives and other printmakers of the nineteenth century marketed images for different classes of people. Among lithographs with political subjects, cartoons were likely marketed to lower classes to view in public spaces and political portraits to respectable people and for private spaces. (Chapter 2 will deal more fully and directly with the political cartoons of the era.)

If we broaden our search for popular items with political content regularly found in the home, we can find other "respectable" examples: sheet music for the home piano, "family" photograph albums, and parlor statuary. The piano in particular stood as a landmark of bourgeois respectability for homes in the middle of the nineteenth century, and sheet music was auxiliary to that product.

In other words, owners of pianos must have provided a substantial part of the market for sheet music, and thus a most respectable segment of society became owners and users of materials whose appeal was sometimes partisan. Sheet music reveals the political penetration of the private parlor as surely as political prints. Political portraits and music with political themes appeared in election years, but the uses to which the sheets were put are as important to consider as the timing of their issue. They must have sat on the piano's music rest, visible to all: *The Douglas Polka*, *The Lincoln Grand March*, and others.

It would be a mistake to infer that political songs constituted a great portion of the vast amount of popular sheet music published in the nineteenth century, as it would be to exaggerate that part of Currier & Ives's production dedicated to political subjects. A large collection of such sheet music—the one at the John Hay Library at Brown University, for example—contains a few political titles amidst multitudes of sentimental and popular pieces. The political pieces nevertheless formed a seamless part of the catalogue of available topics of engagement in the nineteenth century. Politics did not enter into everything, but politics was not excluded from the most important concerns of life. Politics was not alien to respectable pursuits. The boundaries overlapped a little.

Prints and popular music were not new to the nineteenth century, but photography was. Popular photography also provides evidence of the penetration of the home by politics. Abraham Lincoln's presidential career coincided exactly with the introduction and popular vogue of what is called the carte-de-visite photograph, a paper photograph of visiting-card size, about 2 inches by 4 inches, mounted on a stiff card. The albums in which they were collected and displayed were equally popular, featured in Christmastime advertisements as popular gifts. One of the most famous photographs of Lincoln shows him looking at one of these distinctive albums with his son Tad.[36]

A brief exploration of any substantial collection of such photographs gathered in midcentury will prove my political point. The

Henish Photo-History Collection at the Rare Book Room in Paterno Library at Penn State, for example, reveals the seamless absorption of the political in the private typical of nineteenth-century America. The collection contains eighteen albums along with numerous separate photographs. Even though the albums are described in the Rare Book Room finding aid as "Family Albums," I decided to examine them to see whether the concerns of the family reached beyond portraits of blood kin.

I opened the first box, and pulled out an album that was obviously of the right period. It proved to have only family photographs in it. I pulled out a second album and found scrawled on the index page in pencil five family names. Then I turned to the first photograph. When I saw that it was an image of Abraham Lincoln being welcomed into heaven by George Washington, I understood the political orientation of the album. The fourth photograph was of Lincoln himself. Facing it, naturally enough in this family space, was a portrait of Lincoln's wife Mary Todd Lincoln. Next came a portrait of the abolitionist Frederick Douglass. That portrait was facing the first of many anonymous family members to come, a little girl with her rocking horse.

The uses of such photo albums were more private than those of lithographed and engraved portraits. The album had no possible public use. Within the home, it did not appear on the walls of the parlor but was kept on a table—displaying its thick decorative leather cover, its brass hinges, and the gilded edges of the thick cardboard pages—to be pulled out, presumably, for viewing on intimate family occasions, even though images of political figures sometimes shared space with family photographs in the albums.

The example of photograph albums containing political images can be found many times over. Their introduction in 1860, on the threshold of the Civil War, naturally increased their political content, but all collectors of Civil War materials are familiar with such albums and their patriotic and partisan contents.

The pages of a photograph album offered a blank slate on which the family could write about what was important to it. The manufacturers of the albums did not, as vendors of such products would do in later years, offer the empty slots to be filled and then, by printing labels underneath the display windows, *command* the purchaser to fill the spaces with photographs of celebrities, to be sold by the album manufacturer as well. There was space below the display windows to write a label, often, but it was up to the album's owner to decide what to keep in the album. Sometimes, what the family wanted in its album pages was images of political heroes along with those of friends and relatives, affirming for the album's select viewers the political convictions of the family.

❧ The home and the public political sphere in fact overlapped; the boundary was more like a beach than a sea wall, with the waters of politics washing over and receding from the shores of home.

I am by no means the first to examine those boundaries, but the boundary has been most studied to date on the other side of the wall —that is, in public political rituals. Some social historians have discovered in the rituals of nineteenth-century politics some participation by women—in parades, for example, or in the audiences of some political speeches.[37] But evidence of such participation remains modest and suggests that women's roles were often largely spectatorial or decorative (see Fig. 1.4).[38] And in focusing on such exceptional participation, historians should not ignore, as *Rude Republic* is quick to remind us, the many women who stayed at home.[39]

❧ The authors of *Rude Republic* are correct to insist that there were boundaries to political life loosely cordoning off areas into which the work of the political parties of the nineteenth century was not to intrude. The role of the clergy in politics offers an indication of the different expectations of home and public sphere. Altschuler and Blumin maintain that political historians "have not recognized the degree to which politics and religion could be placed by some in an adversarial relation."[40] Yet that idea can be carried too far, for America was a heavily evangelized nation, and there would hardly have been voters enough to match the turnout figures if religion and politics did not mix. Had the clergy ever been scrupulous, in war or peace, about separating the spheres of religion and politics, it is difficult to understand how advancing evangelical religion and democ-

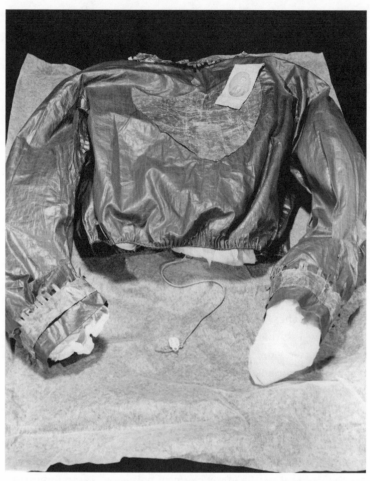

FIGURE 1.4. *Wide-Awake blouse. Courtesy of the Abraham Lincoln Presidential Library and Museum, Springfield, Ill. A campaign ribbon with a paper photograph of Lincoln is pinned to the blue uniform made for a woman to wear in political parades for the Republicans in 1860.*

racy could have marched hand-in-hand across the nineteenth century, as Daniel Howe has argued they did. Surely he is correct to suggest that religion increasingly proved more a spur to public political involvement in the North than a moral barrier to it.[41]

Ideally, religion was not to be corrupted by political concerns, and constitutionally as well as ideally the political realm was to keep itself separate from the religious one. But ideal and reality rarely matched. From the Puritan settlement through the Civil War the relationship of religion to politics was problematic. Puritan ministers believed that church and state should be separate, but they nevertheless delivered "election sermons" on the eve of voting, and these became increasingly narrowly political.[42] The antebellum years were no less paradoxical. Clergymen were not supposed to enter the partisan fray, but some clergy did, particularly on issues of alcohol prohibition and anti-Catholicism.[43]

On this point *Rude Republic* offers a sure guide, noting accurately that the rise of the slavery issue in the Civil War era caused the ordinary boundaries of politics to be expanded into areas previously thought generally to be off limits. Senator Stephen A. Douglas of Illinois reacted with apparent shock to a petition of protest against his Kansas-Nebraska Act in 1854 signed by nearly 3,000 New England clergymen, but his vehement protest was a harbinger. By the time of the Civil War, the alignment of the pulpits of many evangelical denominations was clearly antislavery, and Democrats often expressed renewed shock and bitter disillusionment at the extensive involvement of the pulpit in public issues during the war.

In Harrisburg, Pennsylvania, for example, Democrats denounced the "wild fanaticism belched forth from Sabbath to Sabbath by many of the clergy in our midst."[44] In the spring of 1864, when at a local Bible society meeting the Methodist Reverend J. Walker Jackson maintained that the "religion of Jesus is the purest form of Republicanism devised," a woman stormed out, exclaiming, "I did not come to church to hear politics!"[45] Jackson appeared regularly on the platform with Union Party speakers that election season, eliciting sharp complaints from the Democratic press: "One of the most lamentable evidences of the degeneracy of the times and the corruptions that are creeping into the churches and uprooting the germs of religious faith, is to be found in the fact that ministers—professedly of Christ—are found cheek by jowl with the bloated *habitues* of pothouses, and hob nobbing in social familiarity with the devotees of gilded vice . . . Such ministers are essentially of the church militant. . . . Look in the churches and the thinned congregations, the vacant pews." The problem, complained the same alienated Democratic source, was that "their preachers no longer preached Christ and him crucified, but of John Brown, the apostle of Abolitionism, and for the overthrow of copperheads!" [46]

Republicans defended their clerical supporters as patriots rather than partisans. Exonerating Jackson and another clergyman who helped lead a Union mass meeting in Mechanicsburg, Pennsylvania, Republicans said, "The Reverend gentlemen named are powerful speakers, and are doing a noble work for the cause of the Union. They are speaking for *their country*, and have a higher object in view than the election of men of any particular party. As champions of Freedom and the Right, they have won for themselves a reputation that cannot be attained by the politician." [47] Indeed, Jackson himself felt called upon to defend his conduct. [48]

Other men of the cloth who joined the political fray noted the prevailing strictures against such behavior. A minister named Curran, in his *Sermon Preached by Request of the Pastoral Board of Wall Street Methodist Church, Jeffersonville, Ind., Thursday, (Fast Day) August 4, 1864*, admitted being "benevolently warned off by a certain class of politicians, and told that Churches and ministers should not 'dabble in the dirty pool of politics.' " [49]

Strictures against partisan involvement varied in intensity from denomination to denomination. Episcopalians were less inclined to enter public political debate than more evangelical denominations. Bishop William H. Delancey, of the Diocese of Western New York, pointed out to President Lincoln in the election summer of 1864 that "our Ministers abstain from engaging in ordinary business, from holding public offices, and participating generally in politics." But behavioral limits were everywhere left vague. The bishop admitted that the "common law of our Church" rather than "formal declaration in Rules and Canons" kept ministers from such activities as engaging in warfare.[50]

The presidential campaign of 1864 may have marked the culmination of partisan involvement on the part of many evangelical leaders. The *New York Times* found it "a most significant thing that the religious and moral element of the nation is precisely the element which is strongest for the war." The editors of that Republican newspaper had noticed the many resolutions issued by ecclesiastical organizations such as the American Board of Foreign Missions essentially supporting the Republican administration. The editors admitted that it was "unfit" for "preachers of the gospel to mingle in the ordinary political broils of the day," but the controversies of that day were extraordinary, high principles were involved, and the life of the country was at stake. In such circumstances it was "every way meet" that "Christian ministers who are isolated from the political arena" should "speak boldly." [51]

The Democratic critics were right about one thing at least: to be involved in politics was to use the methods of the politicians, spoilsmen and all. By the time of the Civil War, some clergymen behaved essentially as "pothouse" politicians did, though they did not admit it. Joseph Parrish Thompson of the famous Broadway Tabernacle Church in New York City, for example, visited Lincoln in the White House to speak of matters more than religious. He had sought a transfer for his son in the army. Thompson had gained entree to the president through letters of introduction from the consummate New York City spoilsman Abram Wakeman and from Henry J. Raymond, editor of the *New York Times*.[52] And Henry C. Bowen, an editor of the widely circulated religious weekly, the *Independent*, sought a patronage job in Brooklyn as reward for service to the Republican Party in his newspaper work.[53]

❦ The authors of *Rude Republic* admit that the "conflict over slavery, and over the constitutional issues spawned by it, brought political matters far closer to people's lives, and brought people into the forum of public debate, as nothing had done before." But the evidence from material culture—medals for presidential candidates, popular prints, and photographs, for example—spans the decades and suggests that politics came close to the lives of the people throughout the century.[54] Furthermore, the nature of this particular type of evidence —from material culture—strongly suggests that it was not "issues," let alone constitutional ones, that drew the people to politics. It was also the ritual and group identification that drew them in.

The Civil War also brought previously marginalized voices into the debate, but that is really a concern for another book—one about constitutional change rather than intensity of engagement on the part of citizens. It is noteworthy, however, to see that few spurned the opportunity for participation in the American political system, and many worked hard to gain participation.[55]

Broadened political engagement during the Civil War—a phenomenon that escaped the New Political Historians with their loose periodization of American political history—was a fact. But it was not altogether a matter of issues. Nationalism and slavery aroused some people, but at election time the usual lures of ritual, emotional exhortation, and group activities exerted their force as well.

❦ To identify accurately the boundaries of partisan engagement we need documentary evidence. That is difficult to come by, and much of what we know about the home will have to come from inference from material culture and from other strategies of indirection.

To show how little there is to go on by way of direct witness from the voices of the nineteenth century itself, I can lay out in a few paragraphs nearly everything I have found in three years of research for this book, being on the lookout for the uses of popular political images in the home. These discoveries are always accidental, as there is no obvious place to look for individuals' reactions to political messages.

Occasionally, a letter proves that the purchase of a political print constituted a sign of enthusiastic political identification and ideological alignment with the subject of the portrait. Thus Samuel C. Damon, who was a seamen's chaplain in Honolulu, wrote Senator Charles Sumner in 1863, "Your course as a statesman, has so fully met my approval, that I have your 'likeness' framed and suspended in my parlor." [56]

As for the status of such images as "icons," one Chicago print-maker all but used the term in describing the uses of his product. He sent Abraham Lincoln some complimentary copies of a lithographed version of the Emancipation Proclamation and explained, "I have this day sent you 50 copies of your great Proclamation of Freedom which has been engraved and Lithographed from designs gotten up by me[,] the taste and ingenuity of which have received the highest commendations of all artists who have seen it. The form in which I have now placed it will enable every American citizen to place it among his household Gods & teach their children how you delivered from bondage a nation in a day." [57]

The use of such items to promote the political fortunes of a candidate in an election can sometimes be directly documented as well. Thus Lewis Dodge, another maker of a facsimile version of the Emancipation Proclamation, wrote Lincoln from Buffalo, New York, to ask for a signature to copy in facsimile in his print. He described the image as depicting "your Emancipation proclamation . . . with an acrostical Poem embracing your name and portrait[, and] a Star of Liberty and Union." He added an endorsement of his project by a local political operative named Henry Tanner, who told Lincoln, "I have seen the plan now being Lithographed . . . and I think it will be a very good document and have a Lively influence this fall." [58]

Certainly some in the nineteenth century collected the images of celebrities, as individuals have done ever since. This is obvious from the fact that carte-de-visite photographs were not limited in subject matter to heroes (there are many of the assassin John Wilkes Booth, for example). People attempted to collect the images of all members of Congress, irrespective of party, and Secretary of State William H. Seward sought to bring together print portraits of all the heads of state with whom he dealt—almost none of them republicans, of course. But collecting most likely took a sympathetic ideological path. Thus an African American named David Thomas Fuller, who worked as a messenger in the American consulate in Paris, explained the nature of his collection to Charles Sumner, "Among the collection of Photographs of 'Eminent men' who have from time to time raised their voices in favor of the colored race, I would like to include that of the Hon. Charles Sumner." He had been unable to find a photograph or engraving anywhere in Paris and was now resorting to asking Sumner to send him one himself.[59]

The uses of newspapers in the home—they constitute the political artifact that survives in greatest abundance in today's libraries and museums—illustrate the tensions between public and private, political and family values. Some historians these days opt for a gendered interpretation of nineteenth-century newspapers, suggesting that political papers constituted "a male medium," whereas the religious press "appealed equally to men, women, and children." [60] Surely that contrast in readership is too exaggerated, but it is true that newspapers could provoke tension between the male and female spheres. In a famous and well-documented incident, when a copy of the newly established *Springfield Republican* was delivered to the Lincoln home early in 1857, Mary Todd Lincoln said to Abraham, "Now are you going to take another worthless little paper?" [61]

Evidence reveals that political readership in the home was not confined to qualified voters. Thus Anna Park wrote from Bennington, Vermont, to thank Charles Sumner for donating materials to be auctioned in a church charity bazaar, "Many thanks also for the speeches, which were read, as are all of yours that we get—aloud in our family." [62] Newspapers sometimes enjoyed the same use. Thus a man named Beckwith mentioned to Sumner in passing, "I have just been reading with my wife some account of your work on the Louisiana Question." [63]

Parlor statuary resembled household gods literally, but the difficult three-dimensional medium dictated that creators of statuettes and busts depict mostly successful political subjects and not mere partisan hopefuls. Unlike a political lithograph, which could be produced between the time of a summer nominating convention and the commencement of the autumn canvass, statuary required greater periods of time for fabrication. The creative process included modelling and mold-making, not merely the laying down of a few lines with a wax crayon on a flat surface, as in a lithograph. Life masks or life sittings, almost essential for accurate sculptural likenesses, were far more difficult to find or arrange than purchasing a photograph for a two-dimensional likeness. Nevertheless, some busts and statuettes of politicians who ranked below head of state were manufactured. The reformer Lydia Maria Child, for example, informed Senator Sumner in January 1865, "Mrs. Loring sent me Milmore's bust of you for a New Year's present. I was delighted beyond measure." [64]

Senator Stephen A. Douglas, too, earned the admiration of Chicago sculptor Leonard Volk, who made a life mask and subsequent popular statuettes of the Democratic presidential contender of 1860. Volk covered his bets and enjoyed a greater success with his life mask of Abraham Lincoln and subsequent statuary based upon it.

❦ In the face of such scanty direct testimony, there will always be room for debate. On the other hand, there is much—besides the stubborn election statistics that firmly document voter turnout in the nineteenth century—to support the assertion of widespread and deep popular engagement with politics in the century. Clearly the boundaries were not as sharply drawn as readers of *Rude Republic* might imagine.

By asserting the primacy of community over politics and by drawing sharp boundaries between family and political concerns in the nineteenth century, the authors of *Rude Republic* have written back into that century a dispute that exists more in twenty-first-century university history departments than in the "chimney corners" of the past. Spheres there were, but the boundaries between them were not as well defined or impenetrable as historians seem to think. Family and political life existed in Lincoln's era on a seamless continuum of eager engagement.

Chapter 2 **A New and Profitable Branch of Trade** Beyond the Boundaries of Respectability?

✦ During the heated canvass for the presidency in 1864, a newspaper reporter in New York observed an amusing deception practiced in a nighttime rally for Democratic candidate George B. McClellan. The managers of the torchlit parade marched the various ward Democratic clubs in and out of view among New York's buildings so that they seemed to magnify their number greatly, like a small group of actors marching across the stage, behind it, and back on the stage again so that, to the audience, they seem to form one long file of people. The editors of the newspaper were "not aware that the trick has ever before been played in political meetings."[1]

Such a stunt might seem like grist for the mill of those skeptical of the apparent high level of nineteenth-century Americans' political engagement. Critics emphasize the feverishness and deceptiveness of the efforts on the part of the politically committed to dazzle largely indifferent and apolitical American citizens into interest in voting. Political historians too have long emphasized the importance of party organizations and managers—the sorts of operators who dreamed up ruses such as the one described in New York. But how far must we go in believing that organizational methods and campaign technique periodically *created* a temporary and fleeting political engagement? Does it not beggar the imagination to think that the same little deceptions could produce similarly spectacular results in voting behavior each and every time, as though the people never grew wise to the tricks?

The problem lies in assuming an oversimple model of party that imagines politicians pushing and voters being pushed. The ultimate foundation of such a model is an unflattering portrait of the people. In their description of "vernacular liberalism," Altschuler and Blumin say bluntly that the people were "unreflective"; that their "daily routines of work, family, and social life" monopolized their thoughts; that a "primacy of self and family" ruled their lives; and that they followed an "apolitical way of life."[2] What *Rude Republic* presents, in other words, is the first "me generation," in the middle of the nineteenth century, fast on its way to becoming "generation X."

Ironically, Altschuler and Blumin share with their foes, the New Political Historians, a one-dimensional and rather ugly portrait of the people. The political historical model favored by the previous generation was based on an image of the American voter as a person who did not understand or care about issues and was motivated by "tribal" antipathies toward other social groups in the society.[3]

Without romanticizing them, the people deserve better from historians, political and social alike. Our models of party are too simple and too often left unstated. The politicians, the ward managers who organized the parades in New York, the tireless newspaper editors, and the office-seekers with their oratorical appeals were not the only agents in the nineteenth-century political drama, working on a bedrock of passive, unreflective, selfish, prejudiced, and apolitical people.

Help in revising the oversimplified model of American political life can be found in material culture: for example, a lithograph from the 1860 election campaign, *The Union Must and Shall Be Preserved* (Fig. 2.1), published by William H. Rease of Philadelphia, a lithographer and skilled producer of trade cards (what we call business cards today). The lithograph featured portraits of the Republican candidates for president and vice president, Abraham Lincoln and Hannibal Hamlin.[4]

Rease's lithograph teemed with ideological references. Arching overall was a Union-preserving message, but special appeal was made to Pennsylvania's insatiable appetite for protective tariffs with the image of a shield featuring "Protection to American Industry" in the lower center of the print. Issues stressed by Republicans everywhere in the North—freedom of speech, free soil, and the Homestead Bill—were blazoned on a banner suspended below the image of an American eagle. The rail borders around the portraits of Lin-

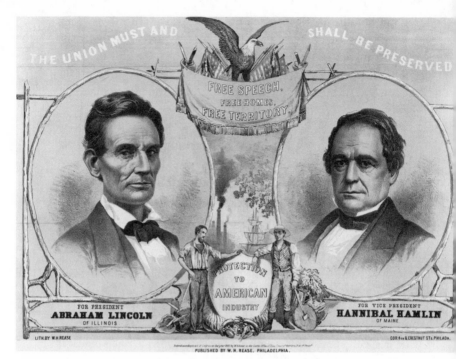

FIGURE 2.1. The Union Must and Shall Be Preserved. *Lithograph by William H. Rease (Philadelphia, 1860). Reproduced from the Collections of the Library of Congress. Although this print made reference to a number of platform planks, both of Rease's lithographs for the campaign of 1860 (see also Fig. 2.2) emphasized Union.*

coln and Hamlin echoed Lincoln's nickname in the campaign, "the railsplitter." The smokestacks of industry, the masts of commercial shipping, and the rural and urban workingmen were pictured above the abundant fruits of their labors, which poured from the cornucopia in the lower center of the print.

Historians are well equipped to explain the political meanings lying in the content of such images, but we do not often enough consider the artifact as an example of material culture. Nameless lithographic artists, necessarily skilled—as anyone knows who has ever visited a printmaker's studio—crafted a polished and appealing product.

And, as far as we know, the Republicans got all that talent free of charge.

In other words, Rease took it upon himself to create the lithograph for sale. Lincoln had no hand in it. Nor did the Republicans in Philadelphia directly initiate or underwrite the endeavor. On the same day that Rease deposited the lithograph for copyright, June 21, 1860, he also copyrighted *The Union, the Constitution and the Enforcement of the Laws* (Fig. 2.2), a similarly formatted lithograph advertising the presidential ticket of the rival Constitutional Union Party, with John Bell for president and Edward Everett for vice president. Currier & Ives also produced political lithographs for candidates of opposing parties.[5]

Such prints were commercial rather than political ventures. Little evidence to the contrary exists: I have rarely seen a letter from a Civil War–era politician initiating the production of a political portrait— and never from the candidate himself. The evidence that does exist points decidedly in the other direction. Like the letters cited in the previous chapter from the producers of facsimiles of the Emancipation Proclamation, most such correspondence refers to projects already undertaken by lithographers or artists. The creators of the products sometimes sought help with some visual detail—a signature or a photograph to serve as a model—or fished for a compliment on the likeness from the candidate.[6] But the correspondence began at the bottom and reached up to the political elite.

By the time the candidate dealt with the product, if that occurred

FIGURE 2.2. The Union, the Constitution and the Enforcement of the Laws. *Lithograph by William H. Rease (Philadelphia, 1860). Reproduced from the Collections of the Library of Congress. Rease's lithographic banner for the Constitutional Union ticket in 1860 could not employ the wide variety of symbols and slogans his Republican print did because the party of Bell and Everett took the Union and Constitution as its only platform.*

at all, the content had already been determined by someone else who was not an active politician. The artist and the printmaking firm dictated the content of the image, picking up all the signals, subtle and forthright, that the politicians sent out to the voters. Presumably the purchasers comprehended the content, or some of it. These items suggest a different picture of politics from the one positing the strenuous efforts of the vitally engaged to persuade the unengaged.[7]

What is true of political prints is true as well of sheet music, of popular photography, and of poster cartoons and comic magazines. Even in the case of other less artful campaign ephemera, like the McClellan medal worn by the barmaid in New York, the politicians did not provide the driving force. Private entrepreneurs did. The market origins of these materials was the lesson that Harold Holzer, Gabor S. Boritt, and I attempted to drive home with our work on political prints in books and articles written over almost two decades. Entrepreneurs aided and abetted the politicians, and the businessmen's market ultimately depended on a bedrock of politically engaged customers.

❧ The combination of eager voters, accommodating printmakers, and strutting politicians necessary for a nineteenth-century presidential canvass would all have been common knowledge to history already had it not been for a curious neglect of political technique as a subject of study. Despite the original emphasis on organization as opposed to issues by the New Political Historians, their efforts turned primarily to statistical voting analysis. The concept of political culture, which was meant to take the focus off the single-minded statistical analysis of election returns, somehow did not serve to turn the spotlight on technique. Instead, cultural analysis took precedence over a look at the methods commonly used by all political parties to win elections in a particular period. And the advent of the "republican thesis," with its emphasis on the political manipulation of irrational fears of political monsters, served to bring the study of political history back to the content of political speeches and ultimately to the political elites and away from voting analysis and the electoral techniques of the faceless party activists who worked well below the level of the speaker's platform. It will be a good thing if the new attention paid by *Rude Republic* to the efforts of the parties to motivate voters at last turns historical attention to the remarkable achievements in campaign technique of the nineteenth-century American political parties.

Still, one thing on which all interpretations of nineteenth-century American politics agree is that the parties made strenuous efforts to motivate voters. And no more strenuous effort than that put forth in the Civil War elections had been made in a generation.

No period achieved more in improving political spectacle than the Civil War itself, but these advances have enjoyed little attention. That neglect is a legacy of the New Political Historians. They never paid much attention to the Civil War, which, as Jean H. Baker pointed out, they dismissed as having insignificant elections that simply "maintained" the same general patterns of voting and commitment already established with the new party realignment of the late 1850s and perpetuated until the 1890s.[8] Joel H. Silbey, the dean of the New Political Historians, said of the period, "despite both the real and apparent discontinuities of American life, the political elements remained pretty much fixed across the Civil War divide."[9]

The authors of *Rude Republic*, finally, failed to pick up on Civil War developments in technique, despite their willingness to acknowledge the heightened interest in politics, because they attributed increase in interest to issues (the slavery issue in particular)—and because they do not respect political technique.

Politics in the Civil War North—unlike the party-less Confederacy—was a fast-moving, innovative, and rapidly changing endeavor. The period witnessed an explosion in the use of visual techniques in political campaigning. The political parties both seized eagerly on innovation in media and method. They increasingly employed pictorial representation in torchlit parades. The *Philadelphia Public Ledger* denounced this development "of late years" for its intensification of the assault on personality in American politics. "Wretched in design, scandalous in character and offensive of good taste and correct sentiment as those political caricatures are, it is surprising that public decency does not at once set the seal of condemnation on them.

. . . It was exhibitions of this kind in the late processions which undoubtedly caused the disturbances which ensued upon every night
display."[10]

The impact of cheap photography probably lay at the bottom of
this revolution in visual political ephemera and campaign devices.
Cumbersome photographs had been available since the 1840s, but
the advent of cheap photographic images printed on paper gave the
medium broad impact for the first time in 1860. Increasingly, campaign medals of the sort that prompted Walt Whitman's reflections
on politics in 1864 utilized small photographs on iron or paper, cased
in decorative frames (see Fig. 2.3).[11]

These attractive little objects were a recent development. In Philadelphia, for example, an independent newspaper observed:

> [The] Presidential campaign of 1864 has developed a new and ap-
> parently profitable branch of trade, and now at almost every street
> corner men and boys expose for sale the miniature likenesses of
> the opposing candidates for the White House. . . . It would seem
> that all the men, women and children in the community feel it
> incumbent upon them to express their political preferences, by
> displaying in the most conspicuous manner, the portrait of their
> favorite for presidential honors. The mania is not confined in its
> operations. The merchant appears to take as much pleasure in his
> badge as does the ragged boy whose entire capital has probably
> been expended in the decoration of his person. . . . The ladies are
> supplied with breast-pins, shawl-pins or finger rings, each con-
> taining the portrait of President Lincoln or Gen. McClellan, while
> the gentlemen can secure a huge rosette, or a neat shirt-stud. . . .
> Silk, cotton, velvet, satin, ivory, gold, silver or imitations of the pre-
> cious metals enter largely into the composition of these badges.
> . . . A collection of the various styles of badges would be interest-
> ing as one of the most curious features of the campaign of 1864.[12]

The appeal of these political novelties reached well beyond enfranchised voters, and their production was market-driven and not ma-
nipulated by the politicians. Thus on June 18, 1864, one John Gault of
New York City wrote Lincoln, explaining, "I intend circulating three

FIGURE 2.3. *Campaign ferrotype of 1860. Courtesy of the Abraham Lincoln Presidential Library and Museum, Springfield, Ill. The new branch of trade in campaign ephemera capitalized on campaign devices with small photographic portraits mounted in decorative frames, like this one of Lincoln, introduced in 1860. The reverse shows the name of the Boston photographer who reproduced the image as well as the pin to attach the item to one's clothing.*

or four million medals or metallic cases containing likenesses of yourself & Andrew Johnson for President & Vice president, and want to ask a perfect Photograph to copy from."[13]

Badges advertising the ordinary person's political affiliation constituted, in the Civil war era, a "branch of trade" and not a system of political management.

The managers of political campaigns themselves relied as much on calculation as on presentation, and the Civil War saw the inception of a primitive form of polling. Politicians pored over the election returns, while newspapers and Horace Greeley's famous *Tribune Almanac* reported electoral results broken down to county and ward level. Yet, politicians and the press usually referred to "majorities" in discussing returns. That is, they were interested in and reported only the number of votes by which the winning candidate exceeded the loser's vote.

The reason for reliance on that primitive statistic lay in political rather than mathematical history: what politicians sought in the nineteenth century was what they have created finally in the twenty-first: what we call "safe seats." Congressional districts so configured as to be safe for one party or another are the norm these days, and in 1988, for example, 98 percent of those who sought reelection to Congress won.[14] Nineteenth-century politicians also thought in terms of identifying and celebrating safe districts, so that they would know where to allocate resources, speakers, and literature for the next canvass. They thus sacrificed statistical precision to the goal of electoral invincibility and held themselves back from truly sophisticated voting analysis. In colleges at the time, no one studied voting statistics as social science—or studied anything else having to do with political parties, which were more likely to be denounced in a course on moral philosophy than analyzed in a history course. Political science was yet to be born.

Despite the lack of sophistication about statistics, the practice developed during the Civil War of asking people on railroad cars to express their preferences for president, with the results then reported in the newspapers. The *Philadelphia Public Ledger*, a mainly financial paper lacking ardent identification with party, regarded the practice as an "impertinence." Similar preliminary "straw polls," as they might be called today, were apparently taken—seizing an opportunity peculiar to the war—among soldiers in camp or hospital to see how they planned to vote. In other words, party enthusiasts thought they had to find confined groups, people in rail cars or soldiers in camps, to poll their political preferences. The indignant *Public Ledger* identified these as party methods for advertising the popularity of their own candidates because the results reported in the newspapers were invariably favorable to the candidate of the reporting paper's own political party.[15]

Josephine S. Griffing, on the other hand, took the polls to heart. She traveled the country raising funds for freedmen's aid and thus was often a passenger on the trains. She informed President Lincoln from Burlington, Iowa, in the fall of 1864: "From Washington here I have noted the vote taken on the cars—generally a respectable majority for us—but between Toledo and Detroit a *tie*. From Detroit to Chicago in a vote of 160—21 Majority for the Republican candidate."[16] Griffing likely found an eager reader in Abraham Lincoln. The president had less than two weeks earlier himself noted the results of a poll taken on a train from Pittsburgh to Harrisburg on September 13:

Lincoln	McClellan	Frémont
172	66	7.[17]

The politicians who led the party tickets could hardly help but be interested in voting—and Lincoln, as we shall see, was more interested than the average politician—but they showed very little interest in image-making. The elite among politicians, the elected officeholders and candidates for important national and state offices, proved backward in making concessions to image-making and advertising techniques.

It is critical to notice the direction of the correspondence about political technique in the private correspondence of the politicians of the era. Thus on June 1, 1860, William D. Kelley of Philadelphia—later nicknamed "Pig Iron" because of his fondness for tariffs protecting Pennsylvania's iron industry—wrote Norman B. Judd, chair of the Republican State Central Committee in Illinois, saying, "A townsman of mine, a clever artist in his line—is very anxious to get out a medal for campaign use with a faithful likeness of Mr. Lincoln. To do this requires a perfect profile and for this he has applied to me." He added, "Can you send me one—A reliable *profile*—or if you have none can you induce Mr. Lincoln as a favor to me, or for the good of the cause to have one photographed. . . . I will cheerfully honor a draft for the cost & trouble as I believe it will result in a creditable work." Kelley concluded with a report on the prospects for the Republican cause in Pennsylvania in the coming presidential election.

Judd passed the letter along to Lincoln with the obligatory gesture to the candidate's assumed indifference to campaign gimmickry, "not . . . so much on account of the picture proposition as that you may know his view of Penn." In the end Judd added, "The picture although troublesome to you, when requested by such a person as Judge Kelley ought to be attended to—Every little [bit] helps, and I am coming to believe, that likenesses broad cast, are excellent means of electioneering."[18]

Note that the medal maker initiated the correspondence because he needed a profile photograph. To that date Lincoln had never posed for one, though it was an obvious prerequisite for producing campaign medals, which, by 1860, constituted a staple of the political novelties circulated in presidential canvasses. Most important, the circumstances of the production of this Philadelphia campaign medal for Lincoln reveal who was really in control of the content of the political messages broadcast at the broadest level—not the candidates. Norman Judd, to whom Kelley wrote for entree to Lincoln, was a politician's politician, an important operator in Illinois politics for a decade at least, but Judd was only now "coming to believe" that medals and such had become "excellent means of electioneering." Much of the business of electioneering was as much a consumer-driven enterprise as it was a matter of politicians pushing and persuading.

All the funding required of the party officials in this episode was the cost of the photograph, which Kelley was willing to pay out of his own pocket. The medal maker assumed the risk of production and hoped to pass on the expense to eager consumers of American political products. He sought no party subsidy.[19]

Throughout that summer of heroic campaigning such activities stirred the surface of American society. On June 28, 1860, Alexander H. Ritchie, an American engraver, wrote Lincoln, "If agreeable to you, we should be glad of the privilege and opportunity to engrave your likeness on steel—with a view to publication of the same." Ritchie included an explanation of the different aims of lithography and engraving: "We notice that the likeness made by Mr. [Thomas] Hicks and that by Mr. [Charles Alfred] Barry [two of the earliest campaign likenesses of Lincoln produced in 1860] are both to be reproduced on stone & in the *lithographic* form. You are undoubtedly aware that a *steel plate engraving* is very much better & more desirable than a lithograph—By the first named process, is secured not only a higher degree of finish, & greater vigor & character, but much better artistic effect." Ritchie also needed an original photograph of the candidate from which to work, and he assured Lincoln that he could "guarantee that no improper use will be made of the likeness you may have sent to us." The entrepreneur, and not the party candidate, would be determining those uses.[20]

◄ The tone of the *Public Ledger* in reporting such "impertinencies" as polls taken on railroad cars recalls the insight of *Rude Republic* in pointing out a certain attitude of disapproval on the part of respectable Americans toward many of the techniques common to political campaigns in the nineteenth century. Some politicians were more successful than others in achieving a stance superior to the less respectable arts of their trade. One of the most successful was Charles Sumner, the antislavery senator from Massachusetts. Typical of the attitude taken toward him by his constituents was that evidenced in the following letter from a man named Rufus P. Stebbins, from Cambridge:

By the way I must tell you of a caricature on president seeking which I saw in a shop window a day or two since. There was a precipice, at the foot of which the candidates were scrambling for popular favor—scattering mottoes and pasting placards on the bottom of the rock, one or two on short ladders reaching up, and uttering catch phrases, *while Charles Sumner was on the top of a long ladder printing, with perfect composure, at the very top of the precipice near the Eagle*, the words *"Amendment of the Constitution."* There was something in your quiet air up above all the tumult below which struck me as very much to your honor— [21]

The cartoon Stebbins saw was a double-page spread pulled from the April 1864 issue of *Comic Monthly*, one of the short-lived humor magazines of the era.

Although Sumner's constituent understood the message of the cartoon perfectly and identified the senator from his comic likeness, he did not recognize the other figures in the image. They were not candidates for office, actually, but famous newspaper editors—James Gordon Bennett of the *New York Herald*, Henry Raymond of the *Times* posting a placard for Lincoln, and Horace Greeley of the *Tribune* boosting Salmon P. Chase or Gideon Welles. The only politician depicted was Fernando Wood, the notorious peace Democrat from New York City, shown in the cartoon as a Jefferson Davis supporter.[22]

Like the man on the street in Civil War–era Cambridge, historians today are likely first to notice the *subject matter* of the cartoon and the attitude it takes toward president-seeking, namely, that the office falls short of true statesmanship, as exemplified by Sumner and his work for the thirteenth amendment of the Constitution, abolishing slavery. In other words, the cartoon, and the comments of the man who saw it in the shop window, embodied a vague antiparty spirit.

Attention to medium and use of the image, however, calls attention to the shop window where the cartoon was displayed. Alas, Stebbins did not say what kind of shop, though it was likely a bookseller or news agent (see Fig. 2.4).[23] We are given a rare glimpse of the similar display of poster cartoons from the other end of the country from Boston. In Dubuque, Iowa, in October 1864, the local Democratic newspaper reported: "On the streets . . . in front of the Postoffice . . . a crowd are constantly in attendance, looking at the caricatures which Kelley [the news agent] has placed in the shop window. . . . Abe and Jeff pulling the Union asunder. . . . Miscegenation in its various phases, with Horace Greeley drinking tea with a beefsteak lipped wench, white

FIGURE 2.4. Abe Lincoln's Last Card; or, Rouge-et-Noir. *Punch (London), October 18, 1862. This cartoon, displayed in a London print-shop window, caught the eye of American Henry P. Tappan, who wrote Lincoln about it. In the humor magazine where it originally appeared it was accompanied by a poem with awkwardly forced rhymes pointing out the inconsistencies of the Emancipation Proclamation.*

men walking arm in arm with colored sisters, white hostlers driving out John Brown's soul with a coach and four, &c."[24] The article referred to a Currier & Ives cartoon, now famous (see Fig. 2.5), and to one of a series of five images published by Bromley & Co. in New York City (see Fig. 2.6).[25]

The letter to Sumner from his constituent about the political cartoon is one of perhaps a half-dozen letters mentioning cartoons that I have seen in thirty years of reading political history sources from the nineteenth century. And I have never seen an instance where the correspondence went the other direction, that is, in which a candidate or office-holder called the attention of someone else to his image in a political cartoon. The elite of the parties tried to stay above the level of the cartoon. Cartoons were a little less than respectable. Some of them were downright "rude."

Any discussion of political cartoons of the mid-nineteenth century properly belongs with considerations of the era's public spaces or workplaces more than in discussions of the home. In modern times editorial cartoons are largely matters of private consumption in one's personal copy of a morning newspaper or a news magazine. But such was not the case in the mid-nineteenth century. Cartoons appeared only rarely in the daily press, and illustrated newspapers such as *Harper's Weekly* and *Frank Leslie's Illustrated Newspaper* were produced only in metropolises. Comic magazines likewise appeared only in great cities and then not for long.

Some of the same printing establishments that produced portraits and landscapes, Currier & Ives in particular, also produced political cartoons as separate-sheet lithographs, and these are occasionally found framed in the same way as domestic lithographs. But it seems unlikely that political cartoons enjoyed the ability to cross the threshold of the home from the more customary realms of the public and political.

Uncertainty about the use of poster cartoons stems from the extreme scarcity of original sources about them. It has never been clear from the meager documentary record what exactly were the uses of poster cartoons in this period—where they were placed and by what means, who saw them, and who was affected by them. Eyewitness ref-

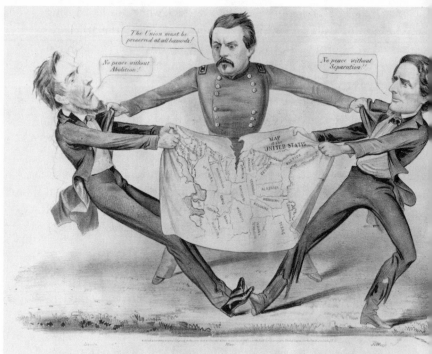

THE TRUE ISSUE OR "THATS WHATS THE MATTER".

FIGURE 2.5. The True Issue or "Thats Whats the Matter."
*Lithograph by Currier & Ives (New York, 1864). Reproduced from the
Collections of the Library of Congress. The national canvass for the
presidential office created a market for political images and ephemera
stretching from New York City, where this fine lithograph was
produced, to Dubuque, where Democrats crowded around the news
agent's window to see it on display in October 1864.*

erences to seeing cartoons are rare, and there is no logical place to look for them. They are happened onto mostly by accident. For the most part, we have only the surviving artifacts, the cartoons themselves, to consider.

To understand poster cartoons, we must keep in mind the boundaries of gender and social class that we cross whenever we move from the home to the public sphere. To be sure, the working classes had homes just as the middling classes did, but as Stuart Blumin has been at pains to show in earlier work, the homes of the working classes did not contain the number and variety of material goods that the homes of others did. As for gender, certain kinds of entertainment and certain endeavors, politics among them, took place outside the home almost exclusively. The cartoons' subject matter was too ephemeral to merit the investment in a picture frame and the damage of a hole in the wallpaper for the hanging nail.

Despite the rather rigid restraints of Victorian taste, scatological language and risqué situations abounded in political cartoons. For example, one of the double entendres found in Civil War–era cartoons about military strategy was the term "movement." The word was used not only to describe the changing positions of troops on battlefield maps but also to describe the action of the bowels.

A Currier & Ives political cartoon thus depicted General Winfield Scott as *The Old General Ready for a "Movement"* (Fig. 2.7), squatting over a hole in the ground from which Confederate animals emerge into his waiting hangman's noose.[26] Another cartoon, *"While the Cat is away, the Mice will Play,"* circulated during the presidential campaign of 1864, made a similar play upon the word "evacuate" to make fun of the checkered military career of the Democratic candidate, George B. McClellan (Fig. 2.8). The scene of the cartoon, a privy in which an Irish carpenter has sawed toilet seats, represented imagery about as crude as one can find in popular culture of the era. Such scenes were surely not intended for proper Victorian parlor walls.

Such cartoons did not belong in the Victorian home. Cartoons formed alien, even hostile, territory for women and children and, for that matter, religion. They smacked of the men's world officially defined by electoral franchise and office-holding qualifications. They

FIGURE 2.6. Miscegenation or the Millennium of Abolitionism. *Lithograph by Bromley & Co. (New York, 1864). Reproduced from the Collections of the Library of Congress. Horace Greeley takes tea at*

center. President Lincoln and Senator Charles Sumner meet at left. Deposited for copyright on July 1, 1864 (the handwritten date in the margin), the lithograph sold for twenty-five cents and was mailed free.

THE OLD GENERAL READY FOR A "MOVEMENT".

FIGURE 2.7. The Old General Ready for a "Movement." *Lithograph by Currier & Ives (New York, 1861). Reproduced from the Collections of the Library of Congress. The "rudest" side of the republic is apparent in this Currier & Ives poster cartoon. The rules of Victorian propriety broke down during presidential canvasses, and the press stooped to employing foul jokes and images. It is a virtue of* Rude Republic *to recall that side of American political culture.*

"While the Cat is away, the Mice will Play."

About this time a **PEACE PARTY** is organized who present *little* **UNREADY** a mansion not "in the skies," but in New York, where his indecision of character is illustrated by the story of the

CARPENTER'S JOB.

Napo. Why did you not cut two openings, as you were directed?

Carp. Why, you see, General, I feared you might come here sometime "taken short," being unable to decide which "hole" to patronise, you might meet with a serious disaster.

Napo. Your explanation is so far satisfactory, I shall recommend you to the President for a Brigadier's commission? But why have you put up that odious picture, in this private room, visited by no one but myself?

Carp. Why, you see, General, that's more of "my strategy." If you are costive at any time, that picture will make you evacuate quicker than anything else.

FIGURE 2.8. *"While the Cat is away, the Mice will Play" (1864). The Library Company of Philadelphia. The verso of this rare little broadside printed a mock call for a Democratic rally. It summoned "WHISKEY HEADS" and those "WHO FEAR THE DRAFT."*

belonged to the roughhouse fraternal side of politics, with its practical jokes, occasional fisticuffs, and alcohol abuse. They found their ephemeral place in public spaces where men dominated and individuals were not walled off from other social classes.

A cartoon that revealed the other side of the image of Henry Clay, the Whig candidate for president in 1844, discussed in the first chapter provides a useful introduction. *All the Morality and All the Religion* featured images of Clay and his vice presidential running mate, Theodore Frelinghuysen (Fig. 2.9). It referred to subject matter that was frowned upon by the clergymen and their disproportionately female congregations. The anonymous artist depicted the candidates standing in Clay's carpeted study as the proprietor shows off his gallery of prints. "Well, worthy compatriot," says Frelinghuysen, "I am much pleased with your study but what do these roosters represent, and what is that horse and his rider and two men yonder who seem to be firing off pistols—and those pictures up yonder on pieces of pasteboard? As we represent the great Whig Party which has all the morality and all the religion, I hope there is no harm in these pictures." Clay assures his pious running mate, "Friend Freely"—with an awkward hesitation and clearing of his throat—that the roosters "represent the Cock that crowed when Peter denied his lord." Other far-fetched but pious explanations follow.[27] Cockfighting, horse racing, dueling, and gaming were the notorious pursuits of fallen men—rumored also to be Clay's pastimes—and the usual realm of the political caricature.[28]

Since only a few images can be reproduced in this book, I shall base the discussion of cartoons that follows on the images described in Bernard F. Reilly's standard work, *American Political Prints, 1776–1876: A Catalog of the Collections in the Library of Congress*, available in most library reference collections. The collection has the virtue of including work by many printmakers besides Currier & Ives, the most famous. This discussion will exclude noncartoon prints and will focus only on the years from 1856 through 1864.

The cartoon artists of that era peopled their images almost wholly with men. The appearance of a woman was unusual, and her representation likely to be unflattering. Many students of the period are familiar, for example, with *The Great Republican Reform Party*, a Currier & Ives cartoon issued for the 1856 presidential campaign (Fig. 2.10).[29] The artist depicted the Republicans as fanatics, cranks, and lunatic reformers. The cartoon did contain rare depictions of female figures, one a thin and spinsterish advocate of free love. Wearing pants under a brief skirt and smoking a cigarillo, another says, "We demand, first of all: the recognition of Woman as the equal of man with a right to Vote and hold Office." A temperance advocate demands to make it a capital crime to use tobacco, food made from animals, or beer. And—in another sure sign of the men's world to which these separate-sheet cartoons belonged—the advocate of "free love" says, in a rough pun, that they are "all Fremounters."[30]

Only imaginary women were likely to enjoy flattering depiction in political cartoons: the allegorical figure representing liberty or Columbia was often a woman.

Domestic scenes gave way to more rough-and-tumble activities associated mostly with men, the very activities depicted in the Clay-Frelinghuysen cartoon as the opposites of piety: horse races, for example, or foot races (commonly relied on for humor about presidential "races"). Boxing, playing ball games, or watching cockfights were more common cartoon activities than doing the washing or planting a garden. Playing cards, another common activity for political protagonists in the cartoons, was a reminder of the gambling that was endemic to American politics at the time. Homes, parlors, and picket fences seldom figured as backdrops: instead the political figures in the cartoons were suspended in open and unidentifiable spaces or shown in proximity to public buildings associated with political office.

The famous presidential campaign of 1860 was, in the world portrayed in political cartoons, a man's canvass almost entirely. Of the twenty-three political cartoons from 1860 illustrated in Reilly's *American Political Prints*, only two pictured women. One was a revisit of the 1856 *Great Republican Reform Party*, now called *The Republican Party Going to the Right House*.[31] The "right house" in this instance was not the White House but the lunatic asylum, and the various lunatics filing in included two women reformers. The other female figure to

FIGURE 2.9. All the Morality and All the Religion *(1844)*. New York Public Library. Lithograph by H. Bucholzer. Print Collection, Miriam and Ira D. Wallach Division of Art, Prints and Photographs, the New York Public Library, Astor, Lenox and Tilden Foundations. To Northerners, playing cards (upper left corner), dueling, horse racing, and cockfighting were representative of the life of a Southern

Oh no – no harm at all, I assure you, friend Freely. Those roosters are meant – ahem! to – to – represent the Cock that crowed when Peter denied his lord. The horse and rider are rather bungling certainly – but they were made for riding into Jerusalem : the men with the pistols – ahem! it only commemorates the time that John Randolph and I shot at a mark one day – perfectly harmless amusement, I assure you. There was no-body hurt! And those pictures on pasteboard etc! they are pictures of Eastern Kings of Ethiopia about whom we read so much in the Bible.

Clay

LL THE RELIGION

planter. Theodore Frelinghuysen of New Jersey, Henry Clay's running mate in the 1844 presidential election, balanced the Whig ticket as a moralistic counterweight to the Kentuckian. Cockfights and horse races were the stuff of which political cartoons were made in the era, but here they became a reproach to the presidential candidate and a comic revelation of Whig hypocrisy.

FIGURE 2.10. The Great Republican Reform Party. *Lithograph by Currier & Ives (New York, 1856). Reproduced from the Collections of the Library of Congress. Women were universally excluded from the franchise and from officeholding in 1856, and they were generally*

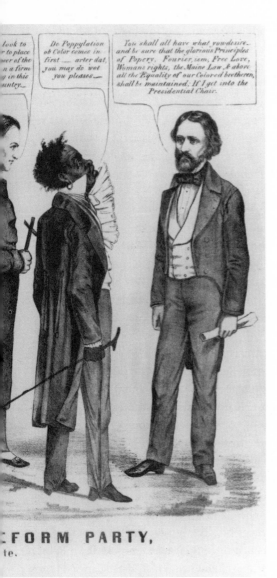

look to
r to place
er of the
n a firm
g in this
untry.

De Poppylation
ob Color comes in
first — arter dat,
you may do wot
you pleases.

You shall all have what vowdesire,
and be sure that the glorious Principles
of Popery, Fourierism, Free Love,
Womans rights, the Maine Law, & above
all the Equality of our Colored bretheren,
shall be maintained; If I get into the
Presidential Chair.

FORM PARTY,

te.

excluded from political cartoons as well. Their rare appearance in
that manly world came as unsexed feminists—in this cartoon,
a pants-wearing, cigar-smoking, whip-wielding advocate of
women's rights and a spinsterish advocate of free love.

make an appearance in 1860 was an African American who danced with Abraham Lincoln in *The Political Quadrille. Music by Dred Scott*.[32] Otherwise the imagery of the cartoons from the 1860 campaign was perhaps the most "manly" ever offered: a baseball game, a gymnasium, boxing, and a cockfight figured in at least one cartoon each. These images can be thought of as offering us a glimpse of the barely respectable world of *Wilkes' Spirit of the Times*, the sporting newspaper of New York City, rather than that of the Congregationalist *Independent* or Greeley's *Tribune*, two respectable papers of vast circulation.

Midcentury political cartoons found family virtues and the uplifting effect of the schoolhouse useful only for groups other than the white American men who engaged in politics. Family images did enjoy brief prominence during the Civil War and Reconstruction. When cartoonists wished to put Republican antislavery policies in a good light they offered images of freed African Americans in family units or eagerly attending public schools. The artists knew that such images were reassuring.

On the whole, political cartoons of the Civil War era stand as solid reminders of the substantially gendered nature of politics. Certain political activities had no place in the home, and the boundaries of political culture are most clearly visible in cartoons.

Rude Republic cannot ignore political cartoons, but the authors skip the era of the poster cartoons discussed here and focus their discussion on those political cartoons produced after the Civil War. The medium changed dramatically. Poster cartoons were lithographs printed on stiff paper, usually in horizontal format with typical dimensions of 12 by 17 inches, and were rarely colored. Though cartoons were separate-sheet prints, like the political portraits, the firms kept the price down to encourage their use, temporarily, in a brief season of intense political excitement. In fact, these cartoons thoroughly embodied the qualities of politics to which *Rude Republic* calls our attention—temporary interest and lack of respectability.

The cartoons discussed in *Rude Republic* hail from what might well be termed their heyday, the post–Civil War era and the Gilded Age, the age of Thomas Nast, the illustrated newspaper, and comic magazines such as *Puck* and *Judge*. Focusing on the 1870s and 1880s Altschuler and Blumin summarize their conclusions about political cartoons this way:

> Politics achieved a larger presence [in print media] . . . in published humor and in mass-circulation pictorial magazines. The character and tone of that presence, however, were most frequently negative, and if these media give any evidence of popular meanings attached to the national crisis and the ensuing expansion of government it is to suggest that suspicion of politics and politicians, and a sense of the separation of politics from the more valued realms of private life, continued to run deeply through American culture. Perhaps they were felt more deeply than ever.[33]

But the difference in medium in the political cartoons of the Civil War period and those of the post–Civil War period is critical.

Political cartoons in the Lincoln era—except for those published as woodcuts in New York's famous illustrated newspapers, *Harper's Weekly* and *Frank Leslie's Illustrated Newspaper*; those appearing in *Vanity Fair* in the North and the *Southern Illustrated News* in the Confederacy; or the few appearing in short-lived and fugitive periodicals (such as *Comic Monthly*, where Charles Sumner's constituent saw the caricature on president-making)—appeared as poster cartoons.

Cartoons of the Grant era, the Liberal Republican era, and the Mugwump era more often betray general disgust with corruption in politics and evince more antiparty sentiment. A greater proportion appeared in newspapers and in magazines that were purchased for purposes other than political ones alone and that allowed for enjoyment in private and perhaps in solitude.

Cartoons of the Civil war era tell a different story from the latenineteenth-century disillusionment with party. They signify, instead, the opposite: commitment to party on the part of those legally qualified to participate in politics by voting and holding office. They belonged firmly to the era of eager and unembarrassed public partisan identification. They belonged in the public areas.

Currier & Ives poster cartoons rarely conveyed an antiparty, plague-on-both-your-houses attitude toward politics. Instead, we see at first a wholehearted pictorial commitment to one party or the other. Partisanship did intensify during the war, with the result that, as Harold Holzer and I have noted previously, the cartoonists often drew a line—literally—down the middle of the print. This bisected cartoon image derived from the sharply defined differences in the political platforms of 1864. The Republicans recognized the Democratic platform of that year—a sop offered to the peace wing of the party because the presidential candidate would be a prowar general—as a major embarrassment. It embarrassed even the Democrats' own presidential candidate, whose letter accepting the nomination in fact denounced the platform. Publishing the Republican and Democratic platforms side by side, with little commentary to sway the voter, became a common Republican ploy in 1864. The side-by-side format carried over into other kinds of broadsides, such as one comparing the platform of the incumbent New York Democratic governor, Horatio Seymour, with a proclamation by the arch-traitor from American history, Benedict Arnold.

In political cartoons the sense of stark partisan contrast developed into the two-panel cartoon, with a contrasting vignette of good behavior and bad behavior. These played off the wholehearted commitment of the politically engaged to one party or the other.[34]

The candidates' correspondence was almost as unlikely to mention campaign finances as political caricature. There too the candidates tried to stand above the fray.

Commerce was substantially involved in nineteenth-century political culture, though not on a modern model. The modern conception of such involvement stems essentially from the Progressive Era and afterward and features the idea of corrupting interest. It is epitomized by the current debate over campaign finance reform. Commerce, on the post-Progressive model, gave money to political parties to protect business interests, and the parties responded by manipulating passive and indifferent voters so that their candidates, indebted to the interests, would win.[35] Revising this Progressive model of party and political behavior is critical for three reasons. First, we cannot otherwise understand campaign finance in the nineteenth century. Second, we will likely retain an image of corruption unfair to the political culture of the nineteenth century. And third and most important, we will otherwise underestimate the level of engagement in political life on the part of nameless Americans.

I have for years been mystified by the scarcity of letters about money in the private papers of nineteenth-century politicians. One rarely finds detailed financial accounting documents in the archives.[36] Unlike today's politicians who complain that they must spend far too much time fund-raising, the politicians of the nineteenth century seldom mentioned the subject.

There were two reasons for the scarcity of documents about party finance. First, the candidates for office, the most prominent political figures and the ones whose papers historians most often read, generally regarded themselves as being above the grittier aspects of political campaigns, including finance. The party elite of elective officeholders and candidates for elective office did not stoop to create medals and lithographs for their campaigns; the same elite spent their own money on the expenses incurred in political campaigns, of course, but they otherwise stood above the scramble for funds.

At the end of the exhausting campaign in Illinois against Stephen A. Douglas for the U.S. Senate in 1858, for example, the state central committee chairman informed Lincoln that he "ran the State Committee upon the least economical plan and it has unpaid bills to the amount of about $2500 — I have written to [Ozias M.] Hatch and [Jesse K.] Dubois about their subscription, but I get no answer, and I am in the boat — Our friends ought to help this matter out, or the party will be disgraced — a personal request from yourself to some of our leading friends throughout the State would help it out."[37] Lincoln had pledged $500 and would more than meet his pledge in the end, apparently, plus he had incurred expenses and foregone much legal business while campaigning. "I am willing to pay according to my ability," he stated, "but I am the poorest hand living to get others to pay."[38]

Not only did those who held "the post of honor," like Lincoln in 1858, feel that they ought not to have to raise funds, elected officeholders and candidates for elective office affected general disdain for the "brass band" aspects of political campaigns. Thus Senator Lyman Trumbull of Illinois told Lincoln in 1858: "I see by the papers that ... [Stephen A. Douglas's] friends are very active in getting up big meetings & making parades over him. I know you despise such appliances & so do I, but still they have their effect. Many persons are dazzled by these shows, & others by being made participants are drawn into his support. I thought that our friends did not pay attention enough to these outside matters two years ago."[39]

The second and more important reason money was so seldom mentioned was that not nearly as much of it was needed in the nineteenth century as would be later. Only assessments of officeholders — or "subscriptions," as Lincoln and Judd termed them — stand prominently in the archives as evidence of a systematic or institutional framework for financing. In 1864, for example, the Union Executive Congressional Committee assessed each member of Lincoln's cabinet $250 to underwrite the printing of campaign documents for the presidential canvass of that year.[40] From Lincoln's cabinet alone came an assessment equal, by my rough estimate, to 10 percent of the cost of running the recent gubernatorial campaign in Pennsylvania, one of the largest and hardest-fought states.[41] The point is not that so much was raised from the cabinet members, but that it took so little, by modern standards, to conduct a major political campaign.[42]

Attempts to get into the pockets of businessmen were even by the time of the Civil War sporadic at best. In Philadelphia the *Public Ledger* noted at the commencement of the presidential canvass in 1860 that "a host of nice young men are running about with books, soliciting aid in sums of almost any size." Despite the reference to ledgers for recording the contributions, these attempts to raise funds appear to have been unsystematic and unplanned — even ad hoc. The *Public Ledger*'s reporter, for example, witnessed a solicitation for money to purchase a flag occasioned by the other party's having just flung one to the breeze.[43]

The *Public Ledger*, mainly a commercial paper, termed the money-raisers "political beggars." In New York one newspaper reported "tribes" of them on the streets, going from "one place of business to another asking for money to hold political meetings and processions." The New Yorkers considered arresting them as other beggars were arrested, but the Philadelphians thought it was up to the businessmen to put a stop to the practice by refusing to contribute.[44] Although Market Street merchants were said to contribute three or four hundred dollars at a touch, the *Public Ledger* could find no reason for making contributions; the paper made no mention of quid pro quos or corruption.[45] There was nothing systematic enough about such door-to-door fund-raising really to explain the funding of the elaborate and showy campaigns that marked American politics in the nineteenth century.

To examine the papers of a nineteenth-century presidential candidate is to be left wondering where the money came from. I recently looked at all the documents in the Abraham Lincoln Papers from the Library of Congress in the period from August 1 through October 15, 1860, the heart of the presidential canvass. Of some 224 letters Lincoln saw in that period, 23, or about 10 percent, mentioned money. The word "mention" is carefully chosen; the 23 letters did not describe fund-raising activities. Many of them did not really deal with the subject of campaign finance. Three came from crackpots asking for money for unsolicited and grandiosely described political services. Another letter, written by the aging abolitionist Joshua R. Giddings, piously sought reassurance that Lincoln had not achieved nomination and political success so far by assuming any compromising "pecuniary responsibility, nor political obligation."[46]

Finances were usually mentioned only incidentally, and but one of the twenty-three letters suggested that the party curried favor with wealthy men. In that letter, James E. Harvey of the *Philadelphia North American* described a problem to Lincoln. C. H. Fisher, the father of the famous Philadelphia diarist and pamphleteer Sidney George Fisher and "our most prominent capitalist, & a gentleman of the highest social position," had been slighted by Lincoln's private secretary, who had acknowledged without adequate ostentation a pamphlet written by Fisher's son. "He belongs to a class most desirable for us to cultivate," wrote Harvey of the wealthy father, "& is now acting from principle, against the prejudices of most of his personal friends. His liberality & sympathy in our cause, & in your election particularly, have been practically illustrated." [47]

The singular nature of the Harvey letter speaks volumes about the funding of nineteenth-century political campaigns. For one thing, it seems as though Fisher's wealthy friends were not funding Republicans. Furthermore, Fisher was clearly unknown to Lincoln, though he was the major Republican capitalist funder in Philadelphia. Even more important, the letter came from Pennsylvania.

Pennsylvania was the source of several of the letters to Lincoln mentioning campaign financing in 1860, and the reason was this: because of the bitter factional feud between the Republican governor Andrew G. Curtin and senator Simon Cameron, two competing committees raised and distributed money for the Republican campaign in that state. The bitterness that arose over this senseless competition caused many to suspect double-dealing of some sort by the duplicitous and corrupt Cameron. Maryland Republican Henry Winter Davis investigated. He reported to his relative, David Davis, who was also one of the Illinois managers of Lincoln's campaign, that the problem "was explained satisfactorily. . . . It grew out of a want of confidence in the pecuniary honesty of the head of the regular committee." [48]

Taken all in all, these letters help put in perspective presidential campaign finance in the nineteenth century. None of the letters that the candidate saw dealt with money in detail. Lincoln did not see budgets, expense vouchers, receipts, or accounts. He did not draw up a budget for the campaign himself, and he had no staff, let alone a treasurer. Second, none of the letters suggested that raising money was a problem. No one complained of shortages or rationing or close budgeting. And the reason was not that the Republicans had tapped the wealthy C. H. Fishers for all a party could need. The reason is that the party did not need much money. Voluntarism and business exploitation of a market of politically interested Americans made campaigning an inexpensive task for state or national organizations.

To express it another way, to read the letters sent to the candidate informing him of possible problems in the campaign—and there were many, of course—is to discover that money simply was not one of them. The Republicans who communicated directly with the presidential candidate in 1860 worried mostly about a fusion of the three parties in opposition to them. They worried occasionally about factionalism in their own ranks, especially among feuding Pennsylvanians. Because of the importance of Pennsylvania's vote in the election, Republicans worried about proving Lincoln's soundness on the protective tariff, an obsession in that state. They worried that Lincoln might unnecessarily make a statement to the public or write a letter for publication on issues, when they should be sitting quietly on their lead. They eventually worried about their own overconfidence. But they had few money worries.

No doubt there were chairmen of committees who did focus on raising money to fund speaking and printing, but the hierarchy of political organization in the period kept the money managers substantially out of the candidate's sight. Out of sight, in this instance, was surely out of mind, and it would be wrongheaded in the extreme to impose a Progressive reformist view on midcentury American presidential politics. And if the chairmen charged with money-raising had suffered many problems, the news, like the feud in Pennsylvania, could not have been kept from the candidate, who would eventually have been approached to deal with the problems. The parties did not have serious fund-raising problems because their funding needs were not large.[49]

← Nineteenth-century political parties ran big, brassy, noisy, and effective campaigns for office. The canvass was typically months in duration and involved many of the trappings of modern advertising.

The important question is not how these parties raised money but why they needed so little to produce so much that was effective. The answer is that private enterprise and its customers provided substantial funding to political campaigns without cost to the parties. Such an answer can be founded only in an assumption of a high level of engagement in politics on the part of the American people. It was so high, in other words, that the people willingly paid for what they got. The people subsidized the parties, indirectly, not on direct appeal of fund-raisers. They purchased lithographs and campaign novelties, as we have seen. But their most important indirect subsidy was the purchase of newspapers.

Newspapers were critical to parties. What a party most needed in the nineteenth century was newspapers. Pamphleteers, like the wealthy Fisher's eccentric son in Philadelphia, had always thrived in times of crisis, ever since the Stamp Act crisis that caused the American Revolution a century earlier. Political pamphlets were a sign of political crisis and feverishly heightened interest in the public sphere, but political parties required, as it turned out, not political arguments produced in excited and brilliant fits and starts. Political parties required the steady and sustained message and creation of identity provided by a daily or weekly political press.[50]

We have not thought as clearly about the institution of the press as we should. When we think of the party organs characteristic of the mid-nineteenth century, what immediately comes to mind is the idea of party subsidy—the money from political organizations that kept so many little newspapers alive in so many little towns in America. The outstanding student of campaign finance in the nineteenth century, Mark Wahlgren Summers, argues that in a typical case "party subsidy" for a newspaper "would give . . . value for money." True enough, but what has gone unnoticed is the modest size of the investment. The newspaper was surely a bargain to the party. The newspaper had subscribers and advertisers, and those other people helped to defray the costs of getting out the editor's political message every day or week. It is true, in other words, that journalism was simply a branch of politics in the nineteenth century and not really a profession or a "fourth estate" of the realm, as Michael Schudson argued in *The Good Citizen: A History of American Civil Life*, but this vital piece of party machinery was not paid for *entirely* by the parties.[51]

Thus Abraham Lincoln, a successful lawyer but by no means a Fisher-like capitalist of great wealth, for a time owned a German-language weekly newspaper in Springfield, Illinois, called the *Illinois Staats-Anzeiger*. For an investment of four hundred dollars, and a tacit promise of patronage if he won national office, Lincoln was able to bring editor Theodore Canisius to Springfield from Alton, Illinois, with his vital press in tow, and dictate the Republican editorial direction of the paper for well over a year.[52]

We have as proof of engagement with politics not only the hard behavioral evidence of voter turnout but also the considerable indirect evidence that masses of people voted with their pocketbooks. At times of election fever, they purchased campaign novelties and lithographs, but in the case of the daily and weekly press the engagement of their pennies and nickels was sustained, week in and week out. The abundance of the political newspapers published in the United States is vital to comprehending the level of political engagement in the nineteenth century. These party organs have more often been read as devices for stirring up the voters, but in fact they were also dependent to a substantial degree on a base of voter interest great enough to defray some of the costs of publishing.

Any model of party for the nineteenth century positing essentially a one-way push from politicians to voters is inadequate. Such a model would fit the evidence, as the introduction to this book pointed out, if the surviving record of political discourse included only the short-lived campaign newspapers of the election season. There were more protagonists in the mix, and the push came from more than one direction.

◆◆ The pushing of the politicians and the voluntarism of the voters led to the most unappreciated result of the new campaign techniques developed during the Civil War: the phenomenal level of voting it sparked. This phenomenon has been overlooked by new and old political historians alike. Jean H. Baker, for example, says, "the contests of 1864 and 1868 have little status. In technical terms, they are maintaining elections in which issues, appeal, campaign techniques, and most important, partisan choices stay the same; in Angus Campbell's alliterative summation, 'the pattern of partisan attachment in the preceding period persists.'"[53] But technique could not stand still in American politics.

Baker herself was discontented with the interpretation but felt compelled to accept the wisdom of the New Political Historians who preceded her on the statistical nature of those elections. "It is clear," she said, "that contemporaries were not particularly excited by either contest, and despite procedures for voting in the field, turnout (the traditional gauge of interest) declined in 1864. . . . Such apathy might be explained by the war, but four years later . . . the lowest turnout in forty years sent Ulysses Grant to the White House." [54]

But national voter turnout in this period is not a very useful figure. The states in the Confederacy cannot be counted, the loyal Border States suffered military interference at the polls, soldiers were allowed to vote absentee in some states and not in others, new classes of voters were qualified and old classes disqualified from voting.

The conclusions of modern historians are utterly at variance with nearly all the commentators who themselves lived through the Civil War presidential election. The best witnesses we have on this point are two of the most ardent students of political statistics in the Civil War era, Abraham Lincoln and Horace Greeley. Putting the astonishing election results of 1864 into a war context, Lincoln boasted in his annual message to Congress early in December that the recent elections

> exhibited . . . the fact that we do not approach exhaustion in the most important branch of national resources—that of living men. While it is melancholy to reflect that the war has filled so many graves . . . it is some relief to know that, compared with the surviving, the fallen have been so few. While corps, and divisions, and brigades, and regiments have formed, and fought, and dwindled, and gone out of existence, a great majority of the men who composed them are still living. The same is true of the naval service. The election returns prove this. So many voters would not else be found. [55]

What this remarkable passage reveals was the fascination with voting returns of a lifelong politician. In fact, the president went on at great length in the message, giving the election tallies from all the states and adding them up.

A seasoned political veteran, Lincoln simply assumed a full commitment and engagement of the electorate in political questions in the republic. He automatically reasoned that an increase in the vote must indicate an increase in the population of the country—something that seemed miraculous, almost providential, in the midst of a shockingly mortal war. At bottom, he assumed full participation of the electorate in any election.

Horace Greeley shared Lincoln's interest in voting returns and could not help noticing the same phenomenon Lincoln did. Noting that the 1864 vote of Kentucky, Maryland, Missouri, and the counties that formed West Virginia (which became a state only in 1863) ran dramatically contrary to the national trend, dipping as much as 37 percent—something the president could not himself comfortably point out because of Democratic accusations of military intimidation at the polls in those Border States—Greeley discounted the Border State vote because it had been artificially depressed, and calculated that for the remaining Northern states the increase in voting was "over eight per cent, which is more than half the ratio of increase of population during the decade immediately preceding the war." [56]

Greeley was right to do that. Once the unusual suppression of the vote in the Border States is eliminated from the comparison, the growth in voting in the North between 1860 and 1864 is truly astonishing.

Altschuler and Blumin, who could not help noticing an increase in political activity and engagement in the Civil War period, suggested that the slavery issue and issues associated with it saved a waning electoral system from death but that people began to lapse into their accustomed indifference and suspicion of political parties when the war ended. A brief examination of electoral statistics after slavery was abolished gives the lie to any such idea. The results of the election of 1868 were once again astonishing, if we take the results regionally or state by state. Pennsylvania, for example, showed a 7.2 percent increase in voting over the figure for 1864. For the decade 1860 to 1870, during which the male population of the state rose some 20.9 percent, Pennsylvania's voting increased (between 1860 and 1868) by some 37 percent.

The explanation of this phenomenon is not yet at hand.[57] But voting during the Civil War is decidedly a phenomenon to be reckoned with. Yet too many political interpretations make us inattentive to voting and to political development from election to election. The New Political Historians have missed these developments because they periodize political activity by party "systems" formed after rare "realigning" elections and persisting for decades. Their critics have missed the developments in 1864 and 1868, too. But there cannot be, upon close inspection of the war-era elections, any excuse for missing the unique level of commitment of the American voter in the nineteenth century.

That level of commitment goes a long way toward explaining party finances and the ubiquitous partisan press of the mid-nineteenth century. But we should not leap to the conclusion that politics entered into everything. The antic enthusiasms and partisan passions of the most zealous party adherents of the period likewise pushed political criticism beyond what many regarded as respectable in the Victorian era. The poster cartoons characteristic of the Civil War era were surely examples of that. They remind us of the important boundaries of political culture as well.

Chapter 3 **A Secret Fund** The Union League, Patriotism, and the Boundaries of Social Class

❧ The Great Sanitary Fair opened in New York City on April 4, 1864. Its organizers, women mostly, put this gigantic charity bazaar together to raise money for the U.S. Sanitary Commission, which underwrote medical care for Civil War soldiers. Press coverage of the event, which could indeed be termed "great," was thorough and came to focus on what was regarded as the most exciting and eagerly watched part of the fair, a competition for richly jeweled swords to be awarded to the public's favorite general and naval hero. The competition for the naval sword never amounted to much, but the army sword became the talk of the town—indeed, it drew national attention. The famous jeweler Tiffany had fashioned the sword with a sterling silver scabbard, its hilt crusted with patriotic red, white, and blue rubies, diamonds, and sapphires. Attendees at the fair, no matter their age or sex, could vote for their favorite general as often as they liked, at one dollar a vote.

The contest narrowed immediately to a race between General George B. McClellan, who had not commanded in the field since autumn 1862, and General Ulysses S. Grant, who had recently moved east to the Virginia theater for the spring campaign.

The independent *New York Herald* covered the contest closely and attributed to it the "deepest political significance." McClellan was widely expected to be nominated as the Democratic candidate for president that summer, and Grant, while not an active candidate, was the *Herald*'s favorite to replace Lincoln on the Republican ticket and a natural stand-in for the president, as well. The sword contest became a proxy for the real presidential election to come in the autumn.

"The ladies are deeply interested in this contest," reported the *Her-*

ald, "much more so than the men."[1] The paper's reporter playfully alluded to the women's rights issues that hovered around such an event: "The ladies are especially interested in it. It is the first time they have had a chance to vote, and they take advantage of it eagerly. . . . This is the only instance of universal suffrage on record, and will supply the woman's rights party with a fine illustration of their doctrines."[2]

In a conversation purportedly overheard by the alert *Herald* reporter, one woman asked the man with her whether he thought McClellan would win. He replied, "Of course he will—that is, if he only gets fair play. But I don't think he will be allowed to win. You see we people of New Jersey consider that this sword question has assumed a national importance and if Old Abe don't send on a secret fund to vote McClellan down, I'm very much mistaken."[3]

As the last day of the contest, Saturday, April 23, neared, fair authorities announced that polls would close at two on Saturday but that votes in sealed envelopes would be accepted until eight that evening. The *Herald* recalled the prediction of dirty tricks to rob McClellan of his Tiffany sword. "There was a good deal of talk yesterday about that Jerseyman's prophecy to the effect that underhand means would be used to defeat McClellan. Much mysterious head shaking and dark hints were indulged in, and there were not wanting those who had seen others who had heard others say that they had been told by others that the Union League Club had subscribed unnamed quantities of greenbacks to defeat McClellan."[4]

When a blue-ribbon panel of trusted citizens opened the envelopes, anonymous "loyal men of New York" had sent some 13,000 votes to overwhelm the lead McClellan had maintained in daily press reports to that time, and in the end the voting stood: Grant, 30,291 to McClellan, 14,500. The *Herald* coverage of the last day of the fair concluded with this sentimental political anecdote about a five-and-a-half-year-old boy, "Little Natie O'Brien," who insisted on casting his one-dollar vote for General McClellan. A woman correspondent thus reported: "I felt as if I should like to hug the little fellow, and thought that, could General McClellan know it he would be more gratified with this innocent vote, than his friends could be chagrined by all the votes that will be given by the Union League Club at the last moment to defeat him."[5]

   Americans would invent a political narrative where one did not necessarily exist, as the sword contest reveals, but even those historians most skeptical of the level of engagement in politics in America in the nineteenth century admit to heightened interest during the war. What the episode also brings to notice is the villain in the *Herald*'s piece, the mysterious Union League Club.

For the wealthy people of the cities, politics surely lacked respectability. The effective electioneering of the nineteenth century could hardly have found a class of voters to bring to the polls who were not already there, but if there was a truly reluctant class, it might have been the people of great wealth. At any rate, what has been said so far in this book about popular lithographs and political medals pinned on barmaids' dresses and men parading in the streets from their ward political clubs would not likely be relevant to a consideration of the upper class.

A sense that the Union Leagues represented something new and significant, even sinister, in American politics affected newspaper reporters in the Civil War—and it has affected historians in our era as well. In fact, the emphasis on the "sinister" note in the leagues' history has obscured the contributions of these remarkable organizations to American political culture.[6] These gentlemen's patriotic and Republican clubs established in Philadelphia, New York, and Boston early in 1863 played an important role in the development of campaign technique. Material culture reveals their surprising role as innovators of political methods.

I first gained a sense of the political accomplishments of the Union Leagues at the Huntington Library in San Marino, California, which owns a nearly complete set of the broadsides printed by the Union League Club of Philadelphia in the 1860s. To examine them with special attention to medium is to realize their role in a dramatic development in political technique, one among many, as it turns out, that flourished in the same brief period of Civil War politics.[7]

The Union League publication committee gradually developed

and perfected the political poster. The wordy political broadside common in the early nineteenth century was aimed at imparting information in public space. It was gradually transformed into the poster meant to persuade with a simple and exaggerated message, and the Union League Club of Philadelphia played a central role in the transformation.

The political broadside had its origins, as did many features of mass politics, in the partisan press. A newspaper would publish some piece afterward regarded as particularly telling, and then it would be reprinted on only one side of the paper, to be pasted on walls and tacked to trees. Those origins left telltale marks on the political broadsides of the Civil War era. Many of them retained the narrow columns of print, like a newspaper sheet. Their origins and format tended to tyrannize over their purpose. The print was small, as in the daily newspaper, and the editors were fond of imparting information — of "diffusing knowledge," as the Democratic organization for publishing documents in the Civil War, the Society for the Diffusion of Political Knowledge, expressed the ideal—with long columns of print.

The publications of the Union League Club of Philadelphia, which was deeply involved in closely fought elections in Civil War Pennsylvania, ushered in a forward-looking movement away from narrow columns of dense type resembling a newspaper page, to large boldface slogans in horizontal headline format, wider than a column. We might term the broadside THE BEGINNING a masterpiece of political poster development, its sensational message imparted in only thirty-one words: THE BEGINNING. / ELECTION OF M'CLELLAN! / PENDLETON, Vice-President. / VALLANDIGHAM, Secretary of War. / ARMISTICE! / FALL OF WAGES! / NO MARKET FOR PRODUCE! / Pennsylvania a Border State! / INVASION! CIVIL WAR! ANARCHY! / DESPOTISM!! / THE END.

The other party proved quick to imitate this, like any other effective method, and the Democrats produced their equivalents for the same campaign emphasizing as their important words, "DRAFT AND TAXES."

The correspondence between a Democratic political organizer in Philadelphia named Henry Phillips and the manager of George B.

McClellan's presidential campaign, who lived in New York, opens a rare window on self-conscious innovation in political technique. Phillips noted late in the 1864 campaign, after Pennsylvania's election in October but before the November election in New York: "Our *experience* [in Pennsylvania] may be useful: all concur that the best thing we did was pasting the State[,] every part of it[,] with placards about 'The Draft & Taxes'—I think they would be very effective in your State & in Indiana—." Phillips had written earlier on the subject with equal enthusiasm and with true advertising acumen: "I send you a hand bill,—specimen of our work—I am of the opinion that such a thing will be effective & ought to be posted so that no man leave his firm or his home without seeing it—You may depend it is more impressive than a long Address, for, whoever read[s], will ponder on the words: 'DRAFT[,] TAXES, UNION & PEACE' even in spite of himself—."[8]

The Pennsylvania election of 1864 provides an unusual opportunity for knowing the numbers of documents printed, at least by one prolific source, the Union League Club. In a letter to President Lincoln, Congressman William D. Kelley reported that the "League furnished the state Committee with 280,000 posters and documents prior to the October election." Kelley did not believe that they had been properly distributed, but he added that after the October election, "the League have *mailed* 306,000 pamphlets and posters[.] Its issues number more than 750,000."[9] Thus the Union League was ultimately responsible for providing, on average, two and a half pamphlets or posters for every Republican vote tallied in the state in November.[10] The Union League had mastered such campaign technique a year earlier. As the league's historian reported, Andrew G. Curtin, who was the successful Republican candidate for governor in 1863, "declared openly that he owed his success to the Union League of Philadelphia, which, as he playfully said, 'had plastered the state with its handbills'" (see Fig. 3.1).[11] Phillips and the Democrats appear to have been following the lead of the Union League Club.

❦ It is difficult to square the creativity and political nimbleness exemplified in the work of the Union League Club of Philadelphia with

FIGURE 3.1. *Union League 1118 Chestnut. Photograph (1863). Courtesy of the Print and Picture Collection, the Free Library Company of Philadelphia. The Philadelphia gentlemen's patriotic club began plastering the state of Pennsylvania with its handbills, as the grateful Republican governor observed, in the tight races in the state in 1863. The wall next to the club in this photograph certainly lives up to the governor's description.*

the image of the Union Leagues to be found in modern books on the subject. There the league's class consciousness, social exclusivity, and old-fogy image reign supreme.[12] One recent treatment says that the "League founders had little respect for the common man and disdained democracy," that they "feared that . . . labor's assertions stood to undermine the war effort," and therefore that they "embarked on a campaign to" instruct the masses "in a more deferential patriotism."[13]

The most influential modern analysis appears in Iver Bernstein's *New York City Draft Riots*, published in 1990. In a chapter entitled "Merchants Divided," the author introduces the Union League Club of New York City this way:

> Merchants were the most identifiable group in New York City during and after the draft riots and, indeed, through the Civil War epoch. Roland Barthes's aphorism regarding the bourgeoisie — "the social class which does not want to be named" — did not apply to New York's lords of commerce. During the riot week they met on Wall Street to devise a "merchants'" response to the violence and form "merchants'" brigades. After the uprising some of these men created a "Committee of Merchants for the Relief of Colored People Suffering from the Late Riots." They sent "merchants' committees" to Washington to advise presidents and supervise legislation. They formed the "Society for the Diffusion of Political Knowledge" and "The Union League Club of New York" to publicize merchants' positions on the issues of the war. In all these instances, merchants made themselves and their programs plain to view.[14]

There follows a class analysis of the Union League Club of New York as a new stronghold of the city's old and "long-established" merchant aristocracy aligned against merchants regarded as "arrivistes." The "anxious patricians," says Bernstein, were losing social ground to the newer merchants, men who mostly "began their careers outside of New York City and moved to the metropolis in the late 1830s and 1840s," and to their city political allies in the Democratic Party.

But the Civil War provided the old elite "their grand moment of opportunity" to reassert a position of dominance.[15]

Though the Union League Clubs of Boston, Philadelphia, and New York City are likely places to look for the political activities of a moneyed elite, in fact an examination of them reveals many problems with such a view.[16] The advent of the "merchants" in the Union League Clubs was indeed something new under the sun. But when examined closely, the clubs do not match their description in modern histories. In the first place, the clubs were not merchants' clubs. In the second place, the views expressed and the political positions taken by the clubs could not easily be identified as "merchants' views." Finally, the views supported by the Union Leagues during the Civil War were not necessarily politically conservative.

My analysis of the Union League Club of New York is based on brief biographies I have compiled of 87 of the 350 original club members.[17] Fewer than one-third of the members I identified could be labeled as merchants, philanthropists, capitalists, bankers, or financiers (28 of 87). As for the "old money" quality alleged in the membership, in fact the club enjoyed a sturdy mix of old- and newcomers, with many members who came to New York in the late 1830s and 1840s (or later). Over 45 percent of the members whose origins are known were newly arrived in New York (36 of 79).

It could hardly have been otherwise, or else the membership would have been too old for the active and innovative roles assumed in the political conflict of the 1860s. Indeed, the early historian of the sister Philadelphia Union League commented specifically on its age mix as an important feature of the organization: "Another element of strength . . . lay in the diversity of ages. Many of the members were in the prime of life; others were getting well beyond the meridian: so that with the glowing force of young manhood was combined the moderation of riper age."[18]

It was equally important that the clubs attract members from other occupations than mercantile ones. The chronicler of the Philadelphia Union League also boasted of the vital mix of minds in their organization: "Not a little of what the League accomplished sprang out of the casual but regularly recurring encounters at the League house of different kinds of minds imbued with a sentiment in common. Dreamers, thinkers, men of practical affairs, met and convened; a suggestion, a passing thought, at once received consideration in various lights, and, if it had value, began to assume substantial shape."[19]

The same was true, surely, of the mix in the New York club. It included the country's leading "political scientist" (Francis Lieber), one of its leading historians (George Bancroft), and at least ten of the country's leading medical figures—who came to the club because of their work with the U.S. Sanitary Commission. There was also a great landscape painter (Albert Bierstadt), a landscape architect (Frederick Law Olmsted, also the executive secretary of the Sanitary Commission), famous newspaper editors such as William Cullen Bryant, and several influential clergymen. One of the founders of the Philadelphia club, its secretary and chief operating officer, was a popular poet and playwright named George Boker. This mix of creative talent led to the potent poster campaigns in Pennsylvania in 1863 and 1864.

The policies the leagues advanced were as innovative and radical as the methods used to advance them. The mix of talent showed to advantage in the league's work with the Philadelphia office of the Supervisory Committee for Recruiting Colored Regiments. Philadelphia Union League member Thomas Webster arranged for the headquarters to stage an elaborate visual celebration of the abolition of slavery in the state constitution of neighboring Maryland in the fall elections of 1864. The club provided transparencies and gas-jet lettering. The transparencies (thin cloth sheets that were pulled taut over wooden frames, painted with images and slogans, and illuminated from behind by torches), he pointed out proudly to President Lincoln, were designed by the artists of the Philadelphia Sketch Club "in the highest style of art."[20] The Union League thus chose deliberately to place emphasis on emancipation right before presidential election day, despite the risk of alienating Philadelphia's conservative voters, who seemed to many Republicans more enthusiastic for Union than for freedom of the slaves. Webster called politicians who suffered such fears "timorous."

These dynamic and forward-looking programs should cause us

to take a closer look at the Union League Clubs. The key source for the internal history of the Union League Club of New York is the famous diary of George Templeton Strong. In its pages lies abundant proof that the Union League was not a merchants' club. At the initial meeting, thirteen men were present. They met at the house of Oliver Wolcott Gibbs, a chemist. The other twelve men included an ophthalmologist; a college professor; Gibbs's brother George, a geologist; two lawyers; two clergymen; a medical professor from the College of Physicians and Surgeons in New York; and a superior court judge. There was not a single merchant of great wealth, old or newly acquired, present.[21]

Only after that conceptual meeting did the men of commerce and capital begin to rally around the men of influential ideas and articulate politics. The most significant addition came a little over two weeks later, when the fabulously wealthy old merchant Robert B. Minturn called on George Templeton Strong to discuss the proposed club. Strong described this meeting afterward in his diary: "He is an excellent man, but impracticable and timid. He sees this movement may possibly prove important and wants to be in it, but objects to 'signing pledges,' thinks we ought to be liberal and admit weak-backed and cold-blooded men to brother hood with a view to their invigoration and conversion, and wants to confer with W. H. Aspinwall and Hamilton Fish. Minturn, Aspinwall, and Fish would be important allies, but if they cannot subscribe to our programme, I think we do not want them."[22] The views did not come from the merchants. In fact, the merchants were coming to the views.

Using class analysis to approach the study of the membership of the Union Leagues breeds confusion rather than clarity. Pointing out that intellectuals with New England roots, the Unitarian minister Henry Whitney Bellows and the landscape architect Frederick Law Olmsted, for example, did not typify the membership of the club, Bernstein says: "But there was indeed a cluster of long-established 'leading merchants,' as George Templeton Strong called them, who helped bring the Union League Club into being. The shipping merchant Robert Browne Minturn and tea merchant George Griswold, whom Strong repeatedly described as the socioeconomic nucleus of the Club were active members; Minturn was the first president."[23] The "socioeconomic nucleus" of the club, though, was not the true nucleus of the club, and Strong considered such men as Minturn mere "allies."

Of course, the merchants were hardly unwelcome. They were needed—for their money, not their point of view. Strong himself later admitted, "Leading merchants are essential to our success."[24]

The men who formed the Union League had seen what money could do in the work of the U.S. Sanitary Commission. Among the merchants who would form part of the first list of members in New York, for example, was the dry goods magnate Alexander T. Stewart. He gave $100,000 to the Sanitary Commission and $50,000 for the relief of the distressed cotton operatives of England, plunged into unemployment and economic depression by the Northern blockade of the Confederacy. The merchants' money would make the political-patriotic program of the Union Leagues effective beyond anyone's imagination. Behind the work of the clubs, which was formulated by professionals, would stand the millions of the patriotic merchant princes like Minturn and Stewart. It was a new model for American political endeavors.

❦ The New York club attracted various circles of well-to-do people in the city. Its roots in the Sanitary Commission, for example, explain the substantial representation of New York's medical community in the club. Not as easily noticed, the New England roots of early club members likely determined some of its appeal. Far from constituting exceptions, the men of New England background appear to have been more nearly the nucleus of the initial group in New York City.

To understand this, we need first to look at the biographies of the club's founding members. Of the members identifiable on the score of heritage—and the club included a heritage-conscious group —people born in New England or descended from New England families made up over half of the club's original membership (55 percent), if the group I could identify is representative.[25] New England culture was as prevalent in the Union League Club of New York as "old" money, and it would not be pressing the evidence too much to say that New England *conscience* was more dominant than old money in the Union League Club.

But we must also take a long side excursion into the chronology of the club's formation. The initial programs of the Union League will make sense in that light, though we must temporarily range far afield from the clubroom to see it.

The timing of the club's origin was important. The context for the origins of all three of the Union League Clubs was the aftermath of Democratic resurgence at the polls in the autumn elections of 1862. Many Republicans misperceived as sedition what was politics as usual. The continuation of political opposition in the midst of a desperate civil war seemed unpatriotic.

In New York, a special circumstance of timing stemmed from an abortive and peculiar initiative of the resurgent Democrats in 1863. They toyed with the idea of manipulating sectional feeling within the North as a means toward partisan gain in future elections. Soon after the November elections of 1862, Kentucky senator Garrett Davis argued in Congress for the preservation of slave property in his home state by pointing to the overrepresentation of New England. The population of the six New England states, put together, was exceeded by that of New York, and thus the loud antislavery voice of the small New England states rested on the compromises of the Constitution of 1787, which guaranteed to all states equal representation in the Senate. New England's willingness to destroy the constitutional compromises that guaranteed safety to slavery, Davis argued, was playing with fire. "You that will not heed this warning," said the Kentucky senator, ". . . may live to witness a reconstruction of the Union that will turn Maine and New Hampshire, I am sorry to say, and Massachusetts, out into the cold and frozen regions of the Northeast." [26]

Paraphrased as "to leave New England out in the cold," Garrett Davis's idea became a political catchphrase. The full assault on New England actually began in New York City in the very weeks that the Union League was forming (gradually in a series of weekly meetings in private homes). On Tuesday evening, January 13, 1863, Ohio congressman Samuel Sullivan "Sunset" Cox came to New York to deliver a lecture at the Democratic Union Association. "Puritanism in Politics," as it was titled, contained a veiled threat that in the states of the Old Northwest much sentiment could be found for reconstructing the Union *with New England left out.*

The image Cox was most concerned to construct was that of the "Constitution-breaking, law-defying, negro-loving Phariseeism of New England."[27] He devoted only one paragraph to economic differences between the sections and dismissed the exploitation of the Old Northwest by New England industry as abuses that "can be borne, but unhappily they seem to be accompanied by an element harder to master—the puritanism of New England."[28] The bulk of the speech dealt with cultural issues. "The grand key-note of the Puritan," Cox said, "is that 'slavery' was the cause of this war, and that as men and Christians we should extirpate it."[29] Cox asserted that, on the contrary, abolition started the war, and he went to the extreme of defending the infamous antiabolition riots of the 1830s: "The riots . . . were the instinctive out-gushings of the Union-loving masses, fearing a speech too free and a cause too reckless for the stability of the Government."[30] Thus Cox willingly put himself in the position of weakening the Democrats' wartime defense of freedom of speech; in a few months' time, the Democrats, Cox included, would not be disposed to say there was such a thing as "a speech too free."

Cox also embraced slavery more closely than Democrats wanted to at other times. Slavery, he said, was not only "part of the practical structure of society South" but also "a part of the Providential order, just as it was in the time of Moses and the Savior."[31]

It is difficult to believe that the Democrats had not collaborated to open this campaign of cultural politics. On the day after Cox's appearance in New York City, Clement L. Vallandigham, also a Democrat from the Ohio delegation, gave a set speech in the House entitled "The Constitution, Peace [and] Reunion." The part of the speech dealing with reunion dwelt on the differences between New England and the Old Northwest as though they stemmed from underlying racial differences.[32]

Like Cox, Vallandigham wasted little breath on the economic differences between New England and the Old Northwest. He made much of the differences between Cavaliers and Puritans and gave more emphasis to peace. Vallandigham agreed with Cox that "slavery is only the *subject*, but abolition the *cause*, of this civil war." "The people of the West demand peace," he said, "and they begin to more than suspect that New England is in the way . . . they threaten to 'set New England out in the cold.'"[33]

There were substantial differences in the practical positions of the two Ohio politicians. Cox would have nothing of an armistice but thought French mediation might work while the armies remained in the field. Vallandigham desired an armistice with vague promises of future reunion. Vallandigham was a lame duck. Cox's career was apparently on the rise. Ohio faced a gubernatorial election in 1863, and anti-New England sentiment might play well there.

This brief assault on New England has never been satisfactorily explained, though it has long attracted the notice of political historians. Those writing in the shadow of the New Deal tended to find an economic thread in the arguments, as if the Democrats objected to New England because that section's capitalist and manufacturing prowess exploited the resources of the Old Northwest.[34] Yet economic themes hardly figured at all in the Democrats' anti-New England speeches, and Cox belittled their importance.

Later, the New Political Historians saw in Cox's "Puritanism in Politics" just the sort of "tribal" signals they expected from the Democrats: there was nothing, according to this ethnocultural school of interpretation of voting behavior, that Irish Americans and German Americans hated more than New England and its intolerant, moralizing "Puritan" ways.[35] This interpretation offered a more plausible explanation of Cox's famous speech, for the erudite Cox did ring the changes on New England moralizing, contrasting it with their hypocritical record of persecution of Quakers, witches, and Roger Williams. Yet Cox said little about Puritan hatred of Roman Catholicism, the driving force in the ethnic identification of many Democratic voters of Irish and German heritage. The central focus of "Puritanism in Politics" lay on slavery and the threat of racial equality.

The debate over Puritanism during the Civil War has attracted the notice of intellectual historians as well. Jan Dawson concluded that Cox's movement was essentially a success: "By the end of the

Civil War . . . Puritan ideology had spent its vitality."[36] But more recently Joseph A. Conforti concluded, to the contrary, that New England emerged from the war in a burst of "Yankee triumphalism."[37]

It certainly triumphed in New York City. Immediately after Cox's and Vallandigham's speeches were delivered, one of the early organizational meetings of the Union League Club was convened at the house of chemist Wolcott Gibbs.[38] Membership as yet numbered only in the teens, and the great influx of members would come, then, more or less on the heels of the controversy over the assault on New England by the Democrats from the Old Northwest.[39] For a week after Cox's speech, the New York Republican press had been refuting and denouncing the attack on Puritan heritage.[40] That may explain the heavy representation of men of New England heritage in this patriotic club.

After the New York club was formed, with its many alarmed and resentful ex–New Englanders, military and political events quickly conspired to bring an end to the Democratic assault on New England. For one thing, Clement L. Vallandigham's association with the idea linked it to the extremist minority in the Democratic Party who did not vote supplies for the troops and sought an armistice.[41]

The argument that the Old Northwest would join its fortunes with the Confederacy out of economic interest was soon made irrelevant. At the time Cox delivered his lecture, the Mississippi River was not entirely in Union hands, but by early July 1863, with the fall of Vicksburg, the North had gained control of the river, which was regarded by many in the Old Northwest as an essential highway for the economy of the region.

In other respects as well Cox's timing was not particularly good, and he should have known it. Jefferson Davis had given a speech to the Mississippi legislature only three weeks before Cox spoke in New York in which the Confederate president had expressed the expectation that "from the Northwest will come the first gleams of peace."[42] The Northern press reported Confederate state papers almost immediately, and knowledge of Davis's speech was easy to come by. Cox risked being seen as a champion of the ideas of Jefferson Davis.

Later developments quickly altered fundamental Democratic

strategies, even in Ohio. In May 1863 Vallandigham was arrested and tried by military commission for violating a military order by criticizing the government in a speech. S. S. Cox himself was on the platform where Valiant Val gave the offending speech, and Cox later served as counsel and witness at Vallandigham's military trial.[43] After that sensational event, the Democratic Party changed its focus back to the plight of civil liberties under the despotic Lincoln administration. The assault on New England was substantially abandoned because New England was more a symbol of abolitionism than of despotism.

The lasting legacy of the assault on New England—beyond the early summer of 1863—was truly ironic. Though after the summer of 1863 little trace of it remained in the rhetoric of the Democratic Party, which now favored more timely partisan schemes, the assault traumatized some Republicans and gave others a political opening to exploit. The Ohio congressmen had been carelessly willing to leave the impression that a substantial sentiment existed in the states of the Old Northwest for secession from the Union and New England. Such an impression did nothing to counteract what *later* proved to be a major Republican contention about the Democrats: that they harbored a disloyal conspiracy to form a separate Northwest confederacy. It is no wonder that so many Republicans came to believe that such a plot really existed—the Democrats had been the first to warn of its existence.

The Democratic assault on New England also played an ironic role in provoking formation of the Union League Club of New York, which became an effective, innovative, and well-funded voice attacking the Democrats.

The response to Cox's speech on the part of Republicans and New Englanders and Americans of New England heritage proved important politically and much longer lived than the brief Democratic anti-New England sally itself. The cultural counterattack appears to have gone substantially unnoticed by political historians, but the Civil War witnessed a conscious reassertion of New England identity that left the region's historical image perhaps as triumphant as it had ever been since the end of the seventeenth century (see Fig. 3.2).

Symbolic triumph for the New England counterattack came na-

FIGURE 3.2. The Politics and Poetry of New England. *Photograph by Alexander Gardner (Washington, D.C., 1863). bMS Am 1340.10(4). By the permission of the Houghton Library, Harvard University. Massachusetts senator Charles Sumner posed with poet Henry Wadsworth Longfellow when the latter came to the capital to visit his son, convalescing from a wound incurred in the war. The photographer supplied the title of the image. It was important to remind Americans that New England stood for antislavery conscience but also played a "civilizing" role (and did not stifle creativity and art, as Puritanism was said to have done).*

tionally, as the cultural historian Joseph A. Conforti noted, in the success of Sarah Josepha Hale's long campaign to make Thanksgiving a national "Union Festival." On September 28, 1863, she wrote President Lincoln, explaining her crusade and enclosing editorials about it from *Godey's Lady's Book*, the magazine she had edited for years. The president issued a proclamation on October 3, designating the last Thursday in November a national day of thanksgiving and prayer. Thus, in a way, even President Lincoln, who knew nothing of his own New England genealogical roots and did not much care about such matters, joined the counterattack by New England culture.[44]

By December 1863 Senator Sumner could tell the New England Society of New York: "Never before, since the Mayflower landed its precious cargo, have New-Englanders had more reasons for pride and gratulation than now. . . . The principles and ideas which constitute the strength and glory of New England have spread against opposition and contumely, till at last their influence is visible in a regenerated country."[45]

Given the New England roots of many of the New York Union League Club's members, its 1864 Thanksgiving project can be termed characteristic, and it played a major role in riveting Sarah Josepha Hale's Thanksgiving holiday on national consciousness and custom. The club decided to provide Thanksgiving dinners for soldiers in the field and sailors on shipboard. Previously, without the organizational ability and financial resources of the Union League, efforts along those lines had been sporadic and limited often to the soldiers of ready access, ones convalescing in hospitals locally, for example. But the Union League had members who knew how to get things done. A committee established on November 10, 1864, eventually collected $56,565.83, which, by persuading one of the leading poultry dealers in the country to forego commissions and profits, they turned into 49,814 turkeys for the Army of the Shenandoah; 30,300 turkeys for the Atlantic Squadron; and 225,000 pounds of turkey as well as many other delicacies for the Armies of the Potomac and James.[46]

Some of the New England counterattacks were anything but heartwarming. The *Atlantic Monthly*, a bastion of New England culture, responded to S. S. Cox quickly and vigorously with an article in its April

1863 issue, written by Francis Wayland Jr. He proved as vituperative as Cox. He knew, perhaps because his father was president of Brown University, that Cox was a Brown graduate, and Wayland enjoyed playing on the ironies of the Ohioan's New England higher education:

> Here comes a little Western Lawyer, with unlimited resources of slang and slender capital of ideas, barely redeemed from being an absolute blackguard by the humanizing influences of a New England college, but showing fewer and fewer symptoms of civilization as he forgets the lessons of his collegiate life; and *he* delights an audience of New York "roughs," adopted citizens of Celtic extraction, and lager-loving Germans, (do not cocks always crow longest and loudest on a dung-hill?) by the novel information, that "Puritanism is a reptile" and the cause of all our troubles, and that we shall never fulfil our national destiny until Puritanism has been crushed. Let us not elevate this nauseating nonsense into importance by attempting a reply.[47]

Wayland offered precisely the sort of response that Democratic politicians might have been seeking to provoke. In this instance, at least, Cox had stirred the cultural prejudices of Anglo New Englanders such as Wayland into slanders against German Americans and Irish Americans. New Political Historians such as Joel H. Silbey have alerted us that such ethnic signals reminded those of immigrant stock of their safe refuge in the Democratic Party and of the innate hostility of the Republicans to them.

The response of the Union League Club proved to be more ideological than ethnic. The veiled threat of secession of the Old Northwest hinted at in Cox's speech triggered the New Yorkers' fear of disloyalty and sedition. The Loyal Publication Society, organized in New York in February 1863, shared many of the same members of the Union League Club. Like the club, the publication society aimed to stimulate loyalty in the North.[48] To answer Cox the society chose an author from the Old Northwest, Robert Dale Owen, son of the famous utopian socialist. Owen, a former Democrat from Indiana, now an ardent antislavery Republican, had written an attack on the idea of a Northwest confederacy for Indiana governor Oliver P. Morton, and the New Yorkers got wind of it from Parke Godwin of the *New York Evening Post*.[49] The resulting pamphlet was *The Future of the North-West: In Connection with the Scheme of Reconstruction without New England*.

Works such as Owen's turned the tables on the Democrats. The fuel lent to the smoldering suspicion that Democratic political organization in fact constituted sedition in the midst of a war was consequential. The publication board of the Philadelphia Union League responded in similar fashion. Among the twenty-two different pamphlets the board published and distributed for the presidential election of 1864 was Henry Charles Lea's *Great Northern Conspiracy of the "O.S.L.,"* which focused on the allegedly secessionist Order of the Sons of Liberty.[50]

Many members of the Union Leagues feared such possible sedition, and patriotism was the principal thrust of their work. But they had a distinctly political outlook on patriotism. The Union Leagues of New York, Philadelphia, and Boston were established to support the government politically so that there would be no more victories like that of Democrat Horatio Seymour, who won election as governor of New York in November 1862 and was assuming office in January 1863, just as the New York and Philadelphia clubs were forming. As a result, the Union League purpose was partisan—they supported the reelection of a Republican president and the election of Republicans to other offices as well—but like the Protestant ministers described in the first chapter, the club members did not necessarily see their work for the Republicans as partisan.

In at least one important respect, the New York club was true to that principle. It forbade expression of opinions on what were traditionally partisan economic issues. As the club's early historian explained, "For an unpartisan Club to become an active political body was not difficult, so long as national questions were all engrossing—questions not of taxation, finance, internal improvements or tariffs, but the questions of the honor of the flag, the integrity of the National territory, and the rights of the Government to protect and save the fundamental institutions of the country."[51]

Surely it is misguided to see in the ideas of the Civil War–era Union League the views of New York's great merchants—the league deliberately suppressed issues of keen interest to merchants in the interest of the nation during the war.

The Civil War programs of the Union Leagues contained little of commercial significance. The national debt and the use of greenbacks as legal tender figured as loyalty issues during the war. Many regarded it as unpatriotic to deny the acceptability of the paper currency printed to fund the war, and, conversely, carping that the debt incurred in the war effort would forever cripple the country was a common Democratic complaint. Therefore, some of the publications of the Union Leagues and the closely associated Loyal Publication Society in New York maintained the sustainability of the national debt incurred to fight the war and the utility of the greenbacks printed to finance it. The publication board in Philadelphia, for example, distributed *Uncle Sam's Debts and His Ability to Pay Them*; *The Old Continental and the New Greenback Dollar*; and Lorin Blodget's *The Commercial and Financial Strength of the United States*.[52] Surely many a member had to swallow his hard-money ideas and his aversion to government debt for the sake of the war effort.

The clubmen did not lack vision for the future of the country that transcended their material class interests. The clubs were, during the Civil War and in early Reconstruction, radical in politics. The Union Leagues helped recruit African American regiments during the war and advocated African American suffrage in the reconstruction of Southern states immediately after the war.

In an attempt to argue the Union Leagues' obvious radicalism out of existence, modern interpreters of the movement have asserted that their sponsorship of African American regiments was a matter of local cultural politics and not of radical national vision. They point particularly to the impressive ceremony of presenting the flag to African American regiments in New York City as the soldiers departed for the war. That, it is argued, was nothing more than a symbolic retaking of the public sphere from the Irish Americans who had rioted in New York's streets against the draft so shockingly in July 1863. In other words, such historians attempt to reduce that event to an episode of the assertion of social class and ethnicity by the upper-class clubmen. For one of the club's founders, Frederick Law Olmsted, as well as for "his patrician allies," we are told, "a Protestant and pious black poor [was] . . . a more receptive audience for their cultural ministrations than an inattentive or hostile white and immigrant Catholic working class. . . . The Union Leaguers did not completely discard paternalism but merely changed the color of its clientele." The message of the league support for African American regiments, another historian has asserted recently, "was intended in part for the participants of the city's recent draft riots."[53]

We can now see the basic problem of encountering the coverage of the Union League Club of New York in the context of a book on the draft riots in New York City: it leads too easily to an image of reaction. It is important to recall the actual chronology: the formation of the Union League movement preceded the draft riots by months.

A close attention to chronology is again critical. The Boston club also sponsored an African American regiment, and the departure of that regiment caused great excitement in the city. But it left before the draft riots in New York and marched through the streets of a city, Boston, whose public sphere did not need to be symbolically retaken from the unruly Irish American Democrats.

In fact, one of the organizers of the Union League Club of New York, Henry W. Bellows, was present in Boston when the African American soldiers paraded, and he told Francis Lieber "that he never saw a more deeply impressive display than the march of a negro regiment a few days ago, through the streets of Boston. The manly bearing of the men; the serious character of the bystanders—everything was . . . a symbol of a most important historic turn of events and thoughts." Sumner's friend Longfellow was a witness also: "I saw the Negro Regiments pass through Beacon Street; standing at the windows of No. 39, with Mrs. Chas. P. Curtin, who clapped her hands and waved her handkerchief!"[54] We can reasonably surmise that there would have been a public ceremony for the departure of New York's African American regiment whether there had been a riot intervening or not. They would have copied Boston's thrilling experience.

Moreover, the radical programs of the Union Leagues entailed the revolutionary consequences to be expected, and the clubs followed them through to their logical and just social conclusions. Because

Camp William Penn, where African American regiments from Pennsylvania trained, was located eight miles from Philadelphia, friends and relatives of the soldiers could not visit them in camp, since African Americans were excluded from riding in the public cars. On New Year's Day in 1865 Abraham Barker, a Union League member, initiated a crusade to open the passenger cars to African Americans in Philadelphia. He succeeded eventually.[55]

A similar programmatic liberalism in matters of race defined the early outlook of New York's Union League Club. The New Yorkers took up the cause of the widow of an African American veteran who was denied seating on a streetcar in the city, and eventually streetcar lines there also opened their cars to African Americans.[56]

In fact, if the views of merchants came into conflict with the social vision of the Union League Club, they were likely to lose out. A dramatic episode of conflict among merchants over reconstruction provides an illuminating picture of that. If there was such a thing as merchants' policy, surely it was the attempt to relieve the people of Savannah, Georgia, after William T. Sherman's siege in the Christmas season of 1864. After Savannah citizens, encouraged by Sherman, passed resolutions of loyalty to the United States in a public mass meeting on December 28, 1864, merchants in New York, Boston, and Philadelphia organized relief expeditions to bring food and supplies to the Southerners. The lure of an old Southern port piled high with bales of blockaded cotton was considerable from a commercial point of view. A committee of the Chamber of Commerce of New York City recommended on January 6, 1865, that "provisions be immediately sent to Savannah for the relief of the suffering people of that city." The relief was rationalized as a reconstruction measure: "It would prove," said the merchant who presided at the New York meeting, "that no vindictiveness existed at the North."[57] The measure carried easily, apparently, but not altogether without dissent. The main protester was the Union League's Charles H. Marshall, who attempted to stall the project, saying that more information was needed before sending the relief supplies. He argued that conciliation would not bring Georgia back into the Union. Only vigorous fighting would accomplish that, he warned.[58]

Later at a rally at Cooper Institute for the cause of the freedmen in the South, Marshall spoke on "behalf of Sherman's Freedmen." As the *New York Tribune* reported the speech,

> Their sympathies were called toward these people far more than toward the "people of the South" they had of late heard so much about through the newspapers. He had told a gentleman who had urged the claims of the people of Savannah, that he should wait till he heard more particularly from that place. He had since heard all about it, and there was not that distress existing among the white population of Savannah which had been represented in the public press. For his part he would give five dollars for the freedmen where he would give one dollar to the Rebels in Savannah.[59]

Members of the Union League were, some of them, merchants, but they did not become members of the club in order to effectuate any mercantile program. They had organizations for that already—such as the Chamber of Commerce. None of the Union Leagues, though located in the three great commercial centers that rushed to the aid of the white people of Savannah and to the site of all those cotton bales, participated in the Savannah relief program. The leagues stood for reconstructing the South, not conciliating it for the sake of the recovery of the national economy. On that score, they were more humanitarian than nationalist.

❦ The bringing together of the merchants' wealth and the Republican antislavery cause in 1863 in the Union League Clubs is, as several modern writers have sensed, definitely worthy of note. The Union League Clubs have become the focus of attention on the alleged connections between the Republican Party and capitalism. In other words, the Union Leagues seem likely places to look for the comfortable and steady infusion of business money into Republican coffers. But what works best to help us understand their origins is political party and not social class. It is a mistake to read the Gilded Age Republican Party back into the party of the Civil War.

But the Union League Clubs did represent something new in

American political culture. Prior to the Civil War, the financing of political campaigns for any party was apparently rather haphazard, degenerating at times into the spectacle of boys running about the streets seeking subscriptions for particular meetings and parades. The party in power assessed officeholders a percentage of their salaries for a campaign. Candidates spent their own money, and the parties relied heavily on indirect government financing through the franking privilege, which allowed members of Congress to send materials free in the mails.[60] Men with money were touched, to be sure, but their participation was sporadic.[61]

The Union Leagues began to bring the contents of the deep pockets of the merchant princes to the party campaigns directly, systematically, and reliably perhaps for the first time in American politics. The parties had rich men in them, but how was one to identify them, and where was one to find them after the mass meeting? The clubs brought together rich men through their interest in public political questions and in congenial club life. There they could be found, year after year, campaign after campaign.

At first that money was available only under the guise of patriotism. The legacy of the Union League Clubs, altogether forward-looking, was mixed. Because the clubs arose at a time when political opposition was suspect—during a war—their members, some of them, were attracted also by an antiparty feeling. That impulse continued into urban good government campaigns and civil service reform, which were league programs from the start. Eventually that path led to liberal Republicanism. The other impulse, once the patriotism and idealism of war departed, may have contained the ingredients of the Gilded Age.

✦ For all the dynamism of political parties and despite all the interesting developments in technique and funding in the Civil War years, with the advent of big money and elite direction to political campaign spectacle and advertising, we must not lose sight, in the end, of the underlying theme of all of these chapters on American political culture: the firm bedrock of political engagement on the part of

American people in the nineteenth century. The Union Leagues may be seen as bringing to the banquet the last of the reluctant, the men of very great wealth in the cities.

And yet one must not go too far in asserting political engagement and activity on the part of Americans, enfranchised and disfranchised. It is a stern reminder of the boundaries of politics in the nineteenth century and of the confining nature of the ideal of the home that among the many and varied letters sent to Abraham Lincoln while he was a candidate for president in the period from August 1 through October 15, 1860, not a single surviving letter that he saw came from a woman.[62] There are many important political activities besides actively campaigning for office, but that one was very important, and it was men's business for the most part.

Most important, the true story of nineteenth-century political engagement leaves a more flattering view of the people, if not of the politicians. The people remained in many respects true republicans, not apolitical but vigilant in both a paranoid and celebrated sense. They were fearful of the fate of liberty represented by a republic swimming in a world of predatory aristocratic and monarchical sharks. They wanted to save it from self-destruction in civil war. They were also eager and energetic at all times in fulfilling their civic duties of public engagement at the polls and in mass meetings. And some of the wealthiest among them were willing to forget about their economic interests for the sake of the imperiled republic.

Chapter 4 **Minstrelsy, Race, and the Boundaries of American Political Culture**

◀ On June 29, 1860, not long after the Republicans nominated Abraham Lincoln for president, the candidate received a letter from a man named Louis Zwisher, a former resident of Springfield, Illinois, intimate enough with the Lincolns to call their son "Bob" and to know the name of their horse. Zwisher was now an agent for the Christy Minstrels. The famous entertainment company was then in Providence, Rhode Island, and their next stop was Boston.

"Our company are all Lincoln men," Zwisher enthusiastically announced. "Our funny men," he added, "are giving you good hits from the stage—all the time which of course before an audience of 1000 People in a strange place every night does no harm. Mr Lincoln as every one is using your name in whatever manner they choose we took the liberty to place it in our Bills."[1]

It no longer comes as a shock to learn that Republicans found support among racists, but to find political support for Lincoln on the minstrel show circuit is a revelation. After all, the most extended historical treatment of the relationship between blackface minstrelsy and American politics is to be found in Jean H. Baker's *Affairs of Party: The Political Culture of Northern Democrats in the Mid-Nineteenth Century*.[2] Whereas one can readily imagine white Republicans chuckling at jokes that ridiculed African Americans, it is commonly agreed that capitalizing on racial prejudice during the political campaign was the stock-in-trade of the Democratic Party. In the great political debates of the 1850s in the North, the Democrats strove to avoid the subject of slavery and to get the conversation around to race, whereas the Republicans loved to talk about slavery and hated to talk about race. It is generally agreed that, though neither party escaped the racial assumptions of the age in their platforms and mass political appeals from the stump, the Democrats became the party of play-ing the (white) race card, of baiting the Republicans on race, and of the most retrograde and pugnacious appeals to white supremacy. It is only natural, therefore, that historians have sought to find the sources of the race prejudice of the Democratic Party.

Naturally, the attention of political historians has been drawn to the phenomenon of blackface minstrelsy. Blackface minstrelsy pro-vided powerful reinforcement to race prejudice in American culture, and, in the study of nineteenth-century political culture, therefore, minstrelsy has been identified as a part of the political culture of northern Democrats.

Baker's work capped the initial two decades of scholarly interest in minstrelsy. The argument, when she took it up, boiled down to this: managers of the famous minstrel troupes of the nineteenth century, such as the legendary Christy Minstrels, as well as the genre's most famous songsmith, Stephen Collins Foster, held ardent Democratic Party affiliations. E. P. Christy's partner, Henry Wood, for example, was the brother of New York's conservative Democrats Fernando and Benjamin Wood.[3] Stephen Foster's father was a federal officeholder under President James Buchanan, to whom he was related by mar-riage.[4]

More recently, blackface minstrelsy has been the focus of atten-tion from cultural historians interested more in its racial and class dynamics than in its exact relationship with American political par-ties.[5] Baker's study still stands as the last word on minstrelsy and politics. Her approach to the subject was more systematic and more concerned with assessing mass opinion than previous essays on the subject. Seeking "to ascertain . . . the invisible attitudes of the Demo-cratic fellowship," she searched popular culture, an "artistic produc-tion free from upper-class correction." Popular culture "not only de-fined the nature of the Negro's inferiority but also provided a domain within which Democrats developed specific public policies. By using its language and symbols, party leaders linked popular sentiments to party agenda."[6] Baker offered a rich analysis of the content of min-strelsy and concluded the description with the assertion that the "two worlds—the one in which racial intentions were expressed in popular activities from minstrelsy to rioting, the other in which Democratic leaders . . . articulated public policies—were connected." Her proof of the employment of minstrel idiom, theme, and form by the Democrats for political gain lies in campaign ephemera—songsters, cartoons, and sheet music—from the Civil War.[7]

All of this innovative work on minstrelsy in America has served to prove its powerful and near-pervasive presence in popular culture as well as the ideology of racialism contained in its performances and in the spin-offs from them, popular sheet music, cartoon images, and song books. But, of course, we can never be sure who sat in the audiences and what they took away from the performances. And when the argument is examined closely, we find that the Democratic obligation to the medium—before the Emancipation Proclamation—is not particularly well established.

Moreover, popular culture remains a big and somewhat vague subject, which has been the object of investigation by historians not especially interested in the history of political parties. Imagine the surprise of readers who encounter early minstrel songsters as prominent sources in Richard J. Carwardine's book, *Evangelicals and Politics in Antebellum America*. After all, the evangelicals in the antebellum North were the source of the moral opposites of minstrelsy —moralistic concerns in general and antislavery enthusiasm in particular. The whole purpose of Carwardine's book was to argue "that evangelical Protestants were amongst the principal shapers of American political culture in the middle years of the nineteenth century." They were "deeply engaged in the processes which tore political consensus apart and which opened the door to armed conflict."[8]

And yet, in dealing with the subject of "Presidential Electioneering and the Appeal to the Evangelicals," which he does in separate chapters for 1840 and for 1844 and 1848, Carwardine likened presidential canvasses to evangelical revivals and quoted here and there from such fugitive campaign materials as *The Harrison Medal Minstrel*, published in Philadelphia in 1840, and *The Clay Minstrel; or, National Songster*, also published in Philadelphia, but four years later.[9] These sources are described in the bibliography as "songbooks produced for particular campaigns," consulted because "campaign songs often incorporated the music, language, and millennialist outlook of evangelicalism."[10]

Nothing in the previous literature on minstrelsy and the song-books its popular performances inspired has prepared us for finding "the music, language, and millennialist outlook of evangelicalism" in such places. Clearly, a profound problem in understanding American political culture of the Civil War era lies within the covers of the little songbooks published for the political canvasses of the time.

The solution is not simple, entailing as it does necessarily controversial interpretation of the crude and often silly songs and lyrics. The contents of the songs are sometimes inscrutably topical, referring to obscure candidates for gubernatorial offices and employing sly references to scandals that made headlines then but that do not make much sense now. And any conclusion drawn from these difficult sources will inevitably fall short of concrete proof of the political affiliations of the audiences at the minstrel shows themselves.

The problem is amplified by the difficulty in gaining systematic control of the sources. Campaign songsters and "minstrels" constituted truly fugitive literature. They were often published in paper wrappers, a sure sign of their ephemeral nature in the mid-nineteenth century—and a ticket to destruction or degradation over the years following. They were also very small in dimensions, sometimes only three inches high, to accommodate the coat or shirt pocket, and therefore all the more easily lost sight of by the twenty-first century. Their scarcity and fragility generally confine them now to the guardianship of rare book rooms. Whatever their survival rate and whatever the difficulties of access now, examining these little works is where the solution to the problem must begin.

⤻ The initial association between minstrel entertainments and political pageantry had been close. Stephen Foster, for example, had been a participant in a political singing club in the 1844 presidential campaign in Cincinnati, where he was working in his brother's office. The club continued to meet after the election, and Foster wrote some of his earliest minstrel melodies for it.[11] Conversely, the traditional date for the first blackface minstrel show in America is 1843, and the American political parties showed their usual alertness to popular currents by adapting minstrelsy to the campaign simultaneously with its introduction to popular culture.[12]

Political and popular cultures thus necessarily overlapped, but the exact relationship between minstrelsy and the racial programs of the Democratic Party was not at all what the historical literature has suggested. First and most important, the Whig Party and not the Democratic was the first to exploit the popularity of minstrel entertainments for political gain. Until the Civil War at least, such exploitation of minstrelsy by politics was a minor phenomenon. Second, it is not clear that the management of such entertainments was Democratic. Republicans managed entertainments that depended on racial stereotyping too.

Third, despite some overlapping of the spheres of entertainment and politics, in fact they can very properly be termed separate spheres. Neither political party ever felt or claimed a close relationship with minstrel entertainments or with the stock characters and themes of their shows. The major political parties, though in conflict with each other on many issues, simply accepted minstrelsy as a part of the landscape of entertainment in the country. Nor did any political party attempt to answer the racial imagery of the minstrel shows. There was, therefore, not exactly an opposing school for racial political ideas. That raises the fourth point: there was no *dialectical* relationship in the entertainment sphere between popular antislavery entertainments and the minstrel shows. These entertainments with seemingly opposing messages on slavery and race existed side by side rather than on opposite sides of some imagined intellectual discourse. They were not in obvious dialogue with each other.

Fifth, the social and ideological content of blackface minstrelsy itself, though obviously dominated by racial themes, was not particularly partisan. And its relationship to politics might be described as exploitive: the performers used the events of politics for their humorous "hits." Otherwise, the content of the minstrel entertainments appears to have been vaguely antiparty. Sixth, after the issuance of the Emancipation Proclamation in 1863, the Republican Party no longer printed campaign minstrels for electioneering purposes, and the Democrats did so, for the first time, with real gusto. Still, the Democratic minstrel songbooks were only somewhat more indebted to the characters and themes of minstrelsy than the old Whig songsters had been.

The important conclusion we can draw from this rather surprising history, is that politics simply did not enter into everything. That was true of blackface minstrelsy, which was a part of the entertainment industry and not a school for politics.

❧ As soon as the form of the minstrel show jelled, the Whigs borrowed from the genre. The presidential contest between Henry Clay and James K. Polk in 1844 saw the use of several "minstrel" songsters. On this score the Whigs proved more alert than the Democrats. The Whig Party, and not the Democrats, introduced minstrel songsters into American political culture. The first campaign songster with "minstrel" in the title, *The Harrison Medal Minstrel*, contained songs celebrating William Henry Harrison, the Whig candidate for president in that rollicking and precedent-setting canvass. With Harrison's untimely death in 1841, the publication of political materials for other Whig presidential hopefuls resumed suddenly, for example, with John S. Stockton's *National Clay Minstrel, and True Whig's Pocket Companion, for the Presidential Canvass of 1844*, published, perhaps in 1843, in Philadelphia. Another version, *The National Clay Minstrel, and Frelinghuysen Melodist* (Fig. 4.1), was also published in Philadelphia, in 1844.[13]

These little books—*The National Clay Minstrel, and Frelinghuysen Melodist*, for example, measured about two inches by three inches—contained mostly typical campaign songs. They used the term "minstrel" for the first time, but they were simply songsters. Nevertheless, the underlying debt to blackface minstrelsy was, here and there, unmistakable. The first song, "Clay and Frelinghuysen," had been sung by a group called the Philadelphia Clay Minstrels at the Baltimore convention to ratify the nominations of the Whig presidential candidates. For the book, Tennessee's William G. "Parson" Brownlow wrote "A Sittin' on a Tree" in dialect (for example, "by de light ob de moon)."[14] Some of the other songs were meant to be sung to tunes familiar from blackface minstrelsy, like "Old Dan Tucker." Still, most of the works were innocent of racial allusions. They were thought of as "patriotic songs."[15]

Despite the similarity in title, *The Clay Minstrel; or, National Songster*, published in New York by Horace Greeley's steam presses, was a completely different book.[16] Its debt to blackface minstrelsy was also clear. "Clare de Kitchen" depicted the visit to Washington from Kentucky by an African American who meets the various aspirants for the presidency one by one. The last verse went this way:

> O hush! who come yonder!—oh! dem's de Whig boys,
> Dey bringin' Massa CLAY—by golly what a noise;
> Dis nigger better *colonize*—but hark, what dey say,
> "You must *all* clare de kitchin for Massa HARRY CLAY!"[17]

The songster measured 3 by 4¾ inches and included a frontispiece portrait of Clay and a woodcut of Ashland. Among some 150 songs, "Clare de Kitchin" was the only one in dialect.

A number of these Clay minstrel songsters survive because the initial production of them was prodigious. The first version of *The Clay Minstrel; or, National Songster* included a *Sketch of the Life, Public Services and Character of Henry Clay* and thus combined the traditional informational campaign biography with the more promotional and rousing songster. Apparently, from December 1843 to April 1844 nearly 15,000 copies of that edition were printed in seven printings. *The Clay Minstrel; or, National Songster* without the biographical sketch was designed to make the songs available more cheaply (and for those who already owned a campaign biography of the Whig candidate in another format).[18]

The minstrel songsters serve to remind us of one of the keys to understanding American political culture: until the Progressive Era there was no distinction in the methods employed by the parties, whatever their platform differences might be. They generally gave as good as they got—and in kind. Thus the Democrats wasted little time in imitating the successful Whig appeal to music in 1840 and to minstrel performance in 1844. The various *Clay Minstrels*, therefore, were met by *The Young Hickory and Annexation Minstrel, or, Polk and Dallas*

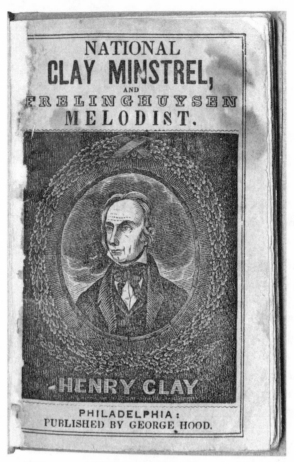

FIGURE 4.1. National Clay Minstrel, and Frelinghuysen Melodist
*(Philadelphia: George Hood, [1844]). Division of Rare and Manuscript
Collections, Carl A. Kroch Library, Cornell University. Despite the
reputation of the Whig Party for having "all the morality and all the
religion" (see Fig. 2.9), in fact Whigs were the first to introduce minstrel
themes into American presidential campaigns. This is one of the first
campaign pamphlets with "minstrel" in the title, a pocket-sized
songster with a woodcut image of the presidential candidate of 1844,
Henry Clay, on the paper cover.*

Melodist. Although this songster contained no lyrics in minstrel dialect, it did contain the virulently racist "Frelinghuysen's Amalgamation Song." The Whig nominee for vice president had a reputation as a moral reformer, and this Democratic song, to be sung to the tune of "My Ole Aunt Sally," described his alleged lust for African American women. Frelinghuysen sings:

> When I am Vice I'll free them all, and kiss their lips bewitching,
> They shall parade the White-house hall, while white gals scrub
>   the kitchen,
> They shall parade the white-house hall, while white gals scrub
>   the kitchen,
> Darkey, darkey, sweet plump darkey,
> Ra-re-ri-ro plump and sassy darkey.[19]

The antislavery Liberty Party in 1844 likewise attempted to imitate the methods of extremely popular campaigning introduced successfully by the Whigs four years earlier. *The Liberty Minstrel*, in which George W. Clark gathered antislavery songs for traditional airs and wed his own music to words by antislavery poets such as Longfellow and Whittier, was meant to have a life for the reform movement beyond the presidential campaign. The preface was signed in October 1844, and it is not certain that Clark was able to get the book to press in time for the presidential campaign. But, deadline or no, it was basically a presidential campaign songster and surprisingly imitative of the songsters of major parties. It contained many "hurrah" songs and celebrations of the Liberty Party candidate for president in 1844, the abolitionist James G. Birney, and featured an occasional dig at the other parties and their candidates, especially the Whigs and Henry Clay. In "We Ask Not Martial Glory," which celebrated Birney, it was noted that "No menial crouches near him, / No Charley's at his heel." A footnote identified Charley as "Clay's body servant."[20]

As befit an abolitionist work, the little book owed no overt debt to blackface minstrelsy except the name, here connoting only popular singing. The songs in which the voice was African American were not in dialect. One song was to be sung to the traditional minstrel tune "Dan Tucker," but such music quickly entered popular culture without its racial baggage necessarily in obvious tow. In fact, "minstrel" in the case of *The Liberty Minstrel* was likely meant as an abolitionist answer or parallel to the songsters more directly indebted to blackface minstrelsy, for the preface to the little antislavery songster stressed the power of "music of a chaste, refined and elevated style" to cross class lines and thus offer "a healthful moral influence" to all Americans. But by "elevated style" Clark actually meant "moral reform content," for the style of the songs was decidedly popular, using some of the same tunes (such as "Dan Tucker" or Scottish popular airs) as other campaign songsters did.[21]

The practice of publishing "minstrel" songsters for the presidential campaign seems to have sagged in succeeding contests. I have been unable to locate new ones published for the campaigns from 1848 through 1856. But when the Republicans, in many ways the heirs of the Whigs and especially so in terms of the tradition of campaign ritual and song, ran a "hurrah" campaign for Lincoln in 1860, George Washington Bungay offered in that year his *Bobolink Minstrel: or, Republican Songster, for 1860*. Bungay was the author of the popular song "Lincoln and Liberty," and his *Bobolink Minstrel* was published by O. Hutchinson in New York, who also published the music of the antislavery Hutchinson Family singers. The contents of *The Bobolink Minstrel* and *Hutchinson's Republican Songster for the Campaign of 1860* were substantially the same except that the *Bobolink Minstrel* contained words to a song making fun of Democratic presidential candidate Stephen A. Douglas, entitled "Poor Little Doug. A New Nigger Song Sung to An Old Nigger Tune." The music was "Uncle Ned," and the words supplied came from the minstrel dialect:

> Dere was a little man and his name was Stevy Doug,
> > To de White House he longed for to go;
> But he hadn't any votes fru de whole of the Souf . . .

Hutchinson's Republican Songster printed the "Free Soil Chorus" where the *Bobolink Minstrel* had "Poor Little Doug."[22] Indeed the "bobolink" in the title offered a clue to the contents, for, as historian W. T. Lhamon Jr. points out, the bobolink, a songbird whose plumage changes from brown to black, was early associated with blackface performance.[23]

◀ As for the partisan identification of the management of the minstrel shows, the Zwisher letter that opened this chapter certainly calls that into question in the case of the most famous of the minstrel companies, the Christy Minstrels. The career of the greatest showman of the age calls it into question as well. P. T. Barnum, like many of the entertainers of the time, had roots in minstrel entertainments. He began his career in entertainment travelling the country with a blackface dancer. Barnum's entertainments thereafter often capitalized on the same racial prejudices of white Americans. By 1860 his museum of curiosities in New York City even made a signal contribution to the racist atmosphere of the presidential canvass of 1860. Barnum's Museum displayed at the time an African American of small stature whom Barnum advertised as the "What Is It?" Visitors to the museum in New York could decide for themselves whether the "What Is It?" man was really human or not.[24]

The image of the "What Is It?" man appeared in a poster cartoon printed by Currier & Ives in 1860 as *An Heir to the Throne* (Fig. 4.2).[25] The cartoon suggested that Barnum's sideshow wonder would be the natural heir of policies concocted by the fanatical reformer Horace Greeley and the Republican presidential candidate Lincoln. The lithographers had likely copied the image from Barnum's advertising in New York (Fig. 4.3).[26]

Yet Barnum himself had become a Republican in politics in the 1850s. He was a Republican all the time he employed the men who played the "What Is It?" man in a long career of humbugging exploitation of racial stereotyping. Barnum apparently sat at a desk and could greet visitors to the museum, so his acquaintance with his African American employee was not at bureaucratic arm's length. Unfazed by exploitation of the man's image to criticize the Republicans in 1860, Barnum ran successfully for the Connecticut legislature so that he could vote in favor of the Thirteenth Amendment and work for the amendment of the Connecticut constitution to guarantee African American suffrage in the state.[27] Barnum's ability to compart-

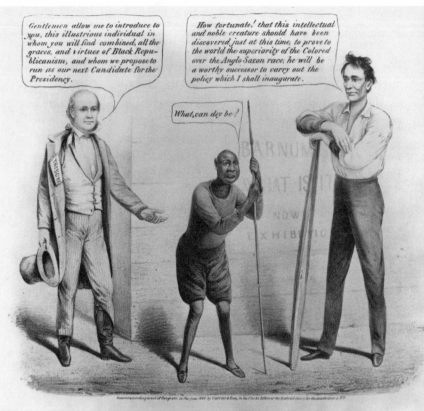

FIGURE 4.2. An Heir to the Throne. *Lithograph by Currier & Ives (New York, 1860). Reproduced from the Collections of the Library of Congress. Despite his famous sense of humor, Abraham Lincoln surely never examined the Currier & Ives political cartoons issued while he was running for president in 1860. Otherwise, he almost certainly would have dissuaded his wife and children from making a prominent visit to Barnum's Museum while in New York City. The African American pictured in this cartoon was featured as the "What Is It?" man at the museum at the time.*

FIGURE 4.3. Living Curiosities at Barnum's. *Woodcut illustration from* Frank Leslie's Illustrated Newspaper, *December 15, 1860. Rare Books and Archives, Paterno Library, Pennsylvania State University. The image of the "What Is It?" man (at right) appears among other images of "living curiosities" from Barnum's Museum in New York City. Currier & Ives likely had other models available for the figure to be copied in their political cartoon for the presidential campaign (see Fig. 4.2). December would have been too late to capitalize on the presidential canvass with a poster cartoon.*

mentalize the different parts of his life, professional and political, was perhaps paralleled by the ability of many other white Americans to draw boundaries between the different parts of their lives when going to the polls on election day or choosing entertainment on another night.

◄ Neither Whig nor Democrat had any particular political affinity for the songs and routines of blackface minstrelsy. The Whigs introduced minstrel songsters into presidential campaigns, not because of their racial agenda, but because the Whig Party played the largest role in introducing music into presidential campaigns. The famous log cabin and hard cider presidential canvass of 1840, which saw the Whigs determined to adopt the organizational and emotional electioneering techniques of the Democrats—and go them one better— saw the introduction of the fullest panoply of campaign hoopla. Partisan songs sung by partisan singing clubs became a major feature of campaigning, and the Whigs apparently excelled in this category. But the Democrats did not remain far behind.[28] In technique, the parties were always alike.

They were alike also in their peaceful coexistence with minstrel entertainments. The best and most consistent proof of the generally nonpartisan appeal of minstrelsy lies in the eager embrace of advertising for minstrel shows by the nineteenth-century party press—a sign, surely, that audiences contained people of all political parties. These newspapers existed primarily to promote a political party, but there was nothing so political in the content of the minstrel shows that any partisan newspaper spurned their advertising on principle or offered editorial critiques of the content of the shows. These newspapers did offer their readers information about nonpolitical events, crimes and natural disasters, for example. Along with advertisements of local amusements, they also offered their readers reviews and notices of these happenings.

Republican and Democratic newspapers made no distinction whatever in their willingness to publish advertisements for minstrel entertainments. This is in itself important proof that politics did not enter into everything. Lacking modern professional standards, the press indulged in the habit of noticing and generally promoting those amusements that advertised in the pages of the newspaper, among other practices now spurned by the fourth estate as a self-conscious profession. And this willingness to advertise and promote minstrelsy across the lines of the partisan press continued unabated throughout the antebellum and Civil War era. Examples of the bipartisan advertisement of minstrel shows abound in the Northern press. In the ardently antislavery *Chicago Tribune*, for example, during the Kansas controversy of the middle 1850s, the editors could thrill to the willingness of the women of Lawrence to enroll themselves to fight the proslavery settlers. That item was juxtaposed against a notice that Phelps's Burlesque Ethiopian Opera Troupe was playing at Metropolitan Hall.[29]

Astonishing proof of the acceptance of minstrel entertainments even by those most opposed to Democratic Party policies on slavery —and in the very midst of the Civil War—lies in the pages of the *Boston Commonwealth*, a radical Republican abolitionist newspaper founded by George Stearns, Moncure Conway, and James M. Stone as a mouthpiece for the Emancipation League during the war. The newspaper's favorite Massachusetts politician was Charles Sumner, and the speeches of Wendell Phillips and those of other antislavery radicals made regular appearances there. In December 1863 the *Commonwealth* advertised Buckley's Serenaders' appearance at the New Minstrel Hall and Aquarial Gardens. In the "Matters About Home" column of January 22, 1864, the *Commonwealth* commended the Buckleys' new program: "Their performance this week is one of more than usual merit and attractiveness, in which all the talented artists of the troupe are engaged." The troupes offered a wide range of entertainments, but there is no mistaking the nature of the show commented on by the *Commonwealth* in this instance. The program included the revival of the risqué minstrel show staple "Sally Come Up" along with "Three Contrabands . . . Esseva of Old Virginny . . . [and] Black Yer Boots."[30] The same issue of the paper contained an editorial in favor of land distribution to the freedmen of the South.

The acceptance of the minstrel genre as entertainment rather than as political expression is surely reflected in the willingness of the anti-slavery and rather high-toned *Atlantic Monthly* to publish work un-critical of minstrelsy. In Reconstruction, even while the magazine's columns were open to Frederick Douglass, an article on Stephen Collins Foster could conclude with this assessment of his work for the genre: "If Mr. Foster's art embodied no higher idea than the vulgar notion of the negro as a man-monkey,—a thing of tricks and antics,—a funny specimen of superior gorilla,—then it might have proved a tolerable catch-penny affair, and commanded an admiration among boys of various growths until its novelty wore off. But the art in his hands teemed with a nobler significance. It dealt, in its simplicity, with universal sympathies, and taught us all to feel with the slaves the lovely joys it celebrated."[31] This is an unusually expressive passage in midcentury social description. Minstrelsy was regularly noticed in the papers but only for its availability as entertainment. The social content of the genre was seldom commented on. In part, that was a telling sign of the deep and unwitting prejudice shared very widely in the white culture of the day. It was also a function of the enter-tainment purpose of the medium. It was meant to amuse and not to instruct.

To Americans of the mid-nineteenth century, even those con-sumed by politics, minstrel shows and similar entertainments were just that, entertainments. The Lincoln family saw no problem with attending them. Indeed, as soon as they had a chance, they sampled the genre. When Abraham Lincoln went to Washington for his only term as a member of the House of Representatives during the Mexi-can War, he and his wife Mary went to Carusi's Saloon to see a group called the Ethiopian Serenaders. As president, even after the issuance of the Emancipation Proclamation, Lincoln again took his wife to see a blackface minstrel performer named Barney Williams at Grover's Theatre in Washington.[32]

Even when all eyes were watching, amusements beckoned. On his inaugural journey to Washington in 1861, Lincoln stopped in New York City. P. T. Barnum invited the Lincolns to visit his museum. Lincoln declined, but his wife and children went. No doubt, they saw the "What Is It?" man (Fig. 4.4)[33]

❧ For those historians inclined to see politics in everything in nine-teenth-century American society, it might be argued that there were competing forms of entertainment for Republicans. Theatrical ver-sions of *Uncle Tom's Cabin* remained popular throughout the period and often played in one house in town while minstrel shows met dif-ferent entertainment needs in others.

Jean Baker, though her book is concerned only with Democratic political culture, suggested that there was an alternative culture offer-ing a different message on race: "By the 1840s an antislavery (though never problack) vernacular had developed, reflected in the fiction of Harriet Beecher Stowe, the travel accounts of Frederick Law Olm-sted, the children's literature of Peter Parley, and the poetry of Lowell and Longfellow. In this 'romantic racialism,' as George Fredrickson called it, Northerners produced a more sympathetic black, created in God's image and sharing with whites a common humanity."[34] There was indeed variety in the theatrical and popular entertainments avail-able to the American people, but the differences were not so clearly partisan and ideological.

The hopes expressed by reviewers of the theatricals focused less often on the need for political enlightenment on racial questions than on the improvement in the overall moral tone of the audience to be found attending wholesome and religious fare like *Uncle Tom's Cabin*.

Popular culture did have upper-class people who wanted to cor-rect it, and the theatrical dialogue had been going on for years. After a long and successful run in New York City in 1853, *Uncle Tom's Cabin* came to Chicago. The Whig *Tribune* was reminded of the play's previ-ous success in New York, where it had also done good for humanity. "Men and boys, whose associations were bad"—those of the "every fellow for himself and the D—l take the hindermost" sort—had their hearts melted by the touching drama.[35] A letter from New York pro-moted the play with rare direct reference to the social reform ori-

FIGURE 4.4. Progress of "Honest Old Abe" on His Way to the White House. *From* Phunny Phellow, *April 1861. Courtesy of the American Antiquarian Society. This elaborate cartoon included one panel (bottom row, second from left) depicting a fanciful visit of the*

president-elect with his wife to see the "What Is It?" man at Barnum's Museum. Actually, fancy came close to reality: Lincoln's wife and children did visit the museum and likely saw the exhibit.

gins in the novel by Harriet Beecher Stowe, saying of its current run in New York that "most would have predicted not only a failure, but a most violent opposition, from the b'hoys, in the form of a row, or something akin to it. The history of the Anti-Slavery, or rather Pro-Slavery excitements in this city, proves that the lower class of boys and young men have been the chief actors, if not original movers in those disgraceful riots against the Abolitionists which occurred here some years since . . . the b'hoys were the foremost to kick and curse the 'niggers,'" but *Uncle Tom's Cabin* nevertheless brought down the house.[36]

The above review contains a specific reference to "antislavery" not as frequently found in newspaper reviews of theatrical versions of *Uncle Tom's Cabin* in the 1850s and 1860s as one might expect.[37] A *New York Tribune* review of 1854 also embodied strong antislavery feeling: "We could not but feel last night as we witnessed this play of Uncle Tom, in its representation at the Bowery, that it must make a gross, robust, unreasoning sentiment of hatred to slavery in the very ground tier of society; that may be the germ of a tremendous social explosion. Do slaveholders count upon the steady support of the masses. . . ?"[38] Half the seats in the house went for twelve and a half cents each.

To some degree, theatrical presentations engaged in ideological dialogue with each other, but it is difficult in the absence of extended reviews like the one just quoted here to be certain what the content of the dialogue was. To some extent, it was a matter more of high and low rather than of white and black. The minstrel shows, often running regularly every night, sometimes featured burlesques of the higher operas, such as *Lucia di Lammermoor*. On occasion, likewise, the minstrel troupe might offer a burlesque on *Uncle Tom's Cabin*, if that perennial favorite was enjoying a run at another local theater. Thus in Philadelphia, in February 1862, the Continental Theatre drew, according to the *Philadelphia Inquirer*, "immense crowds of people of all conditions" to *Uncle Tom's Cabin*. Meanwhile, Sanford's Opera House offered the contrasting "Ethiopian operatic version of *Uncle Tom*."[39] Almost a decade earlier in New York, the same pattern had been visible. The National Theatre enjoyed a very long run of *Uncle Tom's Cabin* in 1853 and 1854. Down the street George

Christy and Wood's Minstrels offered their "New Burletta [of] Uncle Tom" every evening.[40]

But in truth the world of entertainment tended to blur party lines rather than to draw them across American audiences.

It is notorious that Harriet Beecher Stowe's great antislavery novel was widely corrupted in theatrical versions, which often altered the material to racist conclusions.[41] That became shockingly clear to Chicago Republicans eager to be uplifted by a theatrical version of *Uncle Tom's Cabin* in their city in 1854. The review of the first night's performance in Chicago expressed disappointment from the standpoint of moral reform. "It is not Harriet Beecher Stowe's 'Uncle Tom's Cabin,' dramatized by any manner of means," commented the *Tribune*'s reporter. "The version . . . is the one which was gotten up to conciliate Southern feeling," the reporter said, and that was done by interpolating corruptions into the story. "Southern slavery and English servitude" were "compared," and Uncle Tom did not die.[42]

Still Chicago's Republican newspaper was pleased to see that *Uncle Tom's Cabin* drew very well. It was true, however, that "one very great drawback to the interest and effect of the play, is the very conspicuous part which the 'man who plays the banjo,' is allowed to take." There was no such character in Mrs. Stowe's novel.[43]

As the shocking reference to the "banjo" suggests, on the whole, the tendency of the entertainment sphere was not to polarization but to homogenization. A similar phenomenon was observable in Philadelphia's run of *Uncle Tom's Cabin* during the Civil War. The Continental Theatre was shaping their *Uncle Tom's Cabin* toward a common denominator of opinion: "This evening Mrs. H. Chapman, so well known to the public as the celebrated delineator of 'Topsy's' character, takes a complimentary benefit. She has displayed, in her rendition of this character, a marvelous appreciation for the comic in nature. 'Topsy's' genuine love for 'Eva,' showing beneath a rough exterior a good heart, has not been overlooked, but admirably portrayed. This evening the little 'darkie' will appear in all her original greatness, causing the wildest merriment."[44] As was often the case, *Uncle Tom's Cabin* underwent a transformative interpretation whereby its most racially caricatured protagonists were put forward at the expense of its abolitionist scenes. In other words, *Uncle Tom's Cabin*, in its unauthorized theatrical performances, tended to be adapted in the direction of a minstrel show with banjos and comic, racially stereotyped characters and scenes.

The blurring of political messages on race did not run all in the direction of watering down uplifting antislavery sentiments. For example, in New York City in 1854, after months of discussion in Congress of Senator Stephen A. Douglas's Kansas-Nebraska Bill and its final passage in May, the minstrel shows could hardly pass up so rich a topical reference. The result was, in the language of the *Tribune*, that "George Christy, *the* 'darkey' par excellence, will offer a new burletta, tonight, called 'Black Douglas, or the "Lost Babby Found,"' in which George figures as 'Nebraska Bill Douglas.'"[45] We have no way of knowing what Christy said as Stephen A. Douglas in blackface, but it was surely satirical and not heroic.

Minstrelsy remained, after all, theater and not political exposition. It was not easy to separate medium and message in the entertainment realm. The Hutchinson Family singers, for example, were known for their antislavery and protemperance repertoire. In the midst of the Civil War, one newspaper, in alerting its readers that the Hutchinson Family singers were coming to town, said circumspectly, "Whatever may be said of their political opinions, they are certainly excellent singers."[46] Conversely, a rare review of a performance made a similar observation about a minstrel presentation. Commenting on a performance at the Grand Academy of Music in 1864, a time of intensification of racial issues politically, the reviewer for the Democratic *Chicago Times* observed, "Mr. Arlington was loudly applauded at the conclusion of a song, 'You can't wash a black man white,' though it was difficult to determine whether the sentiment, which was that it were best to leave said black man alone, or the singer, was the more immediate object of approval."[47] And surely confusion was added when a minstrel delineator took on the role of Uncle Tom in a theatrical version of Harriet Beecher Stowe's novel, as sometimes happened.

Finally, note the confusing message conveyed in the Hutchinson Family song *The Ghost of Uncle Tom*, which included these lyrics:

Nigger's only made to work, de Sudden people say;
And de nigger's berry willing, but he want his pay;
So he swims across de ribber, and he flies across de plains;
But de Northern people catch him and dey ribbet on his chains!
Knock! knock! knock! when de hour ob midnight come—
Who is dat a'knocking? 'Tis "The Ghost of Uncle Tom!"

The music, an anti–Fugitive Slave Act song sung in blackface dialect, was published in 1854 and was advertised as a number performed by the Hutchinson Family at all of their concerts.[48]

❦ At times, entertainment and politics were in fact not complementary but competitive. During the heat of a presidential canvass, entertainment had to take a backseat to political entertainment. Political spectacle seems to have filled up so much time near the presidential polling day that it made no monetary sense to keep all the theaters in a city open for business. Thus in New York City in mid-October 1864, one newspaper observed, "The mass meetings that are held in the various Wards, night after night, make a visible impression on the theatres,—and their exchequers."[49] For the final week preceding the election in November, New York's Academy Theater closed its doors altogether. That eliminated an opera (*Il Trovatore*) rather than minstrelsy, but apparently all theaters closed on election night: there was no competing with the level of excitement and curiosity about election returns.[50]

It might be almost as easy to see minstrelsy in competition with politics as to see the entertainment medium as supporting one side or the other in the political party discourse of the day.

Categories of interpretation remained primarily moral rather than political. When *Uncle Tom's Cabin* prepared to depart Chicago with its last performance in 1854, the *Tribune* noted the "full houses" the play always attracted in their town and expressed gratitude "that the class of persons who have visited the Theatre . . . had been, to a great extent, members of churches," though one wonders how the reviewer could know such a thing.[51]

The minstrel burlesques tended not to be sharply aimed and politically pointed. Rather, they were as often vague and indefinite in thrust. To examine what proved popular enough to be presented in books and pamphlets that fed off the popularity of the theatricals is to see their somewhat nebulous political thrust.

Christy's New Songster and Black Joker . . . , for example, published in the midst of the Civil War was certainly antiabolitionist, but it was not proslavery. Its contents could not be readily identified as Democratic: the commonest denominator was patriotism. The patriotic note was more sentimental than ideological. "Was My Brother in the Battle?" asked one song, and another celebrated "Our Union None Can Sever." The patriotic songs were not in dialect. The familiar antipolitical note was also retained. "We can raise Politicians nuff to ruin any country," went one comic line. And Stephen Foster, despite his Democratic family heritage, offered a song called "Better Times Are Coming" with this celebratory verse:

> Abra'm Lincoln had the army and the navy in his hands,
> While Seward keeps our honor bright abroad in foreign lands;
> And Stanton is a man, who is sturdy as a rock,
> With brave men to back him up and stand the battle's shock.

Subsequent verses celebrated McClellan and a host of Civil War generals and naval commanders from Franz Sigel to Commander Worden of the *Monitor*.[52] *Bob Hart's Plantation Songster* of 1862 sang of "The Happy Contraband," who came North where "they go for Union." [53] Democrat Andrew Jackson was more likely to be celebrated on the minstrel stage than Abraham Lincoln or some other Republican apostle of Union, but the Union was celebrated.[54] The "shoddy" results of corruption in war contracts also came in for their fair number of "hits" by the minstrels, but criticism of shoddyism went beyond partisan boundaries in the realm of party politics, too.[55]

The direction of the development of the minstrel genre is difficult to identify. It was not a medium that flowed outward to the hinterland from a metropolitan and standard-setting center. There was no real intellectual control of its content. And it does not appear to be the case, despite the intensification of identification of the Democratic Party with racist platforms from the mid-1850s through the

FIGURE 4.5. Brutus and Caesar. (From the American Edition of Shakespeare). Punch *(London), August 15, 1863. Association of Lincoln's Emancipation Proclamation with minstrelsy was common in Great Britain. John Tenniel's cartoon was accompanied in the original magazine by a dialogue in which an "Ethiopian Serenader with a Banjo" enters Brutus's (Lincoln's) tent at night. The minstrel with a banjo falls asleep at left, and the ghost of Caesar appears to haunt Lincoln for issuing the Emancipation Proclamation. The ensuing conversation is conducted in minstrel show and mock-Shakespearian dialect.*

Civil War, that minstrelsy followed the party in that direction. Like Stephen Collins Foster himself, it could be found stressing the patriotic and sentimental rather than the racially satirical.[56] The entertainment sphere had its own dynamic, and that led away from ideological polarization and toward an almost bland patriotism during the Civil War—to the degree that any trend of ideas is detectable in so decentralized, topically responsive, and intellectually slack a medium.[57]

❦ Available evidence suggests that minstrel shows flourished during the Civil War, but this was not necessarily a matter of combating the progressive racial programs of the Republicans or of the topicality of racial debate. It was at least in part a function of the high demand for entertainment. Soldiers in camps of instruction, on leave, or travelling to their assigned quarters were often idle and sought amusement. Even while on duty but idle, soldiers sought minstrel entertainments. Amateur versions were staged on shipboard, even on naval vessels with African American sailors forming part of the crew.[58]

On shore swarms of idle young men from the country swelled the demand for popular entertainments of all sorts. In an army boomtown like Harrisburg, Pennsylvania, with Camps Curtin, Simmons, and McClellan nearby, training grounds for thousands of Union soldiers brought there by the crisscrossing railway network, theatricals enjoyed big nightly audiences.[59] The town sported several music halls, and Democratic and Republican newspapers alike advertised the city's steady stream of travelling and resident minstrel shows.

Sanford's Hall advertised its entertainments with a rare woodcut of a dancing minstrel figure in the ardently Republican *Telegraph* in early March 1864.[60] In April, Hitchcock's New National Hall brought the "popular Negro delineators" Comber and Pettit to the Pennsylvania capital city. Sanford featured "the great Ethiopian comedian" F. Diamond less than two weeks later. Diamond, trumpeted the Republican paper, was "the prince of Negro delineators."[61] Brant's Hall met the competition by bringing Campbell's Minstrels about a week later, and in May, Harris and Clifton's Minstrels.[62]

Notices of minstrel entertainments appeared not only in the Republican newspaper's advertisements but also in the section of the paper devoted to local "news," called "Town and Country." The result was that this stalwart Republican organ, like many others at the time, sold advertising space to minstrel show promoters, promoted attendance at them in local news columns by praising their performances, and at the same time advocated radical Republicanism, the Thirteenth Amendment abolishing slavery, and other advanced policies of emancipation in its editorials. Republicans and Democrats alike must have patronized the music halls in Harrisburg. That was a sphere compartmentalized in people's minds as entertainment and not commonly thought of as a realm of political indoctrination.

For the rest of Northern society, the Civil War was not an all-absorbing fact of life. For many people, life, we might say, went on. As in the novel *Little Women*, picnics, amateur theatricals, and socializing continued. So did the demand for professional entertainment — and as far as anecdotal evidence available in the press of the day indicates, it continued unabated.[63]

Naturally, the salience of racial political issues during the Civil War invited a tendency for the first time in two decades for Democrats to exploit aggressively and more exclusively a genre of entertainment that had, until the Emancipation Proclamation, existed in a nonpartisan or an antipolitical world (see Fig. 4.5).

The *Copperhead Minstrel: Choice Collection of Democratic Poems and Songs, for the Use of Political Clubs and the Social Circle*, first published in New York City in 1863 and brought out in a second edition for the presidential canvass in 1864, was an example of the partisan exploitation of minstrel themes by the Democrats (Fig. 4.6).[64] Even so, war and related Republican measures, rather than race, provided the dominant theme in the songs printed in the pamphlet issued in 1864. Of thirty-nine songs, six dealt mostly with race; but one-third (thirteen) did not mention race at all. Race was only incidentally mentioned in some others. Ten dealt with a mixture of bitterness and sentimentality with death and suffering in the war. Paper money, corruption in government contracts, and conscription were the focus of nine pieces. Only five songs were written in the telltale dialect of minstrelsy.

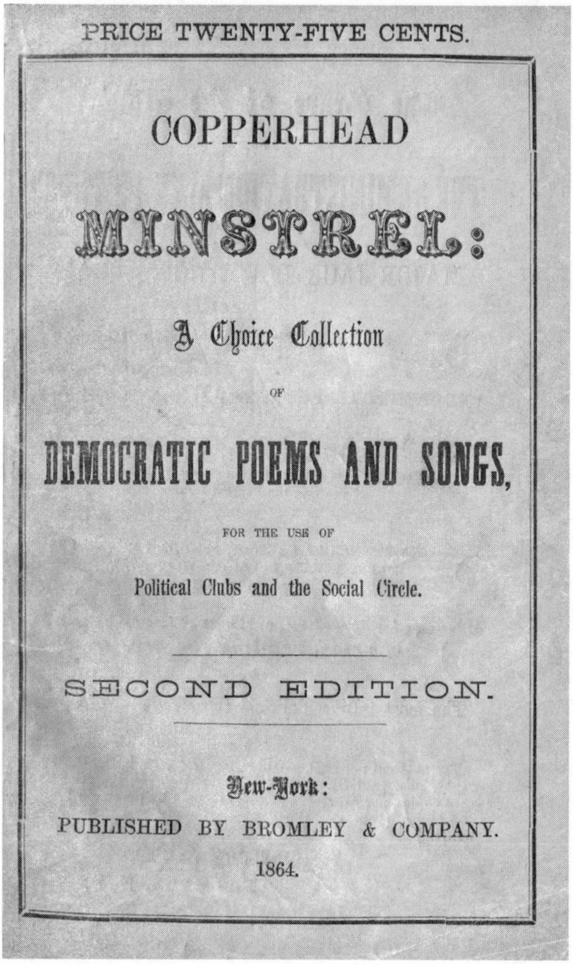

PRICE TWENTY-FIVE CENTS.

COPPERHEAD

MINSTREL:

A Choice Collection

OF

DEMOCRATIC POEMS AND SONGS,

FOR THE USE OF

Political Clubs and the Social Circle.

SECOND EDITION.

New-York:

PUBLISHED BY BROMLEY & COMPANY.

1864.

FIGURE 4.6. Copperhead Minstrel: A Choice Collection of Democratic Poems and Songs for the Use of Political Clubs and the Social Circle *(New York: Bromley & Co., 1864). Division of Rare and Manuscript Collections, Carl A. Kroch Library, Cornell University. Published by the company that produced the* Miscegenation *lithograph (see Fig. 2.6), this songster also sold for twenty-five cents.*

Despite a new tendency toward one-sidedly Democratic exploitation of the minstrel genre during the war, the politicization of minstrelsy was by no means thorough even then. A striking example of its broad appeal to white people in North America was the performance of the Libby Prison Minstrels, apparently held at the prison itself, on Christmas Eve, 1863. Libby was a Confederate military prison for Union officers, and the performance was presented by the Northern inmates for the Richmond public (see Fig. 4.7). All of the performers held an officer's rank of lieutenant or above.[65]

✦ A sign that minstrelsy existed in a sphere of leisure activities widely considered to be outside the political sphere of the parties was the scantiness of the effort made by political activists to answer its "hits." Frederick Douglass chose to denounce minstrelsy in Europe —where the shows also proved popular—more than in the United States. In fact, perhaps recognizing the grip of the genre's popular melodies on American opinion, he once attempted to claim minstrelsy for the antislavery cause. In a speech given in Rochester, New York, in 1855, Douglass said:

> It would seem almost absurd to say it, considering the use that has been made of them, that we have allies in the Ethiopian songs; those songs that constitute our national music, and without which we have no national music. They are heart songs and the finest feelings of human nature are expressed in them. "Lucy Neal," "Old Kentucky Home," "Uncle Ned," can make the heart sad as well as merry, and can call forth a tear as well as a smile. They awaken the sympathies for the slave, in which Anti-Slavery principles take root, grow up and flourish.[66]

When he visited England, however, Douglass felt the weight of minstrel stereotypes more powerfully and sought to blunt their influence. In Newcastle-upon-Tyne in February 1860, Douglass more predictably termed Ethiopian minstrels a "pestiferous nuisance." They had "brought here the slang phrases, the contemptuous sneers all originating in the spirit of slavery; and it was necessary, when we had seen the negro represented in all manner of extravagances, con-

"I WISH I WAS IN DIXIE!"

PLAINTIVE AIR—Sung nightly in Washington by that Celebrated Delineator, ABRAHAM LINCOLN.

FIGURE 4.7. *"I Wish I Was in Dixie!"* Southern Illustrated News, *February 27, 1864. Courtesy of the Western Reserve Historical Society. In this rare cartoon from a Confederate comic monthly magazine, President Lincoln has cast aside the symbols of his humble beginnings, tools for splitting rails, and has taken up the banjo of the "Celebrated Delineator"—a reference to the "Negro delineators" of minstrelsy, as they were called.*

tented and happy as a slave, thoughtless of any life higher than a merely physical one—it was meet and right that some slave should break away from his chains and rise up and assert his manhood and the manhood of his race in the presence of those prejudices."[67]

✦ Thus to a degree the popular culture of the day shaped the political culture. But on election night and at other times popular culture took second place behind political concerns. For most Americans, it seems, it was possible to compartmentalize the various realms of social life, behind boundaries that overlapped and changed with the times. Popular culture could not manage to conquer the political culture, however easy it may have been to make a burlesque of the average stump speech of the day. Popular culture did not move the society in the direction of indifference and turning inward.

It is crucial to recall the voting statistics of 1864. They remind us yet again of the astonishing levels of political involvement among Americans of the Civil War era—figures so high that they astounded even politicians such as Abraham Lincoln who were accustomed to public commitment. Understanding American political culture in the nineteenth century eluded even such participants as Lincoln, but, to this day, understanding American political culture properly begins with the fundamental assumption he always made about his society: one could count on the fullest participation of the people if the politicians made the effort. The politicians made strenuous efforts, and indeed the American engagement with public life in the nineteenth century was without parallel.

Notes

PREFACE

1. Byron E. Shafer and Anthony J. Badger, eds., *Contesting Democracy: Substance and Structure in American Political History, 1775–2000* (Lawrence: University Press of Kansas, 2001), 1. The event was the annual convention of the Organization of American Historians.

2. Rick Shenkman, "Reporter's Notebook: Highlights from the 2004 OAH Convention," History News Network, March 26, 2004, <http://hnn.us/articles/4320.html>.

3. Glenn C. Altschuler and Stuart M. Blumin, *Rude Republic: Americans and Their Politics in the Nineteenth Century* (Princeton: Princeton University Press, 2000), esp. 153–56.

4. Joel H. Silbey, *The American Political Nation, 1838–1893* (Stanford: Stanford University Press, 1991).

5. Iver Bernstein, *The New York City Draft Riots: Their Significance for American Society and Politics in the Age of the Civil War* (New York: Oxford University Press, 1990).

6. Jean H. Baker, *Affairs of Party: The Political Culture of Northern Democrats in the Mid-Nineteenth Century* (Ithaca: Cornell University Press, 1983; New York: Fordham University Press, 1998).

7. Michael F. Holt, for example, said the book "integrate[s] social and political history" in "An Elusive Synthesis: Northern Politics during the Civil War," in *Writing the Civil War: The Quest to Understand*, ed. James M. McPherson and William J. Cooper Jr. (Columbia: University of South Carolina Press, 1998), 128.

8. Among these were Harold Holzer, Gabor S. Boritt, and Mark E. Neely Jr., *The Lincoln Image: Abraham Lincoln and the Popular Print* (New York: Charles Scribner's Sons, 1984; Urbana: University of Illinois Press, 2001), and *The Confederate Image: Prints of the Lost Cause* (Chapel Hill: University of North Carolina Press, 1987); Harold Holzer and Mark E. Neely Jr., *The Lincoln Family Album: Photographs from the Personal Collections of a Historic American Family* (New York: Doubleday, 1990), *Mine Eyes Have Seen the Glory: The Civil War in Art* (New York: Orion Books, 1993), and *The Union Image: Popular Prints of the Civil War North* (Chapel Hill: University of North Carolina Press, 2000).

CHAPTER ONE

1. Edwin Havilland Miller, ed., *Walt Whitman: The Correspondence, Volume I: 1842–1867* (New York: New York University Press, 1961), 242.

2. Joel H. Silbey, *The American Political Nation, 1838–1893* (Stanford: Stanford University Press, 1991), esp. 145.

3. William E. Gienapp, "'Politics Seem to Enter into Everything': Political Culture in the North, 1840–1860," in *Essays in Antebellum American Politics, 1840–1860*, ed. Stephen E. Maizlish and John J. Kushma (College Station: Texas A & M University Press, 1982), 15–69.

4. William E. Gienapp, *The Origins of the Republican Party, 1852–1856* (New York: Oxford University Press, 1987), 8.

5. Michael E. McGerr, *The Decline of Popular Politics: The American North, 1865–1928* (New York: Oxford University Press, 1986), 8.

6. The New Political Historians first called attention to such work. See especially Richard P. McCormick, *The Second American Party System: Party Formation in the Jacksonian Era* (Chapel Hill: University of North Carolina Press, 1966), esp. 349–53.

7. Glenn C. Altschuler and Stuart M. Blumin, *Rude Republic: Americans and Their Politics in the Nineteenth Century* (Princeton: Princeton University Press, 2000), 79. "Partisan imperative" is a term frequently used by Joel H. Silbey to describe the politics of the nineteenth century.

8. Ibid., 9–10.

9. Joseph C. G. Kennedy, *Preliminary Report on the Eighth Census. 1860* (Washington, D.C.: Government Printing Office, 1862), 102–3.

10. Joseph C. G. Kennedy, *Population of the United States in 1860; Compiled from the Original Returns of the Eighth Census . . .* , 4 vols. (Washington, D.C.: Government Printing Office, 1864), 1:88–101.

11. Roy P. Basler, ed., *The Collected Works of Abraham Lincoln*, 9 vols. (New Brunswick, N.J.: Rutgers University Press, 1953–55), 1:202 n. For correspondence about the *Old Soldier*, see also pp. 203–5.

12. Mark E. Neely Jr., ed., *The Extra Journal: Rallying the Whigs of Illinois*, pamphlet and facsimile newspapers (Fort Wayne, Ind.: Louis A. Warren Lincoln Library and Museum, 1982).

13. Altschuler and Blumin acknowledge the cluttered election calendar on p. 4 of *Rude Republic*. For the original insight, see Roy F. Nichols, *The Disruption of American Democracy* (New York: Macmillan, 1948; New York: Free Press, 1967), 20–21.

14. Altschuler and Blumin, *Rude Republic*, 19.

15. Altschuler and Blumin describe the political press as a source on pp. 4 and 12 of *Rude Republic*.

16. The irresistible term comes from Christopher Lasch, *Haven in a Heartless World: The Family Besieged* (New York: Basic Books, 1977), though that book deals with a later period and distinguishes the home sphere from the world of business and work rather than politics.

17. Robert E. Wiebe, *Self-Rule: A Cultural History of American Democracy* (Chicago: University of Chicago Press, 1995), 72–83. I have given the concept a bit less fraternal and more assertively "masculine" characterization. Wiebe is cited in *Rude Republic*; see, for example, pp. 4 and 8. The rough-and-tumble behavior actually marked an improvement over the mortal duels fought in the preceding era of "mixed deferential participant politics." See Joanne B. Freeman, *Affairs of Honor: National Politics in the New Republic* (New Haven: Yale University Press, 2001); Ronald P. Formisano, "Deferential-Participant Politics: The Early Republic's Political Culture, 1789–1840," *American Political Science Review* 68 (1974): 473–87.

18. Barbara Welter, "The Cult of True Womanhood," *American Quarterly* 18 (Summer 1966): 151–74.

19. Philip J. Ethington's review of *Rude Republic* (*Journal of American History* 88 [2001]: 645) compliments the authors for "painstakingly" examining "sources that have been ignored by the creators" of the opposing model of American political engagement. It is true that the New Political Historians were interested mostly in voting analysis and behavioral evidence—numbers, as Jean H. Baker puts it. One of their pioneers, Richard P. McCormick, did make very suggestive observations about the nature of political ritual in *The Second American Party System: Party Formation in the Jacksonian Era* ([Chapel Hill: University of North Carolina Press, 1966], 349–50), emphasizing electioneering "spectacle" as "a satisfying form of cultural expression" for Americans of that era. Richard Jensen was one New Political Historian who followed McCormick's lead, but for the most part, they did not pursue the systematic study of campaign ephemera. The pioneer scholarly work in that field was Roger A. Fischer, *Tippecanoe and Trinkets Too: The Material Culture of American Presidential Campaigns, 1828–1984* (Urbana: University of Illinois Press, 1988).

20. Altschuler and Blumin, *Rude Republic*, 131. They add that Currier & Ives ignored only one notable part of the "American panorama": the "unpleasant reality of working class labor and life"—slaves in the fields or New England factory women and immigrant workers.

21. Ibid., 132–35.

22. That was the point of the books I coauthored with Harold Holzer and Gabor S. Boritt. See, for example, *The Lincoln Image: Abraham Lincoln and the*

Popular Print (New York: Charles Scribner's Sons, 1984; Urbana: University of Illinois Press, 2001).

23. Robert Philippe first noted that popular prints "testify to convictions" in *Political Graphics: Art as a Weapon* (New York: Abbeville Press, 1980), 172. Philippe's statement played a major role in inspiring my interest in political prints.

24. Again I am indebted to Robert Philippe, who characterized the political print of the mid-nineteenth century as the "heir" to "the sacred picture" in ibid., 172.

25. Altschuler and Blumin themselves note that Currier & Ives' banner double-portrait lithographs were "printed . . . in the ordinary lithographic size for hanging on interior walls." *Rude Republic*, 132.

26. An advertisement for images for the American Art Union, for example, featured their American and English landscapes and copies of old masters as "ornaments for the parlor, the library and the public resort." *Harrisburg Telegraph*, May 4, 1864.

27. See Henry Clay Memorial Foundation, *Henry Clay: Images of a Statesman* (Lexington: University of Kentucky Libraries, 1991), 33. Dodge was a New York City miniature painter. See Robert Seeger II, ed., *The Whig Leader, January 1, 1837–December 31, 1843*, vol. 9 of *The Papers of Henry Clay* (Lexington: University Press of Kentucky, 1988), 880.

28. Clay made claims to the contrary. When he sat for portrait painter G. P. A. Healy, commissioned by Louis Philippe of France, Clay "enjoyed the gossip of the courts of Europe, but he would chide Healy that the painter showed no interest in his farm or livestock, of which he said he was prouder than his finest speeches." Clifford Amyx, "The Painters of Henry Clay as 'The Sage of Ashland,'" *Kentucky Review* 8 (Spring 1988): 78.

29. Today, we would be most likely to encounter a print portrait of Henry Clay in a public gallery or museum, but such institutions were virtually nonexistent in Henry Clay's America, and no artist or printmaker could make a living by producing works meant for display in an art museum.

30. Harold Holzer, Gabor S. Boritt, and I examined images of the president in the context of the home in *The Lincoln Image*, 167–88.

31. Altschuler and Blumin, *Rude Republic*, 8.

32. Bryan F. Le Beau, *Currier & Ives: America Imagined* (Washington: Smithsonian Institution Press, 2001), 27. Le Beau emphasizes the cheapness of the lithographs, as did the company's own advertising.

33. Stuart M. Blumin, *The Emergence of the Middle Class: Social Experience in the American City, 1760–1900* (Cambridge: Cambridge University Press, 1989).

34. Ibid., esp. 159.

35. Altschuler and Blumin, *Rude Republic*, 134, cite the great number of racehorses depicted as proof of the insignificance of Currier & Ives' political production.

36. Harold Holzer and Mark E. Neely Jr., *The Lincoln Family Album* (New York: Doubleday, 1990), vii–viii, 41, 50.

37. For a most unusual artifact of women's involvement in public political ritual, see the woman's Wide-Awake parade uniform in John H. Rhodehamel and Thomas F. Schwartz, *The Last Best Hope of Earth: Abraham Lincoln and the Promise of America* (San Marino, Calif.: Huntington Library, 1993), 28. Wide-Awakes were generally young men's marching groups affiliated with the Republican Party in 1860. For other evidence of public participation in campaign ritual see, for example, Rebecca Edwards, *Angels in the Machinery: Gender in American Party Politics from the Civil War to the Progressive Era* (New York: Oxford University Press, 1997), 28.

38. Michael McGerr emphasizes the "typical feminine roles" played in the public realm in "Political Style and Women's Power, 1830–1930," *Journal of American History* 70 (December 1990): 867. See also Rebecca Edwards, *Angels in the Machinery*, 14–17, for an interpretation that mixes the idea of active participation with analysis of the implications for the idea of gender in the rhetoric and policies of the political parties.

39. Altschuler and Blumin, *Rude Republic*, 289 n.

40. Ibid., 7.

41. Daniel Walker Howe, "The Evangelical Movement and Political Culture in the North during the Second Party System," *Journal of American History* 77 (March 1991): 1216–39.

42. David D. Hall, *The Faithful Shepherd: A History of the New England Ministry in the Seventeenth Century* (Chapel Hill: University of North Carolina Press, 1972), 121–55.

43. Mark Voss-Hubbard, *Beyond Politics: Cultures of Antipartisanship in Northern Politics before the Civil War* (Baltimore: Johns Hopkins University Press, 2002), 92–93.

44. *Harrisburg Patriot and Union*, May 3, 1864.

45. *Harrisburg Telegraph*, March 2, 1864.

46. *Harrisburg Patriot and Union*, November 4, 1864.

47. *Harrisburg Telegraph*, November 2, 1864.

48. *Harrisburg Patriot and Union*, November 7, 1864.

49. See p. 10 of the sermon sent to President Lincoln at August 4, 1864, Abraham Lincoln Papers, Library of Congress, microfilm reel 78.

50. Resolutions, Protestant Episcopal Church, Diocese of Western New

York, annual convention, Utica, New York, at August 17, 1864, Abraham Lincoln Papers, Library of Congress, microfilm reel 79. The resolutions requested exemption of ministers from the draft with the possibility of assignment to duty serving as chaplains, performing hospital service, or aiding freedmen.

51. *New York Times*, October 23, 1864.

52. Abram Wakeman to Abraham Lincoln, September 3, 1864, Abraham Lincoln Papers, Library of Congress, microfilm reel 80. Wakeman vouched for Thompson's devotion to "the Union and the Administration" and said that the minister had been making speeches for Lincoln in Massachusetts. See also Henry J. Raymond to Lincoln, September 4, 1864, ibid.

53. Henry C. Bowen to William H. Seward, August 19, 1862 (asking to be collector of revenue for Brooklyn), Abraham Lincoln Papers, Library of Congress, microfilm reel 40; Bowen to Abraham Lincoln, August 21, 1862 ("never asked a favor before"), ibid.

54. Altschuler and Blumin, *Rude Republic*, 152–53.

55. On Anna Dickinson's and Frederick Douglass's speeches for the Republicans during the war see especially Melinda Lawson, *Patriot Fires: Forging a New American Nationalism in the Civil War North* (Lawrence: University Press of Kansas, 2002), esp. 141–56. On the strenuous efforts of African Americans to gain access to the American political system, see especially Michael Holt, review of *Rude Republic*, *Civil War History* 47 (June 2001): 164–67.

56. Samuel C. Damon to Charles Sumner, August 24, 1863, Papers of Charles Sumner, ed. by Beverly Wilson Palmer, Houghton Library, Harvard University, microfilm reel 29. Hereafter cited as Papers of Charles Sumner.

57. A. Kidder to Abraham Lincoln, January 6, 1864, Abraham Lincoln Papers, Library of Congress, microfilm reel 65.

58. Lewis Dodge to Abraham Lincoln, August 1, 1864, with endorsement by Henry Tanner, Abraham Lincoln Papers, Library of Congress, microfilm reel 78. For identification of Tanner, see letters of October 10, 1860, and October 19, 1863, in the same collection. For the use of Emancipation Proclamation facsimiles in 1864 in the way campaign portraits had been used in 1860, see Harold Holzer, *Lincoln Seen and Heard* (Lawrence: University Press of Kansas, 2000), esp. 12–14.

59. David Thomas Fuller to Charles Sumner, May 13, 1864, Papers of Charles Sumner, microfilm reel 31.

60. Harry S. Stout and Christopher Grasso, "Civil War, Religion, and Communications: The Case of Richmond," in *Religion and the American Civil War*, ed. Randall M. Miller, Harry S. Stout, and Charles Reagan Wilson (New York: Oxford University Press, 1998), esp. 316, 328–329.

61. Roy P. Basler, ed., *The Collected Works of Abraham Lincoln*, 9 vols. (New Brunswick, N.J.: Rutgers University Press, 1953–55), 2:389–90.

62. Anna C. Park to Charles Sumner, January 2, 1865, Papers of Charles Sumner, microfilm reel 32.

63. George C. Beckwith to Charles Sumner, March 2, 1865, Papers of Charles Sumner, microfilm reel 32.

64. Lydia Maria Child to Charles Sumner, January 12, 1865, Papers of Charles Sumner, microfilm reel 32.

CHAPTER TWO

1. *New York Evening Post*, August 11, 1864.

2. Glenn C. Altschuler and Stuart M. Blumin, *Rude Republic: Americans and Their Politics in the Nineteenth Century* (Princeton: Princeton University Press, 2000), 9–10.

3. Joel H. Silbey, *The American Political Nation, 1838–1893* (Stanford: Stanford University Press, 1991), 163. The ultimate basis was Angus Campbell, Philip E. Converse, Warren E. Miller, and Donald E. Stokes, *The American Voter* (Chicago: University of Chicago Press, 1960).

4. Harold Holzer, Gabor S. Boritt, and Mark E. Neely Jr., *The Lincoln Image: Abraham Lincoln and the Popular Print* (New York: Charles Scribner's Sons, 1984; Urbana: University of Illinois Press, 2001), 36. Rease did not have direct access to the candidates, who lived in Illinois and Maine, respectively, but instead relied on available photographs for portrait models. The one of Lincoln used for this handsome print was taken by Samuel M. Fassett in Chicago on October 4, 1859.

5. Bernard F. Reilly, *American Political Prints, 1776–1876: A Catalog of the Collections in the Library of Congress* (Boston: G. K. Hall, 1991), 427, 431–32.

6. The Cincinnati lithographers Middleton, Strobridge, & Company, sought such an endorsement from Lincoln in a letter written to him on June 20, 1860, Abraham Lincoln Papers, Library of Congress, microfilm reel 7. Along with a sample of their portrait print came the question, "If satisfactory please acknowledge by letter." If the candidate wrote a response, it was likely to appear in advertisements for the product later.

7. Altschuler and Blumin, *Rude Republic*, 79.

8. Michael F. Holt, "An Elusive Synthesis: Northern Politics during the Civil War," in *Writing the Civil War: The Quest to Understand*, ed. James M. McPherson and William J. Cooper Jr. (Columbia: University of South Carolina Press, 1998), 112–34; Jean H. Baker, *Affairs of Party: The Political Culture of Northern Democrats in the Mid-Nineteenth Century* (Ithaca: Cornell University Press, 1983; New York: Fordham University Press, 1998), 261–62.

9. Silbey, *The American Political Nation*, 9.

10. *Philadelphia Public Ledger*, November 4, 1864.

11. They are called ferrotypes and are discussed in Roger A. Fischer, *Tippecanoe and Trinkets Too: The Material Culture of American Presidential Campaigns, 1828–1984* (Urbana: University of Illinois Press, 1988), 71–73; and in the pioneering J. Doyle DeWitt, *A Century of Campaign Buttons, 1789–1889: A Descriptive List . . .* ([Hartford, Conn.]: privately pub., 1959), updated and revised by Edmund B. Sullivan as *American Political Badges and Medalets, 1789–1892* (Lawrence, Mass.: Quarterman Publications, 1981).

12. *Philadelphia Public Ledger*, October 27, 1864.

13. John Gault to Abraham Lincoln, June 18, 1864, Abraham Lincoln Papers, Library of Congress, microfilm reel 76. There is no endorsement on the back of the Gault letter indicating that action was taken on the proposal, and I have not been able to identify the campaign device by maker, if indeed it was ever actually produced.

14. Silbey, *The American Political Nation*, 247.

15. *Philadelphia Public Ledger*, October 4, 1864.

16. Josephine S. Griffing to Abraham Lincoln, September 24, 1864, Abraham Lincoln Papers, Library of Congress, microfilm reel 82.

17. Roy P. Basler, ed., *The Collected Works of Abraham Lincoln*, 9 vols. (New Brunswick, N.J.: Rutgers University Press, 1953–55), 8:3. Lincoln had been travelling from Washington himself, and it is not known who reported the results to him. Pennsylvania and Indiana, however, were regarded as crucial to Republican fortunes in 1864, and Lincoln was interested in the prognosis from those states. See Schuyler Colfax to Abraham Lincoln, July 25, 1864, Abraham Lincoln Papers, Library of Congress, microfilm reel 97.

18. William D. Kelley to Norman B. Judd, June 1, 1860, and Norman B. Judd to Abraham Lincoln, June 6, 1860, Abraham Lincoln Papers, Library of Congress, microfilm reel 7.

19. Judge John M. Read of Philadelphia commissioned a life portrait miniature for a campaign image and apparently paid for it himself. See John M. Read to Abraham Lincoln, September 3, 1860, Abraham Lincoln Papers, Library of Congress, microfilm reel 8; Holzer, Boritt, and Neely, *The Lincoln Image*, 57–66. Read owned a bust of Lincoln with which to compare the work of the miniature painter.

20. Ritchie never produced a picture for the 1860 campaign, but he did produce a Lincoln portrait for the 1864 campaign. See Derby & Miller to Abraham Lincoln, July 21, 1864, Abraham Lincoln Papers, Library of Congress, microfilm reel 77. See also George E. Perine to Abraham Lincoln, May 6, 1864, Abraham Lincoln Papers, Library of Congress, microfilm reel 73.

21. Rufus P. Stebbins to Charles Sumner, April 6, 1864, Papers of Charles Sumner, ed. by Beverly Wilson Palmer, Houghton Library, Harvard University, microfilm reel 30.

22. Gary L. Bunker, *From Rail-Splitter to Icon: Lincoln's Image in Illustrated Periodicals, 1860–1865* (Kent, Ohio: Kent State University Press, 2001), 259–60.

23. For reference to seeing political cartoons on Lincoln's Emancipation Proclamation in London print shop windows, see Henry P. Tappan to Abraham Lincoln, November 22, 1862, Abraham Lincoln Papers, Library of Congress, microfilm reel 44. Tappan had apparently seen "Abe Lincoln's Last Card; or, Rouge-et-Noir" from London *Punch* (Fig. 2.4).

24. *Dubuque Herald*, October 18, 1864.

25. The *Dubuque Herald* commended Bromley's publications for the local McClellan Clubs in its issue of October 7, 1864. See also Harold Holzer, *Lincoln Seen and Heard* (Lawrence: University Press of Kansas, 2000), 122–23.

26. Mark E. Neely Jr. and Harold Holzer, *The Union Image: Popular Prints of the Civil War North* (Chapel Hill: University of North Carolina Press, 2000), 26.

27. Frank Weitenkampf, *A Century of American Political Cartoons* (New York: Charles Scribner's Sons, 1944), 58–59.

28. For a discussion of Frelinghuysen's selection as vice presidential running mate "to offset Clay's supposed weakness on the 'character' issue" see Michael F. Holt, *The Rise and Fall of the American Whig Party: Jacksonian Politics and the Onset of the Civil War* (New York: Oxford University Press, 1999), 188–89.

29. Reilly, *American Political Prints*, 408–9.

30. Ibid., 408.

31. Ibid., 443.

32. Ibid., 436.

33. Altschuler and Blumin, *Rude Republic*, 206.

34. For examples see Neely and Holzer, *The Union Image*, 146–47.

35. Actually, the relationship between business and political party was more complicated even in the notoriously corrupt Gilded Age. See Mark Wahlgren Summers, *Party Games: Getting, Keeping, and Using Power in Gilded Age Politics* (Chapel Hill: University of North Carolina Press, 2004), esp. 141–48. Robert B. Putnam, *Bowling Alone: The Collapse and Revival of American Community* (New York: Simon & Schuster, 2000), esp. 40, depicts modern parties as Altschuler and Blumin describe the nineteenth century. Putnam says, "The contrast between increasing party organizational vitality and declining voter involvement is perfectly intelligible. Since their 'consumers' are tuning out from politics, parties have to work harder and spend much more, compet-

ing furiously to woo votes, workers, and donations, and to do that they need a (paid) organizational infrastructure."

36. For an article based on one set of documents about funding—these for the 1868 presidential campaign—see Paula Baker, "Campaigns and Potato Chips; or, Some Causes and Consequences of Political Spending," *Journal of Policy History* 14 (Winter 2002). Another example can be found in James A. Rawley, "Financing the Fremont Campaign," *Pennsylvania Magazine of History and Biography* 75 (January 1951). Naturally, the papers of national party chairmen or state central committee chairmen contain a disproportionate number of letters about funding. As examples I will use further on in this chapter the letters of Norman Buel Judd, chairman of the state central committee, for the famous Lincoln-Douglas senate campaign of 1858 in Illinois (located in the Abraham Lincoln Papers).

37. Norman B. Judd to Abraham Lincoln, November 15, 1858, Abraham Lincoln Papers, Library of Congress, microfilm reel 4.

38. Abraham Lincoln to Norman B. Judd, November 16, 1858, in Basler, *Collected Works of Lincoln*, 3:337.

39. Lyman Trumbull to Abraham Lincoln, July 9, 1858, Abraham Lincoln Papers, Library of Congress, microfilm reel 3.

40. Document at August 26, 1864, Abraham Lincoln Papers, Library of Congress, microfilm reel 80. Mark Wahlgren Summers, writing about the Gilded Age, when corruption was a more serious issue, nevertheless acknowledges the importance of funding by candidates and office-holders. See *Party Games*, esp. 148–54.

41. The Union League Club of Philadelphia boasted that it raised $150,000 for Governor Andrew G. Curtin's reelection campaign in 1863, which proved more than enough, and some was returned to the League's publication fund. See *Chronicle of the Union League Club of Philadelphia, 1862–1902* (Philadelphia: Union League, 1902), 79–80.

42. Mark Wahlgren Summers comments on "shoestring campaigns" of the era after Civil War and Reconstruction in "'To Make the Wheels Revolve We Must Have Grease': Barrel Politics in the Gilded Age," *Journal of Policy History* 14 (Winter 2002): 49–72.

43. *Philadelphia Public Ledger*, September 6, 1860. When the citizen refused the request for money to purchase a flag, professing an "absolute distaste for politics," the fund-raiser then asked him to stand him a drink.

44. Ibid., September 10, 1860. The *Public Ledger* appears to have been independent in politics and affected a disdain for political organization and spectacle.

45. Ibid., September 4, 1860.

46. Joshua R. Giddings to Abraham Lincoln, October 15, 1860, Abraham Lincoln Papers, Library of Congress, microfilm reel 9.

47. James E. Harvey to Abraham Lincoln, October 4, 1860, Abraham Lincoln Papers, Library of Congress, microfilm reel 9.

48. Henry Winter Davis to David Davis, September 1860, Abraham Lincoln Papers, Library of Congress, microfilm reel 9.

49. The question of the expense entailed in corruption—particularly buying votes—arises in recent literature stressing the corruption of the ballot box in the middle of the nineteenth century. See Richard Franklin Bensel, *The American Ballot Box in the Mid-Nineteenth Century* (Cambridge: Cambridge University Press, 2004), and, for a later period, Summers, *Party Games*. The weakness of the new emphasis on corruption and money in politics lies in the difficulty of separating allegations raised by party, often as explanations of electoral defeat by the other party, from firm proof that such practices were systemic.

50. Michael Schudson, *The Good Citizen: A History of American Civic Life* (New York: Free Press, 1998); Bernard Bailyn, *The Ideological Origins of the American Revolution* (Cambridge: Harvard University Press, 1967).

51. Summers, "'To Make the Wheels Revolve,'" 55; Schudson, *The Good Citizen*, esp. 121.

52. Robert S. Harper, *Lincoln and the Press* (New York: McGraw-Hill, 1951), 76–77. Canisius's paper failed, and obviously a longer-sustained effort might have required more capital. Likewise, the great and influential dailies in the metropolises required very considerable investments. See George T. McJimsey, *Genteel Partisan: Manton Marble, 1834–1917* (Ames: Iowa State University Press, 1971) esp. 37–39.

53. Baker, *Affairs of Party*, 261.

54. Ibid., 262.

55. Basler, *Collected Works of Lincoln*, 8:150.

56. *New York Tribune*, December 29, 1864, and January 6, 1865.

57. For controversy over the accuracy of the reigning estimates of national voter turnout see Gerald Ginsberg, "Computing Antebellum Turnout: Methods and Models," *Journal of Interdisciplinary History* 16 (Spring 1986): 579–611; and Walter Dean Burnham, "Those High Nineteenth-Century American Voting Turnouts: Fact or Fiction?" *Journal of Interdisciplinary History* 16 (Spring 1986): 613–44. The differences between the nineteenth and twentieth centuries seem solidly proven by Burnham, but his analysis inevitably glosses over differences from presidential election to presidential election within the nineteenth century.

CHAPTER THREE

1. *New York Herald*, April 7, 1864.

2. Ibid., April 8, 1864.

3. Ibid., April 9, 1864.

4. Ibid., April 11, 1864.

5. Ibid., April 23, 1864.

6. Works associating the Union League Clubs with reactionary authoritarian doctrines unfamiliar in republican America include George M. Fredrickson, *The Inner Civil War: Northern Intellectuals and the Crisis of the Union* (New York: Harper & Row, 1965), 131–35; Iver Bernstein, *The New York City Draft Riots: Their Significance for American Society and Politics in the Age of the Civil War* (New York: Oxford University Press, 1990), esp. 156–57; and Melinda Lawson, *Patriot Fires: Forging a New American Nationalism in the Civil War North* (Lawrence: University Press of Kansas, 2002), chap. 4.

7. I had opportunity to examine the broadsides while I was the R. Stanton Avery Fellow at the Huntington Library in 1997–98. I remain grateful for the Huntington Library's support of my research that year.

8. Henry M. Phillips to S. L. M. Barlow, October 16 and September 16, 1864, S. L. M. Barlow Papers, Huntington Library, San Marino, California, box 53.

9. William D. Kelley to Abraham Lincoln, October 27, 1864, Abraham Lincoln Papers, Library of Congress, microfilm reel 85.

10. The Republican vote for president in 1864 in Pennsylvania was 296,389.

11. George Parsons Lathrop, *History of the Union League of Philadelphia, from Its Origin and Foundation to the Year 1882* (Philadelphia: J. B. Lippincott, 1884), 69. I first encountered a reproduction of the photograph of political posters outside the Union League clubhouse in Philadelphia in Bradley R. Hoch, *The Lincoln Trail in Pennsylvania: A History and Guide* (University Park: Pennsylvania State University Press, 2001), 117.

12. On the conservatism of the Union League Clubs see, in addition to the works cited in note 6, Frank Freidel, ed., *Union Pamphlets of the Civil War, 1861–1865*, 2 vols. (Cambridge: Harvard University Press, 1967), 1:1–24.

13. Lawson, *Patriot Fires*, 113, 114. The New York club receives only incidental mention in surveys of New York Civil War history, such as Edward K. Spann, *Gotham at War: New York City, 1860–1865* (Wilmington, Del.: Scholarly Resources, 2002), 90, where he characterizes the group's aspiration to stand as an aristocratic "power above the reach of Democratic politics" but admits to their constituting "an effective lobby of talented supporters of the war and, with that, also of emancipation and black rights." See also Ernest A. McKay,

The Civil War and New York City (Syracuse, N.Y.: Syracuse University Press, 1990).

14. Bernstein, *New York City Draft Riots*, 125.

15. Ibid., 129–31. The argument follows the familiar outlines of the standard interpretation of Northern intellectual life in the Civil War, George M. Fredrickson's *The Inner Civil War: Northern Intellectuals and the Crisis of the Union*. Fredrickson argues that the war represented a triumph of conservatism among American intellectuals. He depicts a displaced old elite capitalizing on the crisis of the Union to invoke a conservative nationalism at odds with the liberal traditions of the Declaration of Independence and antebellum individualism. Bernstein refers directly to Fredrickson on p. 157.

16. I follow Lawson's *Patriot Fires* in treating the three metropolitan clubs apart from the broader league movement.

17. I used standard sources such as Allen Johnson et al., eds., *Dictionary of American Biography*, 11 vols. (New York: Scribner, 1946–58); and James Grant Wilson and John Fiske, eds., *Appleton's Cyclopaedia of American Biography*, 7 vols. (1888; Detroit: Gale Research, 1968); as well as these histories of New York City: McKay, *Civil War and New York City*; Spann, *Gotham at War*; and Edwin G. Burrows and Mike Wallace, *Gotham: A History of New York City to 1898* (New York: Oxford University Press, 1999). Also useful was Allan Nevins and Milton Halsey Thomas, eds., *The Diary of George Templeton Strong*, 4 vols. (New York: Macmillan, 1952).

18. Lathrop, *History of the Union League*, 34.

19. Ibid., 75.

20. Thomas Webster to Abraham Lincoln, October 28, 1864, and October 27, 1864, Abraham Lincoln Papers, Library of Congress, microfilm reel 85.

21. Nevins and Thomas, *Diary of George Templeton Strong*, 3:292–93.

22. Ibid., 3:299.

23. Bernstein, *New York City Draft Riots*, 129–30.

24. Nevins and Thomas, *Diary of George Templeton Strong*, 3:303.

25. Number = 87. New England birth = 37, other birth = 41, unknown = 9. But of the New Yorkers and others in the club, at least six came of New England stock. New England heritage = 43, other = 35, unknown = 9.

26. *Cong. Globe*, 37 Cong, 3rd sess., December 15, 1862, 90.

27. Samuel Sullivan Cox, *Eight Years in Congress, from 1857–1865. Memoir and Speeches* (New York: D. Appleton, 1865), 283.

28. Ibid., 285.

29. Ibid., 286.

30. Ibid., 288. Cox may well not have known, but the riots appear to have

been led by elites alarmed by denunciations of the racism of the colonization movement. See Leonard L. Richards, *"Gentlemen of Property and Standing": Anti-Abolition Mobs in Jacksonian America* (New York: Oxford University Press, 1970).

31. Cox, *Eight Years in Congress*, 288.

32. *Cong. Globe*, 37 Cong, 3rd sess., January 14, 1863, pt. 2, Appendix, 52–60.

33. Ibid., 56–57.

34. Frank L. Klement saw the origins of Granger-like opposition to railroads in the Copperheads' complaints. See his article "Middle Western Copperheadism and the Genesis of the Granger Movement," *Mississippi Valley Historical Review* 38 (March 1952). For a more recent interpretation stressing the economic differences between Republicans and Democrats in the Old Northwest, see Marc Egnal, "The Beards Were Right: Parties in the North, 1840–1860," *Civil War History* 47 (March 2001).

35. Joel H. Silbey, *A Respectable Minority: The Democratic Party in the Civil War Era, 1860–1868* (New York: W. W. Norton, 1977), 74–77.

36. Jan C. Dawson, *The Unusable Past: America's Puritan Tradition, 1830–1930* (Chico, Calif.: Scholars Press, 1984), 77–78.

37. Joseph A. Conforti, *Imagining New England: Explorations of Regional Identity from the Pilgrims to the Mid-Twentieth Century* (Chapel Hill: University of North Carolina Press, 2001), 206. "The war," Conforti says on p. 195, "encouraged the moral rearmament of Pilgrim-Puritan history—the forefathers' crusading spirit now consonant with the righteousness of the Union cause. The war also marked the 'national' triumph of the Pilgrim-Puritan narrative of American origins, just as it advanced the victory of the Yankee identity and of the white village as an iconic republican landscape. In 1863 President Abraham Lincoln declared Thanksgiving a national holiday."

38. Nevins and Thomas, *Diary of George Templeton Strong*, 3:288.

39. Ibid., 3:292–93. Strong was a staunch Episcopalian himself and considered "Puritanism . . . unlovely" (153). For the views of another skeptical Episcopalian scornful of New England's claims to relevant political heritage see Salmon P. Chase to Janet Chase Hoyt, December 24, 1866, Salmon P. Chase Papers, ed. by John Niven, Claremont Graduate School and NHPRC, microfilm reel 36.

40. See, for example, *New York Tribune*, January 14, 15, 16, and 17, 1863; and *New York Times*, January 15, 17, and 20, 1863.

41. "The Constitution, Peace, Reunion," *Cong. Globe*, 37 Cong., 3rd sess., January 14, 1863, pt. 2, Appendix, 52–60.

42. *New York Times*, January 15, 1863.

43. Frank L. Klement, *The Copperheads in the Middle West* (Chicago: University of Chicago Press, 1960), 93–94.

44. Sarah Josepha Hale to Abraham Lincoln, September 28, 1863, with enclosures, Abraham Lincoln Papers, Library of Congress, microfilm reel 59. See also p. 81 of *Godey's* July 1859 issue (part of her enclosures to Lincoln); Roy P. Basler, ed., *The Collected Works of Abraham Lincoln*, 9 vols. (New Brunswick, N.J.: Rutgers University Press, 1953–55), 6:496–97.

45. Charles Sumner to Elliott C. Cowden, December 21, 1863, Papers of Charles Sumner, ed. by Beverly Wilson Palmer, Houghton Library, Harvard University, microfilm reel 77. Hereafter cited as Papers of Charles Sumner.

46. Henry W. Bellows, *Historical Sketch of the Union League Club of New York, Its Origin, Organization, and Work, 1863–1879* (New York: G. P. Putnam's Sons, 1879), 69–70.

47. Francis Wayland Jr., "No Failure for the North," *Atlantic Monthly* 11 (April 1863): 504. Cox apparently retained his New England reading habits and noticed Wayland's intemperate reply. See Cox, *Eight Years in Congress*, 281–82.

48. Freidel, *Union Pamphlets of the Civil War*, 1:8–9.

49. Ibid., 2:611.

50. Maxwell Whiteman, *Gentlemen in Crisis: The First Century of the Union League of Philadelphia, 1862–1962* (Philadelphia: Union League of Philadelphia, 1975), 79, 315 n.

51. Bellows, *Historical Sketch*, 67.

52. Whiteman, *Gentlemen in Crisis*, 315 n.

53. Bernstein, *New York City Draft Riots*, 160; Lawson, *Patriot Fires*, 112.

54. Francis Lieber to Charles Sumner, June 8, 1863, and Henry Wadsworth Longfellow to Charles Sumner, June 2, 1863, Papers of Charles Sumner, microfilm reel 77.

55. *Chronicle of the Union League of Philadelphia, 1862–1902* (Philadelphia: 1902), 110–11.

56. McKay, *Civil War and New York City*, 240.

57. *New York Herald*, January 7, 1865. See John P. Dyer, "Northern Relief for Savannah during Sherman's Occupation," *Journal of Southern History* 19 (November 1953): 461–62.

58. *New York Herald*, January 7, 1865.

59. *New York Tribune*, January 26, 1865.

60. See, for evidence of this, Elihu B. Washburne to Abraham Lincoln, September 5 and 11, 1860, Abraham Lincoln Papers, Library of Congress, microfilm reel 8.

61. On campaign finances before reform see James A. Rawley, "Financing the Fremont Campaign," *Pennsylvania Magazine of History and Biography* 75

(January 1951); Paula Baker, "Campaigns and Potato Chips; or, Some Causes and Consequences of Political Spending," *Journal of Policy History* 14 (Winter 2002); Mark Wahlgren Summers, "'To Make the Wheels Revolve We Must Have Grease': Barrel Politics in the Gilded Age," *Journal of Policy History* 14 (Winter 2002).

62. An eleven-year-old girl wrote to suggest he grow a beard during the campaign. Once Lincoln assumed the mantle of the presidency and head of state, then many women wrote him.

CHAPTER FOUR

1. Louis Zwisher to Abraham Lincoln, June 29, 1860, Abraham Lincoln Papers, Library of Congress, microfilm reel 7.

2. Jean H. Baker, *Affairs of Party: The Political Culture of Northern Democrats in the Mid-Nineteenth Century* (Ithaca: Cornell University Press, 1983; New York: Fordham University Press, 1998), chap. 12 (a nearly fifty-page chapter).

3. Alexander Saxton, "Blackface Minstrelsy and Jacksonian Ideology," *American Quarterly* 27 (March 1975).

4. Robert P. Nevin, "Stephen C. Foster and Negro Minstrelsy," *Atlantic Monthly* 20 (November 1867): 612.

5. See, for example, W. T. Lhamon Jr., *Raising Cain: Blackface Performance from Jim Crow to Hip Hop* (Cambridge: Harvard University Press, 1998).

6. Baker, *Affairs of Party*, 212–13.

7. Ibid., 249 and following.

8. Richard J. Carwardine, *Evangelicals and Politics in Antebellum America* (New Haven: Yale University Press, 1993), ix.

9. Ibid., 53.

10. Ibid., 453.

11. Nevin, "Stephen C. Foster and Negro Minstrelsy," 613.

12. On the controversial origins of the genre see Lhamon, *Raising Cain*, 31, 57, and elsewhere.

13. Carwardine, *Evangelicals and Politics*, 453.

14. *National Clay Minstrel, and Frelinghuysen Melodist* (Philadelphia: George Hood, [1844]), 1, 43–44.

15. The version of the songster published in 1843, *The National Clay Minstrel, and True Whig's Pocket Companion, for the Presidential Canvass of 1844* (Philadelphia: George Hood, [1843]) included not only Brownlow's dialect song but also "De Possum's Tree" and "Honest Farmer Harry," which contained dialect. The reference to "patriotic songs" appears in the preface to this edition, which answered Democratic criticism of the Whigs' extensive use of song and other spectacle in the 1840 canvass.

16. *The Clay Minstrel; or, National Songster* (New York: Greeley & M'Elrath and Philadelphia: Thomas, Cowperthwait, 1844). I examined historian J. Watts DePeyster's copy from the Franklin and Marshall College Library.

17. *The Clay Minstrel: or, National Songster*, 126–27.

18. Ibid., 3.

19. *The Young Hickory and Annexation Minstrel; or, Polk and Dallas Melodist* (Philadelphia: J. M. David, 1844), 7. "Miscegenation" was coined in the presidential campaign of 1864; twenty years earlier, the term used was "amalgamation."

20. George W. Clark, *The Liberty Minstrel* (New York: Leavitt & Alden, 1845), 95. This appears to be the commonest surviving political songster with "minstrel" in the title.

21. Ibid., iii.

22. I examined three closely related songsters at the Abraham Lincoln Presidential Library and Museum in Springfield: George W. Bungay, ed., *The Bobolink Minstrel; or, Republican Songster for 1860* (New York: O. Hutchinson, 1860) ("Poor Little Doug" appears on p. 41); John W. Hutchinson, ed., *Hutchinson's Republican Songster, for the Campaign of 1860* (New York: O. Hutchinson, 1860); and John W. Hutchinson, ed., *Connecticut Wide-Awake Songster* (New Haven: Skinner & Sperry, 1860).

23. Lhamon, *Raising Cain*, 4.

24. Neil Harris, *Humbug: The Art of P. T. Barnum* (Boston: Little, Brown, 1973), 98, 108, 167; Edwin G. Burrows and Mike Wallace, *Gotham: A History of New York City to 1898* (New York: Oxford University Press, 1999), 643–45.

25. See Harold Holzer, Gabor S. Boritt, and Mark E. Neely, Jr., *The Lincoln Image: Abraham Lincoln and the Popular Print* (New York: Charles Scribner's Sons, 1984; Urbana: University of Illinois Press, 2001), 3–39; the "What Is It?" man image is reproduced as a detail from the cartoon in the chapter on minstrelsy and Democratic political culture in Baker, *Affairs of Party*, 236.

26. *Frank Leslie's Illustrated Newspaper*, December 15, 1860, ran a column praising the "Living Curiosities at Barnum's" as a worthy sight to see (Barnum's Museum was a regular advertiser in the newspaper) and featuring a woodcut illustration with the "What Is It?" man's image and others from the show. Currier & Ives made two lithographs of unknown date featuring the "What Is It?" man (besides the cartoon). They are illustrated in James W. Cook, *The Arts of Deception: Playing with Fraud in the Age of Barnum* (Cambridge: Harvard University Press, 2001), 123 and 157. Cook gets the facts straight on the "What Is It?" man and corrects many errors of fact and interpretation (see his chap. 3).

27. Lex Renda, "'A White Man's State in New England': Race, Party, and

Suffrage in Civil War Connecticut," in *An Uncommon Time: The Civil War and the Northern Home Front*, ed. Paul A. Cimbala and Randall M. Miller (New York: Fordham University Press, 2002), 242.

28. Robert Gray Gunderson, *The Log-Cabin Campaign* (Lexington: University of Kentucky Press, 1957), esp. 123–26.

29. *Chicago Tribune*, January 4, 1856.

30. *Boston Commonwealth*, December 11, 1863, and January 29, 1864. The paper commended the Buckleys again in the issue of January 29, 1864. The *Boston Daily Advertiser* celebrated the reopening of Buckley's Minstrel Hall in their September 24, 1864, issue. On "Sally Come Up" see Memorial Hall Museum On Line, Deerfield, Mass., Pocumtuck Valley Memorial Association, <http://www.memorialhall.mass.edu/collection/itempage.jsp?itemid= 15499&img=0> (December 4, 2004).

31. Nevin, "Stephen C. Foster and Negro Minstrelsy," 616.

32. Earl Schenck Miers, ed., *Lincoln Day-by-Day: A Chronology, 1809–1865*, 3 vols. (1961; facsimile ed., Dayton, Ohio: Morningside, 1991), 1:299 (January 6, 1848); 3:170–1 (February 24, 1863). My thanks to Phillip S. Paludan for suggesting that I check this source for Lincoln's attendance.

33. Ibid., 3:18 (February 20, 1861). I first saw the cartoon depicting the Lincoln visit to New York in Gary L. Bunker, *From Rail-Splitter to Icon: Lincoln's Image in Illustrated Periodicals, 1860–1865* (Kent, Ohio: Kent State University Press, 2001), 88–89.

34. Baker, *Affairs of Party*, 213.

35. *Chicago Tribune*, November 14, 1853.

36. Ibid., December 21, 1853.

37. My search has not been exhaustive, but it included the *Chicago Tribune*, *New York Herald*, *Chicago Times*, *Harrisburg Telegraph*, *Harrisburg Patriot and Union*, *Philadelphia Inquirer*, *New York Tribune*, and *Boston Commonwealth*.

38. *New York Tribune*, January 17, 1854.

39. *Philadelphia Inquirer*, February 20, 1862.

40. *New York Tribune*, April 22, 1854.

41. See Thomas F. Gossett, *Uncle Tom's Cabin and American Culture* (Dallas: Southern Methodist University Press, 1985), esp. chap. 14.

42. *Chicago Tribune*, January 5, 1854.

43. Ibid., January 9, 1854.

44. *Philadelphia Inquirer*, March 14, 1862.

45. *Chicago Tribune*, June 19, 1854.

46. *Philadelphia Inquirer*, February 5, 1862. The *Inquirer* was, in fact, a Republican paper.

47. *Chicago Times*, February 24, 1864.

48. *New York Times*, February 13, 1854.

49. *New York Evening Express*, October 13, 1864.

50. Ibid., November 4, 1864.

51. *Chicago Tribune*, January 18, 1854.

52. E. Byron Christy and William E. Christy, eds., *Christy's New Songster and Black Joker . . .* (New York: Dick & Fitzgerald, [1863]). For a facsimile of the sheet music see *Better Times Are Coming* at <http://www.stephen-foster-songs.de/Foster03.htm> (8/13/2004).

53. *Bob Hart's Plantation Songster* (New York: Dick & Fitzgerald, 1862), esp. 5, 11, 17.

54. Ibid.

55. On "shoddy" see Frank Converse, *Frank Converse's "Old Cremona" Songster . . .* (New York: Dick & Fitzgerald, [1862]), esp. 15 and 45; and *Christy's Bones and Banjo Medallist* (New York: Dick & Fitzgerald, [1865?]), esp. 58 (on the "swindlers" in Washington).

56. For a more traditionally racist message for a song with words by George Cooper and music by Stephen Foster see *A Soldier in de Colored Brigade*, published by Firth in New York in 1863, sheet music facsimile at <http://www.stephen-foster-songs.de/Foster141.htm> (8/13/2004).

57. Alexander Saxton argued that "Minstrelsy in 1864 mounted an extensive campaign for McClellan." Saxton, "Blackface Minstrelsy and Jacksonian Ideology," 21. By contrast, in a chapter called "Minstrels Fight the Civil War," Robert C. Toll contended that the war "completely dominated the minstrel show" from 1861 to 1865 and that the war's length and severity gave the shows a more "somber" tone after 1863. Moreover, emancipation and the use of African American troops even "forced [them] to reconsider" their "position on blacks." Toll, *Blacking Up: The Minstrel Show in Nineteenth-Century America* (New York: Oxford University Press, 1974), 104–33. Toll is right about their earnest patriotism but exaggerates the ideological transformation.

58. See Michael J. Bennett, *Union Jacks: Yankee Sailors in the Civil War* (Chapel Hill: University of North Carolina Press, 2004), 174.

59. A reporter in Harrisburg noted that war had been good for the city, with "hundreds" of soldiers landed daily by the railroads there; they "thronged her public places." *Philadelphia Inquirer*, October 23, 1862.

60. *Harrisburg Telegraph*, March 2, 1864.

61. Ibid., April 12, 1864.

62. Ibid., May 5, 1864.

63. J. Matthew Gallman (*Mastering Wartime: A Social History of Philadelphia during the Civil War* [Philadelphia: University of Pennsylvania Press, 1990],

340) concluded that Philadelphians in wartime "did not change how" they "responded to pressing needs." The people met war's "challenges without major changes."

64. *Copperhead Minstrel: Choice Collection of Democratic Poems and Songs, for the Use of Political Clubs and the Social Circle* (New York: Feek & Bancker, 1863). An edition, with the article *"A"* inserted before *"Choice"* appeared in 1864, published in New York by Bromley, and the racist Van Evrie, Horton Press published another edition in 1867. The contents vary. I examined copies at the Division of Rare and Manuscript Collections, Carl A. Kroch Library, Cornell University Library, Ithaca, New York.

65. T. Michael Parrish and Robert M. Willingham Jr., *Confederate Imprints: A Bibliography of Southern Publications from Secession to Surrender* (Austin, Tex.: Jenkins Publishing, n.d., and Katonah, N.Y.: Gary A. Foster, n.d.), 568–69 (item no. 6728). For the "Dixie" cartoon, see Bunker, *From Rail-Splitter to Icon*, 214.

66. John W. Blassingame, ed., vol. 3 of *The Frederick Douglass Papers. Series One: Speeches, Debates, and Interviews, 1855–63* (New Haven: Yale University Press, 1985), 48.

67. Ibid., 3:336.

Selected Bibliography

MANUSCRIPT SOURCES

Salmon P. Chase Papers. Edited by John Niven. Claremont Graduate School and NHPRC, 1987. Microfilm edition.

Abraham Lincoln Papers, Library of Congress. Microfilm edition.

Papers of Charles Sumner. Edited by Beverly Wilson Palmer. Houghton Library, Harvard University, 1988. Microfilm edition.

NEWSPAPERS

Boston Commonwealth

Boston Daily Advertiser

Chicago Times

Chicago Tribune

Dubuque (Iowa) Herald

Harrisburg (Pa.) Patriot and Union

Harrisburg (Pa.) Telegraph

New York Evening Express

New York Evening Post

New York Herald

New York Times

New York Tribune

Philadelphia Inquirer

Philadelphia Public Ledger

Springfield (Ill.) Extra Journal

OTHER ORIGINAL SOURCES

Basler, Roy P., ed. *The Collected Works of Abraham Lincoln.* 9 vols. New Brunswick, N.J.: Rutgers University Press, 1953–55.

Bellows, Henry W. *Historical Sketch of the Union League Club of New York, Its Origin, Organization, and Work, 1863–1879.* New York: G. P. Putnam's Sons, 1879.

Blassingame, John W., ed. Vol. 3 of *The Frederick Douglass Papers. Series One: Speeches, Debates, and Interviews, 1855–63.* New Haven: Yale University Press, 1985.

Bungay, George Washington, ed. *Bobolink Minstrel: or, Republican Songster, for 1860.* New York: O. Hutchinson, 1860.

Clark, George W. *The Liberty Minstrel.* New York: Leavitt & Alden, 1845.

The Clay Minstrel; or, National Songster. New York: Greeley & M'Elrath and Philadelphia: Thomas, Cowperthwait, 1844.

Copperhead Minstrel: Choice Collection of Democratic Poems and Songs, for the Use of Political Clubs and the Social Circle. New York: Feek & Bancker, 1863.

Cox, Samuel Sullivan. *Eight Years in Congress, from 1857–1865. Memoir and Speeches*. New York: D. Appleton, 1865.

Foner, Philip S., and Yuval Taylor, eds. *Frederick Douglass: Selected Speeches and Writings*. Chicago: Lawrence Hill Books, 1999.

Freidel, Frank, ed. *Union Pamphlets of the Civil War, 1861–1865*. 2 vols. Cambridge: Harvard University Press, 1967.

Hutchinson, John W., ed. *Hutchinson's Republican Songster for the Campaign of 1860*. New York: O. Hutchinson, 1860.

Kennedy, Joseph C. G. *Population of the United States in 1860; Compiled from the Original Returns of the Eighth Census. . . .* 4 vols. Washington, D.C.: Government Printing Office, 1864.

———. *Preliminary Report on the Eighth Census. 1860*. Washington, D.C.: Government Printing Office, 1862.

National Clay Minstrel, and Frelinghuysen Melodist. Philadelphia: George Hood, [1844].

The National Clay Minstrel, and True Whig's Pocket Companion, for the Presidential Canvass of 1844. Philadelphia: George Hood, [1843].

Neely, Mark E., Jr., ed. *The Extra Journal: Rallying the Whigs of Illinois*. Fort Wayne, Ind.: Louis A. Warren Lincoln Library and Museum, 1982.

Nevin, Robert P. "Stephen C. Foster and Negro Minstrelsy." *Atlantic Monthly* 20 (November 1867): 608–16.

Nevins, Allan, and Milton Halsey Thomas, eds. *The Diary of George Templeton Strong*. 4 vols. New York: Macmillan, 1952.

Wayland, Francis, Jr. "No Failure for the North." *Atlantic Monthly* 11 (April 1863): 500–14.

The Young Hickory and Annexation Minstrel; or, Polk and Dallas Melodist. Philadelphia: J. M. David, 1844.

WORKS ON POLITICS AND POLITICAL CULTURE

Altschuler, Glenn C., and Stuart M. Blumin. *Rude Republic: Americans and Their Politics in the Nineteenth Century*. Princeton: Princeton University Press, 2000.

Baker, Jean H. *Affairs of Party: The Political Culture of Northern Democrats in the Mid-Nineteenth Century*. Ithaca: Cornell University Press, 1983; New York: Fordham University Press, 1998.

Baker, Paula. "Campaigns and Potato Chips; or, Some Causes and Consequences of Political Spending." *Journal of Policy History* 14 (Winter 2002): 4–18.

Bensel, Richard Franklin. *The American Ballot Box in the Mid-Nineteenth Century*. Cambridge: Cambridge University Press, 2004.

Bernstein, Iver. *The New York City Draft Riots: Their Significance for American Society and Politics in the Age of the Civil War*. New York: Oxford University Press, 1990.

Burnham, Walter Dean. "Those High Nineteenth-Century American Voting Turnouts: Fact or Fiction?" *Journal of Interdisciplinary History* 16 (Spring 1986): 613–44.

Edwards, Rebecca. *Angels in the Machinery: Gender in American Party Politics from the Civil War to the Progressive Era*. New York: Oxford University Press, 1997.

Ethington, Philip J. Review of *Rude Republic*, by Glenn C. Altschuler and Stuart M. Blumin. *Journal of American History* 88 (September 2001): 644–45.

Formisano, Ronald P. "Deferential-Participant Politics: The Early Republic's Political Culture, 1789–1840." *American Political Science Review* 68 (1974): 473–87.

Freeman, Joanne B. *Affairs of Honor: National Politics in the New Republic*. New Haven: Yale University Press, 2001.

Gienapp, William E. " 'Politics Seem to Enter into Everything': Political Culture in the North, 1840–1860." In *Essays in Antebellum American Politics, 1840–1860*, edited by Stephen E. Maizlish and John J. Kushma, 15–69. College Station: Texas A & M University Press, 1982.

Ginsberg, Gerald. "Computing Antebellum Turnout: Methods and Models." *Journal of Interdisciplinary History* 16 (Spring 1986): 579–611.

Holt, Michael F. "An Elusive Synthesis: Northern Politics during the Civil War." In *Writing the Civil War: The Quest to Understand*, edited by James M. McPherson and William J. Cooper Jr., 112–34. Columbia: University of South Carolina Press, 1998.

———. Review of *Rude Republic*, by Glenn C. Altschuler and Stuart M. Blumin. *Civil War History* 47 (June 2001): 164–67.

Howe, Daniel Walker. "The Evangelical Movement and Political Culture in the North during the Second Party System." *Journal of American History* 77 (March 1991): 1216–39.

Jensen, Richard. "Armies, Admen and Crusaders: Types of Presidential Election Campaigns." *History Teacher* 2 (January 1969), 33–50.

McCormick, Richard P. *The Second American Party System: Party Formation in the Jacksonian Era*. Chapel Hill: University of North Carolina Press, 1966.

McGerr, Michael E. *The Decline of Popular Politics: The American North, 1865–1928*. New York: Oxford University Press, 1986.

———. "Political Style and Women's Power, 1830–1930." *Journal of American History* 70 (December 1990): 864–85.

Rawley, James A. "Financing the Fremont Campaign." *Pennsylvania Magazine of History and Biography* 75 (January 1951): 25–35.

Schudson, Michael. *The Good Citizen: A History of American Civic Life*. New York: Free Press, 1998.

Silbey, Joel H. *The American Political Nation, 1838–1893*. Stanford: Stanford University Press, 1991.

———. *A Respectable Minority: The Democratic Party in the Civil War Era, 1860–1868*. New York: W. W. Norton, 1977.

Stout, Harry S., and Christopher Grasso. "Civil War, Religion, and Communications: The Case of Richmond." In *Religion and the American Civil War*, edited by Randall M. Miller, Harry S. Stout, and Charles Reagan Wilson, 313–59. New York: Oxford University Press, 1998.

Summers, Mark Wahlgren. *Party Games: Getting, Keeping, and Using Power in Gilded Age Politics*. Chapel Hill: University of North Carolina Press, 2004.

———. " 'To Make the Wheels Revolve We Must Have Grease': Barrel Politics in the Gilded Age." *Journal of Policy History* 14 (Winter 2002): 49–72.

WORKS ON POPULAR PRINTS AND MATERIAL CULTURE

Bunker, Gary L. *From Rail-Splitter to Icon: Lincoln's Image in Illustrated Periodicals, 1860–1865*. Kent, Ohio: Kent State University Press, 2001.

DeWitt, J. Doyle. *A Century of Campaign Buttons, 1789–1889: A Descriptive List. . . .* [Hartford, Conn.]: privately published, 1959.

Fischer, Roger. *Tippecanoe and Trinkets Too: The Material Culture of American Presidential Campaigns, 1828–1984*. Urbana: University of Illinois Press, 1988.

Holzer, Harold. *Lincoln Seen and Heard*. Lawrence: University Press of Kansas, 2000.

Holzer, Harold, Gabor S. Boritt, and Mark E. Neely Jr. *The Lincoln Image: Abraham Lincoln and the Popular Print*. New York: Charles Scribner's Sons, 1984; Urbana: University of Illinois Press, 2001.

Holzer, Harold, and Mark E. Neely Jr. *The Lincoln Family Album: Photographs from the Personal Collections of a Historic American Family*. New York: Doubleday, 1990.

———. *The Union Image: Popular Prints of the Civil War North*. Chapel Hill: University of North Carolina Press, 2000.

Philippe, Robert. *Political Graphics: Art as a Weapon*. New York: Abbeville Press, 1980.

Reilly, Bernard F. *American Political Prints, 1776–1876: A Catalog of the Collections in the Library of Congress*. Boston: G. K. Hall, 1991.

Smith, Chetwood, Mr. and Mrs. *Rogers Groups: Thought & Wrought by John Rogers*. Boston: Charles Goodspeed, 1934.

Sullivan, Edmund B. *American Political Badges and Medalets, 1789–1892*. Lawrence, Mass.: Quarterman Publications, 1981.

Wallace, David H. *John Rogers: The People's Sculptor*. Middletown, Conn.: Wesleyan University Press, 1967.

Weitenkampf, Frank. *A Century of American Political Cartoons*. New York: Charles Scribner's Sons, 1944.

WORKS ON HISTORY OF THE ERA

Bennett, Michael J. *Union Jacks: Yankee Sailors in the Civil War*. Chapel Hill: University of North Carolina Press, 2004.

Blumin, Stuart M. *The Emergence of the Middle Class: Social Experience in the American City, 1760–1900*. New York: Cambridge University Press, 1989.

Burrows, Edwin G., and Mike Wallace. *Gotham: A History of New York City to 1898*. New York: Oxford University Press, 1999.

Carwardine, Richard J. *Evangelicals and Politics in Antebellum America*. New Haven: Yale University Press, 1993.

Chronicle of the Union League of Philadelphia, 1862–1902. Philadelphia: 1902.

Conforti, Joseph A. *Imagining New England: Explorations of Regional Identity from the Pilgrims to the Mid-Twentieth Century*. Chapel Hill: University of North Carolina Press, 2001.

Cook, James W. *The Arts of Deception: Playing with Fraud in the Age of Barnum*. Cambridge: Harvard University Press, 2001.

Dawson, Jan C. *The Unusable Past: America's Puritan Tradition, 1830–1930*. Chico, Calif.: Scholars Press, 1984.

Dyer, John P. "Northern Relief for Savannah during Sherman's Occupation." *Journal of Southern History* 19 (November 1953): 457–72.

Egnal, Marc. "The Beards Were Right: Parties in the North, 1840–1860." *Civil War History* 47 (March 2001): 30–56.

Fredrickson, George M. *The Inner Civil War: Northern Intellectuals and the Crisis of the Union*. New York: Harper & Row, 1965.

Gallman, J. Matthew. *Mastering Wartime: A Social History of Philadelphia during the Civil War*. Philadelphia: University of Pennsylvania Press, 1990.

Gienapp, William E. *The Origins of the Republican Party, 1852–1856*. New York: Oxford University Press, 1987.

Gossett, Thomas F. *Uncle Tom's Cabin and American Culture*. Dallas: Southern Methodist University Press, 1985.

Gunderson, Robert Gray. *The Log-Cabin Campaign*. Lexington: University of Kentucky Press, 1957.

Harris, Neil. *Humbug: The Art of P. T. Barnum*. Boston: Little, Brown, 1973.

Klement, Frank L. *The Copperheads in the Middle West*. Chicago: University of Chicago Press, 1960.

———. "Middle Western Copperheadism and the Genesis of the Granger Movement." *Mississippi Valley Historical Review* 38 (March 1952): 679–94.

Lathrop, George Parsons. *History of the Union League of Philadelphia, from Its Origin and Foundation to the Year 1882*. Philadelphia: J. B. Lippincott, 1884.

Lawson, Melinda. *Patriot Fires: Forging a New American Nationalism in the Civil War North*. Lawrence: University Press of Kansas, 2002.

Lhamon, W. T., Jr. *Raising Cain: Blackface Performance from Jim Crow to Hip Hop*. Cambridge: Harvard University Press, 1998.

McKay, Ernest A. *The Civil War and New York City*. Syracuse, N.Y.: Syracuse University Press, 1990.

Renda, Lex. "'A White Man's State in New England': Race, Party, and Suffrage in Civil War Connecticut." In *An Uncommon Time: The Civil War and the Northern Home Front*, edited by Paul A. Cimbala and Randall M. Miller, 242–79. New York: Fordham University Press, 2002.

Saxton, Alexander. "Blackface Minstrelsy and Jacksonian Ideology." *American Quarterly* 27 (March 1975): 3–28.

Spann, Edward K. *Gotham at War: New York City, 1860–1865*. Wilmington, Del.: Scholarly Resources, 2002.

Toll, Robert C. *Blacking Up: The Minstrel Show in Nineteenth-Century America*. New York: Oxford University Press, 1974.

Whiteman, Maxwell. *Gentlemen in Crisis: The First Century of the Union League of Philadelphia, 1862–1962*. Philadelphia: Union League of Philadelphia, 1975.

Index